A Doubtful Inheritance

A novel 'autobiofiction'

TED TODD (PHD)

(TIBOR WEISZ)

This novel is dedicated to the father I never knew, Lajos Weisz and to all the children in the world who are missing a parent

A Doubtful Inheritance

2nd edition/issue

A copy of this publication can be found in the National Library of Australia.

ISBN: 9 780994 591906
(Or as Ebook 9 780994 591913)

Published by
BLUESTONE PUBLISHING
Melbourne,
Australia

THIS SECOND ISSUE PUBLISHED BY BLUESTONE PUBLISHING AUSTRALIA is the only authorized version

COPYRIGHT C

Table of contents

This is Autobiofiction

*Much of what came to pass in this story is true,
lots of it is not.
Many people in this book lived, loved and
thought deeply about what happened to them,
some did not.
Several characters are still alive, but most live
on only as a figment of my imagination.
I do wish that some of this story was true, but
I'd rather that some of it had never happened.*

Tibor Weisz

At the Esalen Institute of Human Relations, California 1979

The encounter group session is declared closed. I rush to leave the damn room, stumbling out into the bright warmth of late autumn California sunshine. I'm stunned and numb and yet full of energy, needing to move, to run and climb the cliffs in front of me down to the ocean. I move towards the rocks hanging over the waves of the Pacific, the ocean's waves crashing below me onto huge boulders. Moving is good, it is necessary. Stopping is impossible.

I notice nothing; see no one through my rising tears. I climb down toward the sea, scrambling over the rocks. Frothy waves collide one after the other foaming and toppling over, spraying me, tasting as salty as my tears. Weeping turns to bursts of sobbing, as I stop on the last boulder at the edge of the ocean not knowing what to do. I can't go any further. My feet slip; I grab a jagged rock cutting my hand. A few drops of blood splash down bright red. The next wave washes it away leaving no trace of it, of me.
Stumbling again, slipping between two huge wet boulders, I catch my footing and manage to straighten up. The sea seems to have becalmed, stopped rolling, waiting perhaps until my tears come again.

I'm trying to breathe deeply to calm myself, crying and laughing in disbelief at how or what I feel. Questions and rage come rising and fading away, storming inside my head. Questions I know I will never be able to answer or am too ignorant or stupid to ask. Relief, doubt, insight and disbelief churn in confusion. The sound of my brain yells at me if I fall silent. There is so much noise; so much I cannot comprehend, sorrows and fear, anger and doubt I hoped were not in me, things I wish had never happened.

Where has everyone gone?
Where are the grandfathers and fathers and cousins and aunts and uncles?
Why me?
Because I am?

The sun is declining into the sea, slowly darkening the blue sky above Esalen. I try to focus on the immensely beautiful world of nature – focus on anything, anything as long as it is outside of me. The universe does not seem to have been shaken by what happened to me; the universe is not bothered about me; about what I feel or whether I exist.

God died a long time ago;
Nietzsche said God is dead,
God said Nietzsche is dead...Ha.

The breeze strengthens, rapidly becoming a cool wind. Gulls screech, flying low, searching for a feed in the shallows. No sight of whales today, only a new sight of myself. I'm fixed here to the rocks, wishing I could become like the gulls: unfeeling and simple. I throw stones at them, feeling more and more dread, watching the panic rising within me. I force my breath in and out. Om Namah Shivaya Om... Something else suddenly rises. Yes, better feelings, almost good ones. The panic recedes, my heart warms a little, and wretchedness turns and churns mixing with joy. How can this be?

The good feelings do not last long. Heart and throat tighten again in an attack of emotions. Snippets of memories, sentences and words with no one to speak them, belief and hope boil together in my throbbing head. Enormous tiredness hits body and soul. I am punched in the head and the guts simultaneously. Is this why people commit suicide? But no! I reassure myself yelling, 'Not Me, Not me, you bastards...'

Sitting down is an idea I accept, feeling heavy and still as a rock, hardly breathing again. I suck in the cold salty air and blow it out. 'I've got to hold it together.' Tightening my muscles, I hear someone yell out a terrible anguished scream. It is me. The air is sharply cold now; I shiver and hug my arms around my body, wanting to be warm. Fatigue hits in waves to match the rhythmic movements of the ocean. Dragging air in and pushing it out is having control.

*

Time has passed. Feeling weak is winning me over. Time to go back, enough of this, I can't take or want anymore. I drag myself up the cliff. The exertion warms, energizes but fuels an anger that makes me bellow at the sky like a wounded animal. I howl, swearing in English and Hungarian - where did it come from yet again? Groaning, frustrated, then bursting out laughing all at the same time at the ridiculousness of it, of me? Near the top of the cliff, out of breath, I am crying softly again the pain of feeling sorry for myself.

*

Today it is California in 1979, but for me the time warps back to 1950, late August I think. It was then, a few days before my ninth birthday that Mum told me that my father was officially confirmed dead. In a small squeaky voice, she added "so, your father will not return from the war" …I could see that if you were dead you won't return from anywhere, but mum was not being humorous.

*

I am Tim, 38 years old, married with three lovely daughters, successful enough in business. I was born in Hungary, but now I'm an Australian citizen visiting America for two weeks, exploring the world and myself, trying to determine what I am about, what life means, how to be, how to find the 'real' me. Pain is the motivator for so much I do. I want to know why my life feels the way it does, why I feel so permanently uneasy. I live and cope well enough, but there is a gaping hole in my soul. It does not make sense but I don't feel entirely authentic. I live a life that I often think of as an invention.

I came to this encounter group at the Esalen Institute of Human Relations, the Mecca for psychological, spiritual and personal growth workshops; a big deal movement in the seventies. The beautiful institute is on the coast of California and named after a long dead Indian tribe called the Esalen.

In the jargon of the times the encounter group is called 'Getting in touch with your real self'. It goes on all day and half the night for five long and often trying days. For me the five days of encounter group activities and dialogue are variously serious and meaningful, sometimes cathartic, or hilarious, or even silly at times. Sometimes I think it is destructive and mind-boggling, making more confusion than clarity for each of us – for me certainly. Still, I know it is providing me with at least a handle, a way to see what one's inner workings are about. And yes, it is very revealing about how we live and function. I begin to understand that one has to be able to conceptualize one's psyche and how it works, in order to understand self and life.

On the fourth day I am in the 'hot seat' - finally having managed to work up enough emotional energy and trust of the group, I suppose, to 'expose and explore' myself. To do what? Say what? I have no idea when I start. I hedge, fence and dance around the black hole of my heart, waffling on about my business or wife, children or mother, until I become aware that I am indeed just mucking about in the shallows. I'm looking vacantly at the floor, out of subterfuges, so I stop speaking. Hopefully I can get out of the hot seat. Everyone is silent. Is the challenge over? Oh well, I've done what I could, nothing worthwhile, it's disappointing.

Anton, our facilitator is a famous psychologist, author and guru figure. In the eyes of the participants he is variously arrogant, bombastic, cocksure and yet all-knowing and helpful too. Begrudgingly we love him, hate him and I, at least, envy him.

The silence grows oppressive. Anton the facilitator quietly asserts: "There is more to come is there not?"
Fuck. He is right.
The question is a statement. I sit up in surprise, taking a deep breath, and launch into how I always feel as if some part of me is missing. Now it is just pouring out without

me thinking about any of it. I speak for a long time before I stop, feeling at risk again, wanting to leave the hot seat. Something in me, however, just moves on and on. Even though I want to stop, I hear words floating into the air as if pre-recorded, as if nothing to do with me. Words are tumbling out with a will of their own. Words about my dead father and my original, mostly unknown, dead family.

As my words tell stories, snippets, feelings, thoughts, forty people and Anton the wise-man facilitator listen in respectful silence. This is what it's all about this 'encounter' thing; to help people recall, re-experience and explore buried pain. The idea is that re-experiencing, recalling old buried pain will bring it out of the unconscious into the present time and situation where it might be integrated, seen as the past, so one could let it all go. It is necessary to do this in order to free one from being impelled by the past and its pains. "Only by letting it all out could one be free to make saner choices and to live in a more peaceful way." So Anton, tells us. I resist it at times but the process is beginning to make sense. I can see that it offers hope that one could indeed let go, but of what exactly? What do I need to let go of that I appear to know little or nothing about?

I'm sitting on a small child's stool in the middle of the room, feeling hot and shaky, people are watching, while Anton's shaved bald head nods at me, "Yes" or "yes, but go deeper." Now and then when I hesitate he pokes a mocking or even aggressive comment at me: "Oh poor Tim is lost for words, or is he playing hide and seek with us...?"
Who the fuck does he think he is? What can he possibly understand about me? But while he makes fun of my tears, mocking and challenging my sadness I know he is

also supporting me, wanting to help. I nod agreement, or yell at him, about the things he suggests as possible interpretations of what I say. One moment I'm thinking this is really valuable, and then I figure it is useless bullshit emoting at best.

I don't know how long I have been sitting here. Now, like a bursting soap bubble, an overwhelming sadness comes. I have never known such sadness as I now find boiling up. My heart hurts with an actual physical pain. I want to say how I feel, but I burst out sobbing incoherently. God knows why or what.

Anton pushes again, "What's going on? Put words to it...it is all right, feel what you feel - but do not let the child take it all. Be the adult you are now. Explain what is going on, be in touch, put words to it man..."

"Fuck you! Fuck it all!"

I spit out, angrily but at whom or what? I get more and more upset sobbing, choking in my throat.

Calming a little, I blow my nose, wipe my sweating face and head. After a moment of feeling blank I declare, "That's it. No more". But barely do I utter this, and there are more words tumbling from my mouth. I try to smile at the people around me feeling apologetic I'm taking so much time. Some smile back encouragingly. All these people are still listening intently to every word I say.

The sun has gone lower filling the large room with yellowish rays. Hell, I must have been talking for over an hour. And yet they are listening, some have tears in their eyes. This is empowering, I think, looking around, confirming a sort of right to say whatever I will and have said. Perhaps I'm speaking for many of them, or all of them? Maybe some of my pain is what they all feel? I mean, no one is here just for the fun of it.

Anton shifts in his low guru style seat, "You look like you have gone back into your head." I look at him and an unbearable heat rises in me; I nearly vomit bile and hot tears. Then, I begin to mumble about more things I don't know about. Someone who has my words is launching into something, a story that's new to me, but Anton puts his hand up, his broad palm signaling me to hold it a moment.

"Stop a minute. Your name is not Tim, that's an English name. Your accent might be Hungarian. What is your real name?"

I am taken aback by his question. Before I know it, I snap out *"Tibor Weisz"*. The name I was born with. I had not used it for the last thirty years. The man's shiny bald head nods knowingly, satisfied that this really is my name.

"Go on now, but remember you are Tibor Weisz."
I feel like growling at him again to get fucked. He is a conceited, cock-sure, bombastic bastard, what's my name got to do with anything anyway? I love, abhor and resent him. My strong reaction to him interests me, so I don't say anything for a minute. And then from the belly of my subconscious I heave the stories hidden there. I don't know how long I talk or cry. Finally spent, I sit in silence, in awed wonder at the things I've heard myself say. I try to reflect, to make sense of it all, to put it into a rational context, but nothing fits. Something keeps pushing, pressing me on. There is more to be said. It is oozing up and out, an erupting volcano, a king tide, a must happens, a spirit is forcing me to go on.

I hear a familiar female voice in my head, it's Mum;

"When your father comes back everything will be all right".

Up it comes, boom, bang, crash! Up it comes like bitter bile over and over

"When your father comes back everything will be all right".
"When your father comes back everything will be all right".
"When your father comes back everything will be all right".
"When your father comes back everything will be all right".
"When your father comes back everything will be all right".

I see stars in front of my clenched eyes. My body is rigid and tensed to breaking point.

That is, it: that's it!

"WHEN YOUR FATHER COMES BACK EVERYTHING WILL BE ALL RIGHT".
That was my fantasy, a hope held so tightly all my life, but I didn't know it. I did not know I had this built into me. And everything certainly was not all right in my young life. Nothing much was actually. The little Hungarian boy Tibor is still very much alive inside of me. Astonished, I know with a rush of comprehension that I still believed, at the age of 38, that my father will one day come back and fix everything. Here I was, a grown man who didn't know he

was still waiting for his dad to come back to fix up the world and make everything right.

I'm haunted by unknown memories, by ghosts that lurk in me, unfulfilled dreams.

I suspected it though. Or did I? I am so heavy now, a silent lump of non-sense sitting on a small hard chair. I need a cigarette. I'm confused, unable to think, in awe at the realization of what tumbled out of me. I just want to think about it. All this and more arose from a hidden part of me. It is shocking. Oh, I knew I had memories for sure - or is it feelings - deep in there, the sort of fixations that one half feels without words, sense or concepts. Now I knew I was an orphan of sorts, or had I felt that way all my life? I will never have a father; will never know what it would be like to have one. Or a grandfather, or have roots, a sense of continuity from the past.

I weep a dirge for a long time, hysterical tears, pictures, ideas, feelings flashing, flicking inside me mixing with saliva and sweat. People are watching. I feel guilty but why? And, they are not the jury!

Recovering some, I sneak a look around. There are faces, there is compassion filling the room, and that connection allows more, but gentler tears. In a fog, I finally fall silent. I am now a father myself. The thought of my young daughters cheers me up a little as I relish the love that I feel for them. Tears again, such tired little childlike tears tasting so familiar. I must come to grips with the fact that the fairytale I have lived is just that, a nonsense fairy tale, like a loved 'book'. Why does it still haunt me? What had it done to me? All that happened to me, and all that had not, is driving my life, without my awareness. It feels heavy, ridiculous and depressing.

Sitting so very still, afraid to move, to break the moment, something floats up into consciousness. A lighter sensation, a pleasant breeze flows inside me. I'm a little clearer as if something is explained. Yes, something is illuminated. Not much, maybe nothing in the end. My losses can never be truly explained or replaced. Relief and utter sadness – thoughts and feelings mix devastatingly, now with an awareness that I must learn to live with all this; my one and only life, beware of imitations.

*

Later, walking around the dark paths of Esalen I hear the sounds of a reed flute played by someone who sounds like I feel. I am pushing away feelings. I want to be rational. There comes a time in one's life when the idea of 'waiting' for something - but what exactly - must end. I have always lived as if I have not yet started the 'real thing', as if I was still waiting for my real life to begin. Silly stuff this, life is not a dress rehearsal. The performance is always a premier event, a new narrative. A life is written; but this actor did not know the plot. The actions that came and went, the living that passed so far were as unknown bits of fact or fiction.

What to do now?
Where to go now?
Who am I now?
The same as before?
Yes, and no. I don't know.

Asking such questions is not satisfactory. Is it that I have lost my identity, my roots, my people, or that I have never had these to identify with? Is it the realization that who I am, is not who I intended or hoped to be? Which would have been what or who exactly? Do others know exactly who or how they are? A stupid question I've always pondered, trying to figure it, figure me out. Now, there is more understanding, perhaps I can dig deeper into the well, deeper than the shallow one I've drawn from until now.

*

On an airplane floating somewhere above the ocean, on the way home to Melbourne, such thoughts mix in my mind, pushing me to consider things I'd rather forget, or rather recall? Hell's bells! It is 1979, not the childhood years! Just leave it. Leave it all behind now, the job's done, she'll be right, no worries... Bob's your uncle (who is Bob and why is he my uncle?) A stitch in time gathers no moss, a rolling Tim gathers no stitch. Am I funny? Yes, I am.

In the middle of the night, unable to sleep in the dark droning of the plane, I live thus and muse on. Feeling heavy, lead-like and about that color, I scramble out of my seat carefully stepping over my sleeping neighbors and wobble toward the toilets. I note blank looks on sleeping faces, hair messed, limbs in awkward positions spread in narrow seats. Some snore with their heads at angles impossible to maintain, others just pretend to be asleep, hoping to fool the universe. We do that don't we: try to fool the universe? Pity I cannot do it. Blowing my nose, I curse the cold I think is coming on. Sitting down, again intending to sleep, I light a cigarette, put it out, take a drink and shut my eyes. I want to be out of it, out of existence, out of my never stopping thoughts. It would be good to spend the next few hours blanked out, resting the spirit, but as I try to shut off the exhausted brain box, something else comes.

*

The reality of a dream jolts me back to consciousness as if someone had hit me. My heart is racing; I am hot, dry and rigid. Just a dream, I assure myself. I am in an airplane flying home, I reassure myself. But, I know the dream story, recall the scene. Mum spoke in my dream, looking her usual beautiful self.

"Your father Lajos has been now officially declared missing and probably dead somewhere by the Don River so he won't be coming back..."

And then again as if she spoke in an endless loop the same words. Mum explains.

"A friend of our family, Albert, had made it back years after the war ended and recounted your father's and Uncle Andor's final moments to the authorities and then to me."

Good, hell, ...I am definitely awake now. Another cigarette is lit. I'm in some shockwave though, things are churning guts and my whole body. The dream seemed so real, or no, like a movie, but not one I want to see. I do not want to see again the declaration of my father's death. Do I? Or perhaps I do want to see something new in it? An aspect previously missed or misunderstood? I call a stewardess, asking for a large Scotch. The plane drones on, the darkness outside allows it to do so. My smoke curls upward, I stand up stretching; my hand trembles, tinkling the ice in the glass. No one cares.

I am taken aback at the capacity of my memory to re-project the scene of this old story that no one else knew, for it was never confirmed by anyone else. The man who told Mum was 'pretty sure', but not 'absolutely', that it was my father and his brother Andor that he saw. "But he looked certain," Mum said at the time, trying hard not to burst into tears.

I see the obviousness of why the dream came. Just a memory, turned into a film by my restless mind. A show that didn't have the end I wanted. A movie with a bad story and bad directors; that's the human race. That's my early years, bad narratives are what most of my stories are about.

A Jewish Joke, but is it funny?

In a small village in the Ukraine, in 1935, a terrifying report arrives: a young girl had been found murdered. Realizing the dire consequences of such an event, the Jewish community instinctively gathers in the synagogue to plan whatever defensive action may be possible under these circumstances. Just as the emergency meeting is called to order, the president of the synagogue runs in out of breath and excited:
"Brothers," he cries out, "I have wonderful news! The murdered girl is Jewish!"

Source: Novak & Waldoks, 1981, p. 73

Part 1.

The Father

Near the Don River, Siberia, USSR 1945

The late afternoon sun casts dark shadows as an angry wind blows smoke on a brown and barren land. Relentless sounds of bombs and shells echo from far away. The flat landscape seems to have no edges, no end as it winds away from the eye toward the horizon. Somewhere near, perhaps on the edge of a few trees there is the Don River's muddy waters floating dead bodies and junk downstream.

Silence alternates with catastrophic sounds.
God is not here. Destruction and death rule all there is.

A timber hut, barely upright, leans to the left waiting to fall, but hangs on to that half of itself that is not torn away. It was never more than a makeshift shepherd's shed. Weathered gray, roughly hewn timber walls now smoked charcoal black, hold up half a roof. The other half in tatters flops away down the back. The air blows in misty white smoke and then suddenly clears. Once grassy green fields are covered with ash and rubble, foreign bits of metal and unrecognizable things; the scrap of war. Torn clothing, caps and blood stained jackets, twisted rifles and shrapnel look almost as if they were arranged on the fields. Dead bodies are planted in hollowed out earth, bodies that look as if still moving are frozen in pose. The griminess of the earth and the darkness of the late afternoon clouds cover this world with the gunmetal thick mist of the color of war. Now and then the sun pokes through the haze, smugly shining.

Sounds recede or close in, as if arranged by a director. Fear rises as a noise full silence comes and goes, threatens and surprises. The scenery waits ominously for more devastation. The tragedy of war is not yet finished.

Lajos holds his unconscious brother Andor; his arms are around him as they recline against a wall of the hut. Strangled timber beams and iron give the illusion that the two of them are hidden for now. Lajos is aching, hoping for quiet and sleep, but he is worried about Andor. Lajos prays with each silent lull that it will stay that way. Through an opening in the back of the hut, he can see what is left of his group of 'Jewish work serviceman', and the few Hungarian regular soldiers as they move unsteadily further and further away. They are leaving, straggling back toward where they came from yesterday. Dirt covered tattered uniforms and limping bodies tell the story. Lajos can almost recognize some of them. Suddenly another dark smoky cloud billows across painting the sky red. The sound of shells shatters the earth nearby.

Lajos hopes that he and Andor will not be missed. Not yet, not ever. Andor is badly hurt. A piece of shrapnel is lodged in his thigh and another in his back. Lajos is so exhausted that he can barely think. His ankle is twisted; his nose is bleeding. Pain is shooting through his body. He knows Andor cannot walk on his own and won't survive if he leaves him here. Lajos bandages him up as best he can with his shirt. Minutes ago, when the other soldiers got to their feet to leave, his weary mind screamed, 'Don't move, and don't go on'. In a moment of lucidity he reasoned that he had a legitimate explanation to fall behind. Even that murderous Jew-hating bastard of a unit commander couldn't blame him for dropping out; though of course he would. Lajos had thought for some time now that it would be better for them to take their chance with the advancing Russians. The Ruskis can't be any worse than their own countrymen - hell no one could be.

'But if the unit commander came back looking for us he would shoot both of us,' he spoke out aloud. What they would be shot for seemed nearly funny. 'Shoot us for being half dead?' Would he come back? The terror of the unit commander stabbed at Lajos's bowels. He needed to evacuate, and to satisfy hunger and thirst all at the same time. They've had nothing to eat since when? Yesterday or was it the day before? Andor moaned, his eyes flickering with the pangs of pain. If the commander came back, perhaps they could fake being dead. Lajos drank his last drop of water and then fell asleep.

The Hungarian army, or what was left of it, consisted of the commander, fifty odd soldiers, and a few remaining Jewish 'work servicemen'. They struggled on, retreating. No one cared about anything else now, but to get away from the advancing Russians. The Jewish men were forcibly taken into the Nazi Hungarian army that allied itself with Hitler. The government of the day justified this by saying that this was better for Hungary than being overrun by Germany. These Jews, so called 'work servicemen' were not allowed to carry guns. The army certainly had no interest in the survival of the Jews who were up front during an advance and at the back when retreating. The Jews carried machinery, food and supplies, did the cooking and carried what little equipment there was.

Three bazookas abruptly lit up the darkening sky above the retreating soldiers. The deafening noise and bombs blew holes in the ground, spraying earth right next to Zoli. 'Too damn near' he thought vaguely, dragging himself on, one leg already damaged; the Russians had found them. Zoli was a regular soldier, not a Jew. His friendship with Lajos went back to their childhood when they played soccer in the streets of Budapest. He was very fond of Lajos and his brother Andor. The three of them married about three years ago and they had their first children whom neither has seen for the last, over two years. At this point Zoli believed that neither of them would ever see their families again. He looked around for Lajos but could not see him. He tried to look further into the small crowd running terrified in front of him, but it was in vain. He recalled that just yesterday, or was it three days ago, Lajos had kept asking him to escape and run away toward the front so they might be taken prisoners by the Russians.

Shells rained down so everyone flattened out on the filthy ground, at least it was a rest. Zoli thought of the utterly diabolical craziness of making himself and Jews fight on the side of Nazi Germany who would have the Jews dead. It was breathtaking and shameful beyond belief. Now they all started to run again, Zoli moved on as fast as he could. This was a bad war, unjust and unwinnable and one in which he had no interest. "War is such an absolute nonsense." Bitterly he thought also how the Germans used the Hungarians as the Hungarians used the Jews. Why was the under-equipped and outnumbered Hungarian army sent to the Russian front? And how much worse off the Jews were. Persecuted by their countrymen, in a crazy the world... Something he hadn't truly realized until these last two years.

Zoli, Lajos and Andor had been together for over three years, since leaving their wives, new born babies and families in Budapest. The weirdness and the puzzling fear they knew now was not part of their previous lives. The utter fear and the impossible situation they were in turned to feelings of defiant resignation. Zoli recalled Lajos: "One gets used to everything. But we must not, we must not lose our sense of the fact that we are young men who have a life and a future, as do these Russians, we have a right to live..." Zoli always thought of Lajos as the eternal optimist.

More shells came whistling. Screaming floated in the air, a lone tree was burning a few meters away as Zoli fell into a trench. He scrambled up feeling something digging him in the side. It was his binoculars, but there was also a bit of shrapnel stuck in his leg. He yanked it out with a howl, clamping his hand on the wound. He shut his eyes, recalling Lajos's face. Small brown twinkling eyes gave Lajos a handsome face. Lajos's wife Sari used to say that one of his eyes always cried while the other always seemed to be laughing. Zoli looked back again, toward the hut where they rested last night but saw no one there. Still, Andor and Lajos were likely as not in there. 'Not dead,' he mumbled. 'Please God....'
Moments of utter stillness were again followed by the whistling, crying sounds of falling bombs. The soldiers ran desperately looking for shelter, but there was not even a tree left in sight. A bomb exploded behind Zoli. He tried to get up, feeling for his binoculars again. Stumbling he fell with a vague the realization that part of his leg had been blown off. A shattered twisted bloody stump remained. He grabbed it with his hands screaming, watching the blood gush. He shouted for help, looking behind him. His leg felt oddly numb, blood spurting out. Someone was coming toward him. He passed in and out of consciousness while

his leg was bandaged. Once again he turned back toward the hut. Now he thought he saw someone; was it Lajos, dragging Andor out of the hut? Smoke blew the sight momentarily away and then a shell exploded in front of the hut. Earth flew like feather, black smoke rose.
'That's it, they are gone, my friends are dead', he realized and lost consciousness.

Another Jewish Joke

A short history of the Jews;

Hitler tried to kill us all,

He did not succeed,

Let's eat.

Russians

The shelling stopped. Now there was a deafening calm that comes after unbearable noise. Russian soldiers speedily arrived, cautiously moving in towards what was left of the barn. Deciding to camp for the night, they ignored the dead bodies littering the field, or else threw them out of their way.

It was night by now, pitch black sky. The soldiers huddled around a couple of camp fires. An old bearded soldier wearing half a Russian uniform, German boots and a Hungarian jacket walked away from the campfire to urinate. Looking at what was left of a small bush, he saw two men, one obviously dead, torn almost in half on the ground. The other man's limbs were twisted, his face covered with blood and blackened, but he groaned and moved. The old soldier yelled

"I've found a Hungarian still alive."

"So shoot the cunt and then he won't be," was the laughing response. The old soldier drew his pistol. He looked at the face of a young man on the ground. Dark hair, moustache, eyes now open though obviously unseeing, blank. His fingers tightened on the trigger, but he couldn't do it. He put away his pistol. Just leave him there to die was the easiest. Hesitating, he reached down to see how bad the man was. The old soldier had a problem convincing his compatriots about saving this man's life. What could they do anyway? They had no medicines and barely enough to eat, and they were too tired to argue. He decided to prop him up against the back of the barn and tried to give him a drink. The man came to life for a moment. The Russian tore a chunk of blackened bread from his loaf and pressed it into the lifeless hands, figuring they would leave him there to die.

In the morning the rest of the regiment arrived. The medicos were very young, none of them were doctors. The Russians were battle-weary, having pushed back the German and Hungarian armies for so long that hardly anyone knew what day of the week it was. One medico still had some youthful feelings of humanity, so he bandaged the Hungarian as best he could. It was then decided that maybe this captured man might know something. The Russian unit commander was a communist to whom communism still meant humanism. He understood, having examined Lajos's papers, that this man was a 'work serviceman', meaning that Lajos was a Jew.

The bomb that had hit Lajos and his brother had ripped apart Andor, but left Lajos in a damaged, but not impossible, condition. Lajos had a broken arm and shrapnel in his left thigh, and he was obviously shell shocked. When the medico showed Lajos his papers and a photograph, Lajos didn't seem to recognize them. He looked blank, fish eyed. The commander decided to send him back in a supply truck to behind the battle front.

*

Many days later, Lajos was in a prisoner holding camp. He still didn't know who he was or what was happening to him even though some of his physical functions had improved. After many days he slowly, vaguely, regained some consciousness and a picture of what had happened to him and his brother. He had no memories beyond that. Andor was dead, he knew somehow. Lajos fluttered in and out of awareness. Mostly he had no idea who he was or how he got here. The Russians realized that he knew nothing of value to them; no Jew ever knew of battle plans so he was bundled into a truck full of prisoners of war and taken to a rail head where they were packed into cattle trains and sent on a long, cold and starving journey to a Siberian camp. For most of the journey he was delirious, hovering between sleep and blankness, his body racked by pain as he floated in and out of awareness. Now and then something formed in his brain, bright pictures, colorful and cheery. He'd laugh out loud for a moment and then fall into the daze of non-existence.

In the POW camp, a little food and water, a timber bed to lie on, improved his physical condition. Someone was helping him to eat the thin watery soup and black bread and made sure that the guards knew he was too ill to stand up. His memories were blank still mostly blank. Once he began to recover, Lajos somehow knew that it was better to say little or nothing, better to be thought of as a bit out of it. There were a few other Hungarian prisoners of war and many German soldiers, but the Russians treated all enemy prisoners similarly.

Siberia was icy cold, flat and sterile, hardly any grass, a few windblown trees on fields that stretched out infinitely. The camp was circled by barbed wire even though one could see immediately that escaping would be hopeless. Prisoners were put to work, growing raggedy vegetables, or making army uniforms, digging out rocks and cleaning latrines, or building basic timber huts to house the ever growing numbers of prisoners. The huts were cold and bare; only a few prisoners were lucky enough to have a scrappy blanket.

His injuries slowly healed. Lajos recovered his legs and body. He worked, doing whatever he was told to do. He followed orders, spoke no words, but felt himself physically recovering with surprise. Food was a thin soup and sticky bits of black bread, day after day, and month after month. His mind was numb and empty; if others spoke to him he shook his head, pointing to the dirty bandages around his head. At night he slept the dazed sleep of exhaustion and fear. Still, he became stronger. He resolved to stay silent. Puzzled about his lack of feelings or memories, he had no idea what one would or could say anyway. He felt nearly nothing, recalling little and only about the recent past. All he knew and was afraid of, was the constantly recalled, incessant sound of bombs falling. Now and then Andor's face came momentarily into focus. His brother was dead; this he knew, in a puzzled, emotionless way.

One day, after who knows how long, months later perhaps, while digging the frozen ground, flashes of memories came, as if one switched on a light in the dark. An apartment building painted yellow with red geraniums on window sills; a short street, and a shop came into focus. He stopped digging for a moment to marvel at such recollections, they seemed like photographs. He bent over again pressing the shovel into the stiff ground, sweat pouring into his eyes. There came the face of a woman and a baby. Pictures like on a post card began to float to the surface of his mind. A guard was near, so he did not stop digging. He wanted to remember these faces; they must be important, he figured.

More and more pictures emerged during the following days and nights. In his dreams, he saw again and again the face of a woman and thought her very beautiful. He saw an apartment as if he was walking through it, a small kitchen and a room with open windows, white curtains billowing in the sunshine. Another night he dreamt about the cobble-stoned street again and an older, round faced bald man was smiling at him. Repeatedly, there was the dream of the beautiful woman, and even a baby in a cot, a very young baby. He could almost taste the typical way that new babies smell.

He tried to think about all this, through the long work days during which he carried water or rocks or dug sanitary holes. If you did not work, you got no food. One bitterly cold morning, he woke having had the same sort of dreams. Now, his mind was ready to bring it back. He gasped, with a sudden shock of recognition, like a knife entering his brain; the woman and the baby were his wife and son. The baby was three months old when he last saw him, and his name was on his lips; Tibor. And his wife's name was Sari. He continued working. He wept for hours, for the first time in years. His soundless tears eased his mind allowing more and more snippets of memories to float up like debris, as if on his tears.

Later, he bitterly thought that it may have been better not to have regained any of these memories. But that feeling left as fast as it came and with it a small hope reached forward, a thawing in his heart. Yes, the smiling bald headed man was his father; the apartment was their home, the street where he grew up. With a rush of hope and bitterness, he wanted his life back.

He tried to befriend a few Hungarian prisoners now. One of them turned out to be a confirmed Nazi who took one look at him, "Fuck off, Jew pig". Lajos walked away feeling a surge of unfamiliar anger, a murderous blanking out of reason, a fury and a danger. Most of the prisoners were simple young peasants who, although anti-Semitic, didn't really know what if anything they had against Jews. They thought that this Jew seemed like a harmless, quiet fellow and in any case, even the slightest disturbance to the camp's routine was severely punished by the guards.

It was impossible to distinguish days from weeks, weeks from months. A long time had probably passed. He became more and more aware that there were things he had to fight to remember; that there was some kind of life that he had a right to and that it was taken from him. Painful memories had to be retrieved; memories are what makes a human being. 'This is not real life', he told himself. It cannot be, nor is the war. All this is just hell. There has to be more. He told the two Hungarians, Sandor and Laci, who he was friendly with, "I keep dreaming about a beautiful woman and a baby, I know it is my wife Sari and son Tibor I see and hear in my dreams. And I am so happy, but so scared that they… that they…" He could say no more. The two men looked at him, their faces lined with sorrow, tears in their eyes, and then responded with stories about their families and the way life had been before the war.

The camp conditions were severe and the treatment from their guards atrocious. It was not just the freezing cold and lousy, insufficient food; they were lucky to get more than one small meal a day. The camp was plagued with dysentery, flu, hepatitis and who knew what else. There was no medicine. Every day some prisoners died; some went crazy, or were shot trying to escape. Lajos knew he was in Siberia, and although he certainly thought about escaping he figured it was impossible to do so. Escape to where exactly, and where was he actually?

Outside his hut the sky was clear, his breath showed steamy as he stood looking up at the night sky. He didn't know that it was approaching the spring of 1948. He looked up at the big bright stars and huddled his arms around his very thin body. Lajos counted the days, weeks, months and years despondently, yet fiercely forcing himself to bear the relentless torture of this hard hopeless life.

*

One day a new camp commandant and a few new guards arrived. The prisoners were lined up as the new chief spoke. "My name is Sergei, I can't promise you much, but I will try to improve your situation. We have more food coming and I intend to start a new project of growing vegetables. I was a farmer in the days before the war..." He smiled at them. "None of you, and not one of us wants to be here, let's hope we can all go home someday. Now I want some volunteers for the vegetable project." Lajos and a few others immediately stepped forward, welcoming the idea. The prisoners yelled 'Hurrah, Hurrah," and sauntered back to their barracks with some optimism.

Though the project lifted the spirits, how were they to grow vegetables in the cold hard ground and with little available water? Lajos had an idea. He asked to see Commander Sergei, suggesting that they might at least build some sort of roof above the vegetable patches. The commander listened with eagerness to Lajos's broken Russian and German. Sergei nodded enthusiastic approval, "I will see what we can get for materials" he promised. Then ponderously he added, "Maybe we could build a hothouse, but a big one comrade?" He laughed at the idea with obvious pleasure. Standing up, he offered his hand to Lajos, "You are a smart man comrade," Lajos took the hand of the commander slowly, but with a feeling of pleasure he had not experienced for a while. Trust? Yes, but more, something that made sense, something that was about life, not about killing.

A few weeks later, trucks arrived with materials for a roof and a large hothouse was built. Soil beds were dug and edged up. It was spring time so the prisoners sowed the seeds almost immediately. Lajos found surprising pleasure in working the soil. For a time, he managed to push aside the increasing torments attached to his past life. Daily he grew stronger in body and spirit, making an effort to learn more Russian. His now frequent visits to the commander earned him a book on the Russian language. Soon he was put in charge of organizing the work, in spite of the fact that he was a city boy. Learning fast from the Hungarian peasants about vegetables and fruit, he requested and received a couple of books on agriculture. He developed ideas about many aspects of the work, such as building watering channels rather than bucket watering. Fortunately, the first crop was huge success.

*

A part of Lajos was determined to make the best of a life that was unpromising - although sometimes he bitterly wondered what for? What year was it? Why did anyone bother? His ability to pick up the Russian language was better than most, and resulted in some extra privileges. Out of the three Hungarians he befriended, two died suddenly. One of them threw himself onto the barbed wire yelling, cursing and crazy, trying to escape. He was shot in the leg. He could have recovered, but did not. The other much younger boy died painfully and slowly, perhaps of hepatitis.

One day Lajos went to see the Commander. As a trustee he was by now on very friendly terms with Commander Sergei. "What year is it?" he asked. "1951, March ". Lajos swooned with disbelief. Six years of his life was gone. He recovered his wits as Sergei waited patiently smoking tobacco mixed with tea leaves. Lajos requested to be allowed to write a letter. Sergei nodded, adding, "I'll try to get it through, but do not hope for much."

It took until the autumn of 1952 before Lajos was able to get his letter sent. He was only allowed to write one letter so he wrote to his wife. He waited for weeks and then months, but no answer came. Again he went to talk to Commander Sergei. Holding back his feelings he asked "Was my letter sent? Why have I no reply?"

"I don't know comrade. The mail is unreliable, but I have some good news for you anyway. Your country has joined the communist bloc, so it is now a Russian ally. That should improve the mail and offer some hope that you might be able to go home, huh...?"

Sergei smiled pointing to a chair, "Comrade, I've sent the letter that's for sure, but whether it got there, I don't know. The truth is that our government cares little about prisoners of war, though I should not say that. There are some in high places that hope you all die and save us the embarrassment of accounting for all these camps." Sergei was obviously disturbed as he shook his head, producing a bottle of Vodka, and poured two glasses. "I like you," he said to Lajos. "Be patient, like all the rest of us," and he laughed, "What a stupid thing to say or think..." and he threw the vodka down his throat in one gulp, banging his hand in anger on the desk.

Despondently, Lajos wrote another letter. Again he waited. The commander he trusted, but anyone else out there in the world, did they care or even know about the prisoners? Then the day came when there was a great upheaval in the camp. Word was out that several letters had arrived for prisoners. Alas, none of them were for him. His disappointment turned to anger and he felt a fury with which he was not acquainted.

Commander Sergei watched him sink to the ground, beating the earth with his hand sobbing. He nudged him into his hut. "Easy Lajos, we'll try again, I promise you we'll try again...Maybe you should write to the authorities. Perhaps your family has moved...You know, lots of people are displaced."

"Yes, yes that's what must have happened," Lajos replied, with a wish he tried to feel.

His friendship with Sergei had grown. Often they had vodka and stale tobacco. They spoke of life and of better times. Sometimes they talked of those they loved back home. The commander somehow always managed to get hold of something from real life. With an effort loaded with anger, Lajos demanded; "But why am I being held? Why? I am a Jew who was forced to fight your people. I am not your enemy... Why don't they let me go?" he demanded. Then, Sergei shook his head looking sad and worn as he listened to Lajos.

"Do you think I want to be here?" he gloomily responded. "I haven't seen my family for many years and I am lucky to get the odd letter".

"But when will they let me go home?" Lajos asked. The commander picked up his bottle of vodka again, not wanting to look at his prisoner. He was miserable and visibly shaken. He simply murmured, "I don't know'.

"Can you help me at all? Can you tell me what has happened to Budapest during the war?"
The Russian shook his head "Not much, not really. I don't know much; I think it was bombed"; immediately regretting his words. It took Lajos a while before that new information reached his brain, furthering his fears about his family. Sergei's bloodshot eyes watched, nodding in sympathy.

*

The seasons followed one another in the orderly fashion only nature achieves. Another year, another spring. Now and then a bunch of letters arrived. These were distributed alphabetically. Because Lajos's surname was Weisz he had to wait. Sergei didn't hand him the letter immediately. He nodded at Lajos, murmuring, "Come with me, let's have a drink." They went inside his hut. Lajos's heart was throbbing fearfully about what was to come.

"I hope it is good news," Sergei said handing him the letter. Lajos looked at it, ripping the envelope open. Inside he found his own first letter returned with a note from the Hungarian post office saying 'Addressee Unknown'.

After all these years, if you were still alive in a Siberian prisoner camp you already knew the meaning of hopelessness. It was a state of existence you survived or else. By now, disappointment was often just a numbing sense of mind and body rather than an upheaval of emotion. He sat there motionless, wishing himself dead.

Sergei watched him, feeling emotions he did not want to feel. His prisoner seemed rooted to the spot, his body frozen like the tundra outside. What Sergei knew was that if he could ever help anyone, if there was any way to save even one of these unfortunates, then he'd make sure this man would be free again. He watched his skinny prisoner for several minutes until he saw the man recover something of himself.

Lajos stood up, speaking hoarsely, not expecting an answer, and yet his questions came, his voice barely audible. "What could this mean? Are they all dead? Have they just moved away, escaped from Hungary?" Sergei, grabbing his arm, made him sit, forcing another sip of vodka into him. They sat there a long time, saying nothing. The hut got dark, Sergei silent, Lajos staring into space. Finally, Sergei stood up and said, "Lajos you had better go write another letter. I'll get it through quick, somehow." His prisoner said nothing. "Yes, write another letter, I'll send it to my family," Sergei repeated, "and ask them to send it on. Maybe this time write to the authorities and your family? Or to your other relatives."

"Who?" asked Lajos bitterly, shaking himself angrily back into life, "To who? How do I know who is left?"

"Perhaps you could write to the authorities and list a number of names." Lajos looked at him and saw Sergei's shining eyes. He squeezed out some words, thanking him.

A letter was sent to the Hungarian authorities. He included the names of his wife and child, his brothers, sisters, parents, cousins, aunties, uncles, everyone whose address he could recall. It was risky to do it, but Sergei sent Lajos's letter to his own wife, asking her to post it on. Six months later a reply came from the Hungarian People's Republic. Lajos asked his one remaining Hungarian friend,

Sandor, to read it. He could not bring himself to do so. They sat outside on a fence next to the vegetable garden, now frosted over with winter. Sandor's hand was shaking as he began to read the letter:

"We regret to inform you that there is very little we can say regarding the persons about whom you have enquired. The building where your wife and child lived was severely bombed. This office believes that many in the building died, though it is possible that some have moved elsewhere before the bombing, or illegally left Hungary between 1945 or later. The following people on your list are known to have died before or during the invasion of the liberating Russian army".

The list was long and referred to most of his brothers, cousins, aunts and uncles. Most of these people, it stated, died at the hands of the Nazis, before the end of the war. Almost everyone Lajos had enquired about was pronounced dead or missing, except for his brother Janos, and his mother. Two people might be alive out of nearly forty names, but these last two were also listed as address unknown, or missing. The letter went on:

"Given that much of our records were destroyed there is always a chance that we may be wrong regarding your relatives. As stated earlier, it is also possible that your wife and child or other members of your family have left Hungary in those first turbulent years between 1945 and 1949 when our borders were still open. On behalf of the Hungarian Communist Party I extend my sympathy to you. The Hungarian government has instituted proceedings to ask for your release, as well as for the release of your fellow prisoner Sandor Nagy".

Lajos grabbed the letter as if he hoped that the other man misread it. He tried reading it through the haze of disappointment and pain. He was suddenly lost in anguish, the kind that blanks out all there is in heart and head. Sandor gently shook him, "Lajos, Lajos, look," he said, pointing to the letter, "The Hungarians have promised to ask the Soviet Union to release you and me, Hey," he yelled, "How did they know about me, did you... you must have put my name in your correspondence." He looked incredulous and burst into uncontrollable sobs.

*

Lajos went on working the vegetable gardens in a numb silence, feeling nothing, caring about nothing. Months went by. Sergei spoke with him almost daily, reminding him that he had to live, that there were still possibilities. Lajos contemplated suicide, knowing he would not do it. Slowly and without wanting it, life and a fierce hope, the kind of hope that cannot be killed in some people, returned to him.

*

Conditions improved in the camp. Years rolled by no matter what men did with their time, or where they were. Then, almost as if by magic every now and then a few people were released much to the utter disappointment of those left behind. Twelve years had passed since the end of the war. It was now January 1957. Sergei pushed some old newspapers across to Lajos. He read about the world as it was presented by the Soviet government. In one of these papers there was a short article that said that there was no more prisoner of war camps in Russia. The writer spoke about how the last few men were sent back to their countries and about how their relatives were shocked to find them alive. In another brief article there was talk of how the Soviet army managed to save Hungary yet again, from 'dissident forces', by putting down the revolution of 1956. The Hungarian government, it stated, had asked for help. This was disturbing news, but what did it mean? What revolution by whom and why? Sergei told Lajos that there was an uprising against the Russian occupation and the rabidly murderous and inept Hungarian communist government of the day. Evidently, a lot of people had escaped Hungary during or after the days of the fighting. No one knew the numbers of dead or who had escaped.

As winter's last hurrah a snow storm came, one worse than anyone could recall. It was impossible to work outside, so the prisoners were allowed to stay in the barracks. Late one afternoon, the door to the hut Lajos shared with ten others slammed open. Commander Sergei entered, wiping away snow and sleet, cursing the weather. Lajos saw him shutting the door, walking towards him smiling - he knew something had happened and stood up. Sergei grinned and danced a little jig, putting a bottle of vodka on the table, and grabbed Lajos.

"Lajos, you are going home and so am I... It is over." Lajos stared blankly, hearing the words as if in a dream.

"What? What did you say?"

"Lajos, you are going home! We all are, it is over," Sergei repeated, holding his arms out in joy, twirling like a happy child. "We are going home." Everyone yelled out in excitement, jumping and hugging one another. Lajos was speechless. He gulped down a shot of vodka. Sergei, containing himself said, "Come to my office in the morning. We are going home, the gulag system is over."

A Russian Joke, but not so funny;

"One man's death is a tragedy; a million deaths are a statistic"

(Joseph Stalin)

The Journey 1957

Commander Sergei drove Lajos in a horse-drawn cart to the train station. "A bit of a joke to call it a station; four slabs of cement blocks marking where the train should stop, if it does." As uninspiring as it was, the scenery struck Lajos. For twelve years he had not seen anything but the prison camp. Here, the land strained even further into the distance, but a few more trees dotted the landscape divided by the rail track. Hungry for new sights, he took in everything so intently that even this drab place seemed all right. The rail tracks leading toward freedom awoke feelings he had all but forgotten - joyous anticipation, hope and a sense of vitality. There was going to be a new 'real' life for him after all. This marvelous moment filled his attention, no thought of the past or fear of the future interfered.

The train arrived three hours late, slowly puffing its way to a stop. Lajos threw his small bundle of clothing on the train step. Turning to Sergei, he said his thanks for all the man had done for him: "I will actually miss you, Sergei, and I won't forget that you are a human being of the better kind." The Russian shook his head, "It is a crazy world my friend and a harsh one. It was not fair that you should have to suffer so much, but here we are ready to live on, ready for life." His eyes smiled, misting with tears. They shook hands, and embraced. Lajos stepped on to the train. Sergei, his big red face grinning widely at the thin, brown skinned Hungarian said, "And don't ever come back for a visit will you."

The train was an old cattle truck fixed up to carry passengers. The red paint was worn off to its uneven timber planks and the wheels and undercarriage were rusty. The wagons were jam packed, mostly with soldiers, ex-prisoners and Russian peasant folk holding boxes of chickens cheeping loudly in disgust at being confined. Lajos noted, amazed again, 'people, real people going about their business, living their ordinary lives.' An almost unbelievable sight. He looked for a spot near the door next to what passed as the toilet; a hole cut in the floor, and sat on his wooden box, a gift from Sergei. A very pale skinned, white haired, skeleton of a man smiled at him and he smiled back; the recognition of optimism. The train huffed, wobbled and screeched, making noises enough to frighten anyone, but these people, packed in like sardines, were past worrying about safety. Every few minutes Lajos felt inside his pocket for his papers and the few rubles he had been given. The papers gave him the freedom to travel out of Russia back to Hungary. He was free now, though free to do what? Free to face his losses? No, he forced himself to think, 'No, to find my son and wife and family.'

The train jolted forward, rumbling, gathering speed. The clicking of the wheels became hypnotic and soothing. Every sound was a new song; every movement and face seemed like a new beginning. His eyes shut out the last sights of this damnable place and he fell asleep, his arms crossed over his chest keeping his papers safe.

He woke feeling something unique. Excited! He felt excited, and it was fresh to feel this. But soon, negative thoughts began to brew. He felt sick just thinking about it. He was going home to Budapest, but the idea was full of trepidation and bitterness. He must find his family, his wife and child, brothers and sister, mother and others. The thought stopped and stunned him, 'Do I really still believe that they are alive after all?' It was not a question, he would not ever let go of the possibility of finding everyone, or, or at least...

What would his son Tibor look like now at the age of what, 16 years old? Where were they, he and Sari, and how had she changed? Perhaps she remarried? 'No, no!' his mind screamed, but worse still – what if they had been home when the bomb dropped on their building? He swallowed hard to keep the chill of fear stabbing his bowels. The most horrible must not be allowed to make images in his mind. He knew something about the extermination of millions of Jews, Russians, and millions of others. His heart contracted, leaving him gasping for air, he knew his chances were not good. How to believe or make sense of all that? The excitement of being free and his fears mixed in a heavy brew. What would he find? How to live with all this? He forced back his tears till his throat hurt.

All day and much of that night he sat glued to his timber box, staring at the passing scenery. The sun came up and went down, the endless tundra slipped by as people talked, sang, or argued. A chicken gave out one last quack, dying in the arms of its owner. People came to the makeshift toilet hole next to him. Some looked at him, others did not. Though he was nervous about falling asleep, weariness, the hypnotic rhythm of the train and the torments of his thoughts dazed him into sleep again and again.

The train staggered on. It was morning, crispy cool. Lajos was hungry and thirsty and needed to go to the toilet, but did not want to risk losing this not so crowded spot. Being next to the door was the best place to be, 'in case one had to jump from the train'. He decided to always sit or stand so he could see what or who was coming. 'Never again will I let the bastards take me.' There was still not much that was new to see, nothing but patches of frozen tundra, the odd log cabin amongst three or four scraggly bushes. A day later a few hills, some trees and an occasional field planted with something sprouting a greenish tinge covering the ground. Early another morning he woke to see through the small window, a village; people, cows and carts. It was beautiful. It was magnificent. He watched it with intense pleasure until it was out of sight.

In the late afternoons there were stops when the Red Cross people handed out water, a piece of bread and cans of beans - the only food they had for many days, but much appreciated none the less. The pale white haired man who sat silently in the opposite corner was obviously a German. He tried talking to Lajos now and then, but he shook his head, he had no intention of being friendly to an ex-Nazi. He often felt the other's eyes on him, but this man was not going to hurt anyone, he figured, he looked totally worn out.

The weather was getting warmer. More and more trees and bushes, almost forests, came in to view. Some animal, perhaps a horse was running fast through the trees. Villages and farm lands, fallow or sown to pasture one after the other now; this is real life. Occasionally, the train would chug through villages slowly enough for Lajos to see peasants working on the land. The villages he saw were poor, but full of color and movement. Horses, cows, geese, and little children chasing them.

The next morning, the jolting movement of the train woke him from a nightmare. He was grateful for the stop, hoping they could get off to stretch their limbs. Hunger was also gnawing at him. The doors slid open, a Red Cross man was handing out cans of sardines and stale black rye bread. Nothing had ever tasted so good. Word came that everyone could get off the train. Lajos jumped down with his box, into an early morning sunshine. People stood on the rail siding, eating, looking at the scene, rubbing their sleepy eyes. The puffing of the steam engine was gentle. Some people ducked under the train to see the other side, and the panorama there struck everyone. Thickly forested hills and a river running fast, gurgling and tinkling, the sunlight dancing on the water, astonished Lajos. He saw pebbles and rocks under the clear water. The breeze blew the smell of tall fir trees, stunning everyone and then someone yelled, "let's swim," and people began to peel off their clothing.

A few young Russian soldiers took off their uniforms as the older peasants, holding onto their bags and children, watched. Dozens of ragged ex-prisoners dashed for the water, some jumping in fully dressed, others stripping off, asking their friends to sit on their clothes while they bathed. Lajos also walked to the river. The beauty of the scene made his heart thaw, reminding him of swimming with his wife in the Danube River in Budapest. He washed his face in the cool clear water, drank from it, and took his boots off to stand in the icy cold water. Boots in one hand, his wooden box in the other, Lajos stood feeling the water cooling his body. Sergei told him not to leave anything unattended because people would steal anything. Lajos badly wanted to jump into the fast surging waters. He hesitated, his hand feeling his papers in his pocket.

The thin German from his carriage stood next to him, cautiously watching him. He was about Lajos's age, white to blonde hair and beard, his face and body even sicklier looking than some, his bones poking at his skin. He said something in German. Though Lajos understood some German he answered in Russian, "I don't understand". The man spoke again this time in broken Russian: "I'll watch your stuff and then you can watch mine."

They looked at each other for a while. Lajos was reluctant to trust a Nazi. Hell, could anyone be trusted? The man's blue eyes were vulnerable, pained and yet smiling. Something in those eyes reassured Lajos. As if the other could read his thoughts he said, "I am Austrian, my name is Oscar," and extended a shaky hand that Lajos shook, surprising himself. Without thinking anymore, he nodded acceptance, handing the box to Oscar, taking off his padded jacket and trousers, and jumping in the river. The coldness shocked, but it felt purifying and joyful. He comprehends that he was swimming, 'something one never forgets like one never forgets who one is…' and he stroked the water as fast as he could, feeling strong and agile, just as he used to as a teenager during the many competitions he swam in. He swam hard against the current. It was like a dream, a past life that came back. In Hungary, he and his wife Sari used to go to the river Danube for a picnic. In the summer, swimming there was their favorite outing. Then they would talk and hug and kiss and imagine the children they would have later.

Lajos panicked, looking back at where the Austrian sat on his box. It was all right, Oscar waved to him laughing. For the first time in God knows how many years he was having a good time. 'Swimming was like love; loving, one also never forgets'. He laughed then. Loud, long howls that turned into an ache; how can one love anyone given what had happened? Diving down, immersing himself under water, holding his breath till he saw stars, grabbing at pebbles and then coming up splashing water, up into the sunlight, each drop bright and clear. The feeling was so cleansing that he forgot the icy coldness of the water. As his exuberance lessened, he floated on his back watching the sky and tall pine trees. Realizing he had floated away from his papers and possessions he looked again. Oscar was sitting on the river bank guarding them.

How often did he hear in the army that "The only good Jew is a dead Jew?" Well now, is
the only good Nazi a dead one'. He banished the thought forcing his spirits upward as he came out of the river, amazed at how strong he felt. He put his clothes back on his wet body, as Oscar looked on smiling. The Austrian stripped off and cautiously waded in, Lajos noted many scars on the painfully skinny body. Oscar hesitantly swam around with slow and weak strokes, the water taking him downstream. He never looked back to check on Lajos. Eventually Oscar came out of the water. Three young, heavily built Russian soldiers were laughing and yelling at him, making pointed remarks about his thinness. Oscar smiled and waved to them, walking back towards Lajos. The three Russians followed him. Lajos sensed danger. Oscar was a few meters from Lajos as one of the Russians stuck his foot out and Oscar fell heavily. He got up quickly, legs bleeding, his arms out front protesting, he did not want to fight. One of the Russians lurched forward and grabbed Oscar's boots, which seemed to be in rather better condition than most anyone's, and started to walk away with them. Oscar, surprising Lajos and others watching, leaped on the Russian, bringing him down. The other two instantly jumped on Oscar, dragging and throwing him into the river. Lajos watched hoping that this would be the end of it, but the three burly Russians began to heavily thump the now bleeding Oscar. Then one of them held Oscar's head under the water, which was easy,

as he must have been three times the Austrian's weight. Another picked up a rock as if to strike Oscar's head, while the third one was kicking Oscar's ribs and head. Other ex-prisoners, in and out of the river, watched silently at first, not keen to get involved, but a few started to yell at the Russians.

Sudden, white hot fury that knew no sense, or rational thought, overtook Lajos, as he ran towards the group with his wooden box clenched in his hands. He screamed and yelled in Hungarian and Russian at the men who looked like they were happy to finish off their half drowned victim. With the box in his left hand Lajos hit one man in the head, and then another in the stomach. Wildly swinging the box, crazy with rage, he finally dropped it, grabbing Oscar out of the water. The two young soldiers were hurt and surprised; the third one moved away bleeding. For an instant they stood glaring and swearing at Lajos whose eyes fired fury, his voice hoarsely yelling over and over, "No, never again! Never again will I let this happen..." He became this thought that fired and repeated itself, screaming towards the Russians. Again he moved towards them, his fists tight, still full of fight blinded with fury.

One of the Russians staggered away yelling about a gash on his head. The other two moved toward Lajos, one had a knife in his hand. Lajos stood still, no backing away possible. He would stand and fight, beat the hell out of them, at any cost. His face and body beyond rage, his mind beyond considering danger, he lunged forward, his fist hitting one of the Russians squarely on the nose, as the other Russian kicked his leg from under him. His screams and frenzy was finally enough to motivate some of the onlookers who came running to stop the fight. The three young Russians were grabbed by several of their countryman. The soldiers screamed abuses, cursing both Lajos and Oscar, but realized they were faced with too many opponents to continue. They swore at everyone, spat at Lajos who was also being held back, and finally left, going back to their wagon. A Russian woman apologized to Lajos.

A shrill blast shattered the scene; the train belched a cloud of black smoke. People quickly clambered back on, talking about the fight. Lajos overheard many saying that there had been enough fighting and killing already. 'Encouraging words', he thought, calmer now, but shaking and scared too. And stunned at his ability to care and fight. And for a Nazi? But someone had to, surely.

People helped to put the unconscious Oscar back on the train. Lajos wiped Oscar's bloody face and chest as best he could, and put some clothes back on him. The bruised and battered body seemed so light. There was a childlike quality to the young unconscious Austrian. He stirred painfully, moaning, groping his way back to life. Lajos thought that Oscar's left arm, and possibly a rib, was broken. He opened his eyes, recognizing Lajos, trying faintly to smile, but he passed out again.

Lajos sat back breathing heavily as the train gathered speed. His anger flared again, and again, so much anger, held back for so long, he thought. But 'better anger then fears,' he decided, grinding his teeth, 'better to fight, than to just take it all.' Tears hot and salty ran down his face as he sat cradling an unconscious Nazi soldier. He knew now that he would, he could, survive anything. Conflicting emotions stuck like fish bones in his throat. That he could care for a Nazi was even more hard to swallow, but it was right. It was decent, human behavior. He was still a man who could care. Then, his exhausted mind and body shut down.

When Oscar woke, he was looking up at Lajos' face. He tried to smile, whispering, 'Danke, Danke...' and 'Spaciba,' thanks, in Russian. He coughed, spitting blood. Lajos gave him some water, wiped his face and offered him bread. Oscar tried to sit up and then wailed at the stabbing pain in his chest, "I think my rib broken," he said. Lajos ripped up his one spare shirt, given to him by Sergei, and wrapped a tight bandage around Oscar's chest. He made Oscar swallow two aspirins that he was offered by an on looking Russian, and propped him up in the corner of the carriage. Oscar went to sleep almost immediately. Lajos shook again with fury, 'What if those Russians find us?' Fear and fury one after the other, but he knew that no one would bully him ever again and get away with it! Blood flushed his head and body at once with what had become his new, his only prayer; 'Never again, not while I am alive, no one will do it to me, to us, ever again...'

*

During the next two days the train stopped many times. Lajos watched, alert for the three Russians until at a small town he saw them leave the train. It was a relief and something more: 'A battle won by a Jew,' he mused and laughed out loud, repeating it; 'A battle won by a Jew,' and he relaxed.

Oscar slept on and off a lot, but they managed to have several brief conversations. Lajos looked after Oscar as best he could, often amazed he could still care for anyone. He still needed to justify his caring. 'I saved the life of a Nazi - No, a human being like me,' he corrected himself.

Oscar was going back to Vienna. They were quite well off, in the post war boom. Austria had the good fortune of being occupied by mainly American and English soldiers, as opposed to Hungary, now a communist satellite country. Oscar told Lajos that he had been drafted into the Nazi forces and taken as a prisoner of war in 1945. He never believed he'd survive. These were recognizable feelings to Lajos. Oscar spoke haltingly: "My family had survived the war and spent a lot of money trying to find me, never giving up hope. While most Germans and Austrians had no hope of ever coming back from a Russian prison camp, my family had managed to bribe the Russian authorities to let me go. This was thanks to my brother Wilhelm who works for the Austrian trade ministry. They have very good connections all over the world. The Soviet Union needs food. It is even scarcer here these days than in Europe." Oscar stopped, looking pensive, "I understand what I said might make you feel... I mean..."

Lajos nodded. For Oscar there was all hope for a renewal of life, but what for himself?

The Red Cross told them they were about to arrive in Warsaw and would soon be back home. Neither of them could sleep. Silently, they watched the full moon shining on forests, fields, villages and rivers, each lost in thoughts about the future. After a while and without understanding exactly why, Lajos turned to Oscar. "I'm a Jew."

Oscar looked at him for a long time. His lips trembled, "I think I knew that, and I'm so sorry, I'm sorry for what your people have had to suffer, and for your losses. There was nothing I or my family could do...or maybe there was, but we could not do it." He flinched as his chest heaved with emotion and pain from his injuries. He was also grappling with his guilty feelings; for all those times when he, let's face it, simply did not care that much about what happened to Jews. When the trouble started in Europe, and things got rapidly worse, Oscar's family quietly agreed, behind closed doors, that what the Nazis were doing was terrible. They did not do anything about it, 'What could we do?' A question they all knew was shameful, unless answered by actions. "I suppose that we are all at fault. Our culture and leaders, the churches too, but mostly just us, the ordinary men and women who allowed things to get so bad. I'm very sorry..."

What to say – Oscar speculated, what could be a good enough apology to anyone let alone to someone who saved your life - for something so horrendous. He knew the likelihood that most of Lajos's family was wiped out. And he could imagine that such losses were irreplaceable. Oscar could barely comprehend how it would feel having no hope, never to heal. No real recovery from all that was likely, he supposed.

In the darkness, through the train's noises, Lajos heard what Oscar said. He listened and yet did not hear. The words wafted in the air, lightweight, almost irrelevant. He listened, without saying or thinking anything about this man, and whether he was personally culpable. By now, he suspected that many of his relatives did not die in the war, but were murdered in concentration camps - or else they were lined up and shot into the Danube.

Oscar paused, looking worried. Lajos probed speaking his mind: "Why? In all my years in the camp and in that terrible army, I kept asking myself why? Why was my beloved Hungary so brutal and murderous to Jews? I mean, we were a small minority, why did they hate us so much? How am I to comprehend all this? Why did they make Hungarian Jews fight for the Nazis who wanted us dead? How come innocent children had to die just because they were Jewish? These questions will never be answered, no matter how I think and think and think about them."

He stopped raving, swallowing hard. His eyes burned through his skull, trying to focus on the darkness outside, rather than on the passion-filled mess in his heart and mind.

Wanting to find words, some way of easing the pain, Oscar could not find more than, "I am so sorry Lajos. The world is a terrifying place that you and I must live in, and make better somehow. Look at how you saved my life, the life of a Nazi soldier, and yet you had the humanity to do it." He stopped, feeling inadequate. Lajos felt Oscar's compassion, and with the recognition of suffering they had both experienced. They were just two young men who suffered and survived, when so many died needlessly. No simple answers and likely no complex ones either will ever answer any questions. His feelings cooled a touch, "You are right Oscar, we will all have to accept the past. I must somehow to believe that not everyone in the world is an anti-Semite who wants me dead. Things happened to people who may have had, or thought they had, "no choice." His words bounced edgy in him: "But would I kill, even if I was ordered to, would I kill a child? I think not."

The train wheels clacked on, a few lights out there sweeping past now and then. Oscar moved closer, reaching out painfully, his trembling hand placed on Lajos's shoulder. He had thought about something he wanted to put to Lajos now.

"Lajos, I have to say something. I know from letters - I had three of them in the last year - what is going on in Hungary. We have a cousin in Hungary and they secretly write to my parents, though they are not allowed to correspond with people in the West. They said that no one is allowed to leave the country. The borders are closed; Stalin was, and now Khrushchev is a brutal occupier of your country, and his local henchman are rabid and crooked communists." Oscar paused finding the next words difficult to say:

"You must not go back to Budapest. They will let you in, but they will never let you leave. And...and so, what if your wife and child have left Hungary? My father says that the Hungarian government is full of turncoats, people who were Nazi or Nazi sympathizers now calling themselves communists. My brother Wilhelm travels to Budapest frequently. He has dealings with the Hungarian foreign and trade ministry. He thinks that as far as the Jews are concerned Europe is finished. Lajos you must not go back to Budapest. You must emigrate."

These words came at Lajos like a shattering bomb. Shaking his head, he retorted loudly, "No, no!! I must go back. My wife and son, and the rest of my family will be...some have to be...I hold on to the idea, that some are alive. I have to think that. How else could I continue? What is there when you are torn away from all that meant the world and my place in it?"

"But you can't go back Lajos - it is useless. You have had no positive answers to the letters you sent to Budapest. Your family must either be... I mean... or with luck, they have escaped. It would be easier to search for them from somewhere else where you have freedom and money. And if you do go back, and find that your wife and child have escaped from Hungary, they will not let you go. They shoot escapees at the borders. I'm sorry, but please, oh please, think! You must not go back," Oscar pleaded, his face flushed. Perhaps he said too much?

Lajos could not contemplate it. He repeated, "NO, No!" His body tensed, unbearable pain in his chest.

Oscar saw Lajos struggle to comprehend yet another blow. 'I must make him understand and accept, yes, it is up to me to save Lajos's life.' He silently watched the strain on his friend's face. The night passed slowly. Oscar slept on and off. Lajos was wide awake, his eyes burning, his mind in a spin. 'What if Oscar was right about Hungary?'

It was still dark but light began to pierce the far away eastern sky. The train moved exceptionally slowly, creaking and moaning as if it would fall apart. Just as Lajos felt as he considered his 'choices'.

Oscar sat up whispering, "Are you awake?" Lajos nodded, knowing that Oscar would continue to press him. Oscar's determination to save this man became a fixation, a passionate force, something Oscar had never experienced before. "Please Lajos, it is your best chance to remake your life. Please, you must not go back."

Lajos shook his head, "No," but he knew he could not dismiss the idea. What if Oscar was wrong, what if his information is simply incorrect? He tried to work it out on some sort of logical basis. Oscar pleaded with him further. "Don't let them finish you off like this. Please listen to me and let me help you, I beg you..." Oscar sensed that Lajos was beginning to consider his plan, and he had a plan.

"Please Lajos, come with me to Vienna. I will help you escape when we get to Warsaw. My family will help, I'm certain."

Oscar got through the fog of Lajos's mind. Enough so that finally he agreed. What he knew from Sergei and a couple of letters Oscar showed from Austria, convinced him about what was going on in Hungary. As the morning air began to warm up, he could see more and more good sense in what Oscar was saying. After all, what harm would there be by assessing the Hungarian situation from the safety of Vienna? Yes, and what if his family, like so many others, had left Hungary? Many people had, that much he knew. A few days in Vienna to find out...And Oscar's family would help. But could he rely on them? He must, one cannot live without trusting, at least a few people.

The train slowly shunted on with many stops and starts, belching smoke on a countryside that now seemed more familiar. They were near the border of Poland, now also a satellite communist country. Lajos had not slept more than a few minutes the whole night. In his heart he longed to go back to where he was born, to the way things were. He reminded himself that Budapest is only a couple of hours by train from Vienna. And, 'The way things were, not the way things are now.'

Oscar was excited, his pale face flushed red.

"But how? How are we going to escape? My papers say that I am to be sent to Budapest," Lajos asked, his throat dry and hoarse.

"I know there are trains leaving Warsaw for Vienna, every few hours," said Oscar.

"But I don't have the money to buy a ticket, or a visa," Lajos worried again.

"No problem, I am standing on money," Oscar winked at Lajos, looking down at his heavy boots. "I have money, and as for the rest we'll just have to see what happens."

"You have money? But how?" Lajos was astonished

"I told you that my family managed to bribe a long chain of bastards, and they sent me some clothing and this pair of boots. Amazingly it all arrived. I put the boots on, oh man they felt great and warm, but oddly uncomfortable to walk in. First I thought the boots were stiff because they were new, but then I took them off, putting my hand inside, finding the inner lining was slack. I pulled the lining, and discovered $100 US underneath." Oscar laughed. "That's why I would not let those bastards take them, as you know only too well."

Lajos smiled at his companion's excitement and pleasure. Yes, that was tremendous luck and something more.

The train was running at full speed past suburbs and the debris of war. Half torn buildings spread out in empty spaces that used to be streets and parks. Hooting, the train pulled into Warsaw station. In a few moments the doors were opened. As instructed, all the ex-prisoners got off and stood on the platform to be sorted out as regard to destination. About fifty dirty, smelly, tattered men; gaunt shadows, too tired to be real, stood on the platform, squinting at the sunshine, and even managed to look animated and happy.

'Human spirit,' Lajos thought, and something his father said came to mind; "Where there is sorrow, joy is close by, and where there is joy, sorrow is a shadow". Just like now for himself, a rising excitement and fear about what was to happen next.

Oscar was bright and flushed, glancing around and then, grabbing Lajos's arm, he whispered, "Quick, let's jump off the platform and duck under the train." They scrambled under the carriage. Others watched with curiosity, but said nothing as the two of them disappeared and kept going under another and another wagon. A guard yelled at them to get off the track. They nodded, running to the end of the track, climbing on to the platform. Another train waited there. So far it was easy.

"Stay here," Oscar ordered. "Don't move and don't talk to anyone." Oscar thrust his bundle in his hand and ran off. Long minutes later, he returned breathless, waving two train tickets.

"It is just the next platform. Come, quick, get on the train!" They got on to an empty third class carriage. "When does it leave?" Lajos asked.

"In about an hour," Oscar replied. Silently they sat next to one another with their boxes under the seat, their hearts in their mouths, hoping that the ease of their escape would continue. The carriage filled up with people, a mixture, locals, soldiers or Austrian businessmen returning to Vienna. Soon, the whistle blew, the train moved, gathering pace. Oscar smiled at Lajos, speaking in his broken Russian, "We are in luck so far. When the conductor comes, with a bit of luck he will speak German, so let me do the talking."

Lajos felt amazed at his own excitement, though a foreboding anxiety rose in him again, not of what would happen next, but about whether he had made the right decision. There was no turning back now, not for the time being. Oscar seemed a different man; though his chest and arm was bandaged he was full of energy. A conductor arrived, took their tickets, giving them a long look, but moved on. As the train neared the Austrian border, Lajos asked "What now? There is sure to be border patrol."

"Leave it to me, that's our very last hurdle," Oscar said.

At the border more people got in. A woman and her husband sat opposite them, soon opening a parcel of bread, cheese and salami. They saw Lajos and Oscar looking at their food in a way that both of them recognized. "I think I packed too much food," the woman said to her husband. He took up her thought, "Perhaps we could share it with these two gentlemen."

Most people going to Vienna were well dressed civilians so Lajos and Oscar stood out, still wearing their padded Russian prisoner of war jackets. The woman offered them each a piece of bread with a chunk of cheese and salami. Oscar took the food, "Many thanks, I have not seen food like this in years," and took a huge bite.

"Where are you coming from?" The woman asked.

"Siberia," Oscar replied. The couple nodded with amazement. "There are prisoners still in Siberia?" Oscar nodded yes, busy tasting the nectar of the Gods: salami. The woman handed out more food. Lajos hesitated and then took it, thanking them in German. The woman wanted to ask more questions, but her husband nudged her to be quiet. The train stopped. "It's the border patrol," said the Austrian man looking concerned. Oscar nodded, "I have papers, but my friend does not." The couple looked at Lajos. Having heard his accent, they knew he was not an Austrian. When the guards asked for documents, the two Austrians were quickly cleared. It was then Oscar's turn. He showed them his piece of paper explaining he was a returning prisoner of war. The two guards looked at the documents and shook their heads sympathetically.

"My God," one said, "You have been in Siberia for this long and you have survived. I've heard stories like this about people still showing up, but it is unbelievable..." He shook his head handing back Oscar's papers. "Welcome home, we are a very different country now."

The guards were young, probably army personnel, Oscar thought, but their uniforms were not what he recalled. Lajos dared not to speak or move. One of the guards turning to him said, "Your papers please?" Lajos shook his head. Oscar spoke up rising from his seat. "He is a Hungarian refugee. He has no papers to enter Austria. He saved my life." The young guard looked at Lajos, "I see, uhm well, I'm sorry but we will have to detain you and put you on a train back to Hungary."

Oscar appealed, "Please, couldn't you just make like you missed him? He was with me in Siberia. He really saved my life. My family will look after him." The two guards looked at each other and then stepped outside the carriage to discuss the matter. One came back in. "I am sorry I cannot let your friend go. We will have to report him. Is anyone meeting you in Vienna?"
Lajos did not fully understand but he sensed trouble.

"My family will meet me at the station as soon as I phone them," Oscar pleaded handing the guard all the money he had. The guards looked at money, but handed it back shaking their heads, looking at each other in agreement. The young guard said looking worried, "I don't know if I should be doing this…but do not get off the train until the last minute, I will come and get you, so that way your family can discuss it with the authorities," and they left.

"What's happening?" Lajos asked. Oscar explained that all was well, given his family would collect them. The Austrian woman was visibly upset. Her husband said to Oscar, "They are pretty lenient these days. Your friend will be a bit of a rarity, but that may help, particularly if your family will assist."

The suburbs of Vienna looked clean and orderly as the train slowly made its way through them. Lights began to come on in the late afternoon. Billboards advertised beer, cars or new summer fashions. It was early spring; green trees bloomed with flowering buds, pots of geraniums, carnations and roses sat on windows sills. Peace and normality; the world reinstating itself.

At Vienna station, the Austrian couple said goodbye, wishing them good luck. No visitors were allowed on the platform, so Oscar and Lajos watched in silence as the train emptied. Soon, one of the guards came waving, "Come with me."

"Why don't you just go" Lajos offered. I don't want you to be in trouble now that you are so near to home," and he forced back tears with a greater effort than it took to carry the rocks in Siberia. Oscar shook his head, his face flushed with excitement, "No my friend, come, it will be all right."

They were escorted to an office. A guard quickly explained the situation. They could not hear the discussion. When the guard came out he was smiling, "All is well. We have phoned your family and they are coming to get you... of course I should call the authorities as well but I have not the time just now huh..." and he winked at Lajos.

Twenty minutes later Oscar spotted his family walking towards the office. He yelled out. His mother, father and brother ran toward him. Oscar's brother Wilhelm got there first. He whirled Oscar around, yelling in joy, kissing him. His mother and father grabbed his thin body, hanging on as if they'd never let him go again. Then they were all talking, asking questions and laughing in delight.

The reunion, as Lajos dreaded, broke him. He sobbed as quietly as he could, doubled up in his chair, holding tightly onto his legs, swaying back and forth. The faces of his wife, brothers, sister and parents floated in and out of his vision. 'Why not me, why not my family?' was all he could think. He could not understand much of what was said. He blocked himself, or tried to, from feeling too much, something he had plenty of practice doing.

When things were calm enough for Oscar to speak, he explained how Lajos had saved his life. He showed them Lajos's bloody and dirty spare shirt still wound around his chest under his jacket. His family took a long incredulous, almost shy look at Lajos. Oscar's father opened the office door, moving toward Lajos, his arms extended. Wilhelm also put his arms around Lajos. The mother, in broken Hungarian mixed with German said "Danke, danke. Don't worry we will look after you."

The immigration officer watching, now spoke. "I'm sorry but we cannot let his man go."
Wilhelm stepped forward, "I am employed by the Austrian foreign trade office. Would you mind if I called someone in my office?" He showed his papers to the officer. Lajos was struck by the difference between Oscar and his brother Wilhelm. They looked a little alike, but Wilhelm, obviously younger, seemed strong and self-possessed. The officer, looking sympathetically at Lajos, glanced at Wilhelm's papers, handing him the telephone, "Good luck."

All Lajos understood was that Wilhelm was now speaking to somebody in a deferential tone. The conversation went on for some minutes. The family spoke all at once, fast and excited, often in tears, or at times laughing. Lajos felt faint. The officer offered him a drink of water.

Wilhelm handed the telephone to the officer. The officer listened intently, every now and then saying "Ya, ya, meine herr." Finally, he hung up the phone, "Gut, alles ist gut," and explained what was to happen. Oscar turned to Lajos. "Good news. My brother managed to get hold of his boss, the minister's secretary. He is sending a man with the papers which will release you into our custody, until things can be settled. You will get a temporary visa, and in the meanwhile you will live with us. And, Wilhelm is due to go to Hungary in a few days! He will see what he can find out about your family. Wonderful isn't it?" They all smiled at him, their hands on his shoulders.

It took Lajos a while to understand the situation. Conflicting emotions about his freedom and safety came. A relief, a sort of easing in his chest swept over him. Was there hope, still, after all, has his luck or destiny changed? He might find his wife child and family? There had to be hope, just had to be. Then the reunion of Oscar's family contrasted, conflicted, with his feeling of utter aloneness. His doubts renewed every moment. Had he made the right decision? He was overwhelmed. A blank spin, a dazed life taking on a new shape, overwhelmed him. Pictures in his mind came fast like a speeded up movie, pictures of his wife and his son's round baby face with curly black hair, the curtain billowing in his lounge room window that opened out to the street, the sound of sweet music from somewhere, his father and mother in their home, his brothers and sister laughing at a picnic, his beautiful curly blonde headed six year old nephew Tomi throwing a ball…. pictures and sounds coming faster and faster. Memories came and blew away, … and then his mind went blank and he passed out for a moment.

Consciousness regained, he saw the concerned faces around him and managed a tight smile. Yes, he was safe and the future was ahead of him. His laughter was hysterical, as he tried to explain that the future being ahead, not behind, was funny and wonderful.

*

Within a few days Wilhelm went to Budapest. In his capacity as a trade commissioner he immediately arranged to meet his Hungarian counterpart, Peter Szabo. At the meeting Wilhelm faced three Hungarians; Peter, Laszlo and Joska. There was some fast-talking between them, and Peter reassured the other two officers that he and Wilhelm would finalize the impending deal with Wilhelm over lunch. Laszlo, who wore a communist badge, insisted that either he or Joska had to be there. Peter suggested that Joska might be best, as he had expertise in coal sales matters. Once Laszlo left, Peter re-introduced Joska with a smirk. "This is Joska, or to be more formal Josef Weisz. Unlike the other bastard, he is one of us." Peter shook his head, letting go of a few juicy Hungarian expletives as he saw Wilhelm's edgy looking face change as he shook hands with Joska.

"What's the matter?" Peter asked, Joska also looking surprised.

"Perhaps it's a coincidence. Is Weisz a very common name in Hungary?" he asked.

"Not anymore, but it used to be," Joska replied. "Why?"

Wilhelm quickly outlined Lajos's story, adding, "He wants to come back to Budapest, but we have so far managed to keep him from doing so."

"Yes, keep him away from here," Peter agreed, but now he saw Joska looking astonished as he spoke: "I had an uncle called Lajos, I never knew him really. He is listed as missing, probably dead in Russia."

Wilhelm's heart lurched, "What a coincidence, how sure are you about your Uncle Lajos?"

Joska shrugged. "How sure can one be of anything about anyone, these days?"

Wilhelm jumped in, "Have you seen a picture of your uncle?" Joska shook his head, "No, I was only a few months old when he was drafted into the army, for so called 'work service'".

"Oh well perhaps it is merely a coincidence."

Then, like a lighting strike, Wilhelm recovered his usual well organized thought process. The list of names Lajos had given him! He dug into his case and passed the list to Joska. It only took Joska a split second to recognize the names of his family.

"Yes," he croaked, choking with the words, "I know some of these names; one of them was my father, another is my grandfather..." He tried to say something more but, red faced, he suddenly ran from the room.

A coincidence, a serendipity, marvelous and yet sad since Joska was unable to either go to Vienna or even to contact his uncle. The secret police were murderous and restrictive to the point of ridiculousness. People were reporting on their neighbors, lest they themselves should appear to be 'subversive elements'. The three men thought it best for Wilhelm to deliver a letter from Joska, and hope for a later contact.

*

Wilhelm managed to find nothing else about the Weisz family other than to confirm that most of them were dead. As for Sari and Tibor they were seen leaving the building before it was bombed by one person, he was uncertain it was them. Another woman in the building said Sari and her son and the two grandmothers whom she knew well, were in the building when it was bombed. Down the street where a friend of Sari's owned a tailoring shop, the man working there said that the ex-owner Mr Gross emigrated; he knew nothing about Sari or about where the Gross family went. The next door neighbor was in that half of the building that was destroyed, so most likely dead. Their old apartment survived, just, and was now occupied by someone who was not there before the war.

Wilhelm trod the grey wind and rain swept streets of Budapest, trying agencies and government departments, tracing what few leads Josef had given him, but came up with the same result as Josef had years ago. He tried bribing officials, used all his internal contacts at the foreign and trade office with no result at all. Yes, a lot of records were destroyed during the war and some even during the revolution in 1956, but so many people and not a trace? As an efficient bureaucrat Wilhelm felt very frustrated and only now realized what Oscar had explained to him over and over about the war and the Jews.

He walked day after day hoping, getting to know what hopelessness felt like. Talking to some of these people brought frustration and he could see that many of them just wanted to deny what has happened in the 1940's. But it was more than that. Some old ladies shut the door in his face as soon as he mentioned a Jewish name. The new concierge of the building would not look up any records and lied that he did not have any, or so Wilhelm thought. Some officials were officially helpful but none were really interested. They were all certainly suspicious and disbelieving that someone came back from Siberia after all this time.

Not another relative or Weisz could be traced except for those who were proven dead or had nothing to do with this family! Wilhelm came home sadder and a somewhat changed man. He would have to tell Lajos the facts just as they were. He felt he could not soften the blows or offer any hope, to do that would be an act of silliness and a denial of tragedy.

Lajos heard it all, pale faced and withdrawn. He went into himself, and lost the will to speak or eat for days. The Schmidt family was worried and then relieved when Lajos finally came back to life and agreed to take up the offer to migrate to Argentina where Oscar's Uncle Johan would look after him and provide him with a job. Johan and his family left Vienna in 1938. They saw what was coming to Europe. A few years later Johan changed his name to Carlos. He was disgusted with Austrian complicity in the Holocaust and he wanted to be thought of as an Argentinean. Numbly, Lajos went along with the arrangements made for him.

Yet Another Jewish Joke
A telegram arrives;
"Begin worrying, details to follow".

This was not a Hungarian Joke:
The following picture and text roughly translates as: Jews, defend your Jew honor, don't buy goods from the West.

FORCED-LABOR SERVICE

In 1939, the Hungarian government established a forced-labor service; 'work service' for Jewish men of arms-bearing age. After Hungary entered the war, the forced laborers, organized in labor battalions under the command of Hungarian military officers, were deployed on war-related construction work, often under brutal conditions. Most were sent to Siberia, to aid the side of the Nazi forces that wanted them dead. Subjected to extreme cold, without adequate shelter, food, or medical care, and unarmed, many thousands of Hungarian Jewish work servicemen died before the German occupation of Hungary in March 1944.

Uncle Carlos, Buenos Aires, Argentina 1958

It had been a long journey on mostly stormy seas. Lajos had spent many hours holding tight to the ship's railing, getting wet with spray, watching the rolling grey seas lurch off the ship's bow as it moved him closer to his new life. 'But what is a new life? The same person in a new situation? Does a new place eradicate the past? What was he doing here? Surely he should have stayed and, and...' Over the five weeks of the journey aching hope and doubt churned around in him as usual. At times he felt great apprehension and anxiety, or else the newborn seeds of a fresh sense of aliveness.

He read Josef's letter so many times that he could recall it verbatim; on a particularly difficult day he threw it into the sea. 'If I am to be new, then throw away all the past', but he knew that the past was always present, it was himself and his memories.

*

Buenos Aires waterfront was a profusion of color and movement as the ship neared the docks. Lajos watched spellbound and excited. Dozens of ships and boats were loading and discharging cargo, steam puffing black from their chimneys, small and large vessels mooring or leaving wharfs. On shore he saw cars, trucks, cranes and huge crowds of people busy with their lives. The colorful dress of the people and the range of cultures was also a surprise. He had not seen black or colored people before. The astonishing sights seemed chaotic and yet exhilarating, like his own inner roller coaster turmoil. The cacophony from the shore mixed with some music, creating an air of excitement. People scanned the ship's deck for a glimpse of familiar or perhaps long lost faces. Lajos knew that some of his fellow passengers were meeting family, a painful notion he quickly shook off.

The ship tied up at the wharf. The gang plank was lowered. He took out the picture of Carlos, searching the faces of the waiting crowd. Cars and people, black, white, mulatto, Asian, all dressed in a wild variety of clothing mulled around. A band of five black people were playing the samba now in front of his ship. Oh how much Sari, his wife liked to dance the samba and the tango while holding their baby, singing the silly words of the Hungarian version while the baby gargled and burped away as she rubbed his back. How she would have loved this scene.

Carlos and his wife had a photo of Lajos so they watched for European faces of the disembarking passengers. Carlos pointed to a man coming down the gangplank. He was mid-height, lean, balding but very brown, a hesitant distant look in his eyes. Carlos waved to him as he checked the photo. Lajos felt the focus of the short rotund man standing with a woman. They looked out of place, dressed rather formally in the heat. He looked closely at his photo of Carlos. Were these people his link to the new world, in charge of his future for the time being? Lajos moved slowly with the crowd, down the narrow gangway toward Carlos, smoothing his creased shirt as best he could. The couple came towards him smiling with hands extended. "Willkommen" they said, repeating it in Spanish and then hesitatingly in Hungarian, with reassuring smiles.

Lajos settled in reasonably well. Carlos knew that Lajos had grown vegetables during his time in the in Siberia. He put him to work in the propagation section of his nursery business. This was ideal for Lajos as the foreman Jani was a Hungarian. For a few months Lajos lived with Carlos and his family. His room at the back of the house overlooked vegetable fields and a fruit orchard. This lush scene could not have contrasted more with the endless Siberian tundra. At the end of his work day, he sat looking out his window, soaking in the green life growing before him.

Carlos, his wife and two children were gentle in their interaction with him. They tried to converse with him about the ordinary happenings of life. Lajos rarely said much about his past history or feelings except, now and then, to Carlos. The two of them went for long walks on Saturdays. A relationship of trust and care grew easily. Carlos was amazed at how fast Lajos learned the language and horticulture, and about his ability to innovate in small ways.

Weeks and months rolled by fast and intensely. The comfort of living with this family was always tainted with not having his own family. With help from Carlos, he managed to buy and find materials to build himself a three room shack not far from the nursery. Jani never asked, but eventually Lajos told him that he was Jewish. One Sunday they went for a ride and Jani showed Lajos one of the synagogues in the city. "Thank you Jani, but I've had little interest in religion before the war, and I have none now, and even less interest in God. What is there to say other than the usual nonsense? God can't exist otherwise he would not have allowed all the misery to happen. But wars and terrors are the history of humanity as we know. Still, I don't blame God, I can't very well - given I don't believe in him," and he laughed at his own bitter joke.

*

In the evenings, Lajos studied Spanish and agriculture at a night school. Two years later he spoke good Spanish. His life consisted of work, and studies, and long drives or walks on Sundays, ending usually at dinner with Carlos's family. He was granted Argentinean citizenship.

By now he was in charge of the fruit orchards. As his knowledge and experience grew, he increasingly thought about going into business for himself. This greatly surprised him at first. What was the point of making money or building a business? 'But that is life, one must live, making as much of it as possible.' There really were many opportunities in the vibrant economy of Argentina. Making money, he realized, was having personal power. To buy the things he wanted? Not cars or lavish houses, but the possibility of research for relatives and, like Carlos, to be able to donate to war victims and orphans. Work and money did bring him satisfaction. It proved that he has done something with his life. He did not want to quit working for Carlos, but had an idea that he decided to discuss at their Sunday dinner.

After they finished eating, cigars were lit as they sat in the garden. Everyone smoked cigars, big or small, rich or poor - a habit Lajos grew to love. He excitedly, but carefully broached his idea with Carlos.

"Carlos, all the wealth in the world could never repay your kindness. I am deeply grateful. You have given me a job, a home and a new life. Most importantly you have given me hope and direction. Thank you Carlos."

The older man stood, wrapping his arms around Lajos. "You sound like you have just begun a speech," Carlos chuckled, "Go on..."

"Carlos, over the last few months I have been thinking about an idea that may profit us both. If you don't like it in any way, I shall withdraw it immediately." He stopped, concerned he would jeopardize their friendship, but Carlos, puffing a ring of smoke into the night air, waved him on, "Hm, sounds interesting already..."

Lajos continued, "You have captured a portion of the fresh vegetable market of this city and I believe you, or rather 'we' could and should expand it further. You know how we often spoke about how good it would be to sell vegetables out of season, and maybe even export some to North America in the winter. There is a property available near here that may provide the right environment for successfully growing high quality vegetables. Through my studies, I have come to realize that people would buy - if they could - vegetables when they are out of season. Overseas they are already doing that, storing them in large refrigeration units to make the vegetables last longer than the season. As you might imagine fruit and vegetables sold after the end of the season also bring better prices."

Carlos listened intently, nodding. This was a good idea, but he did not want more work or money.

Lajos took a deep breath. "Would you consider investing in such a venture with me? We could start small. I do not have much money as you know, to set up the business. Would you be prepared to provide the finance? I would be happy if you just gave me a small percentage of the shares for which I will pay you back from the profits."

He then presented Carlos with the business plan he had meticulously drawn up. Over the next week, Carlos looked through Lajos's plan. He made some enquiries. Everything seemed to suggest that the proposal would work. Within three months, they purchased the land and a cool room facility was built. It was not long before the business began to boom. Lajos named the new venture 'Sari's Jardin' (garden).

In just three years they had a very successful venture. It became a major supplier of vegetables to high-class restaurants and grocery chains across Argentina, and there were export markets opening up everywhere. The following year Carlos said that he wanted to sell Lajos his shares. He was ready to retire; his children showed no interest in his business. The deal was done.

*

Lajos handled his life as it came. He immersed himself in his business, spending less energy on the past, refusing to think about it as far as that was possible. Some days, the past was insistent - then he'd jog and run around the property until exhausted. He was known as a loner, a quiet and shy man who had little social life other than his connection with Carlos and the family, and a few friends. Carlos tried to introduce him to some people, particularly to eligible single women, but he politely refused more than brief contacts. Lajos corresponded regularly, if not that often, with Oscar and Wilhelm, as happens when people are not sharing lives directly. Carlos encouraged him to tell them of his success and to go and visit Europe. And though they often spoke about the Austrians, Lajos seemed to be reluctant, even embarrassed, to take up such suggestions. Europe was a place of very bitter memories.

*

On a late Sunday afternoon, Lajos and Carlos sat talking, burning their cigars, sipping coffee and brandy under an exotic old tree. After some silence, Lajos spoke.

"Carlos, I know you are going to want to talk me out of this, but I have made contact with a private detective called Antonio Garibaldi and intend to make yet another search for my wife, son and family, in Hungary, or wherever".

Carlos was indeed surprised. He knew that Lajos had tried this before via several agencies. He had hoped that he had given up.

"I thought you've managed to leave all that behind, amigo, you have to let it go. You know it's useless. You've had no results, only disappointment."

"You are right Carlos. But I can afford to, and I want to try again, perhaps to find some way to stop what haunts me. Every time I hear a story of someone thought long dead turning up unexpectedly in some country, - and this still happens, my heart nearly breaks. Every time I wonder again, why not, why not for me?"

"Is this Garibaldi a specialist in missing persons?"

"No," replied Lajos, "That's exactly why I hired him. The last time I hired a missing person's specialist I could not help feeling that I was being merely entertained for a fee."

Lajos, more animated than usual continued: "I like this Garibaldi, I mean, I really have taken to him somehow. He is a little older, in his sixties I think. He has a quiet and gentle air that is compelling and powerful, and I believe he is a truly honest man. Having told him my story, I found it interesting the way he listened to me. He was more interested in what happened in the days in Vienna and with you here, than in anything else. I guess he was looking for clues that might lead somewhere, rather than just going through the movement of collecting a list of names and such."

"So what was his assessment?"

"He tried to talk me out of doing anything."
Carlos nodded. "Sounds good."

Lajos shrugged. "For long stretches of time I feel like I've managed to leave it all behind, as if I've finally given up. Then suddenly, I don't know, perhaps a dream comes, and I'm agonizing again. It comes back with a vengeance, like a 'jack in the box' it comes flying out once the lid is lifted."

Carlos waited, watching him re-light his cigar, pouring the strong Brazilian coffee they both enjoyed.

"And before you ask for how long I will pursue this, my mind is now made up: for as long as I must... or longer! Why? Because I want to leave something behind, I want that my life continues, that if anyone is alive they should know I was...I don't know, that I existed? Or that they existed for me, no matter what? Because I want someone to know that they have inherited their right to life, and that they have inherited my life too, not only all the bad things that have happened. I want to die feeling I have left my son something, not just money, but that he would know that...that I would have loved him, had we, if we...Do you understand?"

Carlos looked at him nodding. It was astonishing. Even though it made no sense leaving an inheritance to a dead wife and son or relatives, the idea was breathtaking. It could only come from this man. How right it is that not only money is inherited. We leave as legacy all that we are: our lives and stories and continuance, all is left to our children. And it is not only the inheritor who is in this picture. It is a proof that life is truly a mysterious continuum. Yes, one leaves 'love' - by any other name - be that money, pictures, memories of good and bad times. Carlos nodded that he very much understood, and even agreed. What an idea, but of what use... but no, not just an idea this; it was a purpose for Lajos, he realized! The one thing that everyone needs; a reason to live!

Lajos shifted, throwing himself back into the chair, focusing again on Carlos. There was more to come. They both lit another cigar and watched the amber light burn. Lajos spoke again: "I have made a will leaving all I have to my wife and son, nephews or nieces or whoever might be found. I am leaving some moneys to my nephew Josef, who was, is, there in Hungary, I hope - even though Wilhelm couldn't find him again, Josef seems to have disappeared."
"But Lajos, you haven't found anyone else either."

"No I have not, but Josef was there in Hungary in 1955, perhaps he emigrated during the Hungarian revolution of 1956. At least I hope he has." Several letters to Josef had come back 'Addressee unknown.' And neither the Hungarian agency or anyone else could find him.
"You know Lajos; the real explanation might be somewhat sadder. Wilhelm made it very clear that Josef's

sympathies were not with the communist regime, and in the revolution he may well have emigrated or…"

"Been killed you mean?"

Carlos felt awful. Why kill off some little spark of a hope? Lajos buried his face in both palms. Through the haze of the cigar smoke Carlos saw the other's eye softening with a tear rolling down disappearing into that grey brown bushy moustache.

The evening was beautiful. Insects buzzed around the trees and shrubs, the birds were finding their nests and the humidity began to drop to a blissful level. Silently they watched the garden and the sun's last rays on the tree tops. The birds retired, a hush descended on the garden and only the tinkling sound of coffee cups broke the silence.

Antonio Garibaldi, Buenos Aires, a few months later

Antonio Garibaldi's office was one very large room, somewhat faded, but comfortably charming, full of creaky leather chairs and high bookcases. The office had a movie-set like quality and it smelled distinctly of the many cigars smoked, and of the sad stories heard over the years.

Garibaldi was a stocky, strong-looking man, the wisdom of his years born out of much experience of human nature. A curious man, he was interested in why people acted the way they did. To him the main mystery and ambiguity of life was people. Why the human race was still so stupid was a study he never ceased to explore. Other mysteries were fun to contemplate, though likely useless, people and consciousness had to be figured out.

In all his years as a private detective, he never stopped being amazed by the stories his clients brought to him. Humanity consisted of two types of people, he decided. Those who had, and those who did not really have a heart. Oh sure, everyone had a heart for some things, and some people were intelligent while others seemed rather silly. The ones who had a heart incorporated others in their lives. The others were stuck in their own narrow selfish world. People who had a heart, as he saw it, Garibaldi tried to help as best as he could. The others he dismissed, as politely and as fast as he could. His deeply craggy face usually seemed on the brink of being jolly, ready to laugh, or else to reflect on what he saw and heard. He looked at the picture of his wife of over thirty years on his desk. How would he be if his own wife or his family did not exist? What exactly would the world mean?

Garibaldi waited as Lajos settled in an arm chair. 'This client Louie Blanco, originally Lajos Weisz, had fast become a friend over the few months that they had known each other. Occasionally he wondered what it was about Louie-Lajos, this quiet gentle man, that so impressed him. He seemed a wise enough, and yet a sadder man, than anyone else Garibaldi had ever met. The man's melancholy was in his eyes, but there was a tremendous, if odd, sense of humor accompanying it. The sort of humor that only people with some depth have; perhaps only those who have suffered enough and survived it? Yes, it was Jewish humor, no matter how much Lajos denied his Jewishness. Louie-Lajos was usually willing and able to converse about both the serious and the ponderously sillier issues of life. Politics and philosophy, the society around them in Argentina, or the fate of the world was endlessly discussed over meals, wine and many cigars. At such times, emotion and passion came to Lajos, a burning fuse smoldering close to the surface. Yes, there was a depth to this Hungarian Jew, caramba, too much depth for his own peace of mind.

Garibaldi offered him a cigar. "Colombian amigo, just the ones you like so much, though you should not smoke given your recent history."

Lajos had an attack of angina recently. The prognosis was good enough, and Lajos was not bothered. "Nothing can kill me except life," he grinned. As for stopping smoking, or his running regime, he never gave it any further thought. "One is bound to die of a broken heart or else old age will get you," he teased.

Garibaldi knew that what he had to say to this man would bring him no comfort. How to tell him that he was empty handed and unable to offer even the slightest hope? Hope? Hell, he could only offer a vaguely optimistic, ridiculously long shot idea; perhaps he should not even mention it. There was no use in wasting further time. He took a breath, blew a thick cloud of blue smoke, waved it away with a ring-studded hand and spoke.

"Lajos, I am sorry to say that so far I have drawn a complete blank."

His client did not even blink. He sat stone still listening, his face tight, expecting bad news, nothing news, and hoping for something, all at the same time.

Garibaldi went on carefully. "I have nothing to report. There is only one last suggestion I can make and it is thin. If it is all right with you, I have asked the law firm I told you about in Los Angeles, to leave the matter open on their books. I had a long talk to Joe Weinberger, the principal of the law firm, and his suggestion was that we should concentrate on the only possible survivor we know, your nephew Josef. It is slim, this idea, but I think they are right. I've worked with this company for 30 years, with some success. There will be no charge, but if they get lucky then a success fee will apply."

Lajos nodded agreement. He saw what was coming anyway; he could read his friend's face all too well. He tried hard not to feel the usual dizzy sadness welling up. He took a long drag of smoke and swallowed it. It made him lightheaded, helping to mask the sharpness in his heart.

Garibaldi thoughtfully spoke again. "One other thing Lajos, my wife and I are going to Europe on holiday. While there, I will go to Budapest and do some investigative work myself, though I have no idea what I intend to do…as usual." He laughed adding, "Who knows? I might get lucky with some of Weinberger's contacts in the Hungarian Foreign office."

"That's fine Antonio if you think so," Lajos finally squeezed out.

Garibaldi sighed and coughed clearing his lungs.

"Come on Lajos, let me buy us dinner."

They rose from their chairs and, walking out to Garibaldi's car, he could not resist asking again, "I don't suppose you will ever give up?"

Lajos shook his head, "No."

Garibaldi slapped him gently on the back. "Caramba, merde, diablo, shit and fuck," he mumbled. What else could one say?

Oscar 1976

Sunday evening, at the end of a long warm summer's day, Lajos arrived at Carlos's home as usual for dinner. The familiar garden hummed with the music of chirping, screeching birds in the late afternoon sun. The huge mix of tropical and European trees began to turn the color of their foliage to their autumn coat, but the vividness of the pink and red bougainvillea was still brilliant.

Lajos felt excited and a little uneasy. Over the last few weeks he had developed an urge to visit Vienna to see Oscar and Wilhelm. He knew that while he was there he would be compelled to go to Budapest. Visit that damn place but for what? To renew hope or lessen hope? To confirm his utter disbelief about his birth place and what happened there? Or perhaps he wanted to go there out of curiosity; or even maybe to show 'them' that he was still alive and kicking? Perhaps a confirmation that he did not just imagine his first 27 years? The idea of going to Europe was sudden and scary. It was also and undoubtedly exciting, and now he was determined to do it. He mentally shrugged thinking, oh well I do not have to justify this or work it out do I?

When Louisa opened the door, Lajos knew immediately that something was wrong. Her eyes were red, obviously from crying. Carlos appeared quickly, looking disturbed. Lajos addressed both of them, "Is something wrong?"

Carlos nodded brushing away his tears. "Oscar has died." The two of them led a stunned Lajos into the house. It was unspeakable, what he felt, another part of his past was ripped from him. Perhaps, he thought, shaking himself back into rationality, perhaps it was a premonition that made him think about seeing his old friends again. Now it is too late. Remorse and regret came. Why Oscar, a younger man than he was?

They sat down, each momentarily lost in their feelings. Carlos looked up into the air avoiding eye contact. Lajos spoke with an effort.

"I had a letter from Oscar just a month ago and I spoke to him on the phone a few weeks before then. He never mentioned he was not well."

"No," Carlos said. "He didn't mention it to me either, although a letter from Wilhelm did suggest he was having some heart and blood pressure problems. Wilhelm called this morning: Oscar had a massive heart attack and died within minutes. I keep thinking about how his wife and child must feel."

They sat on the familiar sofa, arms around each other. To Carlos, Oscar was a near stranger as an adult, but a dearly beloved nephew, a happy child of long ago, in that stupid old world called Europe. To the other, Oscar and his family represented a connection to goodness and kindness. The Schmidt family gave back to Lajos faith in humanity. He felt a sense of belonging to these people, and now, one of them was gone and he was not there to help to ease the pain of the others.

Lajos spoke with an effort. "I was just about to tell you that I have decided to visit Oscar and Wilhelm, and perhaps go to Budapest. And now, I must go, sad as it is, to the funeral."

*

A gray, tired, and older looking Wilhelm, upset, but trying to be cheery, waited for Lajos at the airport in Vienna. Neither man spoke as they saw each other for the first time in many years. They hugged tearfully, watched by the curious Viennese crowd going about their business. Lajos recalled his first arrival to Vienna. The world went on; life goes on no matter what.

As Wilhelm drove they talked, eager to catch up with the news of their lives. Wilhelm spoke in a flat tone until they arrived at his place. Then he looked at Lajos, crying, "I feel so much lonelier without my brother. All I have left in the world is Uncle Carlos, Oscar's son Andreas and his mother, and you of course."

Lajos knew that Oscar's parents had died some years before, and that Oscar had a son. He had several pictures of the boy, an appealing blonde headed child. Each time the pictures arrived he saw Andreas growing up, and he felt happy for Oscar. But, he only looked at the photos once; it was painful to see happy family pictures.

"How is Andreas and his mother?"
"Devastated," Wilhelm answered. "As we all are."

For a while over dinner they spoke of Carlos and the family in Argentina, business, politics and all those things one speaks of when it is too hard to talk about the death of a brother. The two men told many stories to each other. Near twenty years of life is a lot to catch up on. They told stories of success and failure, fears, needs and hopes. This time they were more equal, and soon began to feel almost as if they had spent their lives together.

Then Lajos asked, "Are Oscar's wife and child well provided for?" Wilhelm shook his head. "Not really. You know that Oscar had a couple of unsuccessful businesses. I think the last one had taken a heavy toll on both his finances and his health. Somehow, he was never cut out to be a businessman. He lost a lot of money and confidence. I have been helping them along as best I could. I've retired from the ministry a couple of years ago, concentrating on the share markets relatively successfully, so I am comfortable enough, but not flush. I have enough to take decent care of Andreas and his mother Heidi, but she is a very proud woman. I suspect she will find it difficult to accept more than a little from me."

Wilhelm lived in his parent's old apartment and, though it was refurbished, it brought back memories of how things were when Lajos first came here. The window was open; curtains wafted a little in the night breeze. Upstairs someone was quietly playing a melancholy piece on the piano, Chopin perhaps. Trams screeched their way around the corner now and then as Lajos lay in bed. Sad thoughts came and went. He pushed them away; by now he was good at doing so. Then his thoughts turned. This time, he had an opportunity to do something for this family. An idea came to him that was not only comforting, it was necessary.

*

In the morning they got ready to attend Oscar's funeral. In Wilhelm's car, Lajos outlined the idea he had developed during the night. His plan was to 'discover' that Oscar had a small share in his Argentinean business, Sari's Garden. They would say it was forgotten and when Oscar died, Carlos suddenly remembered and asked Lajos if he had ever paid out Oscar's shares of the business. Carlos would gladly agree to the idea.

Wilhelm looked at Lajos in admiration. "That is more than very decent of you Lajos, but Heidi will easily find out that it is not true."

Lajos smiled winking, "I have already thought about that. I have a letter at home and I made a photocopy of it and brought it with me. It is the letter that I sent to Oscar acknowledging his share of our business in 1963."

Wilhelm was confused for a moment "What letter?" Slapping his hand on his brow, "You mean you have forged one overnight?"

Lajos nodded "This morning, in your office. I know it's a bit suspect, but perhaps Oscar's wife will be happy enough with such an arrangement and not want to dig into it too far."

"That's true, Heidi is not a businessperson. She is a teacher and a damn good one at that, but she is no fool. Are you sure you can afford to do this?"

Lajos laughed. "Afford it? Obviously Carlos, god bless him, has never fully informed you of our - and particularly my - good fortune. I actually had a plan, knowing a little of Oscar's misfortunes in business, to offer him some financial help. I knew it would not be easy because on occasion, when I raised the idea with him, he very definitely knocked it back. I mean, he wouldn't even allow me to send him and his family the air fares so he could visit us."

Wilhelm agreed that Oscar was very disappointed with his lack of success and how badly his business affairs had gone. And Oscar hated travel, especially airplanes. Lajos went on, "That's settled then. I will suggest to Heidi that she can either have a lump sum of $1 million US or $50,000 a year as the proceeds of Oscar's business".

Wilhelm whistled surprised at the unexpectedly large sum. "But Heidi will surely wonder why this hasn't come to light before."

"Yes, she will. I'm hoping she will skim over it for her son's sake. Do you think we could say that it was forgotten? Or perhaps that Oscar was planning to sell me his shares just recently and waited for my arrival to finalize the deal?"

"I don't know. Let's try it anyway. I know you don't believe in God but may he or she bless you friend."

The funeral was attended by Oscar's friends and a few relatives. Lajos felt Oscar's death as a blow he was not ready for. Is anyone ever ready to lose a piece of their life? Is death not always hard to believe? A renewed feeling of loss and of aloneness enveloped him. He held it all back while the service proceeded. Then he walked away towards the woods and finally he let go, crying. Wilhelm watched from a distance and then came over and led him back to the car.

Wilhelm, Heidi and Andreas and a few others returned to Wilhelm's place. Heidi's eyes were like glass. She said little, busying herself serving coffee to the guests. Her son Andreas sat on the couch with his Uncle Wilhelm quietly, his eyes puzzled and red with the many tears he had shed the last few days. Occasionally, Lajos saw the boy looking at him and then quickly looking away. The boy was near his tenth birthday. Typically, blonde with a lot of wispy hair, he was slight but strong looking. Wilhelm said the child was very intelligent and interested in a great deal around him; particularly, he was keen on literature, plays and the movies.

Soon, guests left, until only a few remained in the small lounge room. Lajos moved next to Andreas, asking in his now rusty German, "You know who I am?" Andreas nodded. Lajos felt at a loss not knowing whether to talk about Oscar. Heidi looked at them:" He knows all that happened to you and Oscar. I think he has been told the story a thousand times. He always wanted to hear it again from you, if you don't mind telling it..."

Her face flushed as she stroked Andreas head. "Talk to him about anything you want Lajos."
Andreas nodded eagerly looking at Lajos.

"How old are you now Andreas?"
"Nearly ten."
"I believe you like movies?"
"Yes," Andreas said shyly, but then perking up, "Is Argentina like Vienna?"
Lajos smiled "No it is nothing like Vienna, it is much warmer and it's full of all sorts of people".
"Refugees?"
"Yes. Refugees from Europe, Spanish, local native born people, black people and many more. I am only sorry your parents and you never came to visit me."
"Papa was very scared of flying," Andreas said, tears welling.
Hesitant, and yet badly wanting to, Lajos hugged the boy. They stayed like that for some minutes. To Lajos, this ten-year-old boy reminded him of the son he never got to hug. To the boy, this stranger was so much a part of his father's tales that he felt like a special connection to his father.

*

The following day Wilhelm told Heidi about Lajos's discovery of Oscar's shares in his business. With red eyes, Heidi looked at Lajos. "I don't believe it. Oscar never said anything. You are just making it up. How come it was not discovered before?"

"I know it is hard to believe but it was only a small share initially, a few percent and it was just simply forgotten. Actually, before I left Argentina, I was looking through some of my old business papers and Oscar's old letters and in amongst them I found a copy of the agreement I sent to Oscar in the sixties. Carlos reminded me as well. You can check with him." As calmly as he could Lajos unfolded a letter and placed it in front of Heidi.

"I know you cannot read Spanish but as you can see it is signed by Carlos, myself and the solicitor who prepared it." Lajos spent half the night rwriting the letter, forging signatures. He even crumpled it as best he could to make it look old, but then decided to say it was a photo copy.

Heidi picked up the document, unable to look at either of the two men. "I don't know if I believe you."

"Look, if it was not true, I would have wanted you to accept some financial help and I would have just suggested that. Please, if it wasn't for the Schmidt family I would not be here today with any good news at all."

Heidi tried to smile. "I don't believe it, but I'll think about it." She wondered for a couple of days whether this man was lying, and why would he bother. Was he just being generous? On the weekend she told Wilhelm and Lajos that she gratefully accepted. "I won't ask any more questions. I accept your great generosity on behalf of my son."

They went to a solicitor to draw up formal papers. The connection between Wilhelm and Lajos spilled over to

Andreas. The boy saw in the two men a bond, like the one between his father and uncle. They took Andreas for walks or to the movies, or to live theatre nearly every day.

*

Lajos went to the railway station to book his ticket and to the Hungarians People's Consulate to obtain a visitor's visa. Afterward he felt unsettled, doubting that he could handle what he intended to do. Which was what, anyway? He needed something right now, something sane and good, something to restore himself. But what? Something to remind him that his world was intact, that this was now, not back then. The idea came quickly. He knew that Andreas' tenth birthday was on the day before he planned to go to Budapest. He found a phone booth, called Heidi, asking if he could take Andreas out for the afternoon to buy him a birthday present. He heard Andreas enthusiastically agree.

Lajos and Andreas walked on the new, thin snow on Mozart Strasse.

"What would you like for your birthday if you could wish for anything at all?"

Andreas small warm hand squeezed his tightly. Lajos knew that this was just what he needed, someone to feel close to.

Laughing and jumping Andreas asked, "Can I have a car?"

Lajos laughed too "No son..." He choked on the word 'son' hoping Andreas would not notice how affected he was. 'Son,' how nice it sounded.

"No you cannot have a car and given you are only ten you would not be able to get a license. How about something just a little bit smaller? A bicycle perhaps? Tell me what your top three wishes are?"

"Well," said Andreas, flushed, "A bicycle would be great, but, but it's too expensive and Mutha said not to be greedy, and uh, ah, my top, top wish in any case is for a movie camera... I would like to make movies like we see in the picture theatre."

"Oh right, one of these new 8 millimeter movie cameras! Do you think you would use it much?"

"Oh yes, and then I could take a movie of mother and Wilhelm and my friends at school and I could take a movie of you before you go, because Uncle Wilhelm said we may not see you again for a long time," he said, his voice faltering. "Will you please, please, visit us again Uncle Lajos?"

The boy had taken to calling him Uncle some days ago. He loved being called Uncle. It was hard to take, but he smiled each time he heard 'Uncle'. His brothers' and sisters' eight children would have called him Uncle. He avoided looking at Andreas so the boy could not see his eyes.

"Bueno, a good idea, the movie camera. Where shall we go to buy it?"

Andreas jumped up and down and pulled Lajos along quickly, "I know a camera store just around the corner."

They practically ran all the way to the store. Lajos recognized he had not felt like this for a long time. Not for a long time? He had never felt like this, one only feels like this when you give a present to a young child. The boy's exuberance and excitement was infectious. Lajos felt like he was doing something real for this little boy. In the store they selected a Eumig 8 millimeter movie camera. The assistant waiting on them asked, "Is he your son?"

'Almost' was what Lajos wanted to say, but he just shook his head. They purchased the camera, 10 rolls of film and a tripod. Andreas was excitedly saying that they should go straight home and make his first movie.

"Oh dear Andreas. There is a problem. How are we going to see your epics?"

The boy looked up worried. Lajos smiled broadly, pleased with his own act, "I think we had better buy a projector too," Lajos said to wide eyed Andreas who was jumping out of his skin.

In the evening there was a small party at Heidi's place to celebrate Andreas's birthday and to say goodbye to Lajos. The child walked around the entire evening, camera in hand. At one time he asked Lajos, Wilhelm and his mother to line up as he carefully attached the camera to the tripod. He pressed the trigger looking serious and intent and ran over to stand with them. They stood there stiff and silent, until Andreas, his face serious and intent, instructed, "No, no, you must move about and talk to each other."

Everyone laughed, trying to make silly or exaggerated movements. Andreas stuck his hand out to shake Lajos's hand. The others watched the handshake, and then Andreas jumped up grabbing Lajos behind his neck. They all stood there laughing and hugging. The camera whirred on and then clicked. The film ran out. The party was over. Lajos was beginning to feel apprehensive and edgy. He picked up Andreas, looking into his eyes. He wanted to remember the boy's face. The child kissed him and held him tight. Lajos smiled a stiff smile. The others saw and understood.

Back at Wilhelm's apartment that night the two of them had rather a lot of drinks. To blot out what each of them feared, the parting and the loss of the comfort each had from the other for the last few days. Connections now remade, and broken again. Letters and pictures did not replace the presence of those you cared for. Lajos made Wilhelm promise he would visit Argentina. He nodded, looking unconvinced. Glasses clinking together, they drank again.

In bed Lajos tried to unwind. He knew well enough that the visit he was about to make to Hungary was likely to be emotionally tough and pointless. 'Why am I going at all?' The question hung in his mind bitterly.

In the morning he decided not to go to Budapest. His heart felt pained, more than usual so he took one of his angina pills deciding that maybe now was a good time not to give in to yet another pointless painful journey.

Yes, yet another – there are so many Jewish Jokes

It is the year 1939. A Jew walking on the streets of Berlin accidentally brushes past a Nazi officer.

"Schwein" yells the Nazi,

"Goldberg" replies the Jew clicking his heels together...

Part 2.

The Son

It was not long after arrival in Australia in 1957 that I first began to wonder how what I sardonically called my 'extremely dead' family affected me. Until my seventeenth year, the old family or my father was hardly ever in my thoughts, had no place in my life except perhaps as a mystery that need not be considered because it was past. Left behind in Hungary. I knew that now and then as a child, I fleetingly had a heart-ache. Other people had a father and I did not, but it never seemed all that important. After all, how do you miss something you have never experienced? Through my younger years I heard a few stories from Mum about what seemed like a huge family. She popped out names by the dozen, but it was all about strangers, people I did not know, or remember.

I have no recollection of my first seven years. The years after the war are also hazy. A fleeting memory confirmed by Mum was that I used to bury my handkerchief and underpants in the kindergarten sandpit when I was perhaps five. Solve that, Sigmund Freud. By my seventh year an actual memory was the recognition that Hungary was a dangerous place for Mum, Grandma and me.

What memories do I have now, and which are genuine? Memories are the stories one hears or experiences and forms into a life narrative, I guess. Some, perhaps most of my memories, were the stories I heard from Mum and her mother Grandma Gizella, and perhaps from others around me like the only two cousins that have survived the war, thanks to mum. One's memories are rarely one's own, I reckoned. By the time of my first actual memories, there were very few people around me that we called relatives. My immediate world was my maternal grandmother Gizella, uncle Janos, whom we barely ever saw, and my two beloved cousins Andre and Agnes. I was only three months old when my father was taken from us.

As I grew older, my yearnings focused more and more on my father. Life had been busy, rewarding, challenging, often curiously empty, and too often depressing. There was an underlying anger in me that surfaced at times, for no apparent reason. This did not help my relationships. Anger was accompanied by depression; the two seemed as one movement. But, I coped as best I could, well enough. Life flowed on, busy and successfully.

My marriage at the age of 21, my three daughters, my young brothers and my mum who lived with us, kept life busy and exciting in a positive way. Building my young adult life left little time for thoughts of the bad old years in Hungary. I put aside thoughts and feelings about the original family and my father as if I had forgotten them. I overlooked my losses and did not dwell on them. Yet I was aware of something dark, scary and venomous in me. It was all pushed under, thrown in a ditch, cemented over. I assumed that I was more or less reconciled, and I just wanted to enjoy my life.

In my early thirties, life was getting better and better in some ways yet I grew depressed more often in baffling ways. Living was fun and exciting some of the time. I was happy to be an Aussie, successful in my own recently founded business, happily married with two beautiful daughters and a third one on the way. I thought that the past could and should be dismissed without regret, for nothing could be done; true enough. But those parts that affect one most are usually hidden. The past may have been out of sight, but it was in my bones, brain and heart, whether I knew or liked it, or not. When the dark stuff wanted up and out, when it turned one's internal wheel, there was no escaping it.

On my 32nd birthday we went to St Kilda to buy cakes and goodies for the birthday party. As I got back into the car an enormous feeling of grief swept over me. It was like a huge heavy wet blanket that fell on me from a great height. I burst out crying and continued for the next hour, bewildering and frightening my wife and myself. I started talking about my feelings of increasing disturbance and unhappiness. I was blurting out things I did not know I felt. It shocked both of us, because I should have been content. Nothing was wrong in my life, yet something was terrifying. In one way I was happy enough; in another I felt lost, devastated and shaky. It was very difficult to have both sets of feelings at once, as if I was two different people.

I took notice of these new feelings and thoughts - had to really. What I used to think of as my hot temper now often felt like immense sadness, melancholy and frustration. I figured that there had to be ways to 'fix' me up. I decided to have therapy, and got involved in human relationship courses and workshops. I set out to explore myself.

*

Why did I still feel so much sadness? What was the sudden onset of dread and wanting things other than what I had, and what I had become? Who was I really? This was the big quest in the 70's and 80's; the finding of one's 'real self'. Ha ha and more ha ha. I mean, I was by now a confident, able man. My family loved me, and I loved them, I got on well with most people. Business was excellent; the customers even liked my silly radio ads. Even my employees liked me. So what was it, with these constant ill feelings and daily struggle? What was the daily struggle, the underlying fact of my existence? That old song by Peggy Lee gave the words: "Is that all there is?" That's what I felt, knowing that not everyone was that way.

The fewer reasons one has to feel bad, the harder it is not to feel bad. I had the meta-feeling of feeling bad about feeling bad. As if one could justify unhappiness only if you had practical reasons. My life was not what it should have been, could have been. But how? Should I have been something different, done some different sort of work? Was I married to the wrong woman who loved me? Why was I so over-interested in sex? What was missing from my psyche? Why be so restless and unreasonable about what I expected from others and from myself? Years of therapy had eventually educated and calmed my worst or silliest parts somewhat, but it was not enough. Nothing ever seems enough. In my greatest mistaken reading of myself when I was forty-six years old I sold my brilliant business just when it was at its best. I thought that would change me. I was bored, depressed, burned out at the time. Perhaps, I reasoned, it was because I am not happy just making dollars, doing business that by now I barely took seriously enough. I sold the business to my everlasting regret. In later years I realized I threw away the proverbial baby, the business I built from nothing; the one good thing I created. I misunderstood psychology, mine mostly and my therapist misread me; as usual for those days he offered no advice and questioned no direction on such matters.

*

Sometimes I still get into what seems like a useless, hopeless rage. The feeling is childlike. Tonight is like that, perhaps because I am writing this. Or I am writing this because I feel this way. I wonder whether I should be writing what I do; will the reader get the right idea of me? For that is the purpose and aim of writing this story. In some way to publish one's self might bring something beyond being this me? I don't know.

But why the rising fury now? What brings it on? Small things or large, but usually disappointments, and with that a feeling that this life I live is not right, not authentic enough. Not me. But this really is my life, the one and only life, 'beware of imitations'. The raging child has surfaced again. He is hitting the keyboard harder, has no intention to accept rational thoughts. The child wants to break things; the old man I am tempers it, so I don't. I drink tea and smoke cigarettes. I feel let down, fake, not entirely sane, alone and lonelier then a prairie wolf howling in the middle of the desert. Howling is what I would do, but one does not in the big city, not at my age. The tea is cold; the cigarette is finished.

*

My rage drops off as suddenly as it came. I laugh at the familiar pattern. Feeling bad is impotent; it is of no use, it works against me. Such things going through one at three a.m. are not good, not satisfactory, not enough, not what is wanted. I constantly remind myself that there is nothing wrong with my life. 'You get what you get and you don't get upset', we tell the grandchildren. I've had so much of what I reached out for, why is it not enough? Does anyone ever feel themselves as enough?

The fury is spent out onto the computer screen. I am tired out of my brain. My back aches and my head is a jumble. Oh yes, I know by tomorrow I will have squeezed it all back into a shape I can cope with. For there is nothing else for it, but to go on, move on, buy more things or less, spend or save, do things or leave them undone. Live on.

I have so many stories I have to tell, and am now compelled to tell. Will anyone listen and understand? Can they, is there one, just one who ever could? I doubt it really, since the only reader who could, would have to be like me, almost exactly. A scary thought in itself; I just said that I couldn't understand me, myself.

I stop now weary and sore. Useless. Once more I have not explained myself to me, nothing new. Oh well.

Have I explained myself to your reader? Maybe now you will get the flavor of my tale in a light that you have not seen before?

Over the bay the light is crawling up into the sky. Grey clouds without color hang out there over the water. Wind blows the palms, no one yet in sight. The whole world is asleep except me. That's comforting; perhaps I have stolen a few hours of extra life.

Let's get on with the story.

Ah, those funny Jews do make a point

The Italian says, "I'm tired and thirsty. I must have a wine. "

The Frenchman says, "I'm tired and thirsty. I must have a cognac."

The Russian says, "I'm tired and thirsty. I must have a vodka."

The German says, "I'm tired and thirsty. I must have beer."

The Mexican says, "I'm tired and thirsty. I must have a tequila."

The Jew says, "I'm tired and thirsty. I must have diabetes."

Budapest 1980

In 1980, one day, who knows why, I surprised myself with suddenly wanting to visit Budapest for the first time since we had left. I justified the suddenly urgent idea by saying that I needed a break from business and home. Within a couple of weeks, I was on the way, at times wondering why was doing this.

Over 32 hours of travel from Melbourne to Budapest offered plenty of time to recall my birthplace and to feel more and more anxious, as if I was at risk. Why anxious? I guessed it was because we escaped illegally, after the revolution of 1956. Did that make me into a criminal in Hungarian eyes? It shouldn't, Hungary had made it very clear these days that expatriates were very welcome to visit, whether they had escaped illegally or otherwise. So why the feelings of discomfort and doom? What did I expect from this visit?

My flight brought me to Vienna and there I changed to a Hungarian airline. As soon as I boarded I noticed something very odd. Every second row of the seats was back to front; 'that's the old continent all right', I thought; 'back to front.' It was early morning and I was hungry. Once the plane leveled off the stewardesses served food. "Welcome to Hungary", the buxom but rather aged fake blonde, stewardess announced. She was dressed in a sort of Hungarian costume, her face painted in rather garish colors. She greeted each passenger thus, handing out a tray with a huge piece of sausage, half a loaf of bread and a pickled cucumber. My spirits rose. There were two Hungarian things I still loved: the food and gypsy music. Other than these, well, I didn't care to be known as having been born there. I did not feel Hungarian and wanted not to look like I was not one of them. That was easy. I was dressed as usual in my Levi's, a white leather jacket and Blundstone boots, and my black and grey hair was cut in a rather large afro style. I certainly did not look like the other, mostly Hungarian business people dressed in suits.

An hour later, we touched down at the Feri Hegy airport at Budapest and disembarked, walking into what seemed to me a laughably small and grey terminal. I read the signs and looked at this, my old world with curiosity. A world that was now alien to me. I only knew it as a child; what would it tell me? 'I might as well be in China,' I thought, except that I could read and understand the language. Hearing so many Hungarian voices for the first time since 1956 was nonetheless a strange sensation. I sensed some nostalgia softening me up, but for what? My fifteen years here, my childhood seemed so long ago. It was 24 years since we had left. Still, the notion of me as a child and teenager pushed memories forward as I stood in a slow line, waiting. Funny what came back suddenly. The last year we lived here, I got a pair of those then fashionable jazzy shoes with very thick soles. It was then that I began to go to a dance school where one could meet girls. But, I also recalled that I knew I would fail my school course yet again for the second time.
The customs line moved very slowly, and I hate waiting in line. Finally, I got to the customs officer, hoping she would wave me on as she now did with many other tourists. But no, with a stern face she looked at my passport and with a forced politeness, speaking excellent English, she told me to open all my bags. She made me empty my suitcase and hand luggage entirely, methodically searching through every sock, unfolding

hankies, searching the lining of the suitcase. She did it all so slowly, every now and then reminding me that bringing goods in for sale was an offence. I kept nodding that I understood, but had nothing to declare. I had my Seiko watch on my wrist and in my bag was my diving watch. Convincing her that I was not bringing in a second wristwatch to sell was impossible. She kept insisting that I was bringing it for sale, and wanted to know what else I intended to sell in Hungary. I was, by now, baffled at all this. We spoke in English until she picked up my passport again, looking at it closely with a sour face. Other travelers had been cleared. Now she looked at me as if there was something wrong.

"So you were born here, yes?" She asked in Hungarian and I replied yes.

"We will speak in Hungarian from now, since you are Hungarian born. When did you leave Hungary?"

I automatically replied in English, "In 1956."

She eyed me with a frown, "Hungarian please"

I replied this time in Hungarian. "All right, but my Hungarian is a bit rusty and I'm not sure whether..."

She snapped her next words out unpleasantly, rolling her eyes as if I insulted her.

"Then you can practice my dear".

I got angry, almost out of control, "I am not your dear, and why are you so suspicious of me? Why are you holding me up?"

"Oh, ho ho keen to get out fast are we? Seems like your Hungarian is good enough to have a big mouth."

I took a deep breath or two, trying to dismiss my anger.

"Can I go now?" She shook her head.

"No. Let's have a look at what else you have to say".

'Stay calm', I thought. I cannot win by losing my temper. She continued asking the same questions: "Why have you come here? What business connections do you have?"

Finally, I lost my temper.

"O.K. lady, I've had it. Get me your supervisor and you know what, keep your stupid country I will get on the next flight out!"

Taken aback for a moment she faked a smile, puffed up her flat chest as much as she could, glared furiously, but called to someone behind. A large, balding and sweaty looking man. His badge read "Supervisor".

"Good morning. What is the problem?" He asked looking at her and then at me. The woman threw some words out about me being impatient and uncooperative. I was fuming, ready to shout at both of them as the man raised his hand to stop me.

"It won't take a minute sir," he said in English, as he flicked through my passport and looked at the contents of the case all over the metal bench. "I'll handle this," he said to the woman and waved her away. She was not happy but, throwing my visa on the pile of clothes, she left.

"How would it be if we kept your diving watch here and you can collect it when you leave?"
I could not believe what he was suggesting and said so but agreed, calmed by his manner, never expecting to see the damn watch again.

"Sorry for the delay and have a nice reunion with your relatives." He helped to repack the case and lifted it off the bench.

"That would be nice if I had any..." I said hotly, but my anger was diffused. I walked away thinking, 'typical of the bastards.' What a stupid thing to have happened. I laughed relieved as well, I could see the irony, figuring it was a minor rip off, them keeping the watch. I walked out of the airport looking for a taxi. I had an Australian passport so they couldn't touch me.

I stayed at the Budapest Hilton, an odd building. The hotel was built on a 15th century monastery site. A sacrilege really, part of what the Hungarians in the 80's called 'goulash communism'; *a bit of this and a bit of that.* The gypsy music in the hotel lobby each afternoon was sensational, less so to me the supercilious kow towing of the staff.

I seemed to have a photographic memory for streets I'd not seen for many years. My memories were those of 1956, existing for me as the reality of today in 1980. I spent the first day walking around, eating cakes and drinking many short black coffees. I was uncertain about where or what to start. Reluctance was recognized, and something deeper; 'What am I doing here? Why had I come back? I'm just a curious a tourist out for an adventure... Nah, not true. Am I looking for something? Or someone?'

That stung. Was I still looking for dear old dad? Had I learned nothing in Esalen just last year? 'But, ah dumb head, that is probably the thing that actually caused this trip' I thought! I had returned to try and retrace my roots. But how? I had very few contacts, a couple of school friends maybe, and a friendly sister-in-law of my step-father. Barely could she be called a relative. Everyone else was dead, other than perhaps one cousin. What was his name, Peter? No, Josef, and no idea whether he was dead or alive, here or in Timbuktu.

It was September, a few days after my birthday. The weather was fine but I was heating up, in my mind at least. A lot of terrific looking women walked past the outdoor café where I sat, in the so called 'inner city', the fashionable part of Budapest next to the Danube river. I nearly laughed out loud - but one does not - recalling how Mum used to watch me turn around to look at a sexy looking female when I was perhaps fourteen. She'd say "Why are you looking at that 'cheap' woman?"
Hm, 'cheap women.' Why were all the ones I thought great looking called 'cheap?

I had made loose arrangements to visit my dead stepfather's sister-in-law Buci and her family. Mother and I were friendly with them and I had good memories of Buci. With some trepidation I hailed a taxi and gave the address in a nearby suburb called Zuglo. Stepping out of the cab, I looked at the familiar house. It was big by Hungarian standards, two stories, with what I recalled as a huge backyard. Now the house looked half the size of my memories and the back yard turned out to be tiny with two fruit trees. Perception changes when you are twice as big and three times as old.

Buci opened the door her face looking almost like it used to, but twice as wide and more wrinkled. Blondish hair, broad smile, arms in the air already. She looked at me: a 39-year-old, black and grey bushy-haired, mustached expatriate in a white leather jacket. She shrieked, grabbing me, tearfully laughing, "Tibor! It is you, my dear child it is you..." The rest of the family came welcoming me as a cherished family member. My cousin Krisztina, with whom I had been in love as a twelve-year-old, her husband and Buci's new husband came rushing forward obviously pleased. They were the nearest thing I had to a family in Budapest, other than that missing cousin.

We talked for hours, reminiscing about the not so good old days of the 1950's. Buci and her husband Geza were equally rotund, jolly, sweet natured and surprisingly intelligent. I'm not sure why I was surprised about that. They were busily refilling glasses with slivovitz and coffee, and constantly offering me all kinds of splendid foods. I asked about my step-cousin Gabor who was one of my best friends for the years between ten and fifteen, until we escaped. I had never written to him either. Or to my very best friend Miklos Zboray, who lived three doors away from us. Why had I avoided contact? Buci put the words out "Why did you never write or call any of us?" The simple answer was that I didn't know.

They insisted I stay with them at least one night so I agreed in spite of my pre-paid Hilton room. It seemed right and comforting to do so. We made plans for them to take me out to various places during my stay. They were so enthusiastic and kind I could hardly believe it. It really seemed that I did mean something to them; "You are, family, why should you be surprised?" But I felt odd about accepting their kindness. Almost suspicious as to why these people were so nice, particularly given that we had left step-father. They asked so I told them a rather brief version of that story.

"Once we were settled in Sydney stepfather drank even more than he used to. Eventually he turned abusive and violent to mother. I was seventeen years old and had enough of the nightly dramas, but what could I do? One night I came home from work to find him drunk. After much yelling and swearing, he suddenly grabbed my one-

year-old brother by the neck, lifted him out of the cot and bellowed "You can't have him." I jumped at him, instinctively knowing that the baby could die. He dropped the baby, luckily into the cot. We fought. He grabbed a knife from under his pillow and stabbed my face, missing mostly, but scraping under my eye. Neighbors came rushing in, separating us. I packed Mum and my little brothers, and a few belongings, into my car and left. We never saw him again. The poor bastard died of liver complications from the booze barely a year later."

Buci certainly understood what it was like to live with an alcoholic given she was married to my step father's younger brother at the time.

In bed, I sat up for a long time, bits and pieces floating up, the room smelling familiar, sort of Hungarian, I thought. Looking out to the tiny dark backyard there was the huge (but in fact small) cherry tree we used to climb. The brain kept ticking away, jammed with memories. I needed the sleep after that damn long journey, but my eyes would not even shut. I sat up in the bed in the darkness, feeling warm and cozy, letting the spinning memories emerge, come to life as if it was now.

It was near my birthday in September 1949. A happy day for me because Mum had come back from one of her many country business trips and that meant we would spend time together. This was always exciting. When she was in town she dragged me around with her - and I loved it - to business meetings, lunches and coffee shops. This day we were going to the Emke, our favorite cafe house. As we walked Mum slowed down a bit and then stopped. After what seemed a long, silence, and a few sighs, she squeezed out the words.

"I've got something to tell you".

I knew something serious was coming, but who knows. I looked up, she was close to tears.

"What's wrong Mum?"

I was dreading another of her often mysterious, or to me totally meaningless pronouncements like, "You know my friend George Zilahy? He has disappeared." Or, "the tax man is hassling me."

There was never any space between Mum's pronouncements, questions and stories, no space to understand what, at my eight-year-old age I could not; no breathing room or time to know how her announcements were going to affect me, or us. Most times there was no 'me' or 'her' anyways. We were like one life, just 'us'. We lived just one life, mainly hers. But that is an understanding that comes only now, not one that existed back then.

She sold costume jewelry at county fairs to peasants. Working for herself was not something you did in a communist country, there was always something, or someone to fear. At the age of twelve I was sent to bribe the tax man, with a Napoleon gold coin. The man gave me an envelope containing money in exchange...None of this was understood by me other than, "Keep it a secret, don't breathe a word, not even to your best friends..." I was proud to be the 'agent' for Mum, but I knew enough to be worried about such excursions.

Every now and then the threat I expected and dreaded when she spoke looking stressed, turned into nothing much; "We have new rings for sale, but they have been cleaned up before the weekend, what do you think, can we do it?"

Words came falling out of her red mouth... all just falling out on me. At times a more serious and gloomy statement came: "If we don't pay tax by the 27th they'll take the curtains and the lounge furniture."

Sometimes I realized in my young-old wisdom, that she needed a non-active listener, certainly not an answering one, and though she had lots of friends, I too, had to hear it all. Somehow I was the main ear for her anyway. We loved each other, whatever that meant for such a damaged and yet beautiful little woman and her only son, who did not understand two thirds of the lives that were hung on him.

Now I was gripping her hand tightly, watching her. She continued slowly and carefully, her words sounding a little squeaky, failing to come out properly.

"I've had a letter from the war office that certifies that your father is...ah, dead, and won't be coming home..."

I could see the irony in this; if you were dead, you would not be coming back, but there was no joke in her eyes. She was looking at me intently. I watched her knowing that I must listen carefully.

"They say he is not coming back - they are pretty sure this time. There was a witness who has just arrived back from Siberia, after all these years, and he says he saw your father and Uncle Andor in a hut, that was then blown up by a bomb. Your father has been pronounced dead."

She wiped away some tears. I gripped her warm hand tighter, wanting her not to feel so bad. If she was upset, I was devastated. If she was worried, I was scared. Something told me that what she said was likely. Most people had come back from the war by 1947, and now it was 1949. I thought we had given up hope, I thought we did not need any further discussion; I thought she hoped no more. Except, she kept telling me incessantly, "When your father comes back everything will be fine."

By now I did not see the need for a father. What would a father do in my life anyway? What did fathers do actually?

There was something I should do or say now, but what?
The tears from her eyes dropped on my cheeks.
She said she was sorry I had no father.
I was, as usual worried, puzzled because she was so sad.

Some tremor inside me started up. This was important, seriously this time. I did not know what to do or say, no matter how hard I tried to think, so I hugged her tight for a while. She wiped her eyes and we moved on silently. Occasionally she looked down at me, wiping away her tears. I hung on tightly to her hand, my lifeline, my entire life.
Then, as we walked on and on, silent, painfully slowly in the cold darkening afternoon, I recognized an occasion, an opportunity. In some instinctual way I knew that something could be made of all this, that I could get something out of this, here and now. Do nine year olds know how to manipulate? I did, though I would not have known what the word 'manipulate' meant. I saw that I might possibly get something out of this, out of her sad face that seemed to apologize to me, as if it was her fault that my father was not coming back to save us.
She was looking at me intently now. Her expression reminded me of when I recovered from nearly dying of

scarlet fever last year. Yes, I could ask for something. Perhaps chocolate? No, a couple of books! And that is what I did. I asked if she would buy me a book. We went to the Athenaeum bookstore, my favorite place. I picked out "The Children of Captain Grant," and something else, both by Jules Verne my favorite writer at the time.

We walked away from the bookstore, her warm hand occasionally leaving mine to carefully wipe her eyes or blow her nose without messing her makeup. I clutched my two new books, looking forward to reading about amazing things. I smiled at her as much as I could, and felt sorry for her. We were both shivering; from the cold or the grief? We did not go to the Emke café. She thought it better to go home.

Did snowflakes begin to drift about us?

*

As a child I was dumbfounded at how my father coming back would work. It was meaningless to me. Yet, I also had something like total faith in the idea that he would come back - in spite of all the contrary evidence. Occasionally, even in the late fifties, people thought to be dead still arrived in Budapest, much to everyone's amazement. It took me another 28 years to acknowledge that the dearly held belief had developed in me as a prophecy; the coming of the 'messiah', who would fix it all: "When my father comes back I will no longer feel bad, scared or confused."

Sleep must have come eventually because Buci woke me up with coffee, warm bread, a fried sausage, butter and jam. The memories lingered on, feelings of melancholy or a warm gladness alternating one after another.

*

Settling into my hotel room I unpacked my case, but I was restless, so I went for a walk. Moving down from the hills of Buda I crossed the Lanchid Bridge to the Pest side. I was surprised at how gray the streets looked. There were still plenty of signs of bullet holes from the war, or were they from the revolution? At first I walked aimlessly, but then I neared an area that was all too familiar. Wanting to avoid this street I decided to go down Rakoci Street to the Emke Cafe. For how long can I keep up moving from one café to another I wondered. That however is a strong memory of mum and me spending time together. No birthday parties or picnics or country trips do I recall, but I am an expert at cafes of Budapest. Hm.

The Emke cafe looked the same as I so vividly recalled. Opening the door, the familiar smells of goulash mixed with cigarette smoke and short blacks came like a whirlwind. The place was nearly full - as usual - I thought, smiling spontaneously; the last 'as usual' was so long ago.

Sitting in the humming, warm café was comforting. My coffee arrived and I noticed a woman to my left. A handsome woman, immaculately groomed, probably in her late thirties. She seemed familiar. Then, I realized she looked a bit like a younger version of Mum. The reveries that had assailed me last night returned fast. I found myself thinking about when Mum had remarried. That was a major change in life for all of us.

It was around my tenth birthday that she first began to talk to me about remarriage. I knew that she had no shortage of suitors. She was a fine-looking woman with a great sense of humor and she earned more than most people. I vaguely recall one or two men she sort of dated. I say 'sort of' because she never admitted it in those words. They were called 'friends'. One of the men, Lehel, was the man for whom she worked before the war. Though she no longer worked for him because he was smart enough to take a job with the communist government, they remained good friends and perhaps even lovers. I believe this now, certainly did not hen; sons did not think such things.

Lehel asked Mum to marry him on two occasions, she told me, but she declined because, she said, "He is too tough on you."

I rather think now, that she thought him too hard on her, that as much as she liked and respected him she was also a touch afraid of him; perhaps she just did not love him. Since anything mum said was a gospel for me, I never questioned it. I actually liked Lehel. He seemed big, strong and confident. His sharp Roman nose had a few black hairs showing. He always elegantly dressed in a suit with a tie. His large hand had a huge gold ring with a red stone that Mum kept referring to as 'very good'. In his deep guttural baritone voice he liked to joke with me a lot, but he turned very serious whenever he asked about my progress in school or about what I did in my spare time. I felt guilty about what I did in my spare time. I barely studied, reading mainly fiction books and worst of all, I masturbated lots. What exactly I was doing was unclear but pleasurable to me, though I knew already that it was a terrible thing to do, but it was enjoyable.

Grandma Gizella lived with us and she kept saying "Sari, that boy needs a father." Mum would nervously tell her to mind her own business. "He is my only business…" Grandma responded.

Mum was unable to get our third floor apartment back at 24 Akacfa street because it was allocated to a communist official after the war. I never did get the full story, let alone understand it; I mean it was our apartment so…? At first we rented one room in an apartment on the first floor in the same building. I suppose that given that my mother was not in the communist party, and because she worked for herself, she was not game to make a fuss about losing our property, which had been purchased for us by my paternal grandfather Sandor.

The people who took our flat seemed nice enough, a middle aged childless couple. Tall, staunch and serious looking, they were communist party members, wore the badge at all times, and they appeared kind and interested in us. Mum met the woman's brother who often came to visit them. His name was Lajos, just like my father's name. To me he seemed tall, gaunt and always tired looking. He had a pointed nose, angular sunken cheekbones, sad eyes and his face always looked gray as if he had trouble sleeping.

Grandma Gizella had something to say about everything. "I'm warning you Sari, this Lajos is a moody sort of character. You watch out Sari, he drinks too much," she kept warning mum. Lajos was obviously keen to see Mum and often came to visit us. Mum decided to go out with him for a while, "He is fun and he likes you," she told me. After a few months, she declared that she had stopped seeing him.

"I told you he drinks too much," Grandma said. "I told you, I told you."

Mum replied, "Oh shut up mother."
I just watched and listened, doing what I did best, worry without understanding or knowing why I should feel bothered.

After a few weeks, they got together again. A few weeks later she broke it off again. Mum explained to me that he wanted to marry her and that she liked him, but she thought he was an alcoholic. Mum couldn't abide drunks; she barely ever had any alcohol. The next thing I knew it was on again and off again. Then evidently, Lajos had a private talk to Grandmother who much to my surprise suddenly turned in his favor.

"This boy needs a father," she stated again like an expert. I never knew why, but Grandma was now keen for Mum to marry Lajos. Perhaps she believed it was safer to have a man than to be on your own, and particularly a non-Jewish man.

Then mum broke up with him again; "This time for good, and we are moving to a new flat". She managed to rent a larger flat for us some distance away. She swore that she would have nothing more to do with Lajos. I was happy to move to the new place, but worried about losing my friends in school and in the building.

Dear old Grandma was instrumental in talking Mum into one more meeting with Lajos. At the meeting he threatened to commit suicide unless she married him. He promised never to touch alcohol again. A couple of days later she explained that she had decided to marry him because, "You need a father."

By then I had grown to like him. He was funny and easy to get on with. We played cards and he'd have a couple of drinks which he couldn't hold all that well, but usually he just got funnier. That he was drinking again was never debated. He didn't bother to ask about my school results which were getting worse and worse. He took me to soccer games, bought me ice cream and stopped Mum from yelling at me at times. He was a skillful tailor and yet he had no qualifications. He made me a beautiful suit, my first one. For a short while I began to see why a 'man' or a 'father' might be a good thing to have around the house.

They got married and he moved in with us. For a year or so things seemed to be all right, but then their relationship rapidly went downhill. I heard and saw everything in our small flat. There was a kitchen, a lounge room which also served as their bedroom, and another tiny bedroom shared by Grandma and me. The apartment was tiny by any measure, but better than many people had, and we owned a new sofa. Mum was doing well at the country fairs selling costume jewelry. At home, arguments, shouting and uneasy tensions lasted for days and weeks on end. Mum started traveling more and more to the country and given that stepfather hardly made a living, it was easy for her to justify the need for more time away from home...

*

The waitress stood in front of me asking if I wanted another coffee. I nodded yes, watching her walk away in her short black satin skirt, white shirt and shiny black boots. Another cheap female? The waitress looked 'available' – I thought, as she smiled at me. Should I chat her up? But another feeling, heaviness and sadness for Mum, for stepfather and for me, came fast. Sadness mixed with nostalgia, feeling good and bad at the same time.

I took out the picture of my family back in Melbourne. I looked at my half-brothers, Tamas and Rob, and smiled. One was a successful marine engineer, the other a lawyer. They were a vital and amazing part of my life, the best friends I could ever have. My wife and three daughters smiled a 'Come home soon, we miss you,' in another photo. I felt vaguely ashamed even thinking about the waitress. But that was my life; thinking about sex all the bloody time.

I looked at Tamas again; his eyes always remind me of his father's eyes.

*

Brother Tamas was born in 1953. Grandma Gizella died shortly after that. Mum was usually away for the whole week, coming home on weekends only, if that. Partly, now I guessed, to keep away from what was a continuous battleground at home. We had a cleaning lady who came in during the day to care for baby Tamas and to clean the flat. Stepfather grew more silent, chain smoking as he sat on the kitchen table that also served as his tailoring work bench. His head down, he stitched suits or repaired old ones, when he wasn't out drinking.

At night, I was often left to care for the baby. Stepfather drank increasingly more. On many nights I would be woken up as the janitor shoved him in through the door. He would simply go to sleep on the floor snoring and muttering, looking limp and scary. In the morning he made like nothing had happened. I was frightened on these occasions. My sleep was often disturbed anyway by having to get up to feed or rock the cot for baby Tamas. Stepfather no longer took me to soccer, or took any interest in what I was doing, other than to yell at me for some minor misdemeanor. One day, uncharacteristically, he gave me a severe beating when he caught me jumping on the couch. I fell and he kicked me several times, frothing at the mouth yelling obscenities and looking wild. I ran out of the flat. At that point he lost me; I wanted nothing more to do with him ever again.

*

Now I realize how unhappy he must have been. He too had been a soldier and had managed to come back from the war about a year after it finished. He never spoke about his war experiences. All he ever said with a shaking head was, "It was horrible."

I intuitively understood the great cultural differences between my mother and him, even back then. In later years, when I questioned Mum about why she married him, she said that she supposed that she loved him, adding, "I thought you needed a father, particularly a non-Jewish one." She also said that in all likelihood she might have done him a great disservice by marrying him, but then again, we'd both agree, "Look what we got in return: your two wonderful, much beloved brothers."

Life is not a predictable journey. Bad things can have good outcomes; or the other way around.

*

My trip to Budapest had become a mission now, I could feel the steam building in me; the past had to be dug up and reconsidered. I flexed my aching back, feeling strong; all those dramas were well in the past! Nothing here could touch me, nothing, but my moods, and the vague, or not so vague really, dissatisfactions I had - and ought not to have - with my life. I sat in the Emke cafe for more than two hours, musing and buzzing, having three short blacks and many cigarettes. The waitress hovered around me, smiling lots, expecting a big tip I guess.

It was laughable that I had questioned why I came to Budapest. I pulled out my notebook and pen. 'That's the way to do it; deliberate planning.' I made a list of whatever names or places I could recall. I rearranged them starting with the earliest memories of my younger days.

Leaving the cafe Emke with the smile of one who had a purpose, I headed for the kindergarten I attended when I was four. On the way I recalled some faces and some nameless faces. There were two school friends I should see again, and of course there was that one cousin from my father's side who might still be here, Josef. Mum did say that in 1956, just before we left, Cousin Josef also left Hungary around the same time. Perhaps Mum spoke to Josef's mother before we left? I didn't think so. Mum did not understand why my father's brother married her. "In any case she never liked me," she added. Dear old Mum and her projections and absolute verdicts, issued with unabridged confidence, reminded me that information from her was never too reliable.

I stood in front of the kindergarten building, suddenly thinking it wouldn't be a kindergarten by now. But yes, it was still here, looking the same as 34 years ago. I walked through the long entrance that led to an internal courtyard, like most buildings in Budapest. Inside lots of children ran about playing. Some stopped, looking at me curiously; I was a stranger and looked it.

An adult can never quite get the feeling of what it was like being a child, but I tried to feel my four-year-old self standing there.

A heavy looking stern faced woman addressed me dryly and unpleasantly, "What do you want?" I told her I used to come here as a child many years ago. She nodded looking even more displeased, obviously untouched by my nostalgia. She waved a hand. "A long time ago so, what is it you want?"

"I just wanted to stand here and look for a few minutes."

"I must ask you to leave," she said.

I was taken aback by her attitude.

"Why? I just wanted to stand here for a few minutes and you know..." I tried to soften her attitude but she wouldn't have it.

"No. You must leave or I will have to call my supervisor."

I was astonished, wondering why the belligerence. I'd argue, but what for? Oh well, fuck them and her. I walked back through the long entrance and as I did, I saw a list of children's names on a notice board. Stopping, I quickly scanned the names, as the woman watching me called her supervisor.

A man came barking at me "What's your business here?"
Again I explained that I used to come here.

"Why are you looking at the names?" he asked with more suspicion than curiosity.

"I was wondering if there was anyone here with the same surname as mine. Perhaps my cousin Josef might have had children?"

He shook his head. "Too long ago, please leave." But his attitude was softer. My eyes slid to the end of the list, to names beginning with W, and there it was; my name and my cousin's name.

Weisz Tibor

Weisz Josef

I pointed to the names, explaining "Look! That was my name, and that of my cousin!" Of course I realized that this was a list of the current children attending. I asked the man who watched me intently,

"Any chance of getting the names or phone numbers of the parents? Weisz is my original family name; these people may be my relatives."

He was not amused. "Absolutely not and I am asking you to leave immediately."

I felt shaken up and walked away defeated. Why was there no compassion here? Why didn't they see what I wanted them to see? Did he not like Jews perhaps? Yes, always this fucking question...

I did not come here to suffer, but I knew I would. What a coincidence, those names. Seeing my real birth name on that list, Weisz, was a shock. I wanted to dismiss the whole thing, but knew I couldn't. At the exit I looked back at two women and the man, staring guardedly after me. Sad people, fat and ugly...Just leave it, I admonished myself knowing I would never forget this scene. And I have not.

*

The next day started with a bright sunny morning, vaguely warm for this autumn time of the year. I watched people rushing to work just as they would anywhere in the world. On the Pest side I stumbled into the Gerbo café, where we used to go whenever Mum had money. There she would show me off to her friends, and buy me a short black with a lot of cream and a tall chocolate cake that looked like a pyramid, called 'the tower'. Eating those with much gusto, I became famous amongst her friends for my good manners, tower cake eating, and for politely and intelligently answering the usual boring questions adults ask children. This place also smelled just as I recalled: of sweets and strong coffee. I wasn't so sure of visual or verbal memories, but smells seemed embedded in my psyche. The aroma of coffee, cakes and hot sausage with mustard were evidently built into these walls. I almost expected to see some of Mum's old friends.

I ordered a short black with cream and the famous tower cake for breakfast. Not a healthy start, but what the hell; I'd run it off back home. This was not the time to restrict the needs of the body. Alas, the cake was not as good as I recalled; it was too sweet and a little stale. The walls were too old too, the wall paper faded, the ornate lights needed something, like replacing - but oh well, I didn't look as good as I did twenty years ago either.

The waitress smiled and brought me a magazine. I glanced through the cartoons. There were signs of political easing. Critical articles and funny cartoons about the government in the magazine. Then, an odd looking scrawny man rushed in through the door. A newspaper boy, except he must be over fifty years old. He had a bunch of newspapers tucked under his arms and in a lilting tone he sang:

"No news again, lots of nothing has happened! No murders, no new wars, no progress in parliament."
He sang nonstop, changing the words, handing out papers to people and casually throwing the money into a leather bag at his waist.

"Buy it now, read it or not, no news again, no good news, no bad news, just the paper. Politicians got married and divorced, the Russians are leaving so new ones can arrive" ...and so on. A good act. Something about him was worrying though, his attitude of bitter cynicism was almost not funny. Everyone seemed to know him. When he got to my table, he looked at me briefly, dancing two steps backwards, and sang on without a break;

"He won't want a paper, not a Hungarian one anyway... hopefully he'll spend lots of money," and turned away. People laughed, I kept a straight face. I was happy not to be seen as a Hungarian, and glad not to be one.

I strolled, ambled or marched variously all over Budapest's streets, not caring where I went. While I hiked the asphalt, I had the initially wonderful and immediately also rather threatening idea of ringing up people with the surname of Weisz.

The day passed me, fading into semi darkness. I went back to the hotel at 6pm. Sitting at the lobby bar with a drink, I saw a fantastic looking young female watching me. I smiled at her, she smiled back. I guessed she was a pro, though that was strictly illegal, but in the Hilton, for visitors, they probably didn't care.

My mind returned to the kindergarten. Maybe one of those children was my cousin Josef's son. I moved to go to my room, exchanging another smile with that beauty at the bar. Too well dressed, perhaps not a Hungarian. She raised her glass to me with a face that looked like a question; will you or won't you? I smiled back wishing I would, but I wouldn't. Or maybe I would, I mean what harm could come from a bit of...But I dismissed the idea fast and went up to my room. It was getting dark now. My window showed a part of the ancient ruins of the monastery, lit up nicely, a romantic scene but my mind questioned me again.

What was the point in calling Weisz's? I defiantly decided that I was just scared of doing so, hence all the hesitation, and therefore, I must do it. 'I'm tough or something', but I hate the idea of having to explain. I finally reached for the phone book, looking for "Weisz" surnames. Unfortunately, there were quite a few. No, fortunately there are still quite a few!

I dialed a J. Weisz, (could be Cousin Josef... ha ha), and an old lady answered. I was hardly into my story when she interrupted, "No, no it can't be my husband because he was born in Czechoslovakia".

A young boy answered the next call. "Is your mother or father there please?" and had to repeat it because it seemed I had an accent.

"Yes," he answers "Who's speaking please?" I am about to say Tim but change it to Tibor Weisz.

"Oh," he asks "Are you one of my long lost relatives?"

"I hope so," I said, heart beating up to 190 beats per second. His mother came to the phone. She sounded cool and strained. I start to explain my story but she broke in with "No. All my relatives are dead".

"That is exactly my point. I think all my relatives are dead too, but I am hoping to find some".

She sounded displeased at the idea but hesitated, so I quickly added "Let me give you a few first names and see if they mean anything to you." I rattled off grandpa's name, my father's, brothers' and sisters' names.

She interrupted, "No, no, no I don't recall any of those. My mother never mentioned those names."

I had an idea. "Is Weisz your married name?"

"No," she replied, "and I don't think I want to carry on this conversation any further." She hung up. Was she afraid, or hiding something, but why would she? Why is everyone so suspicious or reticent in this country?

I kept trying one name after another until I was almost at the end of the Weisz names. The next voice that answered was very deep, the owner very old.

"Is that Mr. Weisz?" I asked.

"No."

The phone went dead. I called him back and tried to explain. This time he listened responding, "My name is not Weisz. It's my son-in-law's name."

"I don't suppose you know anyone called Josef Weisz?" There was a silence and he said, "Well, I knew one, a long time ago. I am no relative of his and I believe he left after the 1956 revolution."

"Do you know where he used to work or his relatives or anything like that?" I asked.

"Possibly he used to work for some government institution, but I'm not sure".

No matter what else I tried he had no more information. Would his son-in-law have some?

"No, he died last year."

Of course, I thought, that'd be right.

More calls ended in futility, so I gave up. My burst of energy for the day had fizzled out. I felt as flat as a thin Hungarian pancake. Aha, that was the way and the meaning of life now; to seek out a famous restaurant called the Corvin, where they used to make the best chicken liver in paprika, and walnut pancakes. To boldly forget the day for the time being, Startrek.

The idea of going to a government agency had occurred to me. Someone must have had a list of names of missing people. I was amazed again that in twenty-four years, neither Mum nor I had tried to trace anyone. Or did she? Perhaps when she was here for a visit, years ago, she tried and finding no-one, decided to say nothing. I took a cab all the way to Pest only to find that the Corvin restaurant was closed. It was being rebuilt, unlike my past. 'You can't have everything', I smiled to myself. I was not hungry anymore, just dead beat tired.

*

In the morning I fronted at the office for identity cards that every Hungarian citizen had to have. The man at the desk explained, "You must know that a lot of paperwork and government officials left Hungary during and after the 56 revolution," and added wryly, "Fake communists." His glasses twinkled, displeased at me, but at least he was looking through some books.
"In any case handing out information is a matter of privacy, not something I can just pass to anyone."
Was he asking for a bribe? I was not interested in doing that, so I tried a different approach.
"Is there any chance of looking up the records pre 56?"
He laughed sarcastically waving his hand: "You expect your expatriate revolutionary friends to have left all records

intact? Even if you were a young fellow in 56, don't you remember that the mob ransacked many government buildings, burning down some, while others were taken over as strongholds from which to shoot? And when the Russians came to liberate us they managed to bomb some of those buildings damn nearly into powder."

I thanked him profusely, writing my name and telephone number on a card, asking him to call me if he came up with any ideas. Hesitatingly, I suggested that there would be a reward if he helped to find my relatives. His raised eyebrows and his voice are similar. "You expatriates," pointedly emphasizing 'expatriates', while shaking his head, "you think money will buy everything, well not here mister."
I noted the use of 'mister' - and he shut the book, indicating that our interview was over. I don't think he liked me.

Trying another department, and another without any success I resolved to 'chill out'. No need to be paranoid, I would enjoy what I could, do what I had determined to do, but take it easy. I felt better instantly. The weather had warmed up surprisingly, so I caught a tram back to the Hilton and changed into lighter clothing. I'd earned lunch. In front of the Hilton I waited for a taxi. I wanted to go to a particular delicatessen that I had spied yesterday, for lunch. A taxi pulled up after a while and I got in. There was a rap on the window; the fantastic looking young female who smiled at me at the bar last night was asking if we could share the cab. I agreed, ('Hm and aha,') and she got in next to me and gave an address to the driver. She started to chat, asking where I was from first in English, and then in Hungarian.

The taxi ride took about 15 minutes. We talked about lots of things. She was vivacious and curious about me. Her long legs were next to mine; her perfume was strong and alluring. 'Maybe one could, ah..., in a foreign country, Hm...'

We dropped her off at her home. As she got out of the cab she turned back and switching to English, her face a touch red and embarrassed looking she asked: "I hope you don't mind but how come you did not hit on me? I mean most men do and I hate it but uhm, oh sorry I am being stupid..."

"No you are not" I said "and you are gorgeous, and I am married and I am also very attracted to you and I don't know what else to say..."
She smiled relived "oh well yes, ah, see you around and thanks for the compliment".

The taxi took me to my designated deli. I felt perked up about the woman. I still had the old magic? What old magic?

Lunch time is a favorite time of the day for me. After all, does anything else really matter after breakfast? I decided to have one of those thick fat sausages these bloody people seemed to be so good at making. The deli was small and narrow and I lined up behind overweight locals. Finally, it was my turn. The one and only male assistant was huge - what we used to call a 'meat tower' - and he was looking at me, wiping his hands on a not very clean apron, sweat beads rolling off his head.

"Nah what will it be?"

"Could I have a sausage please?" and I pointed at what looked like a kransky.

He laughed, his belly bouncing up and down as he addressed the crowd around me with, "Bravo, he wants a sausage."
Focusing on me, his eyes rolled." Any more information will be gratefully accepted." Some people expressed amusement. The man next to me told me to say which bread, and whether it's hot or mild mustard I wanted.
"Oh, ah, rye bread and mild mustard."

"Bravo bravissimo, he can speak Hungarian and so well," the butcher bellowed, picking up a two-kilo loaf of bread in one hand and chopping off a quarter of it. He sliced the bread open with a cleaver and slammed in the sausage. Using the same implement, he slapped the mustard on and wrapped it in brown paper. If it hadn't smelled so good, I might have told him what a smart arse he was, and where to stick it. I held my tongue and paid. He was now busily bellowing at someone else. It seemed that everyone here had an act and making fun of customers was the butcher's specialty. No need for me to be so sensitive.

I ate the wonderful sausage that dripped red fat and yellow mustard as I walked down Korut, one of the main boulevards of Budapest. There was a tiny four treed park around the corner in a quiet street. I sat on a bench eating, and looking at my list of things to be investigated, feeling good. This was real food.

I was committed to this exploration, and then, hopefully, I'd be done with it forever. The cemetery where Grandma is buried maybe ought to be my next destination. I had promised Mum I'd check on Grandma's grave, and visit what was called the 'Fallen Heroes' monument. That title made my blood boil. What bullshit!

Fallen heroes, my sweet arse! Butchered innocents was more like it. The sausage did not taste so good anymore. I have had enough. I threw it in a garbage can and lit a cigarette feeling slowly worse and worse. Why? Grandma? I supposed so.

I hesitated outside the ornate cemetery gates, unenthusiastic now, to put it mildly. Cemeteries all look alike. Dead quiet with dead people and…oh stop it, quiet places cemeteries with a few old trees and many weather-washed graves, large or small. Names and fine sentiments written in stone about people who were most likely not so nice as what was said about them. But hell, you only die once, so they may as well live it - or rather, die it up. I don't believe in any afterlife. Woody Allen, who also doesn't believe in the afterlife, said that he was taking an extra pair of underpants in any case… I should have been a comedian.

I reckoned the task of finding the Jewish section, and, even trickier, Grandma's grave - was not going to be easy. Breathing hard, as if I'd had a run, I walked on. There was a small green booth, a few meters away, hidden by a tree. In the booth there was a woman smoking. She had a very red nose. Everyone smoked in this country; you always saw the smoke before the person. Perhaps because they're on fire…ha ha, eh?

"Good morning" I said as politely as I could manage. "Can you help me to find my Grandmother's grave please?" I was trying to be extra polite, given my lack of success so far with officialdom. She looked at me, cigarette hanging from her half painted lips, sighing as she nodded, ('Ah, another dickhead from the West') – and curtly asked for the name. Leafing through a thick book, she slammed it back down, picked up another that was also of no help. After four of these books she smashed the cover on the last one.

"Nope, not here. You sure you're in the right cemetery?"

"I think so, this is the only cemetery where there is a Jewish section is it not?" She nodded, looking me over, having picked up my Hungarian with an Australian accent I suppose. When Buci first heard me she laughed, she said that I had an accent when speaking Hungarian. Thus there is no language I can speak without an accent.

I slipped a ten dollar note on the counter as the keeper of the dead names lit another cigarette from the old one, spitting grotesquely into a handkerchief.

"What was her maiden name?"

"Gizella Schlezinger," I answered. The spoken sound of Grandma's name shocked me a little. I stood patiently as she checked more tattered books. The sun had gone in and wind was whooshing through trees. I liked the sound; perhaps ghosts would make such noises. Ghosts of my own?

Her fingers came to a sudden halt, "R17 486," and then she added, "By the way, the caretaking subscription you took out in 1976 has expired."

The caretaking subscription? Was this a lead to something? I asked who paid for it, but she couldn't tell me other than it was a Mr Weisz.

There was a sign that pointed to the Jewish section and the rows were numbered so I moved on. Try and think! I was bewildered. Yes, a Mr. Weisz had to be my Cousin Josef. After all, she was his Grandma as well... but no, wrong again, she was not his grandmother, wrong side of the family, so Josef would hardly have known her. I was still excited and hopeful all at once. Who else could it have been? It had to be Josef, maybe doing the right thing. There was no one else, as far as I knew. Could it mean that Josef was still in Hungary? At row 17 I looked at the grave numbers. I expected a well-cared for grave, but 486 was a small sunken headstone, overgrown with weeds. Bitterly I noted that the subscription obviously didn't buy much, nobody had visited this grave for years. At least I could see Grandma's name on the stone.

My eyes fixed to the grave, memories of Grandma washed over, easily overwhelming me. She was a sweet old lady, perhaps 5 feet short and nearly as wide. Long white hair flowed over her shoulders onto her back and round her moon face. A great cook, she was able to make something grand out of nearly nothing. We played cards a lot in the evenings, and we both cheated, argued and yelled at each other, but she was my rock until she died.

Her life revolved around me, her one remaining grandchild out of eight. She loved me, no matter what awful things I said to her, and I did say many things out of my temper and frustration. She was simple, uncultured, uneducated, and not so worldly-wise. Yet, she brought up her six children mostly on her own. Smiling, I thought of the way she stood in front of me whenever Mum threatened to hit me. "Sari, you touch that child and I will give you a bloody nose."

Grandma protected, fed and washed me, took me to the pictures, and for my first few years, she was my best friend. I could picture her easily; even heard her voice now. My short, fat, lovely Grandma, in her usual black dress with the small white flowers. Her long white hair tied in a bun, looking kind of serious; brow usually wrinkled, but when she smiled or laughed her wide face was beautiful.

Without warning, the story Mum told me about how Grandma had saved my life during the Nazi years came back. I first heard the account when I was 16 years old, but Mum did not tell the whole story at the time. Later, when I was 40, I asked her again and it all came out. After I heard mum I ran out of the room, yelling with rage.

"In 1945 perhaps three months before the war finished some of the Hungarian Nazi thugs came to our building in the ghetto and herded all the Jews downstairs. They played a sort of a game, picking people at random, forming them into two groups. Some people were sent to the right, and some to the left side of the courtyard inside our building. We were mainly women and children, perhaps one or two old men. The Nazis would take one group away for what they called 'work service'. In truth these people were taken to the departure ghetto and then shipped out to various concentration camps in Poland and Germany. Most of us didn't know this at the time. Perhaps some suspected it, but it was impossible to believe it. The people taken away were never heard from again. Sometimes the group on the right side were told to go back upstairs to their flats, at other times they were the ones to go.
One morning they picked me, you, and my sister, amongst many others. Grandmother was in the other group, but she dashed over, stepping in front of me, grabbing you, screaming at the Nazis: she is sick and you are not taking my grandson..." Then, she picked you up by the arms and practically threw you behind her, through an open door into the flat at the back of us. She stood in front of the door. You were screaming behind it. I thought they'd

shoot us all right then, but Grandma kept on yelling, "You will have to kill me before you take them."

The Nazi thugs were surprised, and amused? They hesitated and kicked her in the leg, but then moved on laughing, leaving us where we stood. We were very lucky. But then they shoved my sister to the other side. Grandma tried to intervene again, but they just knocked her over. It wasn't till after the war that we found out that she died in the Belsen Bergen concentration camp."

*

There was one more thing I had to do in this old cemetery filled with nearly leafless trees - no matter how I felt - for I doubted I would ever come here again. The air chilled me to a shiver as the late afternoon sun ducked in and out from behind clouds. I walked looking at the path as if I needed to.

There is no walking away from memories. You carry them with you whether you want them or not; the memories of stories hiding inside one's head, or else, the lack of them? Both made me who I am. I'd never know either of my grandfathers. My paternal grandfather died during the war when I was perhaps two. Heart attack or a broken heart, Mum thought. What's the difference when you watch your sons, daughters and grandchildren disappear one after the other...

The ground crunched beneath my feet. The old cemetery had a certain dignified beauty and a definite gloom; like the story of my Mum's father that now came to mind.

"A very sad story, too bad for me to tell you, until you got older," Mum said around my thirtieth birthday. She launched into this one as usual without any warning or reason. I was visiting her in her new house in Caulfield. We were talking about various things; I said I was feeling down. As usual, she stroked my cheek, saying, "Please darlink, don't feel bad, you are all right and better." And then suddenly there was the story coming out of her. Perhaps, I think, she knew that our history was tough, and that was why I often felt down. Or perhaps that was her way of giving me what background or past she could.

Mum's father's name was Simon and he was a small-time, but successful fine arts printer. He owned his own printing shop and was considered a talented artisan in his trade. At some point in his life, we don't know when or why, he took up gambling, which eventually took such hold on him that he managed to gamble away everything. He lost his business, the apartment, everything the family owned within a very short period of time. His wife, Grandma Gizella, kept the facts of his gambling hidden from her children for as long as she could. Mum was nine years old when Grandma Gizella threw out the old bastard. Mum's eyes were angry, her face red, determined to tell me the whole story.

"We were so poor by this time that we lived in a two room rented flat. Your Grandma worked 12 hour days, six or seven days a week just to feed us. One morning I could not go to school - I was only nine years old, because the sole of my only pair of shoes had a hole. It was mid-winter, snowing and bitterly cold. Gizella sent my father to the

shoe repair shop to have my shoes mended. Father went there but never came back until late afternoon.

When he finally arrived he stood at the bottom of the stairs yelling "Sari, Sari come out." Mother and I came out onto the cold and sleety third floor landing to see my father Simon standing down there, snow falling on his bare, bald head. He was crying. He said he was very sorry, but he sold my shoes once they were fixed, went gambling and lost the miserably small amount immediately.

I did not want him standing down there crying.

For a minute there was silence and then mother went crazy with anger. When she blew out all she had to say, there was another silence. My father stood below, his head looking up as he shivered in the cold, his arms hugging his wet jacket around his body, crying. He said he was sorry over and over, and that he was very hungry. Mother yelled and screamed at him again, out of control, scaring my sisters and brothers now huddled around her. Neighbors had come out looking and listening to what was happening. The old man just stood there without a word. Mother eventually ran out of voice and anger, so I thought. Then, I was surprised, she finally and quietly said to her husband: "Come up and eat and then you are leaving for good, I never want to see you again."

That is what happened. My sisters, brothers and I sobbed, holding each other while the old man ate, hardly able to stop his own tears. I was his favorite daughter, and he sold my shoes. He could not understand it himself, did not even try. Now and then he'd turn to me saying "sorry, sorry, I don't know, I did not know what I was doing..."

Then he finished his bread and soup and mother threw him a pillowcase stuffed with what few shirts and things he had.

"You children go to the kitchen and eat your soup," *Gizella said, looking quiet, strong and large for a woman barely five feet tall. We heard her again telling her husband that she never wanted to see him again, as we watched through the ajar door. Without a word, father picked up his stuffed pillowcase and never looking his wife in the eyes, he left. No one ever saw him again after that. No one knew what happened to him. The bastard. I have never forgiven him. I want to but, oh what's it matter."*

I heard Mum, aghast, stunned. Until now I believed he died of natural causes before I was born. Why didn't she tell me all this before? I hugged her and she brushed away her tears.

"In a strange way I feel ashamed of him and unclear about how I feel towards your grandmother either, as far as that goes," she mumbled. "It is confusing."

She stood up and went to the kitchen to make bean soup, my favorite, and her father's last meal. Further questions were obviously not for now, much as I wanted to know what the old man was like otherwise. Whenever Mum finished talking, she was done. I thought I'd better leave her alone and try again another time. I wish I had just one picture of Simon Grandpa. What a bastard! What is to be understood about someone who did such things so long ago?

*

I turned back and put a rock on Grandma's grave, a Jewish custom, and walked out of the Jewish section, past many stars of David on cold grave stones.

The memorial 'To Our Fallen Heroes' loomed tall and stark. There were thousands of dead named, the dates all about the same 1942 to 1945. No explanation or admission that the Jewish dead were not heroes, but victims. People who were forcibly made to fight for the Nazi regime of Hungary at the time. Or else these men, women and children were killed, to 'purify' the Hungarian nation.

I started scanning the names. Klein, Schwartz, many typically Jewish names. At the end of the row of names there were lots and lots of the family names Weisz. Five of them my uncles, two of them my aunts, three cousins between the ages of two and six, a few others whose name sounded familiar, but I was not sure. My father's name was there too; Lajos Weisz. I supposed it was him, but it could be anyone, Lajos was a popular name.

Bile rose with fury. Standing there was meaningless, hopeless and pointless. Enormous grief and melancholy invaded me. I looked at my father's name again, waiting, waiting for him - to speak to me? But only the wind in the tree tops made a sound.

I said goodbye as if he could hear me, as if they could all hear it. What bloody nonsense. I saw nothing but the path I trod. But I turned back for a moment. Perhaps there was an apology from the Hungarians and I missed it? There was none I could find. Only one uncle out of seven had survived, Uncle Janos, and he had immigrated to Canada after the 1956 revolution He died within a year, I barely knew him. I wept tears of unstoppable sorrow. I kissed two fingers, touching each name.

The cemetery was closing; an old man sweeping the paths told me that I must go. He saw I was very upset so he stopped sweeping. I was thankful for the compassion only old people manage to display. The afternoon sun, once again forcing its way through the clouds, sent two rays that lit a couple of trees with a golden glow. Where would our souls go - if I believed in souls?

I was glad I had come here, but it was enough suffering for the day. My shaky knees took toward the exit gate. After only a few steps, I'd recovered. Dead jokes suddenly flooded me; *A reporter asked Arthur Miller why he had not gone to his wife Marilyn Monroe's funeral. He answered "Why should I go? She won't be there."*

"You are in great shape," the doctor said to the old Jew, "you shall live till you are seventy."
"But I am seventy," he replied.
"Nu, did I lie?"

Dead men tell no tales? Not true. And the jokes I recalled seem sour, contrary, but laugh we must in order to defy death, for now at least.

A cab picked me up. The driver, a young man, barely twenty years old, wanted to chat. He asked me questions I didn't feel like answering. I felt anger towards him as if it was all his fault. He knew I was Jewish, having seen me come from the gate of the Jewish cemetery.

"There is no anti-Semitism now," he said, making it sound like an achievement of the Hungarian People's Republic. I mumbled that I doubted that to be the case. He looked at me in the mirror, saying no more until we reach the Hilton; "Will you need me later? I can show you the sights and take you to where the action is."

I declined his offer. As he stopped the car - I was being nasty I guess - I asked him if he wanted to hear a funny Jewish joke. Uncomfortably, he acquiesced, so I told him this one:

During the Second World War, an American southern matron calls up the local army
base. "We would be honored," she tells the sergeant who takes her call, "to accommodate five soldiers at our Thanksgiving dinner."

"That's very gracious of you, ma'am," the sergeant answers.

"Just please, make sure they're not Jews."

"I understand ma'am."

Thanksgiving afternoon, the woman answers the front doorbell and is horrified to find five huge black soldiers standing in the doorway.

"We're here for the Thanksgiving dinner, ma'am," one of the soldiers says.

"Bu... but ... but your sergeant has made a terrible mistake," the woman says.

"Oh no, ma'am," a soldier answers, "Sergeant Greenberg never makes mistakes."

*

Inside the hotel I downed two vodkas and three cigarettes as fast as I could. The girl of one's dreams that I met in the taxi that morning was there again waving to me. Reluctantly, I walked over, saying hello, offering her a cigarette. We chatted. She remarked that I looked drained.

"Perhaps you could buy me dinner tomorrow? Would you like that?" she asked.

"Perhaps," I said.

Maybe I needed some entertainment; I could just have dinner and nothing else, right? I was totally exhausted, light or heavy headed, who knew which, and feeling vaguely sick. Excusing myself, I left her there, though not without noting again how beautiful she really was. I went to bed at 6.45 pm.

*

I woke with the old cliché 'I feel like a new woman', and that of course brought her face into my mind. Hm, a high class prostitute, she was not for me for any number of reasons. But why not dinner anyway? Call it international relations building. I only had a couple more days left in Budapest, which also came as a cheery thought.

What was so anxiety-making about revisiting here where I was born? The only thing, I reasoned, was that my overall memories of my early years had little if any joy. Not many actual memories either. Anxious or not, I was determined today to finish the job. I headed toward 24 Akacfa Street.

Turning the corner, I saw the familiar street. This at least was solidly in my recollections. The scene was like I had never left it. A curious sense of déjà vu, except it wasn't, enveloped me. At number 24 standing there looking up the dirty grey walls I pondered 'What exactly am I doing here? I won't know a soul here, so no big deal, a quick look and that's it.'

Walking in through the entrance I stopped in the square courtyard. Across there, here on the ground floor was the doorway Grandma threw me into. That recollection again made my neck stiff and my head ache.

Looking up, I scanned the doors on the third floor, one in particular. Turning around, there was an iron gate to the left. Stairs lead down to the fuel cellar where we waited out the last days of the war and the bombing. Damn stories quickly filled my consciousness everywhere I looked. Rarely had I heard any stories from Mum that sounded like good times. Hardly ever a fun thing that impressed me enough to retain it.

Here came another tale, about Grandma Helen, my father's mother. I wished this one was not the way it was. I knew that there was hardly any relationship between Grandmother Helen and Mum. I must have been very young when I first realized that, and it left me feeling puzzled as usual. Do parents realize how puzzled and perplexed their children are? I didn't want to be side tracked here, now – neither did the story. It flashed into my mind that not all the Holocaust stories were from wars; some came from parents and the old world that brought so much tragedy to people, Jewish or otherwise.

After one of our very few visits to Helen, perhaps I was eight years old, Mum shook her head, mumbling about Helen becoming more and more demented. I was uncertain what demented meant, but agreed that grandma Helen was strange, nothing like my Grandma Gizella.

*

It was not long after we had settled in Sydney in 1958 that Mum told me this awful story about Helen. I had asked her about what Hungarian papers we had because there was a German compensation case that was offered to Jewish people.

"What papers we have? Very little, I left them all with Helen and now she is dead, so I have no idea what happened to them. Who cares, we won't get any money anyway."

We talked about it and then she had that semi-glazed look about her eyes. She was thinking about something. I asked what was on her mind. "Helen," she said, and that she wanted to tell me something about Grandma Helen. But then she said, "Oh, it does not matter."

I grabbed the opportunity and would not let her stop. I already knew that Helen adamantly opposed the marriage of my father and mother. My father's family was fairly well off, compared to Mum's who were as poor as could be. Fortunately, Helen's husband, my paternal grandfather, loved Mum and the marriage went ahead. But that was not what Mum had to tell me. Lighting her ever-present cigarette, looking away from me, she started.

"In the last few weeks of the war both the Russians forces were bombing Budapest. We were in our own apartment inside the ghetto. Grandmother Helen was evicted from her large apartment that was outside of the ghetto. Rather than being put in with strangers, I asked her to stay with us. Her husband Sandor, your wonderful Grandpa, had died a year earlier. By now there were eight of us living in our two roomed flat. Most of our days were spent in the fuel cellar which was used to store wood and coal to heat the building. Do you remember how cold and dark that was?"

I shook my head; I was only 3 years old, no memories. *"The bombing was intense for the last few weeks and days of the war. The Russians were advancing. Word was out that soon it would be over. 'All we have to do is to survive until then without food, heat, water and air,' a neighbor said, mockingly laughing into the freezing, dank silence of the small cellar, filled with nearly 100 people.*

There was no electricity, no water and everyone had run out of provisions, not that there had been much food for months anyway. In the lull between bombings I used to go out and fossick for anything to eat, exchanging whatever bits of clothing or jewelry I had left for a bag of beans, a packet of flour or a piece of horse or dog meat. By now I had nothing left to barter with, and just about no one was going out into the streets. We had nothing left to eat at all. I did not know what to do. People were hysterical. Adults and children sat on the dirt floor, or on timber logs or on an old mattress. People wrapped in clothing or blankets, frightened out of their wits, waited, trying to keep children from crying, lest the Nazi hordes roaming and looting in the streets should hear us. Sometimes after a bomb fell everyone would scream and then be still and silent, waiting to see if the building was going to crush us. The overcrowded cellar was occasionally lit by a few candles for light and heat. It was damp and smelly and the building would shake and crack as tanks rattled by."

I broke in, "But how? How did you keep us alive during those last few weeks?" She shook her head dismissing the question. It was not something she could explain. Her eyes turned darker and her voice crackly sour.

"If anyone found food, they would share it with at least their next door neighbors. The bombing became relentless, no one had any money and inflation was so high that people used the last few paper notes to light a small fire. We sat like sardines, side by side quietly, in the often pitch black cellar wondering if we were going to die of the

bombing or of starvation. When your Grandma Helen moved in with us a few weeks before, she came with two large trunks, both of them heavily bolted with padlocks. How she managed to get people to help her to bring them was a mystery, but who had the wits to worry about that sort of thing?

One night in the cellar I woke in the dark, lit by a single candle behind me. I tried to shut my eyes again, but I saw your Grandma Helen moving about opening one of the wooden boxes in which she kept her clothes. I saw her rummaging around and then I thought I saw her eating something. 'No, I must be wrong,' I thought. 'I was imagining it because I was hungry.' I watched anyway, I was suspicious, I never liked her, and she never liked me. The old cow was a selfish, dried up crazy woman, never a good word or deed for anyone. How your dear old Grandpa put up with her, I don't know. Anyway, I became rather certain that she was eating. How could it be, I wanted to know, pretending to be asleep.

In the early mornings usually there was a lull in the bombing so people went back upstairs to their flats, looking through their windows at the destruction outside. At least we could boil waste or rain water. Once we were upstairs, I told you to try to get some sleep. You were well cared for by my mother who never put you down for a moment.

I was so suspicious that I decided to sneak back down into the cellar. The more I thought about it, the more I believed I had seen Helen eat something. In the cellar I broke the locks off Helen's boxes and found cans of meat, bags of dried beans, and, a half a side of bacon! I could not believe it. There was enough food to keep us from starving for several days."

Mum stopped, livid with the memory she could barely speak. She lit another cigarette, waving away her feelings. "That's it, that's what the poor old woman was like." And then Mum cried for us, and for Grandma Helen. I put my now soggy cigarette out and hugged mum as we cried.

Though I asked, she never told me about the confrontation that took place between her and Helen. For many years, Mum could not forgive Helen, but eventually we both felt desperately sorry for her, managing to reach some kind of understanding about her. After all, Helen lost her seven children, husband, sisters, cousins and friends, in just two or three years. Enough to turn anyone crazy.

*

Now, here I was trembling, looking at the cellar door, in front of the iron bars. Enough, enough of bad stories. So why did I want to go down to look in the cellar? The gate was locked, thank heavens, so I couldn't. It was strange that I wanted to confirm a nasty memory, even if it was someone else's. What was the point?

Back in the courtyard I looked up to the third floor, top right hand corner. I took the stairs quickly and walked along the balcony, to stand in front of what had been our door. A woman came out of the next door flat. She looked at me, pretending to sweep the landing, and then brusquely asked, "What are you looking for?"

"I used to live here until 1951."

"Oh, you and several others." She turned to go back in the door.

"Excuse me, do you know anybody in this building who has lived here for a long time?"

"No," she said, shutting her door.

I went back down the stairs, looking at the dirty scarred walls. Plaster had fallen off, but the old (was it yellow) paint color was almost recognizable. I stepped slowly, skipping every second stair as I used to when I was nine years old. Back on the ground floor I looked up into the square sky that showed between the walls of the courtyard. 'Oh well,' I thought with some relief, 'I've been here, done it, I can go back home to Melbourne and forget all this.' I felt relieved and curiously lonely as I was about to leave but something made me stop. Once again I looked at the door behind me, recalling Grandma saving my life. I felt sad, lonely and yet lighter.

Not much came from my trip here. Was that true though? I stood there, mindlessly rocking from heel to heel until above me, a door opened and a tiny, old lady dressed in black shuffled out carrying a piece of carpet. She laid it over the railing and began to beat it with a carpet beater. The dust showered down on me. I moved a few steps away and got a better look at her face. She stopped her work, asking in a shaky voice, "Are you alright young man? You don't live here do you?"

"No, but I used to. I left in 1951. We lived up there on the third floor".

"What's your name?" she asked. Spontaneously and immediately regretting, it I answered, giving my Hungarian name.

"Weisz Tibor."

She put her carpet beater down and grabbed at the rail: "Tibor! Oh my god, don't you remember me? I'm Rozsi, come on up here."

I was stunned hearing my name from her. I leaped up the stairs two, three at a time. She waited for me with her arms extended. Yes, Rozsi rang a faint bell.

"I'm Rozsi," she said, and grabbed my hands, "Don't you remember me? It was so long ago. How is your mother Sari?"

Momentarily I was speechless. I didn't ever actually remember Rozsi, until now, but something was coming back about her. In her wobbly voice, eyes pink and watering, she said, "Do you remember how when you were five, I used to clean the flat for your mother if she was away? And how you used to knock on my door many times to ask what was for dinner, because you didn't like what your Grandma cooked. How we laughed about it. And surely you remember my daughter Zsuszi. You said you were in love with her…"

Now it was all coming back. That beautiful blond haired girl, my friend, years older than I was. We went inside and she made coffee.

"Wait, wait, I have something for you. You loved poppy seed cake," and she presented me with a large slice. What an amazing memory you have," I muttered, thinking that she might well remember other things. I sat there sipping coffee, eating her poppy seed cake.

She asked me questions about my mother and what happened to us. She asked why I had come back to Budapest. I told her I was searching for relatives, for memories, for missing links in my life. She sighed, tears in her eyes. "Yes, I well remember the tragedy your family went through, so many people died."

She knew nothing else. My head was filled with the usual sudden rush of hope and despair. How many times can a man feel hope and its opposite? As many times as necessary is the only answer. I asked her a few questions about her daughter Zsuzsi and then thanked her for spending time with me. As I stood up, to leave, she said "Wait, I just remembered something Zsuzsi - who lives in Germany - said some years ago, that a man came here looking for relatives of the Weisz family."

"When was this?" I asked, doubtful that the old lady might be just making up a story for me.

"Oh it would have been about 1970, or 72, I don't know for sure." She had nothing else to add as she looked at me with watery eyes. "God bless you, keep well."
I hugged her, and left.

*

Eight days I had spent in this bloody country, constantly filled with small bits of hope to be dashed by finding nothing significant. I just wanted to be out of here. There was nothing left in Hungary for me.

INTERLUDE

Is Life Really just a Jewish Joke?

"Oh God," Mum said in that way of hers that made me listen and feel doubt, "I cannot remember exactly but my grandmother got it from her mother."

*She was referring to the **"Very Expensive Family Heirloom of a Child Pulling a Cart."***
"Or is he pushing it Mum?" I kept asking, as if it mattered.

"This is a rare and amazing sterling silver work of art," she insisted pointing at the table that filled the living room of our apartment.
*"It's the only thing I managed to hide from the Nazis... Apart from your father's ring that is, and that will be yours someday." Then she sighed, looking sad, repeating: "It is all I managed to save from the Nazis, and then from the Russians, and then from the Communists, so don't ever say anything about any of it! We're not supposed to own such a thing these days," she said, referring, I already knew, to the bloody-minded Hungarian government of the day. I was perhaps seven, when she first told me of things that were: **"Very Important things and Secrets to Be Kept Just between You and Me."***
Looking very serious, she reiterated, "There are things we, only you and I, talk about, these are not for other ears."

At times she mentioned names I had not heard before or could not remember who it was, or what they looked like. "Don't be silly darlink. Of course remember Aunt Malvin?"

Looking at my beautiful mother, breathing in her perfume and cigarette smells, I'd wisely say, "Oh but Mum, that was before I was born."

"Oh yes, yes," she'd say then, "I forget you're only seven."

*

Are there as many Jewish jokes as there are Jews? For this one you don't have to be Jewish:

For your birthday your mother buys you two awful shirts.
To make sure you do not get into trouble the next morning
You put on one of the bloody awful shirts.
You walk into the kitchen to show her and you say
"So what do you think Mum, great shirt huh?"
She looks at you smiling and then her face drops as she says.
"So! You don't like the other one..."

Oh Mum, mama, mamoosh, mush!

On a warm summer day in Budapest in September 1948 Mum and I walked hand in hand from one business meeting to another. It mattered not where we went; these outings were the best part of my life. She breathed perfume, her hair impeccable as always; she was dressed like she was someone. Appearances were not just important to her, they were her life. Because of that, I supposed, there are many, but two particular edicts one is never to forget.

One: always wear clean undies.
Why? Because if one was to pass out or get run over in the street by a tram and was taken to hospital....
Two: Make sure you have a hankie. So the snot does not hang out of your nose? I guess. There were several others, but these were the real important ones.

A not-at-all-Jewish person in practice, but still a Jewish woman, with her curly headed son who had no idea what it meant to be Jewish. The only idea that came loud and clear was that it was better not to look or act like one or be known as one. All those people Mum asked me to remember were Jews taken away and killed by the Nazis or the Hungarian Arrow Cross men. This is what I heard over and over. "Nazis are everywhere, even now. German and Hungarian ones. Some now masquerading as Communists." Some, like the old man one floor down, were Nazis. What is a Nazi? I wasn't sure at the time. I had nightmares about what I had heard about torture and killing. Nazis were bad and worse, to be feared beyond absolutely anything else. These Nazis were not people you made a deal with, even if Mum was very good at deal making.

It took me another 30 years to find out the "deal" she made to keep us alive.

Now and then Mum would bitterly say, "What have the Jews ever done for us anyway?" But this was not a question; she would make the statement to me, a pronouncement into the air, as we walked. Her tone suggested and made me wonder, and indignantly agree, that the mysterious JEWS should have done something for us. But what? And who were they? After all, I usually heard about them as dead. We were Jews, but we appeared no different to my best friend and his family who were Catholics. The man on the first floor looked a bit suspicious because he had a big nose. Big nose equals Jew, but not Mr. Zilahy; nose yes, Jew no, and yet 'he is all right', so Mum told me! Confusing, all that.

I paid total attention to her. So yes, I nodded in agreement. The damn Jews should have done something for us.

Somehow this is very funny now, somehow it is hilarious now. Once in a while I do something for the poor damn Jews, and to this day they have done little for me. I still ask what they were supposed to do for us, particularly if we never went near them.

It does not matter anymore.

*

Basically, if your father was dead it was because he was a Jew, or so some people thought.

One day in school, I was playing in the schoolyard. The new boy who was kicking the ball back to me asked what work my father did. I hesitated, because I had no idea how to answer such a question. It had no meaning to me. Somehow it seemed as if other kids naturally had a father, but we, that is Mum and I, did not. Still, I understood fatherhood, kind of, I was rather bright in some ways. Yet when it came to me or rather us, the 'dad' question was hesitatingly nonsensical. My answer was that "He may have died in the war."

The kid picked up the ball, stepped closer and scrutinized my black hair, asking, "So you are a Jew?"

I wanted to lie but could not.

"Yes," I said.

The boy's reply was simple, "So that's why your father is dead."

This was not a joke; it was more like, 'Ah, that explains everything.' Perhaps the boy meant no harm, but the pain hit me at the time, surprisingly. Perhaps it was the very first time I felt the 'fatherless' Jewish child pain. I wanted to protest that my father was not dead for sure. I wanted to say something vague about how 'Jew does not mean Dead,' but could not formulate the thought.

Red-faced and then crying, I let go of the ball and ran away. The boy looked amazed. His face and the playground have stayed with me as one of the very few actual picture memories of my early childhood. It is written into me as part of my personal narrative. It is my identity, and it is almost like a Jewish joke: "If your father is dead, you must be a Jew."

*

It was 1953. Grandma Gizella lived with us (lucky for me), but the world was in fact Mum and me and our mutual and yet separate, unknown, unsaid fears and pains. Some would say that all the pain was hers. Forty years later I do not mind all that she loaded on me, I do not mind that I was there to help her share her impossible sorrows. As a child, I was the recipient, the bottomless hole into which all things fell. I was the son and the replacement husband, father, lover, and family all rolled into the little short, curly-haired, way too wise but scared me. I was also the "star in the sky", as Mum often told me, the one bright spot in her life without which she could not live. I was proud of it, whatever all that meant. I had partly inherited her life in this way.

I was just the boy who pulled or pushed the sterling silver cart of our lives as it was required looking like the boy of the Very Expensive Sterling Silver Heirloom she saved for me. Meanwhile, the mysteries about the world around me, and about what Mum said or did, multiplied. I would question her at times, depending on her moods; I was not just sensitive, I was an expert about her moods and nerves. I thought extra deeply about this pronouncement of hers:

"You can't have a bicycle because I could not explain to the authorities where I got the money from."

More likely, she was scared I'd fall off and kill myself. I knew I had to let that one *rides...*

Often, with a worried face mum would say, "Take this money to Mr. Fekete with this note, at the tax office, and get there before 10 am on Friday or they'll take our curtains."

Why would a government take our shabby curtains or the half-stuffed chair, and what would they do with it? Sit on it, or use it to light a fire? The world was loaded with such extra unfathomable mysteries. I was serious and took serious care of looking after my mother. I don't remember asking questions about these seemingly very somber things, only about the details of them.

Mum and I walked the streets at a pace, many buildings still bomb-damaged from the war years. Trams cluttered along, overfilled, four, five people hanging out, holding on with one hand, cigarettes glowing in mouths.

Ah, the good old days when you could smoke because everyone did.

My reputation was no joke, but a matter of status. But whose? Mine or hers?
We lived in coffee shops where the smell of smoke, steam, hot sausage, cheap perfume, huge sweets and coffee all mixed into an unspeakable total that was terrific. Waiters ran around delivering short blacks, everyone talked all at once, lovers held hands, business people made deals; communists paraded their badges, secret servicemen looked for subversive activity; a hubbub of noises, smells and action. By now, I was a forty-year-old-twelve-year-old, with a reputation to live up to. This reputation, and to be shown off in these places, ranged from cake eater, to polite, clever, good looking, respectful and mostly, a great caretaker of Mum. All the proper attributes a little boy ought to have, according to the adults. Mum's friends were mainly men with deep voices and yellow fingers, who passionately dragged on filter-less cigarettes or cheap cigars, while lifting short blacks to smoke-filled mouths. Several may have been in love with Mum. (I could already sense something about that.) They had hands which were inevitably attracted by my curly hair. They told jokes, and bought me another short black with cream while I'd sit there and politely glow.

Our lives went on, dropping one day after another into our very uncertain, unplanned, messy future. Mum went away and came home, and then went away again. The love affair between her and me was always renewed by her absence, or perhaps her unrecognized guilt about her part-time mothering? She did the best she could, I know that now, knew it back then too. No one was to be blamed for anything? A lovely idea, but not easy to accept.

Part 3.

Josef

Budapest, December 1956

Josef and Juli were to meet the small group of people who were about to sneak out of Hungary. They packed only his briefcase and her shopping bag, in order to not arouse suspicion, and wore several layers of clothing.

"I'm ready to leave this sad and stupid country," Josef said over and over, using all the juiciest swear words the language offered, punching the table with the clenched fist of his good arm. His wife knew he was in pain and not just physically, his wound was not that bad. Juli was re-bandaging his arm, not convinced that he meant all he said about leaving Hungary.

In the last few days of the revolution Josef was shot while fighting against the Russians. Luckily the bullet passed right through the muscle of his arm and though initially the pain was severe, the bleeding had stopped. Going to a doctor or a hospital was out of the question. They were fugitives now and feared being arrested.

Josef and Juli had married only a few weeks earlier. Josef's job in the Hungarian Department of Trade had been a relatively good one. He had studied foreign trade, was a talented negotiator. His boss, Peter Szabo, had helped him to rise through the ranks. Neither man had been a communist party member until recently. Both joined because they had to in order to hold responsible jobs in the communist government. Their objections were not so much about communism as an ideology, but about the repressive undemocratic government. Josef often grumbled that the government was bloody minded, corrupt and full of psychopaths.

On the second day of the revolution Peter Szabo confessed to Josef that he helped to plot the uprising, adding that there was little hope of success, yet a small chance for a free Hungary, like never before. Josef, as many others, readily accepted the call. Juli was fearful, but supported democracy and freedom. The revolution failed despite the support of many Hungarians. Khrushchev's tanks quickly overwhelmed the unorganized resistance who had little by way of firing power. The freedom fighters were convinced that the West would come to their aid, but all they got were speeches. The revolution was squashed in a few days.

Weeks after the revolution was over confusion still reigned in Budapest and parts of Hungary. Josef and Juli moved to a friend's place, quickly deciding to illegally cross the borders as soon as they could. Josef figured that Peter Szabo, his boss and friend, was most likely killed or jailed. For Josef there was little he was leaving behind other than a few good friends. Juli agreed to leave, but she was distraught at leaving her mother, father and sister. Nevertheless, she could see that it was simply not possible to stay. Josef was likely to face prosecution. The new puppet government, nominated by Khrushchev, could not be trusted. The future of Hungary looked bleak. There would be reprisals and chaos.

Josef found a guide to take them to the Austrian border. This would cost a large sum of money. Juli's parents gave them the few US dollars they'd hidden since forever. The journey was arranged. The plot was to take a train to the Hungarian-Austrian border. From there, they would walk through the night to Austria and freedom.

Russian and Hungarian soldiers guarded the border, but not all that tightly. Confusion still ruled. It was risky as the border guards were ordered to, and sometimes did, shoot at anyone crawling around in the night across the fields, but it was possible to get through at some points. Some of the Hungarian guards could be bribed, some were sympathetic anyway. Over two hundred and fifty thousand Hungarians left this way.

The train journey was uneventful. There were no soldiers on the train and the guide had bribed the train conductor and border guards at the small village where they got off. Once it got dark, they set out on foot to Austria. Exhausted after hours of walking through wet, mud-filled ditches, the group eventually found themselves at the outskirts of an Austrian village. They were welcomed, given food and shelter and some clothing by the international Red Cross. After a few days, Josef and Juli decided they would immigrate to Italy. They had always shared a dream to visit Italy. To see Rome and Venice was something they often talked about during their courtship, never thinking that it would ever be possible, let alone to live there.

It took two months before they arrived in Rome. For a few weeks they were in a refugee camp learning Italian. Then the authorities found them a job. Italy's economic circumstances were not very good in 1957, unemployment was high. All refugees could expect by way of a job were menial tasks. Juli got a job in a clothing factory; Josef was employed as a night watchman. As Josef improved his Italian their circumstances slightly improved but neither felt settled or happy. They worked long hours, and lived in even worse conditions than back in Budapest. Juli often wrote to her parents, but it took months before her letters were answered. Her parents reported that the new government had declared an amnesty, and wanted dissidents to come back. However, there was a lot of witch-hunting of those suspected of taking part in the revolution. As usual in any rebellion, there were sick people who had committed atrocities that no real revolutionary wanted. People were still in jails for having supported the uprising. Juli's parents had been questioned on many occasions about Juli and Josef's disappearance.

Juli's father wrote, "The funny thing is often the same as the sad; you know that Mr. Kadar has been put in place as Prime Minister. He was considered something of a traitor to the cause of the revolution because he legitimized the Russian invasion to crush the revolution. Now, Mr Kadar seems intent, and one might even say - capable, of improving the economy at least."

Consequent letters from Juli's father confirmed that what he had thought previously was actually happening. The witch hunt had stopped. A real amnesty was declared, and many people were freed from jail. The government again asked dissidents to return home. Juli's father warned them about the situation never the less. As much as Juli's parents would have liked it, they cautioned against coming back: "We think you are better off building a new life in a Western democracy. Hungary will be in a mess for many years to come."

Josef and Juli were working 10 hour days, six or seven days a week. They were tired and disappointed, but held their relationship together with the same passion that had been there from the beginning. Letters from home affected both of them. Juli cried thinking about her family. Josef watched her knowing that his love for her was great enough to take him back to Hungary, if she said the word. Eventually he put this to her. She shook her head, "It is just too dangerous."

Life went on in something of a blur even though they began to enjoy the odd train trip to the countryside. The local culture and the easygoing nature of their Italian friends helped. Italian-style fascism had killed a lot of Italian Jews, but, this was not known or acknowledged by many.

After three years, they had excellent command of the language. Juli often spoke to her parents on the telephone. Her mother was not well, but they could not afford the cost of a visit. Then the Hungarian government offered to pay the return fares for some Hungarians living in Europe. Each piece of news made their homesickness stronger.

The Italian economy was still in bad shape. No matter how much Josef and Juli worked, life was hard in every way. She wanted children, but Josef did not. An air of unhappiness, broken only by an occasional outing, settled on both of them, slowly eroding the promise of the great relationship they had in the early years. They were arguing more, hardly ever making love, both feeling more and more alone.

Then Josef had a brief affair with an Italian woman. He felt bad about it, and he confessed to Juli. Now they were even more estranged. Juli asked if he wanted a divorce, but Josef answered definitely no.

Silent, awkward evenings followed. After many sleepless nights, on a bright summer morning Josef suggested a walk in the Uffizi gardens. This time he was determined to convince Juli to return to Hungary. He suggested that life was not so easy in Italy, and that given all they had heard about Hungary, the situation looked fairly positive. He believed he was no longer in danger. His ability to speak good Italian, as well as reasonable English, was likely to land him a reasonable job back in the Department of Trade.

"But the greatest reason of all is that it is enough for me to be an orphan, without you becoming one as well. Let's start a new life Juli, I love you and always will," he said in a trembling voice, hoping for her agreement and forgiveness. Juli cried with happiness, confusion, and still some concern. They phoned her father to ask again how sure he was that it would be all right to return. Within two months they were on the train going back, to live at her parent's place for the time being.

As Josef did the rounds to find his old friends, he had some happy and some sad reunions. Several of his closest friends were missing; either dead, imprisoned or had left Hungary. Still, he managed to find enough of his old contacts to help him get a job, albeit a very basic one, at the Department of Trade. He had amnesty, but the ruling communist officials were not about to trust returning expatriates with great career positions.

Shortly after their return in 1961 Josef decided to change his name. Should a more repressive regime arise again, locating him would not be difficult, name change or not, he knew. Through his contacts he made every effort to remove his original family name of Weisz from documents. Josef believed that his old persona was virtually eradicated from official records. He also hoped that with a new name his career prospects might improve. He changed his name from Josef Weisz to Josef Feher; for no other reason than that Weisz in German meant 'white', and Feher, a fairly common name, and not a Jewish one, also meant white. He felt comforted by the name change. He swore he would never again use or refer to his old name. He asked all his friends, and Juli's family, to do the same. "I will forget my past, the war years, the revolution, and the name I was born with. It feels strange to do this, but perhaps this is the new me?"

Juli stood by him as usual, with concerns of her own. She knew he was in a very mixed emotional state. Every few days he'd hatch a new plot on how to make money illegally, to open a business, or to go back to his studies, but he did nothing about any of it. He was restless, and unhappy. His mood swings and depressions, or abject anger, rose and faded fast. Juli even wondered if he was having an affair again. She decided not to question him, resolving that she would see him through whatever happened. Some days or weeks they were happy and at ease. Other times it was as if Josef had partly disappeared. Then, he'd show up with roses and apologies. He could not promise that he would stay sweet, he was well aware of his moods. Without Juli's knowledge he began to make black market deals, or provide trade information to foreign clients for a fee. He became obsessed with the idea of making more money, knowing he was being unethical. He felt defiant and bitter, bored and lost in his life.

Miklos Zboray 1999

Years went by, many, many years. The revolution was forgotten, as was communism. Instead of things improving in the new Hungary of the late 20th century, the economy, law and order, and the social system seemed even worse than the years of 'Goulash communism.'

Josef was on his way to work, to another day filled with meaningless tasks that did not use his talents. He was tired, bored, and depressed, with little to look forward to. 'The only bright spot in life is Juli. Where would I be without her?' The two of them barely made a good enough living for a day-to-day existence. He smoked too much, and sometimes drank enough to knock himself out. Women looked at him with eyes that spoke of need. He finished one brief affair after another, swearing never to do it again, only to start whenever the opportunity arose. It was not that he wanted out of his marriage, his love for Juli was there; 'could an anchor leave the sea and still be an anchor'? Yet he needed the stimulus that these trysts provided. He felt increasingly bad about it, thinking he was an addict of sorts. Sex was like a drug you took for insistent pain, a background in him that needed something. Like needing to smoke or drink, he could not stop craving these nothing but lustful affairs.

Well aware of his restlessness, for years now, he had read philosophy and psychology with increasing interest. Given that all the books and knowledge never really answered the real questions, he despaired at the human situation. He knew that he studied his own discomfort, to figure out himself. 'What on earth or in heaven makes me and others as we are? Why are people so immensely hypocritical, fearful and murderous? Why the tremendous ego-driven falsity of the world? How is it that capitalism is inhumane, and yet communism had the same problems presented in different ways?'

Such were his thoughts as he walked to his office area. He had barely sat down on his chair behind a narrow desk when Karoly Nagy, his manager, looking amused, came to his desk. With a smirk, he threw some documents in front of Josef, "I believe you can speak some Italian".
Josef nodded cautiously. His boss's face broke into a full grin, "I don't care about where or how you learnt Italian, just translate the bloody thing and if you can make any sense of it, show it to Miklos Zboray, who is a number cruncher economist upstairs. He'll work out if we are getting a crappy deal from these fat, spaghetti eating Italians, or a totally shithouse one, as is likely to be the case."
Josef picked up the documents; at least he could exercise his Italian. He translated the documents, took them to the financial section and asked for Miklos Zboray.
A stunningly tall man with thinning hair, a beaky nose, small sharp eyes and a friendly smile approached him.
"Step into my office and tell me your problems," he said with a beaming smile, as he pulled up a chair for Josef. "Or else lie about them, as you wish. My name is Zboray Miklos."
He was of similar age to Josef, his intelligent eyes alive with humor and depth.
"Josef Feher," and he shook Zboray's large hand. The man was simply huge, rather thin and he must have been over two meters tall, Josef mused. Zboray smiled again, "Yes, I am very tall, if that is what you're thinking."

They chatted about their various responsibilities in the office and then Josef explained the document to Zboray. By now he could see that Miklos was a very approachable and intellectually sharp man.

"Let's have a big lunch over this rather silly Italian deal," Miklos suggested with a smile, "Spaghetti would be nice, but given that neither of us can afford that, how about a sandwich in the park?"

INTERLUDE

An 'heirloom' or 'Inheritance' is a, what exactly?

Once we settled in Australia in 1957, the past was stashed away, put out of my life like a bad dream, sent to the attic of one's brain, shoved into a dark corner, buried under concrete.
I knew that memories were not, should not, cannot be so easily erased or thrown away.

As a seventeen-year-old, I thought little about the future. Life was unpacking itself as it does to immigrants who have arrived to such a new and different place as Sydney, compared to Budapest. I can't recall what 'our new life' meant to me, except I had expectations. Though what about, I had no idea. I was curious about the future, but my main preoccupation was with girls, women, sex, and having to work. Going back to school was never raised as a possibility, not that I wanted to do that anyway. What I wanted to do, or to become, was not a question that presented itself to me in this new situation. We had no plans, no idea about what we should or might do; migrants don't as a rule, I suppose. Things happened and one either fought against or accepted them.

*

In 1971 after my thirtieth birthday I had to reconsider things I had not thought about until now, and I was suddenly astounded. I was startled that I had just washed my past all through without any thought. What could I recall? What had happened in my first 16 years? How much of it was fact, how much just my perception of it? What stories has Mum told me? I had to ask her again. There were big things to recall or to forget. Which memories are actually mine? By now, I figured that one must foster and hug every detail of memories. Because all the past is one's life; the good and the bad bits. Blocking any of it out is not an option. I spent some time writing down whatever I could recall. Like the story of 'The Famous and Very Expensive Sterling Silver Work of Art', the only thing Mum managed to save, that was to be mine when I grew up. Like everything else, it was left behind in Hungary. Everything we'd ever had was gone. Yet I never gave up the 'The Famous and Very Expensive Heirloom' story, even though I recalled that I had never really liked the item itself. For a few years, once in a while Mum would wonder out loud where the 'heirloom' might be, and say that if we had it, we could be rich. Yeah right.

In 1987 Mum came back from a visit to Hungary and could hardly wait to tell me that she had something very special for me. She carefully unwrapped an object that turned out to be 'The Carriage Pulled-Pushed by the Little Boy.' She beamed proudly; "This is your 'Very Expensive Antique Family Heirloom.'"

I looked at it, it seemed all right. I even sort of liked the thing now, mainly for what it meant to her, but I was still not all that impressed with the little sculpture as such.

"Perhaps, you know, vat you think..." she said, looking as if she was thinking hard, "No, actually for sure, you must put this into bank vault?"

I didn't of course. What the hell, the only thing I had from the old days I should put out of sight? I took it home and placed it on the mantelpiece between a Mexican clay god and a Buddhist statue. The room was bright and the walls crammed with all sorts of paintings and ornaments. The statue fitted the room's mixed up mood. I stepped back thinking 'yes, perhaps it is a great work of art.' It is heavy and sterling silver. Maybe she is right for once, perhaps this really is something special, unlike the many things she told me about which were not, or which could have been, but we lost them.

Lots of things happen to everyone between childhood and now. Hilarious, sad, misunderstood ideas, stupid and clever blunders, bad decisions followed by good or bad outcomes. The only thing you get to keep, I knew, whether you wanted it or not, was what's inside you; thoughts and feelings attached to the memories of your stories. That is what makes one who one is and how one is now. Yourself, it is your inheritance. Your inheritance is yourself.

*

Sadness overwhelmed me sometimes for no apparent reason, and then humor brought me back to reality. Now and then I tried to recall what I never knew; rather silly and useless. How can one 'recall' nothing much? Recall having no roots, or losses that feel as if one had no past?

I did not want to, I pushed back, but increasingly I discovered my irreplaceable losses. What I was now seemed to be, was driven by the past, by the holocaust. I knew that by now. I did not want it that way. In a way I had, and had not let go of it, or rather, was it not letting me go? And our lives, the drama Mum and I lived, the turns we took and created as I grew, was by now even more a mystery to me. This too also alive and kicking inside me.

Such thoughts often came to me. Like this time, on my way to the antique jewelry store. Curiously though, I felt roused, something distinctively funny stirring within. I started to giggle.

'Yaiks, what if this turns out to be another one of Mum's unreal realities? The 'heirloom' might be worthless. But surely she was an expert at this sort of thing? Anyhow, why do I want this thing to be valuable now, all of a sudden? What does it matter?'

I had been in a downer for months now; the underlying depression that came and went all my days. I needed something and for some reason today, I was desperate that the little sculpture should be real. That this should be the one thing as promised, that would actually turn out to be, turn out to be, uhm... what exactly? Turn out to be more real than I felt? Turn out to be of huge value and of great significance and what? Save me and the world? Why grab on to this silly thing?

I shook my head to clear it of such silliness. Needy feelings or not, I chuckled at myself (a good sign that I was back to reality) not only about the statue, but also about the fact that un-characteristically, I was going to Balaclava, a very Jewish suburb, to seek out a jeweler. 'You fucking hypocrite,' I scoffed at myself, 'ha ha ha, I am no real Jew, and yet I can only trust another Jew with my 'heirloom?''

I nearly turned back, thinking the city would have better experts; Sotheby's or some such. But too late; I had arrived in front of kosher butcher shops. 'The Jews will have to do.'

The Russian woman serving me in the jewelry store apologizes, "I not know nofink about such idems. My husband, he be, uh ha, here in hour, you like to leave here, and he will look at?"

"No thanks," I say snappily, "I'll come back later."

'Does she think I'm crazy to leave such a piece with strangers?' I was again amused by my reaction.

Later, the husband, all five feet of him and the same in girth, looked at the boy and cart. A Russian man with a heavy accent, probably a new arrival, I figured. He hummed and coughed, and smiled kindly as he mumbled:

"Yes, very nice this, lovely," and asked for his magnifying glasses. He rubbed some solution on the bottom of the statue. He showed what happened, which in fact was nothing. He explained what should have happened.

"I am very sorry, yes but no, sorry, is no sterling silver, no, no, sorry. Is a little age like me yes, hm, no? Not handmade, not expensive, and not made by any known artist, sorry again," he continued, "Maybe piece vas mass produce kind, much mass production eh, around eerly 1900's. If you wish to sell maybe sculptura bring around, uhm, $500, you know, because old look, and dat give some value."

I paid $15 for his work, thanked him, and left quickly, disenchanted.

I became angry and sad alternately, tears wanted to come, but I wouldn't cry over this bullshit. I muttered reminders about Mum, and the world at large. 'Fucking hell. Bloody Mum...' I even had a brief inclination to throw the damn statue in the garbage can next to my car. But that idea shook me back to my senses. By the time I sat in my car it began to seem funny again. I started chuckling, then laughing out loud as I sat in the car. 'Ha ha and AH AH'. Banging on the wheel, 'how bloody funny am I? How funny is poor old Mum? Oh well, bugger it all.'

I did not want to sell the damn thing anyway. I just wanted it to be a real inherited treasure that was meant for me. Inevitable that not much came from this either. Predictable, because Mum's stories were never entirely right, because she had to make the few things she had in her head or in her hand into big things, or hopeful things. Mum was still alive then. I didn't say anything to her about my visit to the store.

Driving home, a deep, fervent silence descended on me, a somber feeling that turned to joy. I realized with a jolt that there were invisible fingerprints on this statue. The undetectable finger prints of aunts and uncles, grandparents and father, and perhaps my little cousins. People who were called my family. They may have touched this silly mass- produced ornament, probably thought it important and beautiful. My people who had never met me had seen it. Who were they, what were they like? Names I had not learned and so cannot recall. No photos, no paperwork, just a few stories shaped my life without any of us knowing so.

The statue sits in my bedroom on the mantelpiece to this day. I am a touch concerned some silly robber will take it away sometime, thinking that it is more than what it is.

Josef, Budapest 2002 : Friends, Ghosts, Memories, Luck, Money

Josef shaved, watching his round brown face, internally conversing with himself as usual. He observed, as he supposed everyone did, his never-ending stream of thoughts, always on the lookout to hear something new from himself.

'What's new?'
'Nothing, and you?'
'Nothing.'
'Don't raise your eyebrows to me boy.'

What he saw this morning was what he usually felt; tired and bored, not looking forward to going to work to shuffle meaningless papers. About the only thing that interested him at work were the rumors about people or situations, or the possibility of making a few US dollars on the sly. Not so few actually this time. In fact, there is a chance of the best earn he had ever managed to make. Maybe even enough to travel a little and perhaps to offer the lovely wife a better life! 'Risky though, if it comes undone I'll lose the bloody silly job...Jail too. Now that would be a terrible.'
Juli in the next room asked why he was laughing.

Washing the soap off his face, a glance at his watch confirmed that he was now in a hurry. Remembering last night's 'affair', which was how he liked to think of his sexual encounters with his own wife, was still pleasant. Actually it was more than pleasant - it was something of a puzzle to him these days. 'Good heavens, surely it's time

to end all that affair nonsense with other stranger females. Growing up finally at my advanced age, is that what's happening?'
He asked the mirror, getting only his brown smirking, deeply grooved face in reply.

At the Department of Foreign Affairs, he greeted the usual faces, often barely knowing who they were. He headed for the coffee urn, and then to his office. He was a few minutes late, so his fellow workers were already busy sipping coffee, discussing last night's TV or the inevitable run of political jokes.

Nagy, his old boss, waved to him. "Well, have I got something interesting for you this morning." Josef just nodded. A little private joke. Every morning, Nagy would say this knowing Josef was bored and restless, and Josef would nod and say 'oh yes.' Nagy would then hand him a bunch of papers relating to various, small-time bureaucratic matters, which justified the existence of their jobs.

By now Josef was dealing mainly with trade concerning Italian and Spanish speaking countries. He should have had a better job, but his moodiness and inability to play office politics, and his age also held him down.
Josef considered himself a realist, a cynic even, usually adding "Whatever a realist is - given that most of reality turns out to be false soon or even sooner than that."
He had a well-developed sense of humor; a man who could and often did see life as a ridiculous situation. He figured that the human race was mostly corrupt, and scandalous. 'And I am no exception,' he admitted. Yet he marveled at the human capacity to create works of art and

great terror and injustice all at once. 'Human beings kill each other, save each other, are holders of genuine love and genuine hate'. Oh well, he sighed.

His hand reached out to Nagy and received two sheets of paper from the man who looked nearly serious now. Josef had worked with Nagy ever since he came back from Italy, Nagy was not so bad, together they made a few dollars on the side.

"Josef, this one really might be of real interest. I got it via your friend Zboray who took a quick look suggesting you should handle it. He, apparently had a phone call from the Immigration Department, because some private detective from Argentina is in Budapest searching for long-lost relatives of a deceased client. He must have a few interesting contacts - know what I mean"?

Josef's interest grew given that Zboray had a hand in the matter.

Nagy continued. "The detective's client lived in Argentina, but he was a Hungarian who went there long after the war. He has not managed to find any trace of his wife and son or any family, though he certainly tried. That did not keep him from searching the world for them on several occasions, and spending rather a lot of money. When he died, he was an extremely rich man. I've no idea why Zboray was so insistent on this file getting to you other then you speak some Spanish yes? So there you are, read it and see what we can do for the good detective...and uhm, see what he can do for us. Know what I mean?"

Josef listened. Why had Zboray asked that the case be given to him? He would ask him that later, but for now an Argentinean detective and a rich ex-Hungarian's story certainly smelled of dollars to be made on the sly. Nagy usually kept the best cases for himself, but of course given that Zboray had a tab on the situation, he had little choice in this matter. He scrutinized his boss's face as to whether this was one of his sometimes elaborate jokes.

Nagy continued, "Miklos Zboray is smart, but he does not uhm, shall we say, do 'deals' with anyone for any money. So my sweet friend, you're the lucky inheritor of this fucking case, a waste of time though it may prove to be. At least it sounds more interesting than the usual inquiry to do with the price of potatoes in the middle of March if bought by another country where they only eat rice eh? Lucky I can trust you."

Nagy winked at Josef, having said all he did in one long hurried monologue.

Josef felt an extra surge of curiosity. He glanced at the brief. On the front sheet was the name of the Argentinean private detective and the phone number of his posh hotel. The other sheet was just an interoffice memo with a scribbled note that said, "Confidential. To Josef Feher, please call Senor Garibaldi at his hotel." It was signed by Miklos Zboray.

He shoved the papers in his briefcase, deciding to go on with his daily tasks, but then he called the Intercontinental Hotel. They connected him to Mr. Garibaldi before he had a chance to ask whether they had an interpreter. The man on the other end of the line had a heavy accent, but greeted him in English. What would this be about? Would there indeed, be a way to improve the balance of the 'Feher retirement fund'?

To Josef's enquiry about the matter at hand, Garibaldi suggested they meet and invited Josef to a drink at his hotel that evening. Josef was reluctant. Tonight he was due at his lady friend's place. He especially didn't feel like canceling tonight's meeting, because he was resolved to quit this, his very last affair ever. Nevertheless, this case was intriguing, so he agreed to the meeting.

The rest of the day went as slowly as a gypsy playing a funeral dirge. Josef could not help trying to guess what this was going to be about. The chances of finding someone so long after the war and the revolution was slim on one hand; on the other hand...? On the other hand, as the hero of 'The Fiddler on the Roof' said, "There is no other hand." But of course, one wan or another there always is, Josef thought.

All this brought back some of his own now long forgotten questions. Why hadn't he himself ever searched again for his relatives more than that one time back in the early 1950's? After all he was in a reasonable position do it, working in this department. He dismissed such ideas, reminding himself that when he changed his name from Weisz to Feher, he swore to forget the past. 'Face it man, before the revolution I investigated what I could about family members and drew a blank, or else confirmed them dead. Except for Uncle Lajos, who was in Vienna. I never followed that up, should have, but did not.' The thought was uncomfortable, 'but Lajos never contacted me either' he thought. And whatever happened to Lajos has not been in his mind for many years.

At home, he left a note for Juli, saying he had a business meeting. He tittered at his note. Given that usually he didn't leave a note when he went 'out', Juli wouldn't believe him. Their marriage has been what they called an 'open marriage' for some years now. It was 'open' for him, because long ago she had told him that she was not interested in other men. Little was ever said between them about his affairs. He picked up his pen and wrote, "I am meeting an Argentinean detective in the Intercontinental – no really I am!"

He placed the note on the table with a bunch of flowers he purchased on the way home.

Los Angeles 2002; Edith and Peter

Extraordinary things can still happen in Los Angeles, Edith thought, and yesterday's call was certainly unexpected. What could Peter Levy want after 20 years? 'Questions, questions that need an answer. Something happening when you least expect it,' she whispered, recalling their relationship. Was it 1979 when she went to Esalen with Peter? They were an item then. Everyone thought they would settle together. He was about 40, with two failed marriages, she was five years younger, her first marriage ended two years earlier. They met at one of those lawyers' cocktail parties that happened too often.

At Esalen, during the second day of the workshop she met that Australian guy whose name she could not now recall. During the workshop that morning, they were asked to look around and pair up with someone they felt drawn to. "Do it without thinking, quickly, use your instincts to draw someone into your life," the facilitator directed.

One quick look around the room, full of forty people, and she moved towards that man, and he unmistakably moved toward her. They talked about how they were drawn together, and that it was not a sexual attraction. They both had the thought that each other's face seemed somehow familiar and agreed to talk more after the session, meeting in one of the hot spas carved out of the rocks facing the ocean.

Sitting in one of the four large spas at Esalen was an extraordinary experience. The natural hot spring water flowed out of the mountain, straight into the square stone spas that were large enough for eight people. The Pacific Ocean sounded as if it was gently breathing, dumping soft waves on the rocks below. An occasional whale breached far away, but still noticeably. The sun was hanging on to the horizon, making the color of the sky change fantastically from blue to pink to purple. It was dreamlike and immensely beautiful. Edith sat in the very hot water, waiting for Peter and the Australian. She was nude like everyone else, relaxed, and happy she was here with Peter, and hoping that this would be the turning point in their lives.

*

Edith sighed as she drove her car toward the cafe where she was to meet Peter. What happened when that interesting Aussie arrived, stripped off, and hopped into the spa, she now recalled with ease. Meeting him was remarkable and the memory was attached to the breakup of her relationship with Peter.

The Australian and Edith chatted, finding out about each other's lives. Talking was easy, as if they were old friends. Edith was immediately interested when the guy said: "I know this sounds a bit odd, but uh, your face is kind of like, like an archetype to me, or like as if we've met before..." He explained that he lost nearly all his relatives and had few memories of his childhood. "Yet, there is a picture in my mind of a smiling face, black hair, a face sort of like yours. A Jewish female face perhaps... like a face I've seen before," he reiterated. "Maybe like an auntie leaning over the cot when I was a baby. You are not Jewish by chance?"

Edith liked his meandering thinking and she was surprised by his question.

"My great grand parents came from Hungary and were Jewish, I've never practiced it."

"Huh, there you go, archetypal all right," he said smiling.

He was interesting and she felt oddly warm toward him. What he said was inexplicable even a bit sentimentally romantic, and yet who knows?

"Do you recall any of your Hungarian relatives' family names?" he asked.

"Yes, I've looked into it a little and found some names. My great grandmother's maiden name was Schlezinger," she laughed. "Sometimes I think she may have been related to the famous tennis racket brand of Slazenger, but I don't know," and she stopped, seeing that the man looked taken aback.

Then he laughed, punching the water with his fist: "Schlenzinger was my grandmother's maiden name. What a lovely coincidence; how about that...archetypes rule, huh?" He breathed deeply and laughed loudly, but he looked disturbed. They sat silently looking at each other. She reached out and held his hand, "Yes, what a coincidence."

Peter arrived, looking awkward. He knew that everyone was nude in these spas, and he was a bit shy about that. He looked at Edith talking with the Australian, holding his hand, and he did not like it. His temper rose, he shrugged angrily, and moved to the next spa, barely acknowledging Edith's invitation to get in next to her. At once she saw that he was prickly, not the happy face of earlier. She knew that face, and saw the moods passing through it very well by now. She asked him again to join the two of them, but he shook his head and looked away. 'Is the silly man jealous? Does he think so little of me that he would be jealous? Oh well, here I am nude with a man in the spa, he'll get over it later,' she hoped, a little foolishly, now that she thought about it.

She reached out, trying to touch Peter; he was looking sullen and moved his hand away. She tried to tell him of her excitement that the Australian and she had discovered they might be related, if a long way back, in Hungary. Peter mumbled, "Yeah, well, keep talking ..." in a tight voice, refusing to look at her. She felt angry that Peter could be so damn silly.

There would be more time to talk to the Australian later. They exchanged phone numbers and he promised that he would call her when going home via Los Angeles.

Peter had already left, without another word. Back in their room Peter was in bed, reading. He spoke in his stifled, angry, public prosecutor's voice that she knew well. An unyielding, almost theatrical sound. Whatever was behind that tight, resentful voice was exactly what she wanted to know more about. She grabbed his hand, he pulled it away. Shocked, she asked, "What's wrong?" The famous words everyone uses when jealously blind came at her like a tornado: "Nothing!"

She tried to leave it, "Please Peter, this is silly," she told him, "You are jealous and it's absolutely not warranted. I am not interested in this guy like that, I am with you, I love you, don't be like this, please give me a hug."

He said nothing, staying turned away from her. Again, she tried to explain the conversation between herself and the Australian. Peter finally turned toward her. His eyes were dark, his face white and tense-lipped.

"I have no intention of being jealous, but now you bring it up perhaps there is a reason for me to be jealous is there? Precisely since you bring it up."

She denied it again. "Honey, please, can't you see what you are doing? Please, please Peter let it go." But she was hurt and angry too by now. He turned away again, saying no more. When the light went out, she did not know that it was also the end of their affair.

In the morning he decided that he wanted no more of the workshop. They drove back to L.A that morning. On the way, in the car, she tried again. It was useless. She resolved to keep things going; perhaps he could ride through his ill feelings. He did not ring her for 2days and when she called him, he agreed to meet for coffee only to call it quits as soon as they sat down.

Oh yes, the other thing that happened or rather did not happen! The Australian never called, though he promised to do so and she lost his name and phone number. Most likely Peter destroyed the note that was left on the bedside table, she thought.

The Australian had not told her his Anglicized surname, only his old Hungarian one, a typically Jewish surname she could not recall. She was sad about the lost connection. And you couldn't find someone in Australia when looking for a name he was not using anyway.

Oh well, it would be interesting enough to find out what had happened to Peter in all these years. She felt no animosity toward him now.

*

Peter arrived at the coffee shop first. He sat at a window seat enjoying the early warmth of the sunny spring day and wondered what Edith would look like. She could have no idea of the interesting twist of fate that made him contact her. That is, if he was right about all that. And he would have to apologize for destroying that note with the details of the Australian on it!

That fine looking woman coming through the door, he realized quickly, was Edith!

After some preliminaries, and briefly catching up, Peter told her of the case he heard about from his old boss Weinberger. Peter's amazing memory recalled the name of the Australian Edith met in Esalen: it was Weisz. Edith's memory was vague and yet they managed to piece together enough once the Schlezinger name was also mentioned. Peter called Weinberger and checked it with him. The answer was yes! The Australian Edith met might just be the man they were looking for!

Josef and Garibaldi.
Budapest 2002

Josef took the tram to the hotel by the side of the Danube, pulling his overcoat tighter around himself, and his old brown hat further down on his head. There was a chilly wind blowing. The lights of stores and street lamps lit up the main boulevard of Budapest.

In the hotel's restaurant he was shown to Garibaldi's table. Garibaldi stood up with a warm smile, extending his hand, "thank you for coming," in surprisingly good English that carried the rich accents of Argentina.

They shook hands. "Josef Feher".

"I'm Antonio Garibaldi and lucky for me, that you speak English," he said. How did Garibaldi know that? Ah, Miklos Zboray. Josef observed the only Argentinean he had ever met. A medium built, well-dressed man wearing a light grey suit and red tie, who seemed to be around sixty years of age and in excellent condition. His eyes were darkly twinkling above a cauliflower nose and moustache going from lack to grey, his tanned good looks accentuated by a mop of snow white hair.

A Gypsy band played famous old songs. The atmosphere was rich with wealthy people, food and décor that said it was a privilege to stay here. Josef knew the price of a goulash here was about that of his daily pay. Outside, the Danube flowed and the lights along the streets showed an idyllic scene for the lucky tourists.

They ordered drinks, chatting about Garibaldi's long journey from Argentina to Budapest. As the drinks arrived., Garibaldi, now looking focused, spoke. "Let's get down to why I'm here. You must be curious yes? But first, do you mind if I ask you a few questions?"

Josef nodded, eager to hear what the man had to say. His first impression of the Argentinean was surprisingly good. There was an air of confidence about the man. He seemed genuine. 'Odd to think someone genuine at first sight,' he thought.

"Ask away." he replied, "Though I'm awfully keen to ask you a few questions. All I know is that you are looking for someone."

Garibaldi raised his glass, drinking deeply, while he observed Josef.

Josef wondered if he should tell this man why or how he got this assignment. He decided not to; better to say little and get a lot of information.

Garibaldi spoke, "May I ask what your position is in the Foreign Affairs Department? And may I ask if you are of Jewish origin?"

Josef showed surprise, but Garibaldi added quickly, "I especially asked for someone Jewish, and though they said no at first, well you know, dollars buy what one wants."

This was rather confronting.

"I see. So much for me thinking that hardly anyone knew I used to be Jewish," he smiled, feeling uncomfortable as he pushed on, but of course, Zboray knew!

"My position is not very high, in fact you got me mainly because a good friend, who does have more authority, handed the matter on to me."

The lines on Garibaldi's face turned serious. "I imagine your family suffered during the war, is that one of the reasons why you say you 'were' a Jew...?"

Josef nodded, taking a deep breath. "Most, of my family was wiped out in the Holocaust, as were most of our possessions. 'Most' is an understatement actually."

Josef hesitated, unsure about all he blurted out. Garibaldi's face was attentive and solemn. 'Somehow,' Josef thought, 'this Argentinean is one of those people who have the uncanny ability to make you say more than you mean to.' And though he couldn't think why, Garibaldi appeared trustworthy, interesting and immediately likeable.

"Sorry, this must be painful for you," Garibaldi said.

Josef shook his head, "I have spent a long time with all my dead now so most of them seem as if they never existed. But what else did you want to know and why the interest in my background?" He hurried on. "My position in the office has the pretentious title of Consultant Investigator for Economic Affairs of the Foreign Affairs Department. In fact, I do little more than the work of an ordinary clerk. Most of it is dead boring. So there you have it. Is it my turn to ask you some questions yet?"

Garibaldi decided to trust his instincts; Josef seemed an intelligent man, as Miklos Zboray said, and obviously a pained one. Garibaldi leaned forward, offering Josef his first Cuban cigar. His craggy brown face serious now, he tried to find the right words to explain his mission.

"Josef, before I go any further, I have to ask you to sign a confidentiality agreement, which I must warn you, carries worldwide legal authority. Don't be too worried about it however; it is to protect both of us. I am in need of a working partner in Budapest. Our arrangement would carry with it a $10,000 fee to start with. I'm aware that you are not allowed to be employed, or paid by anyone other than your government. Our agreement will protect you by keeping the arrangement secret, and guarantee that if the arrangement comes to light affecting your job, we shall pay your current salary for the next two years. Unless, of course, you breach the contract. So you see amigo, it is a good idea for us both to sign this, and the deal may be agreeable for you."

Josef, surprised, looked at Antonio, wondering whether he was lucky, or being drawn into some silly scheme. He had much to lose, because if he lost his job, it would be very difficult to find another even at the miserable level he was at. Most of the time these days he figured that he would live and die there, retiring in another few years. Unless one of his side deals got him into trouble. Just how they were going to live on the meager pension from the age of sixty-five onwards was a mystery to him. What he had stashed away in an Austrian bank was nowhere near enough for retirement. Unlike a few years ago, at least nowadays he could get his money back into Hungary.

Josef replied carefully, "I will look at the agreement, it sounds generous and interesting."

Garibaldi reached inside his admirable suit pocket, and handed Josef the contract.

"Perhaps amigo," he said, "we could have dinner first, on the expense account of course, and then adjourn to my room where you could read the agreement. It is brief and uncomplicated and yes, you need to trust me, which cannot be easy, I do appreciate that."

He added with some hesitation "I must emphasize that we have very little time to do this investigation, and much is at stake. And, truthfully, I have little hope that we can conclude it successfully at all."

"Dinner is an excellent idea," Josef answered. He was hungry and excited, already scanning the words of the agreement. Dinner came and was consumed quickly. Antonio waited. Josef could see that the contract was simple and straight forward. He thought about it. What the hell, ten thousand U.S dollars to start with and maybe more, was serious money. Looking at the two pages quickly he decided that this was an acceptable risk, though he doubted Juli would think so.

"Coffee and brandy upstairs?"

Josef nodded. The Argentinean waved over the waiter to bring the bill. During dinner they were discussing Josef's favorite subjects, on the borderline of philosophy, psychology, relationships, sex and women. Antonio's answers and questions showed that he was a man of some culture, something of a thinker about the human condition.

"Ah," Josef remarked, "Mr Garibaldi, it is obvious that you are a seeker of wisdom and truth," and he laughed.

"Or alternately," he went on, "the next best piece of cow dung will do the job."

Antonio laughed warmly: "And always the two shall meet, but please call me Antonio."

In his room Garibaldi opened the curtains, looking at the lights below that followed the curve of the Danube, and poured two balloon glasses near half full with brandy. Josef sat reading the contract.

"I feel sure," Garibaldi said, turning toward Josef "that I'm not making a mistake with you."

"You are of course referring to the quality of the brandy," Josef answered raising his glass.
As he read the last paragraph of the contract Josef reached for his pen. The agreement was evidently prepared by an American law firm, Weinberger and Company, and yet it was in fluent Hungarian – as well as in English and Spanish. It was brief and straightforward, he assured himself. He signed the Hungarian version and they shook hands. Antonio went into the other room and came back with an envelope.

"Here is ten thousand dollars, Josef, which I'd like you to have as a down payment."
"Would you mind putting it in an Austrian account?" Josef asked a touch embarrassed, wondering if he should give Antonio the current account number, or ask him to open a new one? Ah, he thought, the national preoccupation with not trusting anyone, born out of the fact that actually you could not.
Antonio nodded agreement.

All this was more appealing than Josef had hoped. As Antonio settled in the comfort of the armchair, Josef picked up his glass, offering him one of his cigarettes.
Antonio laughingly protested. "Would you want to kill your future partner even before we start? Let's stick with

these." The Cuban cigar was glorious. They lit up, sitting back into the armchairs. Garibaldi launched into his story.

"I told you Josef, that I am a semi-retired private investigator living in Buenos Aires. Over the last thirty years I have done a lot of work for several large law firms, and I drifted into specializing in cases affecting Holocaust victims, and missing people from Europe who had migrated to the South American continent. Argentina has more than its fair share of both victims and unfortunately, also the persecutors. Some of our leading, well-to-do citizens are ex-Nazis and their wealth often came from what they stole from the Jewish people of Eastern Europe. Although I'm not Jewish, I have developed a strong affinity with Jewish people..., my dear departed friend and client in particular."

He took a drink and continued.

"When I retired from full-time work, I retained contact with two major law firms who occasionally offer me cases. They know of my interest in hopeless situations. Such cases are typically unusual, intriguing, and as a rule, impossible to resolve. However, I have had a touch of success now and then, and that makes it worthwhile for me to do them."

Josef was impressed and more reassured. He nodded, urging Garibaldi to carry on.

"My client was a man called Lou Blanco. His original Hungarian name was Weisz. He became more than a client since he first came to me to investigate his missing family. That was many years ago. We retained a friendship. I was very fond of him."

Garibaldi coughed, but waved his emotions away with his cigar held between two ring studded fingers. "My friend died a while ago leaving his substantial fortune and an unusual will. I contacted a law firm in Los Angeles and we have done a lot of work on it. To be honest with you Josef, I think this an entirely hopeless case, but Lou was dear to me. He asked, and I promised, that I would do this one last search for his family."

Josef reacted on hearing the Weisz name, but Lou was not a Hungarian name. He stilled himself, centering his attention on Garibaldi, who paused, refilling their glasses, and continued. Should he tell Garibaldi his real name now? He held back as the man continued.

"Let me tell you what my briefing is," Garibaldi continued.

"I imagine," Josef broke in, "that with such money and your contacts, you have already gone through every official or for that matter unofficial channel that you possibly could?"

"Exactly," said Antonio. "About ten years ago, and again recently. That process this time has taken nearly a year," he added looking wistful.

"Since Lou Weisz first hired me we have had two thorough investigations and turned up not one person alive. I tried my best to dissuade Lou from any further investigations. Not just to save his money, but to save his heart from all the pain he went through each time we found nothing. He was a decent man. I miss him greatly. Lou had something in him, a sadness that could have moved mountains. He died while healthy, silly as that sounds. A heart attack; one moment he was there playing tennis, and the next dead. Just like that. 'Heart break' means something to me now." Garibaldi sighed, looking disturbed.

Josef waited, respecting Garibaldi's emotions.

"Have you had any success regarding any leads at all previously, anything that could be followed up?"

Garibaldi shook his head, taking another sip of brandy. "No, I have not, or very little. We have already gone down many false alleys in the past, and now once more; I am at the point of announcing that the story is finite, a dead end. But an interesting turn, a coincidence, serendipity - call it what you will, astonishingly surfaced. Might be nothing more than a coincidence but who knows.

Josef jumped in. "Before you go on can I ask a question?"

Antonio nodded, "O.k. amigo, I have a lot to tell you yet, but what is your question?"

"Well," said Josef, "I wonder if you would mind telling me - I'm a fellow full of curiosity - what sort of sum this inheritance comes to. I already imagine it must run into quite a fortune."

Antonio hesitated, "I'm not entirely certain that you need to know that, but I'm equally uncertain whether there's any harm in telling you. Perhaps when you know what is involved, you may even take the case more seriously."

Josef nodded.

"I think you'd better put your glass down Josef," Antonio said, "for two reasons. One is that it's empty, and the other, I would not want you to drop it in surprise. Our deceased client, Lou Weisz, has left a total of over thirty million dollars in cash and investments, and roughly ten million dollars' worth of properties."

Josef had already figured that no one would go to as much trouble, or offer him the kind of money that Antonio offered, without a substantial sum being involved. This sort of wealth was way beyond his wildest imaginings, of which he had plenty. This meeting could be more valuable than he ever imagined.

He raised his glass, "Antonio, I drink to my good fortune in meeting you, and to your health, and assure you that I shall do everything in my power to rise to the occasion."

They clinked glasses and Antonio continued, "The law firm, Weinberger and Company in Los Angeles, has branches in several cities. Whenever there is an investigation of the impossible, every office is notified and asked for ideas and contributions. In this case they had received negative feedback from all of them. It looked like another – how you say - dead macaw, but then something turned up. It is thin as wafer but, who knows? Until now we had absolutely nothing to show for years and years of work. Not a hope."

He waved his arm his face showing his incredulity. "It seems that the head of the Los Angeles office, Joe Weinberger, was having dinner with an ex-employee, Peter Levy, who is now retired. During that lunch, Weinberger, Peter's ex-boss told him about our case. As you might know, lawyers love telling stories and this case is remarkably 'rich', shall we say, in itself. The two men parted, after setting the next dinner date in a month's time. However, much to Weinberger's surprise Levy rang him three days later."

Antonio refilled their glasses. Josef protested that his hangover, at this rate of drinking, would be, "bigger than the Foreign Affairs Department. My head is already buzzing, and not just with the cognac."

Garibaldi chuckled. "Let me continue the story because it is vital you know all the details, and this bit is the only thing we have." He then outlined what took place between Peter Levy and Edith. Josef listened to that a fascinating story, right up until Garibaldi got to the point where Peter Levy asked Edith if the names Schlezinger and Weisz were the connections between her and the Australian.

Josef felt dizzy. The alcohol and the blood ran out of him. His face turned white.

Antonio leaned forward asking, "Are you all right?"
Josef could barely speak but he had to say something now.
"Azanyadistenit...oh sorry, that's Hungarian, means something like 'the God of your mothers. That name... 'Schlezinger', you won't believe it, was also a name in my family...my cousin's grandmother's name!"

Garibaldi raised an eyebrow wondering if Josef's reply was in earnest or...
Josef shook his head, shrugged, calming himself, not wanting to believe a possible connection. He drank a glass of water.

Antonio was apprehensive, interested but cautious. 'If this is true...but how?' He looked at Josef with his years of experience. Was this real? His instincts about people were usually quite sharp and reliable. But not always. It was his intuition together with his intelligence that made him so good at his job, but a healthy piece of suspicion had to be maintained. The money he offered to this Hungarian was substantial, and where there were large sums of money, people did strange things.

He moved on, wanting to test Josef's reliability. "But that would be fantastic Josef, ...if I ever could be, I'd be speechless now. What do you know about the Schlezingers? Can you find out more about them?"
Josef, recovered somewhat, "probably just a coincidence", he mumbled.
 "I'm sure you have done lots of research on the Schlezinger name already? What can you tell me about it?"

An intelligent approach, Garibaldi noted, 'throwing it back at me, obviously neither of us are too drunk.'
"We know that there were Schlezinger families living in Budapest between 1905 and 1945. One Schlezinger family consisted of six sisters and a brother. And this particular family is notable for one big reason, and that is that Gizella Schlezinger had a daughter called Sari, and she was the wife of my deceased client Lou Weisz and..."
Garibaldi stopped, seeing Josef move forward, knocking over his glass, red faced, jumping up, tears in his eyes.
Josef could barely speak. "Gizella was ... and Sari, that name, Sari is common enough, but my Cousin Tibor's mother had that name."
Swallowing air hard, he threw himself back into the chair, looking for another of Antonio's American cigarettes.
Then, he dashed for the bathroom and vomited holding onto the basin. Antonio rushed to get a towel and water.

When Josef calmed down Antonio asked "are you all right? What is all this about?"

Several deep breaths later Josef spoke.

"Antonio, there is something I must now tell you. My name Josef Feher was originally Josef Weisz, I changed it to Feher. And Sari Weisz was, may have been, oh hell, sounds like she was, one of my aunts. She had a son called Tibor who was my cousin. Her mother's name was definitely Gizella Schlezinger."

He rushed it all out in a loud climax, expelling again. Antonio took the words in silently, his mind in a whirl for a moment, and then reacted like a volcano. He yelled "Caramba, Hijo de puta," and then grabbed Josef's shoulders.

"I have searched the world on behalf of my friend Lou for so many years Josef, I can barely believe what you are saying - and this twist of fate…, you would not, you wouldn't lie?

Sorry, I apologize, "he said, looking flushed and excited.

"But, but if this is right, then you are the Josef we had looked for all these years…"

The bathroom mirror reflected two wound up, exultant and yet distressed men. They went back into the lounge.

Garibaldi shook his head. "I can't believe it! At last, at last some contact is here and poor Lou, is dead…" He turned very serious and hesitant, "Josef I must ask you for some proof, I am sorry to be distrustful but…"

Josef waved, "No, no it's all right, I'll give you some names of relatives, like Sari's sisters or brothers." He rattled of some names by now familiar to Garibaldi. The detective's eyes were red and moist as he recalled his friend's obsession with finding someone in the world he could call his family...

Then, Josef asked a question, wanting the right answer, "But Antonio, I do not understand, the name Lou, my uncle's name was..."

Antonio broke in, "yes, Lajos, but in Argentina he changed it to a sort of translation, calling himself Lou Blanco which, by the way, also means 'white' just like your new name of Feher."

Their faces suddenly turned from serious to hysterical laughter, and then to tears, and laughter again. Slapping each other's back, they managed to calm down.

"So much for my cool, hard headed detective image," Antonio laughed, wiping his face. He walked around the room, shaking his head, unable to keep from muttering over and over, "I can hardly believe it. Why oh why could we not find you while dear Lou-Lajos was still with us...Oh God...And I, Estupido, who never believed in serendipity, but knew that the universe is full of chances and luck or the lack of it, I should have done more."

He sat down weary, feeling more than either of them could hold.

Josef needed to stop. It was 3 am. He looked at Garibaldi.

"What do you think? Where to now?" His emotions in his throat, he did not know whether to laugh or cry as the implication of it all hit him. "Cousin Tibor? Would he, could he be alive? He'd be about my own age, or a few years younger. I don't know what to think Antonio."

Was he, were 'they', going to inherit more money than he ever dreamed of?

Garibaldi held himself, trying to think, till Josef spoke again.

"One last thing Antonio."

Josef recounted Wilhelm's visit to Budapest a long time ago. Though Garibaldi knew this from Lajos, here was the final proof that this was tangible and real. Josef also recounted how he had left Hungary, and changed his name on his return. All the terrible mistimed coincidences of life coming together now.

Garibaldi felt bad, blaming himself. That was how fate worked, a never-ending, unpredictable, chaotic piece of fiction that sometimes offered at least partial resolutions. Lajos had always insisted that a nephew named Josef was alive. 'Why oh why could we have not found him before. How good would that have been for dear Lajos?' Gathering his senses, he had one more hard thing to say to Josef before they parted.

"Josef, I hope you realize what this means? If we can be certain that Tibor is dead, you would inherit a large portion of the wealth. But given the probability that he may be alive, and perhaps in Australia, we cannot settle the inheritance until…. well, I am sorry…"

He saw Josef's face contort - hell, who would not feel disappointed? Josef was taken aback by the realization of what that meant. To have to find a cousin maybe alive - or to hope and prove he is dead…

*

Josef sorted the documents for the importation of oranges, and the export of locally grown turnips. What a laugh to be dealing with vegetables when his mind was elsewhere on the bigger things of his own existence. He was incessantly considering the events of the past days. The exciting meetings between he and Antonio had brought a new lease of life, but with awful misgivings. The events affected Josef in startling ways. Eagerly, he kept repeating to his wife bits of their meetings, and the dumbfounding story that was unfolding. He could barely contain himself thinking about finding a live cousin. This was mixed with the fear that they, that he, may lose the inheritance. The will firmly stipulated that if the rightful inheritors were not found by the end of the allotted two years, then the whole estate would be immediately divided amongst a number of charities. Time was running out for claiming the inheritance, with barely a few days left. Josef figured, hoped, that even if they were late they could still claim. Missing out was out of the question. Yet, there was more than inheriting money or cousin; it had changed him in ways he could barely believe, or trust. He felt lighter, stronger and clearer in his mind than he could recall in many years. Sometimes also he felt awful, half wishing they could quickly prove his cousin dead - if they could not find him. What a dilemma, the dreadful fickleness of fate; but even with that, he now coped differently.

After sleepless nights, he settled a little, truly hoping to find his cousin, shutting out other thoughts.

"Money or not, there is an inheritance here Juli, and much as I'd rather be rich than poor, this is the first time the past has acknowledged me. Do you know what I mean?"

Juli was cautious and worried that all this would come to nothing. Fearful that all Josef would get was another disappointment. She nodded, trying to be enthusiastic. All this was after all truly remarkable, and it was not another of Josef's mad schemes…, but such a twisted tale?

"Darling, do you understand what I am saying about being acknowledged by the past? "Josef asked.

"I have a feeling for what you mean, rather than an understanding," she replied ponderously, thinking that Josef has changed. 'He is more like his old, younger self, but no, he is different to that too,' she acknowledged, feeling even more love than usual.

*

Josef re-checked everything he could about his Cousin Tibor and Aunt Sari, looking for clues about where they could be. He found nothing. 'Did they die or leave Hungary after the war? Might Tibor be in Australia, as seems the case? How come the Australian consulate has no trace of a Sari and Tibor Weisz?'

"No such persons entered Australia," he was told. Sometimes he was desperate, but the feeling was not the depression he had known all his life. "I must do anything necessary to find Tibor. This in itself will be my legacy, and for both of us," and then his heart sank. "Unless there is no Tibor. And if we are on time."

Juli gently stroked his head. Now he seemed far away, sitting as if in a trance as pictures of his mother came to him. Juli asked what was on his mind. She had to ask him twice before he hesitantly answered.

"I don't know why but now I recall mother sitting, silently shelling peas. She was never big, but now she looked shrunken and pasty, tired and sick as usual. There was nothing I could do but watch her disappear into herself. I used to sit there as an adult or as a child, helping with the damn green peas that were her main diet - I never knew why. The older she got the more withdrawn she became, breaking out of her remoteness only rarely to tell stories, and then usually about prewar years.

I tried talking to her to keep some connection going between us. One minute she looked like she was listening, and then she'd stop shelling the bloody peas and looking up, she'd might suddenly break into a tale that had nothing to do with what I was saying. In her last few months as she was losing her grip on reality she just spoke out loud at times, as if her story was a continuous narrative that went on inside her head.

I imagine that is how it was. She mentioned many names. Some were vaguely familiar to me like Aunt Malvin, or cousins Tomi or Vera, but I could not put a face to who they were. The only names that meant something I was sure of were cousin Tibor, Grandfather Sandor on my father's side, and yes, another two cousins Agnes and Bandi, all children of a similar age to me. All these names bore about the same weight of memory as the smoke drifting away from my cigarette.

Don't know why now, but now I'm thinking of a particular story that she told me several times. I rarely recall much, if anything of the childhood days, and yet here is one story that is so with me now, ah, well, obviously because of this inheritance thing. The one story mother kept babbling about on and off, was that there was a lot of money deposited by our grandfather Sandor Weisz in a Swiss bank. At first this meant nothing to me as a child, yet I retained it, though never believed it. Later, I wanted it to be true, and desperately so as I got older, but I didn't, could not believe it.

Grandpa Sandor died in 1944. He was a good man, nice to us, but his wife Grandma Helen was, according to mother, a nasty old woman. I have a vague memory of Grandpa's ever-smiling round face...I can almost recall the way he grabbed me with obvious delight each time he saw me.

Mother insisted on telling the money story again and again; not surprising, given we lived so poorly. She said that one time, a year or two after the war, she visited Grandma Helen, who survived the war thanks to Aunt Sari, Tibor's mother. Helen survived and even got her flat back, although how that happened remains a mystery. But Helen was, not surprisingly, much the worse for all that had happened.

Mother was on a mission on this particular visit to Grandma Helen. She asked the old lady about the money in the Swiss bank, reminding her that Sandor deposited US dollars there each time a grandchild was born. At first Helen denied any memory of it. But then, as my mother insisted, Helen said that the money was there for her, not for the grandchildren. Mother argued with her vehemently. Helen finally said that the money was, in any case, withdrawn in the early years of the war, because they were running out of money themselves. Helen remarked, 'How would we get hold of it anyway? I have no records of it.'

This made mother even more suspicious. She wrote to various Swiss banks."

Josef burst out in loud hilarity. Juli smiled, knowing he was right to think it funny. Josef continued.

"Yes, she wrote addressing it to 'The banks of Switzerland, Zurich'. I can well imagine what they said. One bank actually was decent enough and replied with a short note; they were unable to act without account numbers or other proof.

That was the end of getting rich for mother. I actually asked her, a few months before she died, why she was so sure about the deposit. I wanted to believe in this little financial escape hatch, even while I thought it was nonsense. I mean, why is it so ridiculous? Many grandfathers leave something for their grandchildren. This time, surprising me no end, mother replied, "I saw the papers, your Grandpa showed them to me just after he signed them. "

I asked why she had never told me this fact before, but mother just shrugged, saying it made no difference now, and went on talking about all sorts of other things that made little sense.

That story was my main and only connection with Grandpa Sandor, other than what I recall about his smiling face. I have one picture of him. When I think about him or about my feelings for family, but particularly about grandparents, it feels like the distance between me and 'family' is as far as the distance between Budapest and the moon. I never fail to feel a disappointed sadness at not having experienced a grandfather, not even to mention a father."

He stopped, words lost for a moment before continuing.

"I often wonder about how one can miss something one has never had? How can I feel such a need for a person I never knew? For a father or grandparents or cousins and all that? And now you and I shall never know what it is like to be a grandparent either. I'm sorry Juli."

His energy was spent, but he had more to say.

"I can never stop wondering whether I have the right story anyway about anyone, there is no one else ever to confirm or correct any of this stuff in my head? No one damn it!"

"So my dear" and he lifted his eyes toward Juli, "I am going to put in a claim with these bank bastards in Switzerland. You see, I do believe the story after all. I want to, feel compelled to. And, I will do everything I can to get that fucking money, even if I have to do a few things I would not normally think of as entirely ethical. They owe us, the greedy prick bankers. They thought it would be nice to keep all that money, but now there is a chance they will have to come good."

He was angry and energized about his scheme. Juli was already apprehensive, but thought it best to leave it for now. She asked, "How much, how long is involved in this claims business that is likely to be a total waste of time?"

"Well whatever it is, it's running in the right direction, even if nothing comes of it. I shall give them as much pepper in the eye as I can," Josef went on.

"Between the money we have stashed away and what I might earn from the generous Mr Garibaldi, and a bit more from the cheesy Swiss, we might be able to eat after we retire until we die - after which we don't need to eat..."

He laughed uproariously at his own joke.

*

An email arrived to Josef from Garibaldi.

My dear Josef

Something amazing has happened. News you must know. You recall the story I told you about Edith and Peter and how from that meeting we had learnt two small, I think vital facts. You recall that at first all Edith and Peter could recall about the Australian was that although his original name was Weisz it was not that when she met him in Esalen. She knew that he had changed it to an English name which, worse luck she could not recall. However, after some further thought she believed that he worked at something to do with pictures, art gallery, or perhaps he was a photographer? She was also more certain that our man lived in either Sydney or Melbourne, the two largest cities in Australia.

We are now making enquiries of course but so far there are no photographers, art galleries or anything like that by the name of Weisz in Sydney, there is one in Adelaide, but he is not our man. In any case chasing the Weisz name is a waste of time, unless someone in Australia happens to know him by his old name. Unlikely I think, but who knows... There is a fair few Weiss names even down there at the end of the world.

Today I have contacted a private detective in Sydney to investigate the matter and offered him more money as a success fee than he earns in a year. If he comes up with nothing, given we do not know what your cousin changed his name to, we are done for. Time has all but run out, as you know. Any ideas? I imagine not, since I've not heard from you,

>*Regards*
>*Antonio Garibaldi*

Josef read the email first with hope rising, and then a sickly disappointment. The idea of a dead end was too much to swallow. He replied instantly.

>*Dear Antonio*
>*Can one check every photographer in Australia? And what if he was not a photographer, but something allied to that? Like a printer or an artist? Alternately, is it possible to check every Weisz in case my cousin has relatives there?*
>>*Regards*
>>*Josef*

The response from Garibaldi:
You had some good ideas there amigo. We have checked with the Australian authorities, who do have excellent records, to no avail. No Sari and Tibor Weisz arrived and changed names. I think, and have an intuition, that we are missing a vital clue. Perhaps Edith is wrong about our man being in Australia; though according to Peter, she is adamant about that, and he is also certain. My hope is that the Australian detective might turn up something. I have, on your suggestion, asked them to cast a wider net than just the 'photographer' search. Keep thinking. There is something here that is so close, I can almost smell it.

>*Best wishes, Antonio Garibaldi*

Josef's Dubious Plan

Juli knew Josef was up to something. His little brown eyes were twinkling like the stars. She knew that look whenever he considered a new plot of some sort. She saw on his still handsome face what they jokingly termed the 'face of concern' look. So they laughed, whenever one of them was about to make a serious pronouncement.

There he was now, deep in thought, the computer of his brain ticking over. And what a brain he had, she thought. Now, he was about to tell her something that was going to be challenging. She lit the thin cigar he held between his lips. Josef spoke with a certain deliberation that showed he has been preparing what he had to say.
"Listen to me Darling. There are two ways I can go to improve our life, and I am absolutely determined to do that. No more just living with whatever the world chucks at us. First there is finding Cousin Tibor and the inheritance. That looks painfully unlikely now. The chances of getting the legacy are practically nil, unless by some miracle the detective he hired in Australia turns up something.
You know I've spent many days trying to find my cousin. I suppose that means that Tibor and his mother are dead. In any case we are out of time. If we do not claim, and prove our claim within a few days, the money will be lost."

He paused looking worried, rushing out the words.
"I have evolved two clever-stupid plots. The first one was to find someone to be Cousin Tibor, yes to fake it."

His eyebrows raised as Juli looked at him, shaking her head with surprise and dismay.

"I know that would be tricky, illegal, and most likely to fail, and I cannot lie to Garibaldi, who would see through it. And there are lots of other problems, so that idea is as silly as you think it is." Juli sighed as Josef carried on.

"The alternative is the Swiss banks claim. This too is doomed; given we have no papers to prove anything. I have looked up on the internet, the beneficiaries' names, and, how about this; the only one listed is a Tibor Weisz, him yet again. Our future depends on this one likely dead cousin huh? You'd laugh, except it isn't funny.

I have spoken with Garibaldi, who knows something about the Swiss claims. I asked for information from the American lawyers handling the claims about the strictness of the rules regarding proof of beneficiaries or depositors. I'm informed that the bastard bankers, who are offering a miserable amount as compensation to all the Jews in the world, would be happy to go through the process of identification fairly quickly, to be rid of the problem.

If Tibor is dead, and we would have to prove that first, then it might be possible for us to claim some Swiss money, as his nearest and probably only relative. But first we'd have to prove that the Tibor Weisz listed is actually my cousin. Even if we managed do that, it is likely that there will only be a few thousand dollars allocated to shut us up, once and for all. But these few thousand dollars can mean more to us than what we have to look forward to otherwise."

Looking uncomfortable, Juli asked what he was scheming. He nodded, "Yes my dear, I do have a plot, and you won't like the sound of it at first. Please don't say no immediately, think about it hard. I want to do this; I want to risk it because it is our only chance to improve our future. I am sick in my heart and body that we should have to live another 20-30 years in our lousy circumstances."

Juli was about to protest but Josef went on, "I know you don't think it's that bad, but for me the only good thing has been your love and loyalty, which has never ceased to amaze me. You know it took me a long time to really trust it, to really, really trust your love."
He stopped, touching her face.
Juli held his hands in hers, feeling what he put into words.
"What I am proposing is not legal, actually it is very crooked and totally unethical; I could finish up in jail for it. Even if I don't, it is not right or fair to Cousin Tibor - if he is alive. Here is what I propose as our only way to escape our crappy financial situation."

He took a deep breath, "I can get hold of the pro forma copies of birth certificates and the like, that's easy. What you don't know is that I have some, shall we say 'interesting' connections with people. Amongst these people is a master forger. I am proposing that I falsify papers that show my family connections with Tibor, and with Grandfather Weisz, and about the moneys he banked in Switzerland. So far there is no sin in doing this, it is true. The trick is to somehow prove that money was deposited by Grandfather and that it is a substantial amount. We can't forge Swiss bank papers, that's for sure. All I can 'find,' are 'letters' written by Grandpa Weisz, confirming that he had indeed deposited money for his grandchildren. I am not going to go for too much, I am thinking in terms of the original deposit being around say five or ten thousand American dollars. That by now would probably be worth at least a hundred thousand dollars, perhaps more. You don't have to take any part in this, but I need your help. You need to decide if you wish to help, or not."

Juli was taken aback and apprehensive, already hating the idea.

"Oh Josef please, this is so risky and so scary. Please don't do it, please, we're all right as we are!"

"No Juli we are not, not for me or for you. We both work at silly meaningless jobs that are badly paid, with no financial security or future. Please listen to me, I have more to say."

There was no stopping him.

"This is where you might come in. Our case would be a lot stronger if I could get you and your mother to sign an affidavit saying that you both knew my mother - and you did - and that you saw copies of letters regarding deposits in my mother's hands. This would greatly strengthen the case."

Josef stopped. Juli was visibly distressed. "Please oh please Josef! I am pleading with you. I'd really rather you didn't do this. Our life is not so bad, I don't want you to go to jail, I don't want to lose you, and I think this is a rather stupid chance to take now. Please Josef how can you do something so dishonest anyway? Please give it up!"

She was choking back her tears, shaking her head. "The ideas you come up with…" He had suggested various odd schemes in the past and she knew he did some work off the record with firms from Western Europe. But this was just too much, too big a chance to take. Yes, it would be nice to be better off, and yes it would be nice to visit her sister in Canada. But not like this, not by taking such a risk. They looked at each other for a long time.

"Is there no way I can talk you out of this?"
He shook his head.
"Look there is a very good chance that the fuckers at the Swiss banks will not accept the whole thing any way and will find the loop-holes in my claim. And even if they found that my paperwork was a bit 'creative', there is a good chance they would not bother with legalities. As far as the Hungarian government is concerned they won't give a fig about it, unless the Swiss put it to them, which is unlikely. And if we happen to get either a little or a lot of money, I will buy you as many figs as you like..."
He snickered, knowing that figs were either impossible to get or would cost a day's wage. Their mood lightened momentarily. Juli found words to say.
"The funny thing is that even while I am trying to talk you out of it I know what you are like when you get your teeth around an idea. I suppose that if I cannot stop you, then I'd rather help. Let me think about it for a while? But this is dangerous. Jail is not a place for you, not even for a short time. Think of me, what in the world will I do without you?"

She stopped for a minute. Josef was smiling at her as she continued.
"You know I will do it if I must. I'll help, you know I always do nearly anything you want. I don't know about Mum, but I am willing. You know what she is like. She's old, but still has all her faculties, I don't know whether she would agree... In fact, Yes, I think that it might be better if I only told her half the truth."
"What do you mean?" Josef asked, surprised.

"Well you know, I'll explain to her about the Swiss claims, but I'll present the rest of it as if it was true, merely asking her to 'remember' seeing your mother with the letters, and then hope that she goes along with it and actually believes it is true."

Again she looked very uncomfortable. "What documents exactly do you need to uh, create?" she asked.

"We need at least one, perhaps two letters written by Grandfather to a Swiss bank. There will have to be a copy of Grandfather's signature on a document that will also show the signature of a witness. The trickiest one is the will Grandfather made, because that would have to say that he had deposited X amount of moneys in a Swiss bank, and that the beneficiaries would be his grandchildren. One big problem is whether to nominate a particular bank or not. I do not know how to tackle that at this stage. That's about it, I think."

"When will you start all this? After the investigation about your Cousin Tibor?"

"I may as well wait and see if anything eventuates from the Australian detective first. In the meanwhile Garibaldi is paying us well. He is a good man. If by the slimmest of chance we do find Cousin Tibor – I'll give up the idea. But if the inheritance is not claimed very very soon... well, that's it."

The room was nearly dark now. They sat listening to the traffic noises, watching the last rays of the sun yellow the corner of the room. Josef felt the proximity and yet the gulf that separated them from a better life. Juli was lost between her fears and yet some of Josef's defiant excitement was contagious. Josef, perhaps to reassure himself said, "Do you recall my mother, admittedly a bit vague in her last year, did in fact speak about some money that her husband told her was deposited in Swiss banks?"

"Oh yes," she had to laugh, "at the time you said she was going nuts, now all of sudden it suits you to believe her."

Josef laughed too. "Fair comment, but darling, who can you believe if not your own mother?"

Henry Bodowsky, Melbourne, Australia 2002

Henry took the ever-present cigarette out of his mouth and picked up the phone. "Henry Bodowsky Investigations!"

The voice at the other end was immediately familiar.

"How you going you old prick?"

"Fucking Robo!" Bodowsky answered, instantly recognizing the voice, pleased to hear from him at any time. He always answered with, "What the fuck do you want?"

"Eh mate, we're having another Tim's reunion on the 15th and your scintillating presence is indicated. I've already called the others including Tim, and everyone is coming. So be there, or be square. You in for a nosh and a piss up?"

Henry laughed. The rough language was how they communicated, it meant nothing, but it was funny. "Ya whol. Yeah I'm in," he answered in his best fake German accent.

"So you want your old job back or what?" Robo asked the usual standard joke.

Bodowsky leaned back in his overpriced director's chair. He had just moved into this new office in the third and very successful year of his newfound profession. By now, he was a well-known private investigator in Melbourne.

"Henry S. Bodowsky Private Investigators. Your Secrets Are Our Business" it said on his door, situated in a flashy new all-glass office block.

He cackled, as he recalled the time, maybe ten years ago, when Tim called him into his office to offer him the job of manager of the newly proposed duty-free department. Bodowsky had been pleased and asked, "Exactly where would this department be, given there is no room in the existing store?"

Tim sat smirking, while Robo who was the general manager, announced with a straight face, that it was to be 'upstairs'.

"But," said Bodowsky, "there are only two unused toilets upstairs."
There was a silence. Robo could hardly hold his mirth as Tim burst forward, obviously enjoying the discussion.
"Well what do you think Bodowsky? You reckon I'm gonna buy the fucking empire state building for you?"
"Oh no, no, no," Henry said. "You're not serious, you can't be...shit you are? But surely, not the two upstairs toilets? You can't convert those. Surely not? What about the urinals?"
"Oh come on mate," Tim said, hardly able to contain his mirth, "Come on mate, you're pretty fond of pissing my money away by discounting, you are always selling stuff too cheap. Here's your opportunity to piss for free, and make money at the same time."

How they all laughed at the whole idea.
"Anyhow Bodowsky, shit finds its own level," Robo threw in.

"You'd be the one to know, Dick," he countered.

"Get on with it you so-called salesman! Go and sell something," Tim waved at them. "And try to sell something with a bit of profit in it for a change, huh?"

Tim managed people with much delicacy.

The mobile buzzed, and he answered "Bodowsky Investigations."

"Ah g'daymate. It's Andrew. How ya going?"

"Not bad Andy, but speak fast mate because I'm on the way out to an assignment. Or would you rather I ring you back?"

"No, this won't take long and it is very urgent. I got an interesting little job that's come in from a firm of attorneys in LA. They're working with a bloke called Antonio Garibaldi, a well-known sleuth in Argentina. They're looking for a bloke who they reckon used to live in Australia, and worked perhaps as a photographer or a printer. Someone who was born in Hungary, and he is Jewish. I remembered that you used to be in the camera-selling game so rather than flick through the phone book, I thought I'd lob it on you, knowing that if you had any clues you'd give 'em to me no charge, eh?"

"I wouldn't give you fresh air, you amateur," was the replied jest.

"Andy, clearly it is all too hard for you, so that is why you are so generous about giving me the job. Anyway, what can you tell me about the missing bloke?"

"Not much, but I've emailed the details to you. They think his surname is, or used to be Weisz, though he may have changed it. He left Hungary after 1945 they think, or after the 1956 Hungarian revolution. He'll probably be somewhere between forty and fifty years of age.

"Which city does he live in?"

"Most likely in Sydney, but who knows, he could be at the back of Burke or whatever," Andrew answered. "I'll let you go. Read your email, but note we only have two days for the job."

*

Bodowsky sat around the corner of a park for more than two hours on his assignment, but no one showed up. At home he checked Andy's email. He knew of no photographers at all in Sydney, very few in Melbourne and none in other places. Yet, something moved in his brain. 'Aha Sherlock,' he mumbled, 'Ho ho ho, there is a clue here that might lead somewhere: the name Weisz, even though it was spelled a little differently to 'Weiss'.

A George Weiss used to have a bunch of camera stores in Sydney. He might know some names because a lot of his business was done with professional photographers. If he knew anyone with a name similar to his own he might remember. In any case that was all he could think of, given the scant information from Andrew.

Bodowsky decided to immediately to call George Weiss in Sydney. George was surprised; "Well, how the hell are you lad?" he asked. "And what can I do for you, or rather what can you do for me? Or has my wife hired you to investigate my extra-curricular activities?"

'Always the joker' thought Henry.

"No George, but it is an idea, except your extra marital affairs are only in your mind huh?"

"Unfortunately you are quite correct," George quipped in his usual high pitched voice.

"But seriously, what's up? You want a job or something?"

"No thanks George, not a job, but I have come across a request in my work which I thought you might be able to help me with."
And he told George what he knew.

"Oh come on Bodowsky, you're the private dick, don't tell me you can't even give me a name."

"I was coming to that George," Peter commented dryly - as usual Georgy Porgy did not wait till one finished.

"As I said George, I have few clues, the only one being a name, and this is the fun part actually, because the missing man's surname is the same as yours, and his given name in Hungary was Tibor. However, the person we are looking for may have changed his names to English names. Please tell me it is a relative of yours I'm looking for. Now that would be fun."

There was a brief silence, long enough for Henry to ask "Are you still there?"

George answered, "Yeah, I'm here. And surprised. You Kraut bugger you've just given me your ex-boss's real Hungarian name, well sort of anyway."

"The what? You're kidding! Tim? But he is not a photographer and he is a lousy snap shooter... George, are you sure about his name? I mean I know he changed it from his Hungarian name, but that was Toth, not Weisz... so... Are you certain?" he asked jumping out of his chair.

"Yes!" came back the emphatic high-pitched voice. "Of course I'm sure and serious, except that of course he's in Melbourne. But he used to live here when he worked for me. You know that."

"Yes yes, well of course that makes sense, but no," said Henry quickly, "he can't be the one. But was he ever a photographer?"

"Certainly not," said George. "Matter of fact, though I consider him the best photo retailer in Australia, he would have starved to death as a photographer, as you already so beautifully outlined. Of course it could be a coincidence, but it's almost too good not to be true. His real name, the name he was born with was Weisz – unlike mine which originally was not Weiss. When Tim's mother remarried in Hungary it was changed to Toth. In Australia he changed it again. 'Tibor' he changed to Tim, and he changed his Hungarian surname because he disliked the idea of having a Hungarian name - he wanted to be a real Aussie."

"Oh yeah? Holy mackerel, and all the other fishy saints," Henry said, "Amazing if it is him. You have given rise to my further interest George. We will ask more questions," and he mimicked a German accent.

"It's my pleasure Bodowsky that your interest rises like a 17-year old's dick in a brothel, but well, yes, well," George sounded somber now, "If it is him, it's not anything bad is it? What this is all about?"

"I don't actually know much. I was contacted by Andy, who works for a large agency in Sydney. They were contacted by an Argentinean detective. I figure that there is a lot of money involved, because the company Andy works for doesn't take on work without a huge minimum retainer charge up front."

"Is there anything else known about the man they are looking for?" asked George.

"Not that I'm privy to."

"See ya man, let me know if anything further comes up." George hung up and immediately dialed Tim's number. The phone rang three times and then the message machine kicked in:

"Hello this is Tim. I am away sailing in the Whitsundays. Don't try my mobile, I have drowned it. Leave me a message or call me next month."

Bodowsky called Andy in Sydney.

"This conversation has to be off the record. You have to tell me whether the man they are looking for is in trouble or what? If you won't or can't tell me, then I know nothing."

"What have you got man, you sour kraut? I detect you know something." Andy asked with some attention.

"I need to know more. Don't waste my time mate, yes or no, do we have a deal? What I have is either thin, or it is amazingly correct. No, actually it is phenomenal, so off and on the record, is it a deal?"

"Yeah yeah, go on we have a deal," Andy answered, curiosity rising. Andy told Bodowsky what he knew, that there was a lot of money coming to this man if he could be found, and no problems.

"Shit. What a lucky bugger," Henry replied. "Are you sure? Because if my info brings a drama to dear old Tim, I'll have your neck."

"No, I am quite sure, uhm, you know, I had a peek at the email that my boss was reading after he briefed me, so don't worry, it looks good."

"All right. What I found is real cute, like so many of the silly things that come our way in this profession. As you said I was in the camera game, for many years. At Tim's I got to know a George Weiss, better known to you in Sydney as Georges Camera Stores."

"You're joking, "Andy replied. "Is it him? Nah, too easy."

"Hang on, not so fast. Let me unpack it for you lest you miss the point Sherlock. Since he is the only Weiss I have ever known is in the photographic trade I called him up."

Andy broke in again, "So a relative of his?"

"Don't interrupt me you amateur. Just listen, learn and marvel at how a real investigator operates. I put the miserable little bit of information you gave me to George..." and he recounted what he heard from George.

Andy was amazed, "Too good to be true huh? Wow, no, it is good enough to be true. But have you checked with this Tim-Tibor?"

"Elementary my dear Holmes. I called Tim, but he is away sailing in the Whitsundays, where the bloody mobile doesn't work. And even if it did, he wouldn't answer it."

Andy sounded thoughtful: "Nevertheless, the names fit plus the information regarding his profession that comes from twenty years ago from a woman he met once... it is feasible, even fabulous I reckon. I'd better pass this on to the Yank attorney immediately."

Bodowsky still had concerns. "Oh I don't know. Maybe we should wait until Tim gets back"

"Nay buddy, I happen to know that the Argentinean detective has been to Budapest to see what he can dig up there. Evidently time is running out for the case. My instructions are strictly to let them know whatever I find within two days."

Bodowsky thought about it for a moment. All he had heard appeared good enough. He had to agree with Andy.

"As usual you are going to try and get hold of your fees whether you get your man or not," he teased Andy.

"Thanks for that man. Just remember that your fees for the information provided will not be in the mail in seven days or ever."

"Pig's bum Andy, my invoice is in the mail already for $5000 of the best," Bodowsky retorted and they hung up.

*

Andy immediately emailed the law firm in Los Angeles. Weinberger stared at what he read in disbelief. Taking his cigar from his lips he yelled to his secretary "Amazing things still do happen. Get me Garibaldi on his mobile and quick."

Josef and Garibaldi 2002

Josef felt an excitement he could barely contain. Garibaldi had suddenly arrived back in Budapest and just finished explaining the latest news. Josef forgot to be amazed as excitement took over. "How do we find out if this man is who we think he is: my Cousin Tibor? Can we telephone him? His name is Tim now?"

Josef was far too wound up to know what else to ask, or whether to believe the astonishing turn of events. Garibaldi waited patiently for Josef to calm down. "Let's call him on the phone now?"

Garibaldi smirked, "You forget amigo, I just told you he cannot be contacted at the moment. A major problem that, but I have let the Argentinean lawyers who handle the Will know that we may be onto something. Unfortunately, the attorneys in charge of the inheritance make it entirely clear that there can be no extensions to the date of finalization. I've also put it to Weinberger and he said he will see what can be done, by way of challenging the will's timing. He thinks that we may be able to issue an injunction about distributing the dollars to charities, and then try the case in court. A very messy affair in Argentina. Weinberger is not hopeful, but he promised to try everything he can."

Josef's stomach churned. "Good news and bad news in one lump, as usual," he said, trying to keep hope. "So what do we do now?"

"Oh, that's easy amigo. You should go and sit at Tim's doorstep until he gets back." Garibaldi sounded upbeat, "I'm sure you would want to go, yes?" And he placed an envelope and some cash in Josef's hand.

*

It was easy to confirm that a Sari Toth and son Tibor arrived in Australia in July 1957. There were two other details. Sari and Tibor evidently arrived with her second husband and another son, Tamas, aged three. Now it all made sense. Josef found documents showing that only a few years ago his Aunt Sari wrote to the Hungarian government from Melbourne, Australia, requesting birth and marriage certificates. Her birth certificate showed Josef's grandfather's name, Sandor Weisz, and the marriage certificate showed that Sari had married a Lajos Weisz in 1940, the same year that his own mother married his father Andor Weisz.

No doubt remained; this Tim was indeed Cousin Tibor. Josef saw that the reason for the request for the certificates was that Sari was making a claim through the Swiss banks. The addressee was a Tim Tyler and the address was the same Garibaldi had supplied from the Australian connection.

"My cousin's name is 'Tim Tyler'."

It sounded funny as he repeated the name aloud several times, his heart beating furiously. Two days later Josef was flying to Melbourne Australia. The only problem he had was what to do if his cousin was not back from his holidays yet.

INTERLUDE

"If on a Winter's night a traveler…" (after Italo Calvino)

If on a winter's night a traveler calls it could be good news or bad news or no news at all. The visitor may have made a mistake; actually he wants someone else you don't even know. Disappointing, given you got out of your warm bed where you vaguely contemplated making love to your woman.

Then again, if it was going to be bad news it is good that the door knocker was not looking for you. Some people bring bad news only. Others have a story to tell. As Charles Ritz said, "The guest is always right - even if we have to throw him out."

However, a visitor in the middle of the night is another story, it is potentially dangerous. Good news always waits for the light of day; it has no hurry to get to the target. Bad news like the darkness and are always like a fast blowing hurricane.

Josef at the Door

We've arrived home on a cold and wet winter evening, at around 8pm, from the shortened Whitsunday sail trip. The weather has turned foul; a minor cyclone was forecast. I am so tired I can barely move. Marilyn is making a cup of tea in the kitchen – where else. "Tim would you like a sandwich?"

Rain drives relentlessly, lashing against windows and doors. The wind howls and moans. It's only 9pm, but we've gone to bed. I am restless, tossing and turning. Looking up from her reading Marilyn asks, "What's wrong darling?"

"Don't know, I feel edgy, just tired I guess." Needing the warmth of a good night's sleep, I hug up to her. What a blessing a good woman is, and this one is the best. I'd like to make love, but I am stuffed, bushed and whatever

.

After a while, finally settling down, I begin to doze off, only to wake with a sudden coughing fit. Have I been asleep? It is after 11 pm, damn it, hopefully a cold is what I am not getting. She is asleep now. The window frames the gum tree out front of the house, swishing this way and that, the wind whistles and the rain is powering on.

I'm nearly back to sleep - how can one be nearly back to sleep – no thinking man, just sleep o.k.? Floating, drifting, slipping away, arms around her, comfortable.

I hear urgent footsteps shattering, clattering, on the wet pavement. I sit up listening, is it next door or here? More hesitant steps coming closer. Damn. There is an indecisive knock at the door. Fuck. Is there something, someone out there? Bloody hell.

I get out of bed warily, unsure of what may be on the other side of the door, but why worry? It will be a friend in need of a cuppa, or a daughter? At this hour? Yes, that's it, a daughter in some trouble who knows my door is always open to them. I feel cautious, half asleep, shivering, and even angry. I listen and hear the tentative knocking again at my door. Bugger it.

The wind wails, drops of water seep in under the door. Marilyn is behind me now, asking who and what? I shake my head. "Who is it?" I ask sternly. I hear someone saying something, a name? I can't see who it is through the glass, but it's not a woman. I open the door a little, guardedly, it's on the latch, flicking on the outside light.

There is a stranger.
A foreigner, obviously.
He is wearing a brown overcoat.
On his head, sits a brown hat.
There is a small suitcase in his hand.
His hat has a black band and a flag pin.

It's a real hat, like they wear in Europe. Thin brown leather gloves cover the stranger's hands. Nobody around here wears hats like that, and who wears gloves in Melbourne? Or do they? The pin in his hat is a flag I note, but why?

There are no hellos or questions from the man. He is smiling, or trying to. I just stare at him. "Yes, what do you want?" I growl, glad of my gruff tone, "What do you want?"

The rain is pelting down on him and on me as well. In a deep hushed voice with a heavy accent he speaks with an effort. He brushes water from his face; the rim of his hat drips. The pin in his hat is the Hungarian flag, I see now.

I try to hear him; his voice is coming clearer; I'm adjusting to the accent. He wipes water away from his face again and speaks louder.

"Josef, my name Josef. I am looking for a lost cousin who I hope knows about me. I have wrong place? But no, you must be him? Yes, must be you, Tibor...? Yes?"

I hear what he says, but I'm not taking it in. He talks in a rush; his English is laden with a familiar accent that's hard to... a Hungarian accent? Of course! I've no time to think as he goes on.

"Already I recognizing face, even though I not really know, or seen you for more than sixty years! It is yes, Tibor-Tim?"

He wants to shake hands through the narrow door gap; I am taken aback unable to speak as he rattles on. I'm unable to get my brain moving, shivering cold too, but nothing stops him talking.

"I can't believe I am now is..look at... because family is familiar - you know, my name is Josef, yes sorry...ah, me your Cousin Josef. I are your Cousin Josef."

He repeats it all in his broken English, then hesitates, looking concerned. His hands gesture through the air, his eyes pleading, wanting, hoping.

'He is who?'
'What fucking Josef? Who the fuck is Josef?'
'What the hell is this?'

"So who... who do you think I am?" I manage to shoot at him. He has said my name. Still, my foot is firmly blocking the door. My stern face shows that I am no fool. Is he a weirdo? My heart hammers away.

Then, like a church bell dropped from a great height something arrives with a bang to the brain box. I recall, as if I could have ever forgotten, that a Cousin Josef did exist, a lost one, the only one left. I looked for him in Budapest, what, thirty years ago.

He stands there looking at me. Raindrops drip from his hat on to the doorstep. "Tim...Tibor it is, god help, is you?" he says now in Hungarian, his brown face grinning widely.

Tibor – my Hungarian name hits me, I have not been called that since Mum died.

He smiles on, making an effort to reassure. He pulls his coat tighter. I am indeed speechless, or no, I have too much to say.

"I know this is all, uh...a bit uh, how you say, not usual, but you is Tibor, please, yes?"

The wind and rain sighs one last blast, suddenly stopping. An hour seems to have passed, but it was only a few moments. My brain is beginning to take in what he is saying. I nod, "Yes. I am Tibor," making an attempt to talk. Marilyn grips my arm and says something about the police. I shake my head, no it is o.k. She looks wide eyed and incredulous.

"Josef? Josef?" I can't believe it, I mumble again, "Josef?"

Could it be, or is this the rip off that it has to be? But for why?

I should ask him in. Can't think properly. I swoon in and out of thinking power. There is a long silence. She nudges me now to ask him in, or something, I don't know, I suppose. I'm shaking cold. Josef's smile is stuck on his face, his eyes are fixed on mine, eyes that are warm and brown. Not the eyes of a weirdo? Awkwardly, we watch each other.

I tackle him again. "What is your full name please?" I demand, almost pointing my finger at him, wanting to project a solid existence of myself, one that tells this brown European that I am no fool...I try to sound controlled, efficient, and ask well considered questions. "Do you have identification?"

He shakes water off his hat. "My name is Josef Feher" Josef responds brightly, "but that's not..."

Weary and impatient I jump in shaking my head, "Never heard of you."

"Yes, no..." he nods agreement vehemently, "No, sorry, name no mean anything to you, my real name is Weisz; W E I S Z," he spells out.

"My name changing, sorry, like many Jews in Hungary. Weisz, translates to Feher in Hungarian or White in English."

He laughs. "Like you change Weisz to Toth and to Tyler, yes?"

"Josef Weisz!"

Oh my god! Bullshit, I am not convinced, but hell I should be, "What do you think darl?" I turn to Marilyn. She says "oh I don't...I think it is all right. Let him in."

Josef keeps nodding in agreement. Oh well, I feel a little relieved, come what may, so stepping aside, I beckon him in.

Josef takes his hat off revealing a half-bald head and a somewhat familiar-looking face. A familiar face? Like from an old photo? But I don't have one of him. Familiar faces? Nah, I push the thought away.

"Where did you learn such good English?" I ask stupidly, still trying to sense if this is real or some sham, but why? What would be the point? Hey, we'll soon find out, I reckon blowing my chest up with air.

Josef stands there in the middle of the hall in his long brown coat and hat, dripping water, looking at me, still anxiously smiling. I feel confused, I don't know what to think, I have always craved for just this, for something just like this to happen. I've imagined that someone would show up sometime and say 'I am a relative of yours.' Waited for that past blast that would blow away the sadness...oh whatever...oh fuck...Don't know what difference it would make to my life now.

The encounter suddenly takes on the expected, dreamed of, familiarity, and yet, I cannot comprehend it. Am I dreaming? Is this a recurring dream, a kind of self-fulfilling prophesy?

I look at Marilyn. She is there real enough, looking perplexed, but now more relaxed than I feel. I've often had dreams that seemed totally real; layers on layers, sometimes waking up twice, thinking I was already awake before.

And now here is my dream. It is here. Or is it?
It is, it isn't, yet it is.

My body feels heavy, my head foggy at having to accept the possibility. I recall a favorite book by Russell Hoban, who said something like; "Nothing that's ever been completely lost, can ever really be found again - but nothing that's ever really been found, can ever be lost again."
Forget the philosophy man, I admonish myself. This is happening. Marilyn brings a jacket and puts it on me. That's good, I trust her instincts.

*

The discovery at that bloody workshop in California in 1978 comes detonating through me. That's when I first realized that I unknowingly wrote a kind of story in my head when I was only eight years old. My story, the wish about the dead father and the dead family who were looking for me, someone alive who would come back, who would one day show up and save me from my uneasiness filled days. A grown man should not have such silly ideas, yet there it was, another sign of what I knew was my troubled soul. I must give it up - I thought at the time - I must, but to this day I have never stopped craving for at least a whiff of some past momentous event.

*

Will the man standing in my hall, looking silly with that half smile he tries so hard to maintain, will he prove I was always right? That I was right to think and believe my own sad dreams? Why should I be thinking that this is such an outrageous story? No-one else knew about my fantasy. It was my secret. How could it be known to anyone? How could it be used by a crook or a madman - and to what end?

I feel vaguely nauseous, vulnerable and distrusting, and ashamed that I feel this way. I need to fart, take a piss, and I'm suddenly famished hungry. The brain scrambles... looking for a logical way to tackle this, searching for enlightenment, wanting it.

Marilyn stands next to me. She understands what is happening. She does not speak, just watches. Her face is red; she looks excited, unsure, ready to do what is needed. She shuts the door, "Shall I make some coffee, what do you think darl?"
She tests me, but does not move away. I nod, "Yes, that would be good."

The sound of the rain intensifies again, even heavier now. Usually I love that sound on our tin roof but it is so loud I can barely hear myself. We are still standing in the hallway. Don't know what to do, I guess I'm shocked. What's next?

Josef's old-fashioned hat in his hand splatters water on his shoes. I'm focused on his brown homburg, a real hat, a memory? Is it a homburg? It looks like something one would call such. No one wears hats and gloves like this anymore... never mind all that again.

A gust of wind rattles the door. That's what happens when ghosts show up, isn't it?

"Could we have a sandwich, maybe?" I mumble.

"Look" Josef starts again. "I see you suspicion, and I must, should have telephone first, but I just arrive. I could not wait, so I come from airport hoping you get big surprise, I come for big reason, I must tell..."

He stops. His brown eyes are pleased, eyes not unlike someone else's; mine actually, I recognize with a jolt. Josef's cheeks round out, just like mine - and he rattles on.

"I come to see only cousin I know, or not know, actual," and he laughs at his joke, pausing. "And other big, big thing to talk for. Can sit down?" he asks politely.

Josef is brown. Everything about him is brown, his suit, overcoat, hat, gloves, eyes, and skin. He smells faintly of wet wool and breaths of stale tobacco. He looks more significant now; a man on a mission. He is about my height, a little paunchier perhaps, and has a bit more hair than me.

Marilyn waves us into the lounge, telling us to sit down. I'm standing there looking for cigarettes, trying to believe Mr Brown. Mr fucking Feher, Weisz, whoever the hell...

No, it is Josef. It's Josef, my cousin, that's who it is.

"I think it is my Cousin Josef. I'll be damned," I say to Marilyn, and beckon Josef to an armchair. He sits down gratefully, pulling his case closer. 'What's in it?' I wonder, noting his proprietary movement. Hopefully not a gun, or bomb, for crying down the sink, stupid me.

"I make you some food?" Marilyn asks Josef, but I know she is asking if it is safe for her to leave.

He smiles and emphatically.

"Much coffee please, also necessary. And I hungry am, thank you. So much to speak you, I have, so much to say about..." he stops hesitant, swallows whatever he was about to say. I jump in, asking.

"What? What have you to tell me?"
Ha, I'm back, I can think, now let's see; "How did you find me?"
I blurt out the questions. He is not to think I'm a pushover. I alternate between belief and joy and total distrust. Awkwardly he hands me his passport; Josef Feher, just as he said, but Weisz to Feher? Yes, aha, the translation is correct, both mean White in German, near enough.
I try to relax, breathing as deeply as I can, and sit down opposite him.

"What have you come to tell me, how did you find me?" I fire at him.

Josef looks uncomfortable, slides forward to the edge of his chair and he blurts it out.
"So many thing to catch up yes, and you, and me, we have a large inheritance, maybe, and but, we have it if only..."
He stops, knowing he has said too much, but it's too late - my guts jump to my head.

"What...? Whaat did you say? Inheritance. What inheritance?"

My heart thumps against my chest. Fucking bullshit, another smart-arse rip off, by another fucking crook. Yes, I must deposit ten thousand into his account so than we can claim the million, yeah right. I get angry so quick but, but hey, how could he know all he does? This is it, here it comes, the rip off. Money is mentioned so that's the scheme. Now he is going to ask for my bank account. I'll fucking kick his face in if he does. Fuck.

But no, wait. He is who he said he was. Blood rushes to my head just the same:

"If this is some sort of rip off scheme I am calling the police now," I blurt out angry, and immediately feel abashed, but Josef just laughs:

"No no, real this, real Cousin, real. I am your Cousin Josef, believe please."

Real?

My life is real enough these days. But then why do I still feel at times as if I'm just drifting through my days waiting, always and still looking for something? How can one expect what one has never known? And what is that? Why do I feel lost so often? Lost in what sense? No matter, I'm being ridiculous, this is not a hold-up.

Let's hear him out. Anger goes, excitement rises; here it comes, the missing link to my old lost and found fairy tales. My moods change fast this way and that.

Why is it so quiet suddenly? Ah, the rain stopped. My spirit soars upward.

This is going to be the story where Dad comes back from the grave, the one where Dad saves his son from everything or something, the one where Dad went to America or to Africa, made a fortune and has now finally remembered his son...the one where he simply...? Fuck him, where was he when I needed him?

Sweat rises on my balding head and runs from my armpits. Tears well up in my tired eyes. I choke them back. This is crazy.

"Of course," Josef hastens, "So sorry you upset. You don't know, you can't know, so many thing to say, no? I have much to tell you."

Impatiently, I gesture to Josef to get on with it. My feelings go up and down, zooming through everything, boiling away; belief and doubt chase each other.

No, I think, stay cool.

This will be another dead end story.

They always are.

Except he is actually here, a real Cousin Josef...That's if it is really him. I focus.

"Go on," I squeeze out, wanting to allow the story and Josef into existence. I mumble apologies to Josef.

"Can't be too careful, take your coat off." Then I realize Josef's coat is already hanging on the rack. I'm shaking, cold and nervous, so I switch on the heater.

Josef sits back deep into the chair.

"I don't know what to say or think," I say over and over as I wipe the sweat from my face, choking back tears.

"Yes, yes," he nods, seeming to understand, and waits for my storm to pass. Looking pleased and comfortable, he peels off the wet leather gloves carefully, putting his hat down beside himself. He stands up, leaning toward me, extending his hand, which I shake doubtfully. Our eyes connect; this is Josef, and somehow I manage the awkward hug he asks for.

We sit again. My focus returns to his gloves and hat. Memories of feelings - feelings of memories?

Europe and water steam off the hat and the gloves.
Secrets and stories peel off them.
Fear and hope wrapped in this brown Josef.

I used to be so proud of always being a deep brown suntanned child, because everyone commented on it... But focus man. 'Listen,' I reprimand myself.

I am too scared to ask, whatever? How can one ask questions about something one does not know? Does he know anything about anyone? I cannot ask about my father - that does not come up. He is dead, always was, has to be.

Inheritance means someone is dead. Why would Josef know about him anyway? No, that is really mad. An inheritance? From whom? One of my uncles? But no, they are all dead.

I say no more as Marilyn returns with coffee, cheese, salami and bread.

"Thank you," Josef nods approvingly, and states with certainty: "I see now you and I looks a bit alike."

He might be right actually. But I resent him saying so. I nod for him to eat and he grabs some food. The more I look at him the more he seems like an old faded family photograph - if I had more than the six have.

I must be careful, I caution myself again.
We are munching on thick sandwiches, as if our life depended on salami. We watch each other eyeball to eyeball. It is fine; something is all right here. I breathe out, much relieved.

Josef swallows hard and fast, laughs, pulls out some papers from his leather case, and slaps them on the coffee table.

"Yes, this good," Josef says, then reaches inside his jacket. "Is smoking permitted? I am all shaking up."
Josef lights up one of those awful cigarettes and starts to read aloud from the papers.
"You understanding Hungarian, yes?" I nod yes.

It takes me a few moments to adjust to Hungarian words. Words that say Tibor Weisz, Josef Weisz and others in the Weisz family are to collect an inheritance of many millions of dollars in cash, bonds and shares. He reads all this like a public servant or a solicitor who knows what is in the paper, quickly, dryly, without emotion.

It is all too much to register other than it is all too much - this cannot be happening - but hopefully it is.
It's an effort to maintain attention. Where does the money come from? Who from? My insides contract, grabbing my wits. I feel very hot, sweat drips from head into eyes. The urge to vomit overcomes me and I rush for the bathroom. Josef follows me, face flushed, profusely apologizing. The disturbance brings Marilyn running from the kitchen, looking concerned. She is ready to fight if necessary.

Back in the lounge, I tell Josef to slow down. I take deep breaths. Am I having a heart attack? No, it just feels like it, stomach in the mouth, as everything churns away.
"Who, just tell me who left all this?"
I ask, heart beating like a conga drum.
"Who could have left all that money to us?"

Josef sips his hot black coffee as he continues telling the facts.

"It seems your father died two years ago and..."

I stand up too fast, feeling ready to faint. Dry retching, I cough and grope for air. Blood charges through me like soda water so I fall back into the sofa. Both rush to me.

"Should we call a doctor?" Marilyn asks.

"No I'll be all right," but I'm not convinced. I need to breath slowly to stop my hyperventilation. Josef waits, looking alarmed. Marilyn, pale and worried, pours a Southern Comfort for all of us.

"My father died a long time ago, not two years ago." I recover as fast as I lost it.

"No. This has to be a mistake."

Josef shakes his head.

"Sorry, you could not know, but oh so sorry, I don't know how to tell you, not know what to say...I was going to slow do it, telling, but you know..." he waves into his smoke.

"Tell me what, tell me more."
I want to hear it again; I need to hear everything now.
Josef nods.

"It has taken a detective and attorneys long time to find you." Josef says, watching for my reactions.

What he has said is sinking deeper into my belly. It is impacting on me, twisting my guts, and I'm doubled over, trying to speak through a rush of foggy tears.

Somewhere from deep inside of me I want to explain that I already know what Josef is saying, …but I didn't know! How could I have known. But reasoning rises quick.

"Of course my father is dead, otherwise surely he would have found us! And not two years ago… Bullshit. No I can't believe this shit, no I don't want to believe all this."

We cry.

Josef wants to move to hug me, but I wave him away, reaching for Marilyn. She holds me tight. I stop my tears and laugh, surprised that I can laugh, even if hysterically.

"I don't suppose there are any other shocks to your story, go on with it?"

But it strikes me again:

He said that my father died.

Two years ago.

Boom boom.

Only two years ago?

Did he say that?

I take a deep swallow of the sweet liquor. Haltingly, carefully choosing his words, Josef explains.

"I'll tell you about how I find you later, you want to hear about father first right?"

"What? Yes," I mumble, and then it strikes me that he has died again; twice in my life. It takes me a long tearful time to recover.

"Your father had actually think everyone dead. That was information he was given on several times when he try to trace your mother and you with authorities in Hungary, or via detectives and agencies. It was around

1953 when still in Siberia, he first writing to authorities in Hungary."

This is what being shot in the head must feel like. We were in Hungary in 1953, why were we not found?
No time to think now. Josef scrutinizing me carefully, continues to tell it all quickly.

"Actually, your name changed twice times, yes, correct am I? Including when you arrived to Australia. Your father couldn't find anyone. Hungarian paperwork was a mess back then, and still now."

Oh God, this would be a good time to believe in you so one could ...I am flabbergasted and feel shots of pain.

Josef pauses. How come he is so cool...ah yes, he has had time to get used to it all. He takes more coffee, lighting another cigarette. He looks apprehensive that he is pushing me too far. Then he tells me about his friend, my old buddy Zboray, who handed him this case. I am bewildered and unbelieving. I tell him he was my childhood friend too. Of course he knows that already having told Zboray the whole story. Don't know which of us is more incredulous. Zboray certainly was!

Josef waves that away and goes on.
"Ze inheritance,"
Josef asserts, his eyebrows thick and grey, face tight and sad, "really is from your father."

He has said this before, but he is keen to repeat it, keen to make a point of great importance. Each time he does I cringe and feel faint. He then hastens to add half in

English half in Hungarian, "I have no idea why he left some to me, and everyone, I hope you not mind."
He inhales his foul-smelling Hungarian cigarette as only a Hungarian does. The smoke drifts through his mouth and nose at the same time.

"Slow down you two." Marilyn says, and pours three more glasses of Southern Comfort. We drink it like water. The alcohol appears to have no effect on any of us. There is blissful silence for a while. She has taken charge now and we're grateful.

My storms change to lightheaded hilarity. This actually is all too fucking much. The Southern Comfort must kick in a bit sooner or later I figure.
"I reckon I need a cigar, Darl. Could you get us a cigar?" I ask Marilyn; there is a cause to celebrate. "What do you think? Is this ridiculous? Ah god..." I ask her as if she knew more than me.
I want to get up, but feel heavy as lead. We sit smoking cigars now as if that helps to get air into lungs.

There is much more said. I barely hear most of it and yet hang on every word.

*

When I wake up in the morning my head throbs. I jump out of bed, dashing through the hallway toward the lounge to look in on Josef. It was a long night. It was not, surely a cheap delusion...Was it one of those bloody dreams? Was it? I want to believe I am wrong. I want to believe it was real. I know there will be no one in the room but I look anyway. Sure enough the room is empty; the sofa is undisturbed.

I turn around with an unbearable disappointment. I wish I was dead for a moment. In the lounge I dump on the couch. I can't believe it.

I hear Marilyn stir, getting up. I go to meet her for a hug, my eyes teary.

She asks, "Is Josef up yet?"

Huh, the what?

Then, my eyes see a hat hanging in the hall, the brown rim wet. On the stand below a wet brown coat and a suitcase... I jump into the air, not wanting to let it get away from me. I grab the hat carefully, placing it on my head, turning to show it to Marilyn behind me.

"I am awake yes?" She nods, "of course."

"The hat is Josef's?"

"Yes" she smiles. "You know it is."

"So it is really true?"

I know I need no sensible answer. No mind, no voice to speak or hear is needed. Nothing else is necessary for now. Nothing at all. She looks at me, smiling wide.

"There he is coming out of the kitchen with a tray of cups and coffee."

Telling the stories of our lives?

Here is Josef attentively listening to me. His curiosity is obvious and is more than that. He has no baggage about me, does not know me, and has no idea whether what I say to him is fact or fiction. He wants to hear my life, wants to know me, and wants me to know him.

We have caught up on the ordinary facts; marriages, kids, work, and other things. Yet, there are some things that matter even more. What each of us recalls as our lives. He has filled in some gaps, astonishingly enough, confirming some things Mum said about our original family. This is a relief and sadness at once. Josef told me about the years after the revolution, his time in Italy and return to Hungary.

We have examined and marveled about the coincidences that brought us together. His and my friend Zboray, Edith, the woman I met in 1978 in Esalen who was a bridge from nowhere to here. And Bodowsky, the bloody kraut ex-employee who had the good sense and luck to put it together with Garibaldi, my father's very own friend.

What is one to think about the chances of life, living its chaotic nature, in such a converging and organized way? Coincidence and fate doing a job in a disordered universe, where one word uttered, or left unsaid, might make all the difference.

Even if that word is uttered much too late.

*

So, what can I tell about my life to a total stranger? What do I tell or hold back? How does one tell enough to declare, 'this is, was, may yet be, me'? How well does one know one's life story anyway? I know that one knows the ten percent tip, while one suspects the ninety percent of the submerged iceberg under ice, out of sight.

Will I start with the years of the child I was, or rather, the child I never had time and space to be? There was no time for the child I must have been. The child I was, and perhaps still am in some ways, could say so much, but about what must he speak exactly? He can still cry a lot, hysterically, out of control, and like back then, still unsure of what he is crying about.

The enormity of explaining all this is overwhelming. Josef waits, patiently smoking my cigarettes. I stopped him using the Hungarian ones. He observes me gently, without staring, but his eyes are on me most of the time. Now and then, he glances around the streets we stroll in, and then he returns to focus on me encouragingly. He knows I am struggling to begin.

I always expected to explain my life to somebody sometime, like perhaps as a reckoning? To whom though? To my father? Myself? I never expected it would be to Josef.

We sit down on a park bench; Josef is looking happy, warm and cozy. The lines on his face are breaking, I fancy, in similar places as mine. I don't know how long I meandered within myself. Josef is there, expecting, unhurried.

We have talked briefly about the 'inheritance'. I believe, and think it is gone, but I am not pushing it. Josef has great faith in Garibaldi and the American law firm. We have managed to let the potential disaster of losing it go for a number of days. There is nothing more we can do but wait and hope. I am waiting as usual for a minor miracle. That at least seems familiar.

"I'm searching for a good opening line as if there was a proper script and I simply forgot the start of it."

Josef smiles, nods his head. "Maybe start from early time."

I must tell simple stories as I know them, never mind whether they make sense or not. "Yes," I say. "After all, I never knew the start of my story, no one does. We know only what we have been told. And if you have nearly no relatives, there are fewer stories inherited! This is even truer for me than for you, because leaving my birthplace meant forgetting a great deal, I know." Josef agrees, and I continue.

"I don't remember anything about my first 6 or 7 years, nothing at all. All I know or recall are Mum's few stories. I hate that this is how it is. I wish I had more early tangible memories of my own. I don't even have vague first-hand feelings or recollections of those years. Sometimes I feel sort of ashamed about my lack of recall, as if it is my fault. I suppose everyone is like that?" I ask, hopeful that I am not a freak.

Josef shrugs. "Most people do not realize that their cherished memories are based not just on facts, but also on the interpretations of parents, relatives, and culture. We had few relatives left to interpret anything. On the positive side, this way they sold us less of their nonsense and rubbish."

Josef is sensitive, intelligent, cultured and quick. I've learned that already. He seems open to an exchange of our lives. My fears recede, my trust grows in him hour by hour. And so I tell him a few facts as I recall them, the main turning points of my life. Chopping and changing time frames, I go on talking about my children, how my first marriage seemed to work well for a long time, and what I did after it was over. I'm a bit anxious that I might bore him, keen to get the facts over with. Truly you cannot get to know another person fast.

Like a river, I flow into my life deeper and deeper. As I tell him more and more, I start adding feelings, ideas and regrets, and all the baggage one carries as a grown up child. He listens, never breaking in, attentive.

At home we drink a lot of coffee. I'm out of words. "Josef, your turn." We sit comfortably outside looking at the back yard.

Josef speaks a mixture of Hungarian and English just like mum did.
(It would be near impossible to write down how he speaks, and it would be confusing for a reader, so I have decided to use straightforward English from now on to transcribe his speech, even though it loses some flavor.)

Josef tells me about his life in Budapest, and then, going backwards in time, speaks with more emotion. He also feels, just like me, that he is not the potential 'self' he may have become. He speaks as I did, dryly, though with some humor here and there.

I have to stop him now and then and search for the meaning of a few Hungarian expressions. I speak the language well enough, but it is fading since I never use it.

The mix of Hungarian and English reminds me of Mum, who used to insist that some English words were Hungarian and vice versa. That was funny sometimes. As was her pronunciation of some words like 'sheet' which her accent turned into 'shit', so her sons would often ask, "What you doing Mum?" knowing she'd answer, "I'm hanging the shits up in the garden."

When Josef speaks about his wife he does it with some wistfulness and a lot of warmth.

"I wish she was here. It would be such a thrill for her to have the holiday and the journey of what we are doing."

I ask him why they had no children.

"I made mistake," he shrugs, looking sad. "I was so bitter about this world; I could not see why I should bring another person into it. Then in later years we realized this was silly thinking and worse. It was too late then."

He stops looking a bit embarrassed and explains his open marriage, emphatically saying that the affairs are now over. "Juli is a sweet woman; she accepted that I am a restless soul in need of whatever sex gave to me. You think I'm an idiot?"

"No Josef, definitely not. I think I know what you mean. I've done my fair share of silly shit about sex and women."

We grin at each other. It was our first shared secret and understanding. He talks more about his wife. She sounds good; so does their relationship now. We stand up and stretch.

Josef is suddenly looking strained. His face gets flushed when he is about to talk about touchy subjects. Sitting down again, looking bothered he tentatively says, "You don't know about Wilhelm do you?"

"Who?" I dread more new details and yet want to know every little thing about anything or anyone. Wilhelm? It is a German name I don't recall. We are sitting on the swing bench chair. I pull my jumper tighter around myself. Its cooler and I am edgy now. Josef 's eyes are on the bougainvillea that has gone rabid over the back and side fence. He loves the purple brightness of it.

"Well Josef, is this gonna be a cigarette story or a cigar story?" I ask, wanting to lighten up. It's a running joke now. We both smoke way too much; how else to survive but to hide behind the fume at such times?

Josef looks troubled, his cigarette lit already.

"I should have told you already, but I don't know..." He launches into recalling the time that Wilhelm came to his office in Budapest in 1951 and how they all decided to dissuade Lajos from returning to Hungary.

I am staggered by his words. Josef could have met my father. He knew all these years that my father was alive. I did not. Lightning has struck again. Strangely, I also feel as if I should have known. Had I not looked hard enough? Was it my fault, my doing, that I missed knowing my father and Josef all these years?

What Josef had just told me turns my life story upside down and inside out. A rage of frustration sweeps over me. Wrath and blame rise toward Josef. He should have known I was still there, living not so far away from him in Hungary.

But he did not. He should have kept in touch with my father, he should have... Bloody mothers, his and mine should have kept contact even if they hated each other.

I'm blown into a mist of sorrow. Damn the world, damn, blast and fuck - it could have been so different. Blood rushes up in me and my teeth are clenched painfully tight. Anger...rage, fury...a tsunami of it hits me.

I half listened to what Josef heard from Wilhelm, but I cannot go on hearing this. I get up, aimlessly pacing around the garden, bashing trees with a stick, ripping at bushes, kicking bits of dirt around, yelling "Fucking Hell."

Marilyn comes to hug me. She sees how upset I am and that Josef, his face in his hands, is crying. With her arms around me, after a long time I finally relax.

Josef sees the impact of his words. His eyes tell how he is feeling. I force myself to calm down. A sea breeze comforts my heated head.

A little calmed, I drink a rather large dose of vodka... Josef watches, looking afraid and unsettled. The grooves in his face are deeper, his eyes dark, as he stares at me. He is wearing one of my jumpers. His arms are around himself, hugging himself together, lest he too falls apart.

"It's all right... I breathe out, "Give me a minute."

He stands up, not knowing what to do, wanting to move, but stays, still hopping from leg to leg like a nervous school boy in my stretched jumper. Words tumble from him. "I am so sorry, it was not my fault, I had no contact, I did not know you..."

It all comes out in a rush, with tears flowing from his eyes. His face is just so like mine when I cry. Child-like.

"What must have your Mum felt after the war? Mine was damn nearly crazy for years before she settled enough to go on with her life, but never happy, always confused till she died."

He reaches for the bottle, takes a swig of vodka, tries looking firmer.

"I know you must be thinking that you were, or could have been so close, and it must be dreadful to know that. And yes Tibor, I never phoned or contacted your father, first out of fear of the authorities, perhaps even out of anger that Lajos survived and my father did not. Then time went on and I sank into a lethargic stupor for the next few years. Nothing mattered, I just lived on aimlessly. That is when I met my wife and if not for her, I am not sure I'd be here."

Josef weeps into his hands with a sudden sob. "You have no idea how ashamed I am..."

Anger comes again and goes, one following the other fast like a spinning wheel. I understand and do not, all at once. I want to hear more, so I press him on, my voice forced,

"Go on now, I want to know everything. Is there any more?"

It is crisp and cool later. The smell of the sea, as usual in Elwood, is mixed with salty, rotting seaweed. In the fading light we stand rocking silently as if movement could calm us. Josef recalls what he can. It is hard, so hard, but it is also something like a release to hear what I do.

My cousin is a messenger who has things to tell me; the man who will help to re-write my life? New chapters are being inserted into me; but how to make sense of it all? My childish dream about father coming back is not so silly now. Premonition is not for a skeptic like me, but did I somehow intuit his existence? Ah bullshit! Life is a rigged lottery.

My resentment gradually evaporates. Josef is here for me.
I grab him by the shoulders.

"Too late to worry about what I missed. You are part of
my inheritance, the surprise, the gift. Even if I don't like
what you tell me."
I am not so sure it is all done, but I know that I have to let
it go; I am certain.

We embrace for a moment. He sighs, relieved. The
storm in me goes as fast as it came. I will feel devastated
again and again, about what I had heard, but I will handle
it.

*

The following day we went for a walk by the sea shore.
I don't know how many kilometers we walked, stopping
now and then to eat or to have coffee.

"Clearer air here than in Budapest and living so near
the sea is good," Josef said.
"You should see the Whitsunday islands, Josef. I will
take you there some time."

He smiled like a kid, his pleasure obvious. Now and
then one of us told a joke; sometimes they did not
translate all that well, but then we'd think it even more
funny. Joke telling became part of our communication, a
relief from the heavy stuff. Oddly, we two non-believing
atheist Jews nevertheless told mostly Jewish jokes. "It's
part of the blood," Josef asserted, "that we are Jews and
best laugh at jokes aimed at ourselves. In fact, I got one
for you:

Mrs. Stein goes to the rabbi and asks for Hebrew
lessons because she is dying. She wants to learn perfect

Hebrew and fast. The rabbi is curious. 'But why do you want to do this Mrs. Stein, you've not been to synagogue for years.'

'Well rabbi, when I die shortly, I will go to heaven and will want to talk to God in his own language,' she says.

'I see,' the rabbi replies, 'but what if you finish up in hell?'

'Ah that's no problem rabbi, Hungarian I speak already.'

Mirth was followed by silence until we found more questions. I asked Josef about his teenage years. "What teenage years? I doubt I had them. Do you recall 1954 when that butcher Stalin died?"

"Oh yes, I do. I even wrote a short story about that." His eyes lit up. "You write stories? So do I…Will you tell me your story? Why did you write it?"

"I have written down some life stories for many years now, perhaps as if that would prove my life stories were worthy? Or make them more solid or something. Stalin falling from grace shortly after Khrushchev took power in the Soviet Union made a big impression on me. Why exactly, I don't know. I figure I wrote it to make sense out of the nonsense narratives that I took as gospel while very young."

We sat on some rocks looking at the flat, oily sea that seemed like a mirror. I thought about how amazing all this was. I was about to tell one of my tales, the one about 'Father Stalin' to someone who might make more sense of it than to anyone else in the world:

"One lousy heater pretended to warm our schoolroom, letting out more stink than heat. It was mid-winter and very cold, the snow was icing up. Freezing drafts of wind

swirled behind our backs from the rattling, ill-fitted windows that ran the length of the room, blowing sheets of paper off the desks, but helping paper airplanes fly further.

The class was in pre-teacher chaos as usual; but the fat old bugger was uncommonly late. I was entertaining the class with some of my favorite impersonations of the janitor. As I demonstrated how he walked pushing his head forward and back, I stood at the window. Turning this way and that, enjoying the class laughing at my performance, I made a large swing turning toward the window, slipped and banged my head into the glass! It did not break but nearly knocked me out, which was greeted by howls of laughter…. Little Weisz – as I was known - has done it again.

The noise increased. I felt dizzy, but didn't want to show the pain. Suddenly it was silent. The door swung open, squeakily banging against the wall, and our arithmetic teacher strode in. His face was red, arms ready to strike, potbelly riding high in front of him.

"Silence you hooligans," he yelled, hurling his worn case on the desk. He peered at us for a moment and turned back toward the blackboard, looking uncommonly hesitant, and coughed his long and juicy smokers' cough.

The door opened again and the headmaster appeared. A short and pale man with a shiny bald head, he never smiled; in fact, his face never showed any emotion. He strode in looking purposeful, but now he seemed to make an effort to grin at us. He spoke with some care.

'Boys, I have a very important announcement to make today. You probably noted that pictures of Stalin have been removed from the walls?' He looked around as if waiting for us to confirm this. I had noticed, but to us, the removal of Stalin's pictures was about as conspicuous as

the wind whistling in through the windows. No-one spoke. A moment of fear shot through me, I was immediately concerned that we were about to hear something worrying.

He told us that Stalin, who until now was called our 'Father and Savior', was no longer our 'Father'. Stalin was now disgraced. I knew nothing more than what I was told about such things. I had grown to this age being told that Father Stalin and the glorious Soviet army had liberated us from the Nazis. Stalin was the 'Father and Savior' to us all, but particularly to Jews. He and the magnificent Soviets were very much part of my security system. Now, suddenly Stalin was 'disgraced', no longer thought to be a good man.

"Premier Khrushchev told us so just this morning," headmaster continued, looking around to make sure we were listening: "That's why Stalin's pictures are off our walls. You will see it in the newspapers and that is how it is. Now get back to studying." Looking prickly, he abruptly left the room.

I felt scared and confused at break time. Some of the boys were talking about it, most did not care. As I believed it, Stalin had made sure there would be no killing of the Jews, no anti-Semitism, and now he was gone. What did this mean? What would mother think? I knew that all was not what it seemed to be in communist Hungary or the Soviet Union. Strange things used to happen that made Mum cry. But the assurance Stalin and his regime represented to me, in those days anyway, was strong. An assurance that the war was finished and would stay that way. No more Nazis.

"Except for the Hungarian ones who were now masquerading amongst us as commies, just waiting for their opportunity." That's what Mum told me and that's what was whispered now and then, even by the children. Some kids even repeated what they heard at home: "It was a pity Hitler did not finish the job about the Jews and the gypsies."

I tried not to let in that sort of talk. I tried to think that it was just kid's talk, and that they did not know what they were talking about. Mum told me not to worry; they just repeated what they heard at home. I was already smart enough to be puzzled by how was that a good reason that I should not feel worried? In later years I realized how much the fear was embedded in me. The horrible stories about the Nazi years fed on my young consciousness. I could not help recalling all the horror stories I heard and read about Jews being tortured, shot and killed, and about children being taken from their mothers.

I had other problems too, ones that seemed to me to be far worse. Like masturbating twice a day and being unable to study. 'No doubt, as a result of my wanking,' I figured. For sure I would fail school, never have children, and most likely go mad, or at least to hell. Now that would be a terrible disgrace. What would mum's friends say? And making Mum unhappy was dangerous; she could die if one upset her.

During the midday break, a couple of kids started saying that now; the Nazis might come back and finish the job. By the end of the next day, I was worried sick. Mum was away in the country, making a living by selling fake jewelry. I asked my stepfather about all this Stalin business. As usual, he sat on the kitchen table, his legs dangling. The table served as both his workshop and as our dinner table. He was looking grey and tired, his face thin, lips tight, chain-smoking cigarettes. He was sewing the shoulder of a suit he was making. He barely looked at me at first, but then he noted my anxious voice.

"Not to worry Tibor. It's just a change of government, and Stalin has been dead for a while now anyway. The new man, Khrushchev may well be better than Stalin ever was."

He said some other things about politics, which I did not understand, but I felt a touch reassured and asked if he wanted me to make him a coffee. Of course it was only hickory not real coffee. He looked at me then and gently repeated: "Do not worry, and no thanks for the coffee, I can't stop now." He went on sewing; I went to my room.

We had a tiny three-room apartment. I had shared the bedroom with Grandma, but she had died last year. I missed her terribly, she was my rock. Mum and stepfather slept on a fold-out couch in the lounge room. The third room was the tiny kitchen, but we had a bathroom, and overall, it seemed to me that ours was a very nice apartment, compared to some.

Our adult friends never tired of saying I was so good-looking and clever beyond my years, and how I would do very well in life. I, on the other hand, thought of myself as stupid, weak, scared, and very short for my age. Any good things they said about me were only because they had no idea of the truth. And doing what well in life? That was another riddle. I never asked, knowing clearly that I should know, given they thought I was so intelligent. Oh yes, that word 'intelligent' seemed about the best attribute anyone could have. I was short for my age and envied others for their height or strength, or the fact that they had blonde straight hair, not curly black like mine. Mostly though, I envied other kids because they did not seem to be afraid of everything I was.

No matter how I tried to think, I felt that there was something dreadfully wrong about Stalin and what had happened. How did we know Khrushchev was not a Nazi? What was really going on?

*

"Good story Cousin. I know what you mean. My mother was very worried about all that Stalin business and if a mother is nervous, then the child is petrified."

"You know Josef, what interests me is why this particular story has embedded itself in me. Why this one? I mean I have worked it out somewhat, but still this is one of those memories another might not recall at all."

Josef's eyes narrowed, his mind supplied the answer.

"But no wonder you felt so much about this. Just think of the words, 'Father Stalin saved you' while you had no father, and yet your imagery is that a 'Father saves his children...'

I was surprised, even dismayed, that I, the great would-be psychologist had not thought of such a simple answer. Josef was right. To me 'father' was an unknown concept, except for Stalin, and at the time, my stepfather. "I must be an idiot not to have thought of that Josef," I muttered.

*

"I've got joke for you," I said as we sat down to eat. "Where do you get them from?" Marilyn asked.

" I've been looking them up for the story I'm writing."

"What story?" both asked in unison.

"Well," I said a bit embarrassed, I had an idea of writing a short story about when Josef arrived here. I called it 'Josef at The Door'...What do you reckon?" They thought this a good idea, and I did not want to say more about it so I went on with my joke:

"It is Solomon's birthday and Hilda, his wife of 40 years, says he can have anything he wants. He is embarrassed but explains that once, just this once he'd like to go to a prostitute and assures her he has never cheated on her in his life.

Graciously she agrees and gives him a hundred dollars. Off he goes to the girls. When he gets home that night she asks 'Nu how was it?' She is feeling not as charitable by now.

"Well, it was wonderful actually," he says sheepishly.

She frowns asking "So, Soly, what made it wonderful? What those girls do we don't do already?"

"'Nothing really darlink, we do almost everythink the same but..." he answers.

"'Well but, she must have done somefink different and I vant to know wat!"

Sol can see she is getting upset so he waves "All right all right already...well you know uhm, she moaned during sex..."

"She moans?" Hilda asks surprised. "She moans, that's all?"

Solomon just nods. "Yes, that's right, she moans and that was so exciting yet."

The next night Hilda and Sol are in bed and she gets amorous. They start making love and she asks "So, do I moan now?"

"No" he replies, "not yet."

A bit later she asks again "Now do I moan?"

"No wait yet already" Sol answers puffing hard.

Finally, as he is coming he says,

"Now darlink moan now..." and Hilda goes "Ah what a day I had. The butcher cheated on the price and your sister wants to borrow money..."

*

We were out walking in the hills of the Otway's, now standing on top of the rise, sweating, breathing hard. Josef asked, "Your daughters, brothers, nephews and nieces mean so much to you. Something I am only just familiar with, since my wife has a small family and they have accepted me as their own. That helps to lessen the loneliness yes? And they all seem to be lovely people."

"Oh yes, my daughters, brothers and their children make me feel like I belong in this world, and that I am worthwhile as a life exploiting the good earth. They are all good people, really good people and I love them dearly. Sometimes I disagree with what they do, but that does not matter. I wish they would do better for themselves in their lives, but I have enough acceptance of who or how they are; just as they have it of me. It is a comfort, Josef, I can't even describe."

We were silent for a while climbing a hill. When we got to the top I lay down and Josef took a long drink from his water bottle. He seemed lost in thoughts, looking around at the beauty of the hills. On one slope, the green of growing vegetables, on another heavy woods. We listened to the song of a magpie broken by the laugh of a kookaburra. The world was all right today. Were we? Not entirely. Questions had to be faced.

"Where to now Josef, I mean about the inheritance?" My heart was pounding with more than the uphill trip. I was afraid to restart that conversation, and yet it had to be done. We had not said much about it for days. There was no news from Garibaldi. The inheritance question came to me like a bullet that had been slow to find the target.

Our 'Inheritance'.
Talking about it was ripping at a scab, peeling the skin off one's insides. Garibaldi thought it best to meet in Los Angeles for a final reckoning. He felt ok to pay for that out of his expense fund. I readily agreed to going, hopeful that there, I might find out more about my father's life from Garibaldi. What if I did not like some of that story? What if he was not the man I wanted him to be? What if…?

Josef took off his hat, looking somber.
"We are officially too late cousin, you know that, but we simply must get the money Cousin. We must, I must. You are well enough off, but I am tired of being poor, working for a pittance. I can never buy what you call your 'toys', or look forward to a life of reasonable leisure. And damn it all, it is not just the money. This is our inheritance. We have a right to it."
He sighed, the lines on his face worried with the burden of an unacceptable loss.

"My wife said on the phone that I sounded different. She is right. Between you and the inheritance I feel like I can breathe a new air, one I've never tasted before."

"Why is the money so important given I've already 'inherited' you, Josef, and some life story of my father? But I want something more than bad old stories and outcomes. I have seen others get a legacy always with a bit of sadness, and envy. If one inherits then one is acknowledged? Not just by the one who left the money or property, but by the world that says, 'Yes, this was your parent's and now it belongs to you.' And with that, one has officially inherited the whole story of lives, the continuing narrative that stretches far back and will go on and on. Human lives are an unfinished book that's hard to explain."

Josef nodded. "Perhaps it is that we have inherited little by way of roots and pasts of family stories, and even our birthplace denied us as being part of its narrative? Maybe that's why the money is even more important than usually?"

Yes, I thought, that's part of it. My mind went elsewhere, to a story that insisted on being told. Why was it here, now? Josef wanted to hear it. The big story about My Sister. But, I never had one! I began:

"This is something I had not known until I was over forty. Another awful, but alas, as it happened, a proven and true story. Not the only 'bequest' I've ever had from dear old Mum, but... Funny, I've felt more love for mum since she died than ever before. Of course by now mostly I recall her sense of fun and forget her ever ongoing illnesses, paranoia or manipulations". The story rose up into my mouth as another instance of present pasts, about something I had never known, and then did, and it has enormous power even now.

"My father's mother, Helen, didn't want her son Lajos to marry my Mum. Once in a while I went to see her on my own. Mum insisted on it. The visits were always very odd, leaving me to think Mum was right; Grandma Helen was a bit crazy.

On one of these visits, Helen gave me a drink and a biscuit; I mean one biscuit, not a plate full, and then asked how Mum was. Barely waiting for an answer, she'd talk on and on about her illnesses, her bad leg, or about how rarely she saw her one remaining son Janos, and how this was because his wife didn't like her," Just like your mother, she never liked me either."

I sat in her tiny kitchen on a small stool listening, making like I understood, but trying to figure out if it was alright for me to leave yet. In the middle of such diatribe, she surprisingly and without any introduction grandma Helen turned to talking about the end of the war.

"Do you remember how we all waited for your father to return?"

I shook my head.

"But surely you recall your sister?"

Surprised and annoyed, I meekly I said, "But I have no sister."

"Oh yes, but you did."

I was nine years old. I was very surprised and bothered by what she said; I had no sister! Never had one! What was she talking about? I'd know.

Her question sunk in, as she peered at me above her glasses, waiting for my answer. Feeling confused and embarrassed - for her I guess - I said again, "I don't have a sister," thinking that perhaps she mixed me up with Uncle Janos who had a daughter.

Her flat was even smaller than ours. The kitchen was perhaps a meter wide and three meters long. Next to it was one room and the bathroom. She was washing dishes as she talked, glancing back at me. Her tone of voice was matter of fact, as if she was noting the price of turnips. She went on somehow importantly, speaking in a kind of posh voice now.
"Oh yes, yes you did. You had a sister. She died just after the war. Surely you remember?"

I sat as still as I could in her steamy kitchen, disbelieving, worried as usual, and yet somehow interested; but convinced she was wrong. There was no sister, no pictures, and neither Mum nor Grandma Gizella, or family friends, ever mentioned any such thing. I would surely recall such a thing anyway. Still, something strange from adults always got my attention.

I had no idea what to say. She sounded so definite. She looked back at me again, wiping her hands and looking worried.
"Oh dear me, I shouldn't have said that. You don't know, do you? According to your mother it is a big secret. Better if you don't tell her I said anything about it," she added shaking her head. "What would she have said if your father did come back? I do not know."

She said a few more words I don't recall, but it got under my skin. Much as I was stunned at her craziness, unable to recall any sister, I was taken aback by the tone of her voice.

By the time I left her I was wondering whether to tell Mum. If this was true, why didn't I recall it? I was over 4 years of age at the end of the war; surely I would recall something. And why would Mum keep it as a secret, given she had told me so many awful things already?

As soon as Mum came home two days later from one of her trips I asked her. She was seamless and perfectly calm.

"Oh don't be silly darling, God she is a stupid cow," she said casually, turning away. I thought she looked flustered, flushed in the face. She added, "You know Grandma Helen is crazy, and in any case, don't you think you would remember?"

At the time I took anything Mum said as gospel. Well no, actually I wanted to take it as gospel, but I already suspected she was often wrong. Still, Mum had to be right; as a four-year-old I would have had some memories. Mum denied it, and I took her word and forgot the idea for thirty years.

Helen's words made a big impression on me, enough so that I unknowingly deposited them in my head – another good example of writing stories into the brain, without awareness of them. Thirty years later in Melbourne on a Sunday morning I recalled the story. I don't know why, except I had a couple of weeks of feeling lost and very down. I drove over to Mum's place and asked her again. She denied it vehemently. She mainly wanted to know what made me think of all that again.

It took another five years before I confirmed that I did have a sister. I asked her again on my birthday because I had recently visited my only living relatives – as far as I knew - my two cousins André and Agi who lived in the USA. I had not seen them for over 20 years. I asked them about the sister story and about other whispers from childhood. Reluctantly, they told me the whole thing. They said that Mum managed to save their lives and she was their hero, a woman of fantastic courage.

*

For my 40th birthday, Mum cooked bean soup that was better than anyone else ever could make, including myself. We talked about many things. Who knows why, I asked her again. She looked at me long and said, "Yes, all right I tell you. You did have a sister."

I waited, stunned at mum's willingness to tell the story.

"She was born in 1945 on the day the Russians liberated Hungary and she died six months later, probably of hepatitis."

Her voice strong, this time without hesitation, she recalled it all. "I get us a coffee," she said.

"No, wait, tell me more." She looked upset now, her face ashen and weary, her eyes perhaps recalling the face of her baby. I sat on the arm of her chair and put my hand on her shoulder. She continued, her eyes focused looking through the window.

"During the closing stages of the war, I had to have an affair with a Hungarian Nazi policeman. Twice he helped us to escape from the trains that would have taken us all

to Auschwitz. He used my jewelry to bribe the officials. He gave this help only on condition that I slept with him, saying he had been in love with me for years. I knew him vaguely as a neighbor from the building next door."

Wiping away her tears, she said "I could not tell you, I felt so ashamed, I am so sorry."

I hugged her. What could I say? She was sorry? I told her she was the bravest woman ever, that there was nothing to be ashamed of, and that none of us would be here if it was not for her.

She smiled then, took a few deep breaths and smiled again, looking amazingly relieved.

"You really don't mind do you?"

"Mind? How could anyone mind? You have done what you had to, you are an amazing survivor and we are alive, thanks to you."

She nodded, relieved, rushing out more details. "My daughter's name was Judith. She looked like you as a baby, lots of black hair. We had very little food, dirty water, I could not feed her, had no milk... Things were very hard in 1945."

I buzzed with amazement at her courage and at the burden of the secret grief she had carried for so long. Once again, as often since, I marveled at how my silly little mother was such a big brave woman. How would her life have been if it had unrolled in some normality? But there was more to hear.

"Your Grandmother Helen, and even my mother Gizella, felt shame about what I had done. Gizella understood on one hand, and yet she could not comprehend allowing anyone to know about it. I accepted *the shame that she made me feel. We all hoped that your father would return. Gizella was worried about how I would explain a baby to him or what I would say. In spite of all that, she loved the baby, just as she loved you."*

Mum was silent then. We cried and laughed on and off, smoking cigarettes, drinking her strong coffee. Then she sighed and gathered herself together, smiling at me. "I am a lucky woman to have you and your brothers and all your families. The funny thing is that if life would have been otherwise, then you and I would not have your brothers and their children. So, what can one do? My life is good now thanks to you all."

I readily agreed, thinking how rich my life was thanks to my brothers and all our families. We laughed again at her fear about telling us her 'shameful story'. I could see she was relieved and happy now. We went out for a schnitzel dinner to celebrate the end of that saga.

*

Old tales made more sense to Josef than to those who had never seen Budapest and the old Europe. Memories came to me of school years that seemed like moments, not years. Overall I had an awful time in school, always afraid of being found out to be a Jew and a stupid one at that. That reminded me of a joke;

In an Australian school room after the war the class was asked to write an essay on elephants. Later the teacher read out the titles.

The English lad wrote: The British Empire and Elephants.

The French boy: Love life of elephants.

The German boy: We will ask ze elephant questions...
The Russian: Elephants drink a lot of vodka.
And the new Jewish arrival from Europe: The Elephant and the Jewish Question.

Misery your name for me was 'School', in 1955-56

I told Josef about the last two years of my education, or rather the lack of it. An aimless, pointless time that I knew was a total waste and worse.

"Because Mum was not a communist, we knew that it was going to be impossible to get me into what was called in Hungary a 'gymnasium'. This was where you went after you completed your primary education at the age of thirteen. My school results were well below middle of the road, just above not good enough. That did not help either. My only real interest lay in literature and theatre.

I never wanted to be a fireman or a doctor or anything other than an actor. I was street wise, witty and had the gift of the gab, and used it to the amusement of anyone willing to listen. I read books voraciously, sometimes stealing them out of the library if they weren't available to children. I read everything; the stories of Jules Verne, old Hungarian authors, a lot of poetry, grown-up books about Greek philosophy, Sufism, French books about sociology, stories of ancient Rome, Grimm's fairy tales, Dickens, Freud, anything at all, indiscriminately, often understanding very little. My interest in philosophy and psychology became stronger. Not that I knew exactly what either word meant at the time. I knew there was something called wisdom, and reading good books was how you obtained wisdom.

So there I was, 14 years old, and life spilled over me, coming in ever larger or smaller disasters. Mum was a sensational hustler; she could talk the birds off the trees according to her friends. She managed to bribe enough people to get me into the Institute of Food Technology.

"But Mum, I hate chemistry," was greeted with, "Higher education is necessary, and later on when your results improve, you may be able get into the Academy of Arts."

Never mind the fantasy, feel the width. Her arguments convinced me? No, but what was I to do? I had to go to the Institute of Food and Cooking Technology knowing my worst subjects were science and particularly chemistry.

Oh God, that damn Food and Cooking Technology school. I knew from the very first day that I would fail. The only subject I did any good at was cooking practice. I had to cook at home and quite liked doing it anyway.

Soon, I was failing every subject except practical cooking. I could and would crack eggs open when most of the girls and boys were scared to do so. I'd make pancakes using three pans at a time, throwing the pancakes up high with the most casual air and let them fall back into the pan without even looking. I could make Hungarian goulash like no one else. And I would rip a chicken apart using one foot to hold it down - if the teacher wasn't looking. Alas it wasn't enough; I failed all subjects except cooking and had to repeat the year.

In 1955, having to repeat a year was shameful. Mum said not to tell anyone. In 1956, on my birthday, the 1st of September, I started, for the second time, the new school year, knowing that I'd fail again...

Josef interjected, "And then came the revolution!"

Thanks for the Revolution...

One evening in October I was on my way home from the national swimming pool on Margit Island to the tram stop on the bridge. Usually trams came every few minutes, but not this time. Figuring on some mechanical breakdown, I decided to walk the length of the bridge to the Pest side. At the end of the bridge there was more noise and rather more people than usual. I had enough money to buy my after-swimming favorite: a hot sausage in a roll from the street vendor.

I waited, eating the sausage, but instead of trams there were increasing numbers of people on the road and no cars at all. People were marching now, a huge crowd that seemed to be aimed towards the Hungarian parliament by the side of the Danube.

I asked somebody what was happening. "The revolution son! We are having a revolution," the man smiled, "It's about time..." Then I saw a few men carrying the old Hungarian flag, not the communist one, and even more remarkably, there were guns, never seen in the hands of stern looking civilians. Curious now, I joined the crowd moving towards the parliament. This was exciting. I was fifteen and I knew enough to know that communism in Hungary was a horrific and lousy affair, enforced by the occupying Russians, and the communist government of the day. At the parliament, a hundred thousand people filled the large square, singing, chanting slogans and demanding that a jailed political leader be released from prison, and that he should take over the government.

Several trams were banked up in the square. Two were overturned, an amazing sight, lying on their sides. I needed to be up higher to see what was going on, so I climbed up on one of the trams. As I watched, I suddenly realized that it was getting late and dark. 'Mum will kill me if I don't get home soon,' so I climbed down and ran toward home. As I left the square, running around the corner, I heard machine gun fire. It sounded like it did in the movies. The next day I found out that over a hundred people had been killed by the secret servicemen who had opened fire from the building behind the tram that I climbed onto.

If it wasn't for my abject fear of upsetting Mum I may well have died. Mum saved my life again.

The revolution went on. For a few days Hungary was free, and then Khrushchev sent in the Russian army to 'liberate' us from the subversive elements, as we were called, for there was no doubt whose side we were on. Everyone in our building was suddenly a revolutionary sympathizer, even the ones we knew until now as diehard communists.

During the days of fighting, gunshots could be heard; tanks rumbled past and at times there were big bangs as tanks blew away top stories of buildings where freedom fighters were resisting the Russians. One afternoon, ten men came to our third floor door. Knocking politely, they asked how to get to the roof. Mum told them it was the staircase next door to us. This was a bit worrying, the Russians might bomb us, but we were all in this and hopeful.

'Hurray', I thought, as a teenager who never thought of dying as real. Fortunately, the men soon returned; our roof did not offer a good vantage point from which to shoot.

Three, maybe four days went by. The radio kept asking Western countries for help. Sporadic gunfire would be followed by rumors about how the revolution was being *won or lost. Meanwhile, everyone ran out of food. My friend Miklos Zboray and I decided to sneak out to try and get some food. At the age of fifteen we thought we were cannonball proof. That morning there was a lull in gunshot sounds as we took off from our building; no tanks or Russians anywhere that we could see.*

Mum thought I was at Miklos's place and his mother was told he was at my place. We ran to the market as fast as we could. It was full of people carrying food and whatever else, looting. We grabbed a large sack of potatoes. On the way out I spied a big can of dill cucumbers, my favorite, so I grabbed that as well. Miki and I held the bag of potatoes, one on each end by the corner. It was very heavy, but we slowly dragged it crossing the width of the Korut Boulevard.

Without warning the ground shook, trees trembled, the rumbling noise of tanks came from close by. We stopped, the tram tracks wobbly underfoot. Distant tank sounds were familiar, but we'd never heard them this close. Five Russians tanks came around the corner speeding towards us. We froze. I pissed in my pants with fear. All I could think of was what Mum would say if I died here.

The five speeding tanks were so close now; blowing out black smoke that we could taste. They pulled up ten meters from us with a screech and a thump. The lid of one tank flew open. A Russian soldier appeared in a fur hat waving and yelling at us. We understood nothing, in spite of the fact that for the last few years learning Russian was compulsory. It took us a couple of minutes to realize he was telling us to nick off.

I suppose he saw that we were kids and carried no gun, but in retrospect this was amazing because many fifteen and sixteen year olds were fighting as freedom fighters.

We dropped the sack of potatoes - but I held onto the can of dill cucumbers - and we ran for our lives. Back in our street there was no sign of the two revolutionaries we met earlier. But there was some blood on the pavement.

*

I found out after the revolution was over that three of my classmates had died fighting. The euphoria of freedom quickly faded into fear. The bit of bronze I broke off from Stalin's statue was hidden outside, on the top of the staircase. Everyone realized that things were going to be tough. Police came and took men away from buildings. Word got around fast that thousands of people were leaving, illegally crossing the borders into Austria. Mum was worried and stepfather speechlessly scared.

Time seemed frozen for a few days, but everyday life soon returned. The rubble of bombed buildings and the bullet holes told the story, as people ventured back out into the streets. Like everyone else I was amazed at the amount of damage everywhere. This was war, I realized with a bit of a thump, like the movies. What will happen?

Then, smart little me figured out that the news about illegal emigration could also be my salvation. If I could talk Mum into escaping, I wouldn't have to fail in school again. I was fortunate enough to finish up living in Australia thanks to my worries about failing school and the Hungarian revolution. Fate, chance, chaos, it is the way life is built, like brick upon brick, without an architect or plan. But, there were more elements at work on our destiny.

For the last few months before the revolution my stepfather's drinking worsened. He was constantly drunk, hardly able to work. After years of enduring this, Mum finally decided she had enough. I certainly agreed. I used to like him, but he was getting more and more abusive. Just a few months ago and admittedly for the first and only time, he gave me a severe beating for the minor misdemeanor that I was jumping up and down on our couch. He chased me to the front door and caught me, punching and kicking me. I fell and he kicked me, repeatedly yelling with a fury I've never seen in him before. I wet myself and was bleeding a little. I was finished with him, wanted nothing more to do with him.

After the beating Mum screamed and yelled at him and would not talk to him for several weeks. Eventually, she told me that I must apologize in order to keep the peace, because she was so 'nervous', she could not cope with any more tension. This I understood, but resented in a big way. My entire life was filled with Mum being nervous, often looking like she was getting a heart attack that was not imaginary or faked. She often had low blood pressure and dizziness, and that always scared me out of my wits.

I could not understand why I had to apologize, and felt it a great injustice having to do so.

*

By now, the revolution was well over and I was as focused as a fifteen-year-old can be on talking Mum into leaving Hungary. The three of us would escape, and no more school worries for me. Mum agreed to leave my stepfather behind and quickly found a guide to take us across into Austria. She told my stepfather nothing about our intention, saying only that she was leaving him and he could keep the flat. He was distraught and drunk again.

While he was sleeping, we packed a few pieces of clothing and moved in with my Cousin Agi for two days, expecting to leave a day later.

The day before we were to leave Hungary, I heard Agi and my Mum having a heated discussion. I was sent out of the room, but listened in. It turned out that my stepfather phoned Agi, figuring we would be staying with her, and made all sorts of promises if she could only talk my mother into taking him with us. By now Mum was scared and was having second thoughts. She was afraid to leave the country, alone with two children, so she agreed to meet him. To my absolute amazement and against her promise that she wouldn't, she reconciled with him.

I was so angry I could hardly speak. It was another life lesson proving I had little control over what happened in life. In hindsight much of what happens that seems a disaster turns out better and this was one of those things; if it weren't for that reconciliation I wouldn't have had a second brother whom I dearly love.

Stepfather readily agreed to come with us to start a new life. Once again he turned into the man I used to like, if only for two days. I was still angry with him, but he made efforts to be nice to me. I even began to agree that it might be better to have a man with us. In the morning we boarded a train. The railway station was very busy with a lot of people, heavily over-dressed, just like we were, in two sets of clothes. Or had everyone suddenly got fat?

We carried one little bag. The idea was that we would travel to a border village to visit 'relatives'. "What relatives?" I innocently asked.

"Don't worry it is all arranged. Some people will act like family when we get there, and look, you might even be able to use your acting skills."

I could see she was anxious and trying not to be. We knew people were shot or jailed for trying to escape. Many stories were circulating about thousands of people getting caught at, or before, the border towns.

On the train we sat in a compartment, stepfather and mother obviously apprehensive. I played with little brother Tamas who laughed delightfully at my magic tricks and face-pulling antics. The country side rolled on, patches of snow here or there, clean and white. The door to our compartment slammed open. The ticket collector had a policeman with him. I wasn't particularly worried, having complete trust in Mum's ability to get through anything, and we had train tickets.

"Well, well," said the police officer "And where is this lovely family going to?"

"We are visiting my husband's aunt," Mum answered smoothly.

"Right, aha," said the policemen, "and this aunt, she just happens to be living at the border is she?"

Indignantly, Mum answered, "Yes she is. There are people living at the border, aren't there, and it just so happens that one of them is her."

The policeman was a little taken aback by my mother's fearless front. "Identity papers!" he commanded. Mum handed all our papers to him. It wasn't until we got to Austria that she told me that she gave him a large amount of money folded into our papers. I think it was her US ten-dollar bill that she had kept hidden for years. According to her, 10 dollars was enough to have brought us ship's tickets to New York.

The policemen took ages to flick through our papers; I never noticed that he had taken something out of them. Handing the papers back he said "have a good trip" and left. Mum sighed, smiling; stepfather looked as if he turned into one of his tailor dummies.

We arrived at the small station of an old Hungarian village. I saw many policeman and customs officers hanging around the platform. That was worrying. Standing on the steps of the train, Mum was uneasily looking around. I held baby Tamas. An older lady, dressed in somewhat traditional Hungarian peasant clothes, and two other younger girls approached us. "Sari," the old lady yelled, "here we are, welcome, and look how much Tibor has grown, and I haven't seen your new son yet."
Clearly the old lady had been to the academy of acting I could not get into. She grabbed little Tamas, who looked near to tears as she was kissing him. We walked out of the station arm in arm and went to their house. We had potato soup with sausages, and were told to go to bed because we wouldn't be leaving until midnight. It would take a long, hard walk of about three hours to get across the border.

When I was woken, we hurriedly put on our two layers of clothes. A horse drawn cart took us into dark, snowy and muddy fields. We got out at a shed and saw about twenty other jittery people there. The guide came to greet us and assure us everything was ok.
It was very cold now; the time was near 1 am. There was at least two feet of snow on the ground. It was going

to be very difficult to walk, given that I looked and felt like a dumpling, dressed up in all the clothes. We began walking towards the border. The guide was a tall, gaunt man with yellow fingers, lighting one cigarette from the other. He explained that Russian and Hungarian soldiers were guarding the area. He was reassuring us as we moved on, "It will be okay because I have bribed the guard at the point where we will cross, and the barbed wire is down. But you must pay attention to the rockets. They fire up rockets to light up an area and if they see any movement they machine gun in that direction."

We watched him anxiously.
"You can't bribe them not to fire their guns, so as soon as you see any light rise, or hear a shot, fall forward and lay flat on your stomach. Do Not Move! Do not get up until you hear me hoot like an owl, because sometimes they will fire a rocket as a decoy, and then fire again a minute later."
I supposed this was worrying to the adults. To me it was unreal, a movie or story and besides, soon we would be free. What freedom exactly meant I was not sure of, but I had a few ideas; no tax collectors, no policemen showing up at our door, no fear of people disappearing out of our lives without any trace...But mainly, no bloody school to fail.

Sleet began to fall heavily. We trudged in and out of the deep trenches the Russians dug to make it harder to escape. A rocket went up, lighting the area remarkably bright. We fell forward into a deep trench full of snow, water and mud. This happened on three or four other occasions. Our clothes were now caked with mud and frozen. I had to constantly dig mud off my boots so I could walk.

A machine gun fired, it wasn't aimed at us, but it was close enough to hear screams. Stepfather hurt his back on one of these fall-forward maneuvers. I took over carrying Tamas, who was blissfully asleep, having had some knockout medicine. He was tied on my back. Briefly I wondered why no one else offered to carry him. There were several single men in the group.

We shuffled on with our boots sticking to the mire for over four hours. All the rocket lights seemed a long way behind us. Stopping, the guide said he thought we were a little bit lost; that was greeted with much derision and cursing. He suggested that we wait until first light to make sure we were across the border.

We sat in a muddy trench quietly, wet and freezing through all our layers of clothing. No-one said anything for an hour and a half when in the dawn light I saw a building. I whispered to the guide, he stood up stretching, taking a cigarette from inside his jacket.

"The boy is right. There you are. Your new life is about to start," he said, "with God's help and mine, you are now in Austria. The building young Tibor saw is a guest house. It will be open when you get there. That's the arrangement. I will leave you here and make my way back."

We scrambled up, unsure and shivering. Some adults wanted to argue with him that he should come to the pub with us, but he wasn't having that. The group walked on, and in twenty minutes we were inside the warm guesthouse. There were Austrian policemen waiting there to write down our names, religion and Hungarian addresses. My mother gave out the wrong address and said we were Catholics which I thought was very clever.

Changing our few Hungarian notes into Austrian money was enough to buy me a piece of real chocolate. Stepfather decided to treat himself to his one and only, and 'last', brandy, and Mum had a short black. They took us to a nearby building, which had bags of straw as beds, pillows and blankets, and they fed us hot stew and rye bread.

What a wonderful thing the Hungarian revolution was if you survived it.

Refugees in Austria, 1956-57

Serendipity, Stupidity? America, Argentina, Australia? What's it matter?

After a few weeks in a refugee camp on the outskirts of Vienna we were to immigrate to the United States. But six months later, by 1957 we had been stuck in Salzburg. The Americans suddenly closed the Hungarian refugee quota to the US, just as it would have been our turn to go.

Around 100 people, men, women and children lived in each of 15 dormitories, side by side with no privacy, just a curtain between beds. After many months of inactivity, bad food, lousy conditions the refugees decided to go on a hunger strike. The dormitory blocks were barricaded. Refugees who used to help in the kitchen didn't go to work. No food could be brought into the buildings. A day and half later this was resolved with the usual promises, but nothing happened. Meanwhile our immigrant solidarity took a darker turn. The Catholics overturned newly arriving Jewish or Gypsy refugees. In turn these people reacted, fights broke out, anti-Semitism, thinly disguised till now, raised its well known head.

Peace was somehow re made and a few weeks later another hunger strike arranged. People just wanted to get on with their lives in a new country. Some few even went back to Hungary. Again the authorities promised better food and a new look at to which countries people could emigrate. A few trouble makers were moved away, but nothing was achieved.

The children and us teenagers played soccer or went for long walks, but the adults were more and more distraught as more weeks passed.

One sunny, summer morning, in June 1957, the loudspeaker boomed out: "The Australian government has decided to take refugees. If you would like to go to Australia, line up at bus stop four, at 2 pm tomorrow afternoon. Bring all your baggage so you can be transferred to the trains, which will take you to Marseilles and from there on ship to Sydney, Australia."

I dashed back to see Mum and persuaded her to go to Australia. I don't know how I did it. I imagine she was as sick of being in the camp as everyone else. Most of the camp's population decided to go to a country many has never even heard of, and non us knew much about it.

After a two-day slow train trip via Italy we were unloaded at the docks in Marseilles, and walked straight on to the ship. Beds were allocated in large dormitories deep in the bowels of the ship. No windows anywhere. It all looked daunting and too full. Each dormitory held around sixty people. Men were in separate dormitories to the women, but Mum was with brother Tamas who was only three. In my dorm there were bunk beds. I had the bottom bed, and above me was a boy called Tom who became a lifelong friend. Above Tom was a twenty-five-year-old fellow called Gyuri, and my stepfather in the next bunk. We went to the dining room where we were given our first taste of American hamburgers, chips and ice cream.

The trip to Australia took four and half weeks. The weather was stormy for almost the entire trip. Just about all the adults were sick and in bed. My new mates Tom, Gyuri, Bela and I roamed the ship having a great time. This was the adventure of our lives. I had never even seen a sea let alone sailed on one.

At night I slept like a log – if logs can have physical pains, nightmares and dreams. Repeatedly, I kept dreaming about a postcard picture Mum showed me years ago, whenever we were troubled. It was a beautiful harbor with a huge bridge across it. Small boats sailed on a blue bay. One night I grasped, in a kind of a I way, what my recurring dreams were about. I had spent the last six years dreaming and praying that I could live in that beautiful place, near the harbor with the big bridge. Through my childhood I had prayed to a God I didn't really believe in, promising all kinds of good behaviors, if He would let us live in that harbor.

*

Sometime around 1950, a picture postcard arrived in Budapest. It had traveled for over six months and it was addressed to Sari Weisz and it was sent by a Lucy Jolesz to her second cousin, my mother. Lucy and her husband had smartly left Budapest in 1941, just after I was born. They sent the card to Grandmother's old address, the only address Lucy could recall.

Mum looked at the water-damaged postcard. The right hand corner was torn making the sender's postmark illegible. She strained to read the few words, realizing it was from Cousin Lucy. She couldn't make out Lucy's address. All she could see was that the picture depicted a most beautiful harbor with a large bridge spanning across the water. Mum showed me the card.

"One day we will go to this place and leave this stupid country behind. We'll just wait for your father to come back."

When I asked where that bridge and harbor was, Mum replied that the address started with A, so it must be Argentina.

"Many Hungarians immigrated to that country before the war," she explained.
Mum replied to Lucy, but never heard from Lucy again, not surprisingly, since she simply addressed it, 'to Mrs. Lucy Jolesz, Buenos Aires, Argentina.'

That beautiful harbor on the card became a fixation for me, yes yet another fixation but this one I was aware of; an escape, hope and fantasy. I thought about that postcard picture every time I got a bad mark in school, every time my stepfather came home drunk late at night, or when I had to get up in the middle at night to look after my baby brother. Or, whenever Mum, with eyes red from crying, told me that another of her friends had disappeared. Or that on her last trip she had made no money and the taxation authorities were hassling her. I'd console myself each time, thinking of that picture. Mum and I would look at the harbor photo, our escape and dream, wishing we could go there.

I never believed we would ever get there, and yet an obsession developed about it. Now, on the ship, who knows why, deep dreaming, the picture kept rising, coming back into my mind. The actual card was left at home, forgotten in the haste and drama of our departure.

*

We were only four days away from Sydney now. Weather calmer now, the ship gently rolled on small swells.

A couple of people received cables from relatives who lived in Australia. That gave us some extra information. It all sounded pretty good to me. We envied the people who were to be met by long-lost relatives who said they would be waiting at the docks in their cars. Everybody, it seemed, had cars in Australia. Sunny days followed, the sea was flat now and the weather was cooler. Tomorrow we would arrive in Sydney.

The next morning at 6 am everyone was on deck watching the cliffs of the Australian coast. Tom and I went back to the kitchen to say goodbye to our American sailor friends. They gave each of us a liter container of ice cream, which we took up on deck. With a loud hoot, the ship turned left and entered Sydney harbor.

Mum and stepfather stood next to me with little brother Tamas. We were anxiously looking for our first view of Sydney harbor as the ship came through the heads. I saw a coat hanger bridge in the distance. I dropped my ice cream container in surprise; looking at the beautiful hills, huge ships and sailing boats… but that bridge? I looked at Mum as she turned pale and then flushed red. This magnificent harbor and city before her eyes, this place called Sydney was to be our new home. Mum muttered, "That's funny, it looks so familiar, as if I've seen it before."

I already knew, could hardly speak for a moment, but I knew:

"That's our postcard Mum, not Argentina… but Australia," I enthused loudly, and she nodded, "Oh my god yes. Oh my god."

"What postcard?" Stepfather asked. Mum and I burst into uncontrollable hilarity. He never knew about the postcard, because we were not going to escape with him.

*

The ship moved into Sydney, the harbor looked more and more fantastic, colorful and alive. Sailing boats everywhere, big homes on hills, fish jumping, and the blue of the sea made 1200 people as silent as in a theatre. I kept repeating "You'll see Mum, this place will be terrific, and look there are no kangaroos anywhere."

I recalled her often-said words: "As soon as I save up we are going to migrate to where Lucy is, you know that beautiful harbor," and we would look at the postcard again. And now, here it was, my obsessed dream became real. Seren-bloody-dipity?

Two years later, walking on a street, looking around the suburb of Bondi, we came face to face with Lucy and her husband.

Australia is more than just the best wool, but no salami! 1957

Eventually we moved from camp Greta near Maitland to Sydney's Camp Wilawood. The camp was large and the accommodation slightly better. My stepfather had a job, Mum quickly found one working in a cafe where they actually had Australia's first coffee machine. There was full employment in Sydney in 1958. You got a job in five minutes if you wanted one. I was sent to an electro-welding company as a factory hand. They gave me no eye protection gear, and I guess I did not understand that I was not to look, while holding a bit of metal as they welded it. The next morning, I could not open my eyes, I thought I was going blind. I never went back to that job.

Many jobs followed. In a factory I had to drill holes in a small metal block. It was rather boring so I started to whistle and sing songs, pushing the drill harder and faster, resulting in many broken drill bits. On my fourth day the foreman came up to me, after yet another broken drill bit. Grabbing my arms, he must have said," Too much muscle mate." I mistook 'muscle' for 'whistle', so I stopped whistling, but went on breaking the drills. They fired me later that day.

Next came the butcher's block factory. A few weeks later I broke my finger hitting it with a big hammer and had to stop work for two weeks. When I came back it was o.k. for a few weeks, I did not mind mucking about with wood, but then my mate accidentally dropped a huge butcher's block he was hoisting up, and broke my small toe. They fired me; too accident prone.

Several meaningless jobs followed, but I learned a few things at the Dunlop factory in Bankstown. A machine would spew out a never-ending length of warm rubber which I had to cut with a knife at every twelve inches. This was not just boring; it was also very smelly. I quickly devised a way in which I could cut off my required 1500 pieces a day by lunchtime. My English was still ordinary at the time. I found it hard to understand why whenever I went to the foreman - whose nickname was Spag, because he was Italian - he would frown when I asked for more work. With much waving of the arms and a few words he would tell me, "Bugger off, you prick." I made enquiries about what "bugger off" meant and was surprised at the answer. I thought Spag liked me.

We moved into a rented house with another family in Chester Hill. Fortunately, my friend Tom and his family did the same thing, ending up just three streets from our place. Stepfather could only get a job as a factory hand at the glassworks in Botany. He worked night shifts, long hours and was usually dog-tired by the time he got home. Both he and Mum were very unhappy and thought they had finished up with something worse than what they had at home.

This was a common reaction amongst new migrants who found it hard to learn the language, or the customs, and usually worked so hard to try and rebuild their lives, that they could not enjoy anything Australia offered. Pictures of Mum in 1959 show her looking worse than she did 20 years later.

A Hungarian acquaintance offered me a job as a milkman. The pay was high, but it was only for four hours from 5am until 9am. The boss's brother offered me a job in the afternoons in his fish and chip shop. I was earning a small fortune for three weeks, until one dark early morning, sitting in the milk truck, my boss switched off the lights and put his hand between my legs.

"Shit, no," I yelled, jumping out of the truck and running away as fast as I could. In the afternoon I showed up at the fish and chip shop. I was fuming with anger, so when the milkman's brother asked me what was wrong, I told him what had happened. He didn't believe me and telephoned his brother who told him that I was caught stealing money. I grew up very fast that day. I'd never had such experiences before. I heard a year later that the milkman stabbed his brother in the stomach and then committed suicide.

By this time Tom and I had managed to put a down payment of 3 pounds on Malvern Star push-bikes. This changed our lives, making us mobile, and a wonderful target for the bodgies every Saturday night at the Bankstown pictures.

"Bloody wogs! Go back to where you came from." Or "Yalookin' at my girl, ya want a bloody nose?" And, "You stole that bike from my brother, you wog bastard. Give it back," as they tried to run away with my bicycle. Fortunately, by this time we had teamed up with an older and larger Hungarian boy, and managed to keep our bikes.

We got plenty of eye from the girls. Tom looked like James Dean, and I suppose I looked like a younger Dean Martin, or so I hoped. We wore black leather jackets and Levis. None of the girls would dare speak to us on these Saturday outings, unless they were migrants.

Then came the Sebel furniture factory where both Tom I got jobs putting metal chairs together. One Friday afternoon I heard an almighty scream from Tom, who worked at a large electric saw, a couple of machines away from me. The machines had no guards. Tom had somehow left his hand in the way. His middle finger was gone; the rest of his hand was mangled. He left the job and so did I.

For a month I had one or two days of employment here and there, until I was hired by Exclusive Chocolates, a small concern in Newtown, owned by Hungarians. There were only four employees, and, it seemed to me a job made in chocolate-heaven. I was to be the assistant store man. My boss was an alcoholic, tough but very kind, and whenever I asked him what this or that chocolate tasted like he would wink at me. "I got to have a drink to silence my sorrows for having employed a left handed faszfej (dickhead) refugee like you who keeps dropping boxes of merchandise." I looked at him puzzled; I've never yet dropped anything. He saw my confusion, went and got his bottle and took a long swig of whiskey.

"Go on then," he said, "drop that bloody box while I am not looking, segfej (bumhead)..." Catching on now, I cautiously let go of the box, but it didn't break open. He gave it an almighty kick, laughing. "I said you were awkward."

Some days the boss would be so drunk by the afternoon that he would lock himself in his cubicle. I could hear him snoring for hours on end. I worked like a mad man, sometimes emptying large trucks by myself. The truckies sat on the curb rolling cigarettes, and asking how much I was getting paid to work this hard. I soon got to know most of the delivery guys. They were older and often offered me a beer or a cigarette, which initially I politely refused. Eventually I realized that in this country to refuse was not polite, but unfriendly. I didn't drink at all in those days. Stepfather's drinking cured me from touching alcohol for years. I'd invariably tip my beer into an empty box while they were not looking.

The job suited me, the bosses were impressed, and I kept getting one wage raise after another. For the first time in my life I discovered that I could be good at something and my self-esteem rose. After 10 months I was earning the princely sum of 10 pounds a week, not bad for a young migrant in 1958. When there was a lull in deliveries, I innovated by rebuilding shelves so they would take more boxes. We had lots of problems with the chocolate deliveries because in those days the trucks were not refrigerated. During summer, some of the chocolate would melt. I offered that if trucks arrived on hot, late afternoons, I would unload the truck no matter how long it took. This seemed to be such a radical and amazing suggestion, they even hired me an assistant. Some nights we wouldn't finish until 1 or 2 in the morning.

Someone told me about grape picking in Mildura, and how a small fortune could be made in just a couple of months of hard work. I told Tom and we decided to go. We signed up; I resigned my job at Exquisite Chocolates. The boss was unhappy, but he said, "Come back any time after you've got this silly grape picking out of your system."

We returned from Mildura after eight weeks of the hardest physical work we had ever done. I earned more money than I thought was possible in a year. Enough to put a deposit on a used Hillman car. I went back to the chocolate factory for a while and Tom got himself a job as store man in a new camera store in the city. After a few weeks his boss asked him if he had a hard working friend, because Bernie, the bosses' friend, was also opening a new store and needed a good worker like Tom. Enthusiastically, Tom said I should take the job. I thought he was crazy. Why would I want to change my well paid chocolate store man job, where I could eat all the chocolates, and where they were still tempting me with becoming a part owner of the business? I only sort of understood what they were offering me: an education and a job as their first company representative. The big boss said they would cut me into the business as their children were not interested in working there. All four owners were over fifty years old. They all appeared to think I was something special. Perhaps I did not believe or comprehend all this, I shall never know. I

Tom went on and on, trying real hard to talk me into taking the city based camera shop job. Fate as usual intervened again, by using my friend's mouth as the catalyst to change my life. Tom lit upon the idea of tempting me by suggesting that if I took the job we would be going into town together every day. We'd be wearing a tie and suit, and after all, town is where all the girls are! That did it. I thought hanging around with him to chase girls would help my shyness. His latest argument won me over immediately. I resigned from the chocolate business. My English in 1958 was still rocky, enough to get by, but not much more.

In Bernie's camera store I was employed as store man - cleaner, on a lesser wage than I earned at the chocolate factory. But I had my priorities right. It was not more money I needed, but a girlfriend.

Sydney was an amazing and somewhat backward city back then. There were perhaps three shops where you could buy a cappuccino, nobody sold salami or brown bread, and the pubs closed at six. But the city was full of people and to us it was exciting, and vibrant in a way that Budapest never was.

I became very successful and well regarded in the camera business. Bernie and Russell my new bosses were great teachers. Eventually I was head hunted by a short Hungarian fella called George. I worked for Georges Camera stores as a salesman now, eventually becoming the general manager. George and I, even after I left him, formed a rare and certainly one of my most important lifelong friendships.

*

So much more has happened since then, but that's another story.

No doubt you will be keen to see what happened to the inheritance.

Part 4.

...And some un-wholly ghosts

Los Angeles 2003

I had not reconciled to the idea of a lost Inheritance, but I was trying to. The great hope was that there was some loophole found or could be created, even if a difficult one. No inheritance would be far worse for Josef than for me.

The fourteen-hour flight from Melbourne to L.A was sleepless. Much was said between Josef and me. I told him again how important it was for me to have found him, and that I felt some kind of completion in spite of everything. I was also well aware, and tried to put into words, that like Josef, I didn't quite feel the closure I hoped for.

I wanted to get Josef out of his glum mood.

"Josef I know the loss of the money is far worse for you than for me. But look, I am going to help you to whatever degree I can anyway."

Josef shook his head, "Cousin I know you mean well, but I am not, don't wish to be a charity case."

After a long break, he added, "You know, I do have some plans."

"What plans?"

"Well let's not talk about that now, but it has to do with the Swiss banks. As you know your name is on the claims, but unfortunately you can't prove anything either. However, your name is on the fucking list and mine is not."

I wondered and asked why he made that last point. Josef shut his eyes.

"Forget it."

What he said concerned me, but I let it go.

*

Now, Josef and I were sitting in Harry Weinberger's office waiting for Garibaldi to arrive. Weinberger was about our age. He was a large man with a strong, confident-looking face that had seen much, and made many decisions over the years. His office was American huge. Not modern or old looking but full of knick knacks. Perhaps he was a collector of oddities. Like us? He smoked cigars. I gratefully lit one of his huge Cubans.

Weinberger's manner was easy and personable. His smile and tone of voice changed fast from jocular to serious as he spoke. When he laughed, his jowly face reverberated like jelly. I liked him, he was obviously some brain. Josef looked worried and impatient, wanting good news; and I reckoned there was no good news. If there was any upside, Weinberger would already have said something.

Garibaldi arrived. He walked in briskly, his brown face tensely smiling as usual, hands extended towards us. Weinberger buzzed for coffee. It was obvious immediately that we were done for. I could feel it, and smell it. It was on Garibaldi's face. I waited for Weinberger to speak. Josef was perched on the edge of his chair, his face taut and lined.

Weinberger spoke quickly.
"Gentlemen, I had the best brains in this office look into this matter. We made a big effort partly because Antonio and I go back a long way, and partly because I love the high fees he is paying me out of your father's account."
His smile broke, realizing his joke was not welcome, and he continued.

"There is only bad news. I am sorry. Unfortunately, the courts have now awarded all the monies to the charities. Most of it is already paid out. I am afraid all you can do is to either take it on the chin or - and I am not recommending this course of action, or you could try to build a case to get the monies back."

"Who would we sue and what are the chances of winning?" Josef asked impatiently.

Weinberger shook his head," No," and offered fresh cigars. Leaning back, his chair creaked; he drew a large drag of smoke, his eyes told it all.

My mind became ice-covered, hearing that my fucking inheritance was lost. It was now impossible to accept this. It was as if I was not really there. I could not relate myself to this, this should not have happened. No this cannot...The loss was - no matter all my earlier rationalizing - an unexpected bombshell.

I looked at the others intently, wanting this not to be true.

I thought how life was like a movie: unexpected and expected things happened all at once. Four men, sitting in a stereotypically book-covered law office in huge green leather armchairs, with a great view over the smoky hills of L.A., all looking like they have turned to stone as the story ends.

FINISH. No credits rolling.

Antonio's voice brought me back into existence.

"Amigos, Weinberger and I have been through this kind of legal exercise many times. We lost most, won one, and the cost of such an exercise, well frankly, could be more than all your current assets put together, and your chances are not good, hell, it is hopeless! We cannot use your father's money to mount a case. No one thought of doing that when Lajos died."

Weinberger jumped in, "Look, I am very sorry but I am too old to bullshit you people. Even if you got the best legal talent, your chances are still, at best, lousy."

Josef looked stunned, grieved, but something more. Again he asked, "Who would we sue?"

Weinberger answered.

"Well, first we would have to go to court in Argentina and that is already devilishly hard. We would have to find an angle to argue that the fact that you were only a few weeks late due to the circumstances. This is not a legal or really any argument. We have already explored what else we could use, and this office could not think of anything. Then, in the unlikely, very unlikely case that we won that case, we'd have to get dozens of charities from all over the world to refund half of the moneys. Imagine the press putting your faces on front pages as the two bad men wanting to take money back from the hungry...But, we'd never get past the first hurdle. Can you imagine these charities in twenty different countries - many of which have dubious legal systems - can you image mounting a challenge in all these countries, to agree to Argentinean laws, and go against the local charitable organizations? I'm really sorry." Weinberger looked genuinely gloomy.

Garibaldi stood up and went to the window; his usually straight back bowed. Turning around he said, "I'm really unhappy and for you both, and for dear Lajos, but Weinberger is right. We are at the end of the line. I don't know what else to tell you."

His eyes were red, fighting back tears. Josef was silent, his dreams lost. He looked far away. I stood and put a hand on his shoulder, wanting to say something, to him, to me, but nothing came.

Josef suddenly re-animated, spoke.

"No. This is wrong, there is a way. We must find the second will, the one dated after this one...!"

"The what?" I asked, but Josef hurried on.

"The Inheritance belongs to us, surely if Antonio and Uncle Carlos 'find' another will..."

We all caught on now, Josef wanted us to cheat. Antonio and Weinberger looked at each other aghast, speaking almost at the same time.

"You are asking us to falsify a new will and that is not going to happen. Sorry Josef, but no sir, can't be done, that is grand larceny," Weinberger stated.

Antonio continued, "Even if we agreed, the Argentinean attorney's contract shows that no will could supersede the current one unless they wrote the new will with the client. This is standard practice where large fortunes are involved, so no later challenges can be issued."

My feelings went this and that way. What fucking feelings, more like non feelings, like a stone dropped into deep water. Yes, we had a right to the inheritance and no, larceny was not in my wildest dreams and yet...but what was I thinking? No this was not on.

"Easy for you lot to give up, so easy. None of you are piss poor..." Josef burst out and quickly left the office. Antonio and I followed him out.

"I'm going for a walk," Josef mumbled. Antonio put an arm around me.

"Let's go and have a drink."

A Jewish Inheritance Joke.

Moshe meets his best friend Solly and he looks awful, "You look terrible. What's the problem?"

"My mother died in August," Solly replied, "and she left me $500,000. Then in September my father also died, leaving me $800,000."

Moshe is sympathetic: "Both parents gone in two months, no wonder you're depressed."

"Yes," his friend added, "and then my aunt died October and left me $1.5 million."

"Oh hell" Moshe says, "This's shocking, three family members lost in three months? How sad, but time will heal..."

"Then this month," Solly rushed in, "absolutely nothing!"

The Inheritance is lost. Josef has a darkish side?

We had three days left in Los Angeles. I had the disconcerting feeling of not knowing how or what to think, or feel. How would I know about feelings I had never had before? I had never lost this much money before, and especially my inheritance, the outcome of my father's life. My legacy. My fucking inheritance. My goddamn blasted right. A feeling of having lost some of my recently gained heart dropped on me. This entire dream turned out like the usual mirage of Mum's old stories. Well, perhaps not all – I kept reassuring myself. Much was gained. Stories, memories, a life; a contact with the past.

I told Josef all this. He listened absently, not like before. He shook his head in agreement or otherwise, I was not sure.

I rented a car, and together with Antonio we drove Josef around, showing him the sights. Josef didn't say much, he looked, his eyes red. One could tell he was forcing himself to be polite - as one might with people who are not in touch with your reality. It was true that practical reality for me and Antonio was very different from what Josef lived. No matter what wonders we showed him around L.A, he saw it through the eyes of one who would never be able to experience what this world had to offer.

During the day Antonio also tried to cheer up Josef. He suggested he could push a bit of extra work Josef's way, but Josef just shook his head; that was not the point.

I felt increasingly removed - or was it clogged off - from the inheritance dream. I should be used to having such feelings of incredulity. Again I concentrated on the idea that what we had already gained was huge. Yet the missing bit of my psyche was rising to the fore again, like food stuck in one's throat. How can a 'missing bit' be here, I mused, pulling details, words to pieces. What isn't there? What was never there to be mine cannot and should not hurt, should it?

'What's it fucking bloody matter?' I yelled into my brain. 'Shut Up! Leave it!' But I could not leave it.

Back at the hotel I asked Antonio to stay for dinner. "What else?" he tried to joke. "Would I leave you two boys on your own amongst all these beautiful American women?"

My spirits rose a little. Maybe we should get drunk. While getting dressed I started to think about how to help Josef. There had to be a way to make him feel better about his life. Or me about mine.

I suggested dinner at the top floor restaurant with the great view. Josef said he'd rather have dinner in the room; he wanted to discuss something with us. This sounded ominous, his words darkly slurred. Antonio and I readily agreed, phoning through our orders and opening a bottle of fine Napa white wine. Antonio wanted to stay jolly and he said:

"Gentleman, we're gonna die here today, asphyxiated by cigar smoke given that no window may be opened in American hotels. So you wish to smoke, or will we pretend not to, for the first five minutes? "

Antonio's attempt at humor was answered by Josef shrugging as he lit a cigarette. I tried to follow Antonio's tone, "No worries man, you gotta die sometime and I know my time won't come for another sixty years..."

The food arrived. We were all hungry, wanting some sort of filling up, I figured. Josef ate quickly, obviously ready to talk. I turned to him. "What's on your mind?" He looked at me pale faced.

"What I want to discuss with you two is not easy, and don't worry, it is not the second will idea... You know we have spoken before about the Swiss bank claims. You know that unless we can prove the amounts of money deposited by Grandfather and unless we have papers to prove his will, we have no chance of getting the money."

Josef was brewing something I figured I would not like. I had given up on the Swiss claims. I would only look at that again to help Josef get whatever he could get. Unfortunately, I could not see that we could substantiate any claim.

"Go on," I urged him.

Josef outlined his idea. He explained about his connections to a forger in Hungary, and that he had access to the kind of paper work that may have been used in the 1930's. To my amazement he also told us that his wife was willing to be an accomplice, as was his wife's mother. He argued his case strongly and convincingly; having obviously spent quite some time thinking about it. He slapped some yellowish looking, old and worn papers on the table.

"I have gone ahead already, just in case! I got the forger to make up our birth certificates and a letter from Grandfather, stating he left money to Tim and me...the forger is a crook, but a good one. He is now in the process of finding old bank documents from a Swiss bank, and then he will produce a deposit slip or whatever..."

I was dumbfounded. I glanced at Antonio who sat dead still, attentive as usual, his face impassive and yet thoughtful. Josef came to the end of his plan. I didn't know what to say. Antonio broke the silence.

"Oh amigo you can't be serious. What exactly are you asking us? You could go to jail for something like this."

Josef explained why it wasn't such a bad chance to take, and that jail was unlikely even if the plot failed. I was very uncomfortable. "Josef are you just asking us for an opinion?"

"Well, no, not only that. If I can't get you and Antonio, to cooperate, the whole thing gets harder for me, but I'll still do it. Antonio is needed to say that he had some knowledge, via Lajos, that his father left money to his grandchildren."

Antonio lit another cigar, a sure sign that he was pondering. I shook my buzzing head.

"I can't do it Josef. I mean, not only is it dangerous, particularly for you, but it is totally unethical. What you suggest is a major scam."

Josef turned to me, his face distorted and red: "Scam? Sham? How do you know that Grandfather didn't leave a hundred thousand US dollars in these fucking Swiss banks? In fact, you agreed that he had left some money; damn it, you know he did. Maybe all I'm asking for is what is rightfully ours, yet again! Scam, my arse! Is there a bigger scam than what the Swiss banks and their Nazi patrons pulled on us?"

"He has a point there," Antonio agreed, "Some of the bankers were a bunch of crooks during the war, and unethical since. However, that's not the real point, is it? The real point is that we cannot prove that your grandfather deposited money. And I am prepared to believe that he did."

I could not believe it. "Jesus Antonio, don't fucking encourage him."

"I'm not. I don't want him to do this either, but he has a point. Let's just think about it, let's see if there is anything that can be done. As for recalling Lajos saying that his father did leave money in a Swiss bank, I think that is correct, I do believe he said that".

I was angry and sick at hearing this.

"Fuck man, can't you see that this might land Josef in jail and make both of us into crooks for the rest of our lives, whether it succeeds or fails?"

Josef started again, a little softer this time.

"Look I don't give a fuck about jail! I'm sick of being poverty-stricken! I'm sick of working in a dingy office, I'm sick of all the things that might have been!"

This I understood, and I searched my brains for something sensible to say. There had to be a better solution for Josef, but I couldn't think of anything sane. I poured the remaining wine.

Josef turned to Antonio, "Would you be willing Antonio? There is not much risk in it for you."

"Caramba, damn and Diablo and fug..." Antonio muttered, blowing out the heavy blue smoke of his cigar.

I don't know, but you two hombres and your dear departed father - and your whole miserable story has affected me in a big way. I'll consider it, so long as I can believe you won't finish up in jail, but only if Tim goes along with it."

I panicked hearing this, speaking out more harshly than I intended.

"No! No bloody way am I doing this. I love you like a brother, but I cannot do this to my family or to yours. I cannot do this morally, not even if I justify it by saying yes, you are probably right, that Grandfather left some dollars. I can't, and won't do illegal bullshit... All I can do is to say that I do have memories of something like it, but I will not falsify papers. Sorry..."

"Fine," said Josef, icy cold.

"I'll do it on my own. In fact, I have put a claim in already. You just don't understand, in all your comfort, sitting on your boat, what I have to live with."

I pleaded with him.

"Oh shit Josef. No, but why, why have you already started it? I am very sorry about the money but look, perhaps if we think hard..." I muttered.

Josef stood up, his face enflamed.

"I knew this would happen! I knew you comfortable bastards would not cooperate, if it came to the crunch! Well fuck you..." He sprung towards me as if he wanted to punch me, but turned away, storming out the room, slamming the door behind him.

"Oh caramba, here we go again. In all these years dealing with people and money it is very rare that there is a happy end to the story."

"Do you think I am wrong Antonio? Do you think I am being too cautious"?

"No amigo you are right. But we must consider it, in case there is some way to get what he needs. If there is no way we can make him financially secure then, though I understand where Josef is coming from, we must find a way to stop him from doing this. He is certainly determined."

He phoned down for another bottle of wine. We talked for the rest of the night about what we could do, or how to stop Josef. Over and again we went through the possibility of claiming the inheritance money. He even called Weinberger again. Then we tried to formulate a safer plan to cheat the banks. I realized that I would do the bank scheme if I did not feel threatened, or worried about Josef. So much for my ethics and morality.

Suddenly I had an idea.

"Antonio is there any money left from the expenses account? I mean, how would it be if you suddenly found that there was say 200, 000 dollars left in the estate that hadn't been used?"

His answer was definite, "No, I'm afraid not. Any money that is left in the estate has to be distributed to the charities. It is controlled by your father's lawyers."

"I figured as much. I have already offered to help Josef, but it's an 'Inheritance' that he wants not charity. I could put the money into your account. You could say that you have managed to get hold of this money from the unused expenses, and that I didn't want it? Or better still that you have given me the same amount."

Antonio thought about this.

"Hm, aha, not a bad idea, and it may well work. Would it stop Josef, given that as you said it isn't just the dollars?"

I shrugged. "Don't know. He is so angry, and his anger is focused now on the banks - and me. You could say that you are only going to give him this money if he doesn't go through with his plot."

"He might see through that; he is smart enough. Or he'll agree that he won't go through with it, and then go ahead anyway. He wants revenge! Revenge on the world... He wants to satisfy the feeling that the banks, and the world, owe him. And they do. Or he will knock the offer back cold, knowing we are trying to fool him... I don't know, maybe it would work, it certainly has merit."

I was pleased with my idea. Antonio's face turned to a warm smile, his hand in the air grabbed at something, "Just a thought amigo, this suggestion of yours, it is a bit like what your father did for Oscar's son. You have inherited something from your father, that is clear."

What he suggested pleased me. I could have shed a few tears.

We talked on endlessly, trying to refine the idea. I suggested that we find a Swiss connection that would suddenly write to us saying that they had found $200,000, and that if we accepted this offer, and so on.
"Yes, that's another great idea," I yelled, immediately knowing it was a stupid idea. Josef would laugh at us. But would he?
"Good, but this would be rather difficult, amigo," Antonio pondered.
"I can't see how we could manage that one, unless we hired an actor, or a real Swiss banker agreed, and I have no connections with them at all. It needs more work, as the Egyptians said to the Jews working on the pyramids. Let's think again tomorrow."
I laughed at his joke. He raised his glass, "Let me drink to you. You are a decent man, that means much to me."

We called it a night. I went to check on Josef. He either was not in his room, or he didn't answer my knock. I spent a sleepless night tossing and turning, trying to find some way of reconciling myself to Josef's idea, but I couldn't. I was scared of trouble; Josef was right. To jeopardize my comfortable situation was not something for me. I was a coward? No, I was sensible, I reassured myself, squirming anyway at my reasoning.

By the morning I was even more resolved that I didn't want to play any part in Josef's scheme. Neither of us needed trouble. I could not let him go to jail, that was for sure, no matter what he thought of me. I was equally resolved that somehow, something must be done to make us both feel better about all this. My own plan of 'finding money' for him seemed better and better.

Antonio had to go home. He asked repeatedly that I should visit him there soon. My response was enthusiastic. The idea of seeing where my father had lived was exciting and bitter all at once. Of course I would go, to see his house and chair that might still smell of him. To breathe the air and to eat the food he did, to see sights he loved, would be emotionally tough, but of course I would go. I phoned Marilyn and asked her to make bookings to Argentina.

I never left the hotel all that day and evening waiting for Josef. There was no answer whenever I called Josef's room. Later at the hotel desk they said he had checked out. He was due to fly back to Budapest a few hours before my flight left for Melbourne. At the airport, hoping to catch him there, I asked the airline if he had already checked in. They would not provide the information. I tried to explain why I was asking, but she just shook her head, "All I can do sir, is to page him for you."

I nodded yes. He did not answer the paging. I quickly scribbled a note asking him not to go ahead with his plans until we spoke on the phone. I said we had some great ideas. This of course was a lie but I was desperate to keep in touch with him.

Boarding Qantas, I found my seat. 'Don't think just be,' I thought, 'preferably asleep.' Eyes shut, body tired as if I had run twenty kilometers. Sleep was not coming, one had to suffer awake.

As I shut my eyes, Josef's face flashed up, making me remember that back in Melbourne he had given me a bunch of his short stories. I had brought a few with me on the trip to America.

I'd told Josef that I always found the stories of my own life to be the ones that I thought of as my best stories. He had laughed in his deep throaty way.

"What else could one's best stories be about? That's certainly what mine are about, though with more than a touch of added fiction."

He was right; I too, increasingly fictionalized whenever the truth did not suit. We talked about what we termed the 'scripting' or re writing of our lives, relating that to the question of who, if anyone was the 'author' of it. I loved those heady conversations with Josef.

I retrieved Josef's stories from my backpack. It was difficult reading at first, because my Hungarian was rusty, but after a few pages I began to enjoy it. The first surprise was that I had thought of Josef as witty, sardonic, and often cynical. There was some humor in his stories, but mainly they were rather gloomy and melancholy. The stories were compact and brief, a straightforward recounting with a terminal and usually gloomy fictional ending. His work was good, perhaps better than mine. I felt a twinge of envy but recognized that he was writing in his own language, while I was not. In Singapore I emailed him, "Your stories are terrific. Have you had any published?" Hoping but not expecting a reply.

Budapest 2003, where a bit of bad luck is never enough for a Hungarian

By the time Josef arrived in Budapest, he felt like he had been hit with a hammer on several occasions. Agonizingly divided, confused, angry and uncertain as to what to do next. He knew Tibor was right. He was also troubled about his behavior with Tibor. The positive mind set he found since meeting Tibor was worryingly evaporating. 'Still,' he thought bitterly, 'my cousin just does not understand my situation…But surely he does, he must actually,' he thought flicking back back and forth, with a sigh.

Could he do it? Could he go through with the plot without Tibor? It was not possible to mount a strong case without him. The plot he hatched last year, just before Garibaldi showed up and changed everything was all right, but it was thin.

Juli met him at the airport. She knew that Josef had left his cousin in anger, and without any resolution toward anything hopeful. Her arms gladly welcomed Josef. She smiled her usual smile, trying to make him feel better, knowing she would not succeed. She chatted, but did not look well. She handed him mail from his office. He was listening to Juli while opening the letter. The correspondence said they were retiring him. They wished him well and congratulated him on his long service to Hungary. His pension was approved and would be forthcoming. Without saying a word, he handed the letter to his wife.

"Oh God," she said. "I thought it would be something like this. Something else will turn up. Perhaps you can get another job in the private sector."

He shook his head, "Fuck them."

Juli did not want to tell him just yet that on and off, she hadn't felt well for the last few months, and had taken the opportunity to see a doctor while Josef was away. The news was bad. She had a stomach condition that was potentially fixable, but it needed a lot of rest and preferably no work. Her condition would worsen unless she maintained a very strict diet, and was able to use some rather expensive medicines. They had basic medical insurance, but that would not cover all the costs; in fact, there was a large shortfall. All their savings would be eaten up by what was needed. She would tell him later.

There was more bad news to come. In the next few days Josef went back to work to finalize his retirement. His pension was to be smaller than he expected. After his last day at work he felt washed-out and concerned, but being out of his bloody silly job somehow made him feel a relief, in spite of future money worries. Julie had set a nice table, suggesting they enjoy dinner.

Later, Juli explained what the doctors had said. Josef listened intently, his face stiff and turning to ash. This was truly a desperate blow. He decided now that there was no choice. They needed the money now more than ever.

"That's it Juli! The Swiss caper is now officially on," he said, trying to sound light. "In fact I may as well tell you that I have set things in motion."

Juli had thought about the plot, and had grave misgivings about it. She would rather be sick than risk losing Josef. He shook his head.

"There is no way you will have anything less than the best treatment available. Meanwhile I will ask Cousin Tibor to lend us the money."

This blow added to his desperation and yet also to his resolve. The next day he called the forger, but could not get an answer. He tried for several days without any success, so he went to the address only to find that the man had been arrested.

"That's it then," Josef told Juli, "Everything has well and truly fallen apart. Unless I can find someone else." She was relieved, hoping the whole thing would be dropped.

Over the next few days Josef investigated his wife's illness. They went to another specialist to get a second opinion, only to find out that the prognosis was not good, it was indeed life-threatening. He felt lost and cheated by the turn their lives have taken. The only avenue left open was asking for Tibor's help. He sent an email.

Dear Tibor
It seems that the universe does not want me to go ahead with my silly plot; it is now dead - you'll be happy to hear. Dead and buried as is our inheritance. The forger I mentioned has been arrested. I could only do it if I found another crook. If you are willing to help us, I promise to give up the idea. You are the only one I can turn to for help for Julie's medical problems.
Josef

He pressed the send button, not knowing what else to say, feeling ashamed about having to ask.

*

I was much relieved to hear from Josef, and was about to phone him anyway. Marilyn and I had already decided to go to Hungary if that was necessary. Reading the email left me with a sense of his despair. Of course I would help with the costs, that was easy and not that much money. But even then, there was nothing I could do about Josef having lost his job or his finances, unless I resurrected the 'found money in the inheritance account' scheme that Antonio and I had discussed in Los Angeles.

*

My deepening disappointment about the lost inheritance was nothing compared to what Josef must have been feeling. Yet the part of my heart that opened to my own ever-hopeful child began to retreat, freeze over, back to how it used to be. My hope and wish was that the bond with Josef would remain. Would that be enough? Quickly I replied to Josef's email, making no reference to anything else, other than to Juli's illness, and how pleased I was to assist, offering the money as a gift, not as a loan. Josef replied that although he would like to think that he would be able to repay the money, it was now unlikely to happen.

A day went by and Josef found another e-mail from me.

My dear Josef and Juli,
We have thought more about your situation and hit upon the idea of asking you both to come to Australia for

an extended visit. If you like it, you may be able to settle. If not, you can always go back to Hungary. During a year, Juli will be able to have a proper rest. I am sure it would give us a terrific opportunity to discover a great deal more about each other and our families.

I am very excited about the idea. We are retired; both have plenty of time, so we can show you a great deal of this beautiful country. I think what we have to offer here might even improve your outlook on life (and mine!) We have plenty of room. We have just bought a new place, but are not selling the old one. Please Josef, I want you to accept this as my lifetime gift to you. After all I haven't ever bought you a birthday present.

Your loving Cousin
Tim-Tibor

Josef showed the letter to Juli. She cried. "What will we do? How do you feel about it? Why not accept it Josef? Your cousin is genuine and generous, why take this away from him? I'm sure if he could not afford it he would not have made the offer."

Josef needed little persuasion. Juli was right; why not accept such a piece of good luck at least for a year. His email accepted my offer. Within a month, they had visas and tickets to Australia. Meanwhile Antonio has put our secret scheme into place so now Josef and Juli had over $200 thousand dollars to their name. Josef did not question it. Months later when he did say something about it I knew that he figured it all out, but I denied having anything to do with it.

*

Australia was an amazing sight for Josef and Juli, who has never been out of Europe. They settled into our old apartment. Josef knew that it was too late to change country and culture at their age, but they certainly enjoyed the weather, the sea, the hills and the freedom, and the ability to live a lifestyle they had never experienced before.

After her operation in Melbourne, Juli rapidly improved. She got on very well with my partner Marilyn. The two women spent much time together shopping, talking and doing some work for the farm that Marilyn's family owns. Juli started to go to the gym and took quite a liking to exercise, which also assisted her recovery. She would have to be on medication for the rest of her life, but her cheerful calm outlook assisted both of them to feel more hopeful about their future.

But something else again confirmed for me, that the universe is a chaotic, random and curious affair. The chaos we call life sometimes falls into focus like a camera zoom lens, bringing what we call 'good or bad luck'. Here it was again.

Garibaldi phoned me and was very happy to hear that Josef and Juli were staying in Australia. Just a day after our last chat, he called again with what he termed laughingly, as "one of my brilliant ideas that I cannot help having. The stories that you had sent me, were the catalyst for the idea. You and Josef should write what took place throughout this inheritance saga. Make it into a book! At the very least I am sure your families would be interested. I also figure it would help to bring some kind of completion to this whole process, for all of you."

Garibaldi heard a quick intake of breath from me. We certainly needed some kind of resolution. Was that at all possible? I had doubts about that. We had hardly spoken of the fucking dead inheritance – speak well of the dead or forget it - and now maybe we could do just that; speak well of it. But why rip at scabs? And yet, to be done with it by writing it seemed yes, a good idea, sensible. Otherwise, we'd have to live with the whole drama forever. Not a great prospect, I thought.

Garibaldi asked "are you still there?"

"Oh man oh man...Really odd that you should suggest this Antonio because something has been moving around in my brain along similar lines, about how to settle the shit dust. Now you have said it, I think yes, this would be a great process for both of us."

We chatted on about the sorry state of the world, about the rise of terrorism, and the financial crisis. I promised Garibaldi that I'd send him a copy of our writing as we progressed if Josef agreed to the project. However, if he did not, I had already decided, I would do it myself.

After I hung up I thought about the mysterious connections between people. Garibaldi and my father Lajos were close friends, and now that friendship was passed down to us; it became part of our lives. We were inheriting it?

I began to hate, or was it love, the word 'inheritance', our doubtful inheritance.

I immediately told Josef, about Garibaldi's suggestion. At first he didn't seem keen, saying he just wanted to forget it all. Juli and Marilyn thought it was a great idea. I persisted, more and more convinced that doing this, might bring the needed closure to both of us.

"Josef these things are never really finished until they are purged out of the system. The only way to do that is to recall and clear away as much of it as one can, even though going through the process may be painful, yet again. The more I think of it, the more I like the idea of treating the whole exercise like a novel; a fictionalized memoir. Like you've already done in your stories."

He looked more interested. "You mean, tell the truth, and then tell the rest of the story as we wished it to be, rather than how it actually was?"

"Yes! Why not make out the story as we would have wanted it, rather than how it was?"
Josef pondered the idea for a short time, and then smiling broadly, he nodded yes.

"Yes, at least in that way I can feel I am making myself useful. You might be right, we write it as we want - and then close the fucking book as if..."

"I think I'll open a bottle of red so we can celebrate the birth of a new epic," Marilyn said.

*

We launched into writing like men who had been celibate for twenty years and now found themselves in a harem. The gusto that enveloped us was so energetic, it felt so good, that we could feel the process working, clearing our brains. The more we wrote, the more we had to say.

The book was progressing fast, the writing full of sweat, tears, emotion and false starts. How much fiction, and how far to press good or bad luck? What else to add or take away from our characters? From whose point of view? Mine? His? Both? The characters were us, Josef and me, faulty, fun, deep, silly and whatever. What history was correct in hindsight anyway? This felt a good way to view our fictionalizing. We also found that when the facts did not fit, changing them could be surprisingly easy or unexpectedly hard, sometimes even painful.

At some point I realized that all the facts we left in were the bad stories we shared. There was no need to fictionalize bad things; the only time we needed fiction was to dream up good turns for our narrative. Marilyn, my beautiful sane optimist, heard our banter: "Hang on you two. There were and are good things in your life story that are facts. Your story is not only about bad facts, not by a long shot, is it?"

We thought about it and agreed, "After all, you and me would not be here otherwise - so Marilyn, you are right as usual. I don't know how she does it. What a woman you got Cousin Tibor-Tim," Josef teased.

*

The first draft was ready. It was rough, but still, the story was on paper. How to end the novel was puzzling to the point of impossible? It was perplexing and agonizing to actually stop and close it. To find an ending that was acceptable to our story, for the two of us, was one thing. To find one for readers, was also problematic; for we certainly hoped we would get it published. Meanwhile, each chapter was mailed to Garibaldi as promised. Each time Antonio replied.

My dear Amigos

I'm not too sure about your literary quality, but your writing gets to me. I encourage you to continue. I note with interest that you call the book 'A Dubious Inheritance', and I think that's good. What you have to say, after all, is not just about inheriting money, but about inheriting lives. The lives and stories of people you never knew. The book already says a great deal about connections between people, and about the amazing synchronicity that the universe brings to lives.

For me this has been far more than a remarkable investigative journey. For you two, to tell Lajos's and your own stories, fact or fiction, gives me a great joy.

Keep going. I can hardly wait for the next chapter.

As we continued, the story seemed to take over. Parts of what we wrote played themselves back to me as if they were really true, in a disturbing way. Was I losing it? There were discussions and ideas flying all over the place, even during trips to the countryside. Endlessly we found and admitted our feelings of sadness, anger and needs, now mixed with a kind of self-fulfilling prophecy; our book. What we had been through could never be forgotten, but rather, we had to learn to live with it as best we could; we had to 'choose' our own lives! Ye Gods and little finishes...how I hate the triteness of 'choosing my own life'. But, there was nothing else for it.

Josef admitted to some odd feelings, because it was my father who managed to come through the war and leave at least the connection of an inheritance. He quickly added how grateful he was for all we'd actually found. Although neither of us could be certain about what had happened to our fathers, it gave Josef some comfort to know that at least in our story his Uncle Lajos was trying to save his own father. And that may well have been true.

*

It had taken us around nine months to give birth to this 'baby', to feel we had completed a draft of what I now thought of as an interesting story that was worth telling, and that others might want to read. I was even more convinced that 'Life' itself is indeed a narrative.

Josef and Juli had to decide whether to apply for an extension of stay in Australia. They chose, with many misgivings to return to Budapest, for the time being. I badly wanted them to stay. The closeness we had was not going to be replaceable. On the other hand, the famous other hand, I did not want to stop Josef from doing whatever he thought was right for him.

Garibaldi smokes, reads and thinks 2004

Garibaldi relit his cigar.

"I'll be dammed. The two amigos have actually managed to write a story way beyond my expectations," he said to his wife, as he finished the last chapter of "A Doubtful Inheritance." Shaking his head, feeling pleasantly surprised, he sat down to send an email to Tim, but there was an incoming email from Harry Weinberger. The old buzzard was saying hello, and asking if he knew how Josef and Tim were getting on.

Garibaldi briefly explained.

Harry, the writing is rough, but the two amigos had dreamed up some most interesting turns and infused it with a great deal of pathos and passion. It is part memoir and yet it is in the end a fiction, a novel. The result really sounds like a true story. I wonder, if somebody gave them a bit of a hand, perhaps it could be pulled together into a publishable novel.

Knowing about your many years of connections to publishers, I am pondering whether you could assist them. Now Harry, I haven't said anything to them, and I'm not going to, not unless something comes of it... Don't feel obliged, but if you are interested in those two guys, I'll send you a copy to see what you think. In any case, you are a purveyor of stories of human nature, and you have taken a great deal of interest in their story. Let me know if you want me to send the manuscript."

Regards
Antonio

The reply was almost instantaneous.

Dear Antonio,
I would like nothing better than help put their story on a happier basis. Publishing is not easy these days. If it could be done, it would certainly give them something as close to a miracle as we mere humans can manufacture. Therefore, as we lawyer say, 'without prejudice' I will certainly assist. Don't say anything to them, they don't need another disappointment.

Harry Weinberger

An hour later another email came from Harry Weinberger:

I often worry about my passing brainpower. But, man, once in a while a good brain wave washes up into my consciousness.

You recall that Edith Schlezinger and Peter Levy were a major link in the chain of finding Tim and Josef. Tim was not the cause of their breakup, but he has been the catalyst for - can one believe it - their getting back together after all this time! Anyway, the brain wave: Edith was a publisher! Although she retired long ago, she still has contacts, enough that if she is willing, she may be able to open a few doors.

Email me the whole book immediately, and I'll give a copy to Edith, while I read it. If Edith can see merit in the book, I imagine she might just champion the case.

Regards

Harry

A discovery in Los Angeles 2010

A book, "The History of Love", by Nicole Krauss, spoke to Andy as soon as he randomly read a few lines in it. He took it and walked towards the check out. The only other book he chose was "Broken Silence" by Andre Stein, a book about victims of the holocaust. He paid for the books and moved towards the door, eyes still scanning the shelves. At the very end of the row he saw a display of books facing him. On one cover the title: "A Doubtful Inheritance", and below the author's names jumped out; Weisz & Weisz. That is a name he would never forget.

He was about to walk past, but turned back, reaching for the book. As he turned the pages his thoughts wandered back to the old 8mm film he had taken of his mother, Uncle Wilhelm and Lajos Weisz in 1952 at his own father's funeral. 'Better dig it out and have it digitized before it fades away,' he thought, 'and I better have another look at it, it's been years.'

Then another piece of amazement came back. A few years ago, while visiting Wilhelm in Vienna, his uncle told him that Lajos had supported his mother and himself for a long time. His mother never told him that.

He forced his eyes to refocus on the pages of the book he held. Like a magnet the name Lajos was right there at the beginning of the second chapter titled: 'The Father's Story.'

"What the hell..." he murmured out loud. 'What chance... Lajos is a common name in Hungary but....' Common or not, he was intrigued enough to want the book. Moving toward the cashier, he was flicking a few pages further into it. His eyes took a moment to adjust as he saw another name on a page: the name of Oscar Schmidt, his own father.

Late night phone calls worry Tim

I get home about 11 pm after the usual Thursday night Human Relations program where I am a facilitator. It has not been a good session. I feel edgy. Outside it is a beautiful clear night as I watch a ship slowly moving between rows of the red and green lights of the shipping channel; I call it the stairway to heaven. "Green on the right on the way in, red on the right on the way out." Sheer poetry this, I told Marilyn, but she says it is not even verse, only a good way to remember the rules of the sea when sailing.

A drink settles my churning guts. Marilyn's key rattles in the door and my mind and heart relax, welcoming her soothing presence. I stretch and smile, things are okay. My lover is at home. She is my home. She yells, "Hello darl," and as I yell back, the phone rings suddenly, making me jump out of my chair. 'The phone rang suddenly'; but how else could it ring?

My first thought is always that a late night phone call spells trouble, and it's nearly midnight. My heart beats fast as I say "Hello."
A sick grandchild or an accident? It will be nothing more than a friend reminding me about lunch tomorrow. I am jittery.

There is a moment of silence and then an unfamiliar American voice says something, there is crackling on the line. It's a long distance call, obviously. An accent of sorts tells me it is not a straight Yankee voice. Surely, they are not going to say at this time of night that I've been specially chosen from millions of names for a free dance class membership.

I barely hear what he says.

"Please repeat."

Patiently the man with the accent asks, "Is that Tibor Weisz?"

It takes me by such surprise, that first I say no - is Josef having a joke?

"Who? No I'm not…well…Yes, I am Tim, or Tibor Weisz, who is this?"

"Oh great," he says.

It flashes through my brain that this might be bad news about Josef. The voice on the other end picks up my concern.

"Please don't worry, it's not bad news I am ringing you about. My name is Andreas Schmidt".

"Do I know you?"

"Sort of, we have never met, but I have read your book".

The realization of the name Schmidt hits fast. "Schmidt? Really? Are you a relative of my Schmidt?"

"I am Oscar's son."

I am staggered by the reply. "His son? Uhm, his son, ah Andreas?"

"Yes, I am Oscar's son, Andreas. Are you okay? Is it alright to talk?"

"Yeah, well, right, yes, please go on." Of course I don't believe him but he says, "I lost track of your father after his visit to our place in Vienna on my tenth birthday. I have never forgotten him. I could not believe reading your story…"

Waves of responses run through me. I can barely hold the phone with my trembling hands. I can't believe this.

Hard to comprehend yet another real connection. Joy rises too; this man met my father. I can scarcely speak, but I ask "When did you meet him?"

"It was in 1951."

I'm still a bit suspicious.

"Is this some kind of a hoax? Are you some dickhead who has read the book and decided to have a bit of fun? How do I know you are for real?"

"I understand your concern but I have a lot to tell you and your Cousin Josef. As a matter of fact, I have an old 8mm movie, the very first movie I ever made. It was taken at my father's funeral on a camera your father bought for me, and your father is in the film."

I laugh out, hysterically "Oh yes really?"

I am speechless, doubtful, but beginning to believe him.

"You have a film of my father..."

I finally grind out. 'He has a film of my father...' I think over and over.

His voice comes warmed and happy,

"Yes. I don't know if you are a movie fan, but partly because of your father's gift, I have become a reasonably well-known movie director."

Andreas Schmidt. Oh shit, sugar and shandy! He is a director. The name is indeed familiar. Funny how I never related the director to my Schmidt, but there must be millions by that name. His voice now sounds German-ish with an American accent that seems right.

Andreas continues.

"I chanced upon your book, 'The Inheritance,' and really liked it, loved it actually. More than that, I feel almost as if I too have inherited something by knowing more about your father, his son and nephew. It is, you all are also my narrative, my inheritance...

Through my tears I can say nothing, so I wait to hear more.

"I have been in touch with Antonio Garibaldi and Joe Weinberger, knowing what I had to say to you would sound improbable. I asked them not to call you until I did, but if you call either, they will confirm what I am telling you."

"I don't know what to say..."

"Well then," Andreas sounds more confident now.
"Let me say more. I would like you and Josef to come to L.A. I can tell you all that I know, and you can see the movie of your father. And mainly, unless you have an objection, I wish to make a movie of your book."

Marilyn has her arms around me, guessing at the conversation. I glance at her, grinning and whooping with joy, tears pouring from my happy eyes. I assure Andreas that we would love to see the book turned into a movie.
I simply cannot go on talking now. I have to tell Josef immediately.
I thank Andreas, promising that we will be there within two weeks. I have to get off the phone.

*

All my life, I had lived waiting for something, but for what exactly I never knew. What I did eventually come to know was that in my heart there was, and is a hole filled with a dark deep sadness and sometimes with a terrifying amount of anger and frustration. I came to visualize it as an endless tunnel, so deep you could see that there was no end to it. Now I feel something so satisfactory that it is barely plausible to feel this way. I laugh and cry, babbling on to Marilyn's questions. Then I thought of that sad old Jewish joke about the difference between the Jews and the Christians;

The Christians always see the light at the end of the tunnel,
The Jews always see the tunnel at the end of the light...

The past is present; if you got a film to prove it

On my way to Los Angeles I sit impatient to get to the destination, a target that for once feels like an actual one. Because of what it means, because of what I hope it might do for me. Something new, amazing…and what if not? What if this turns sour like so many hopes, what if I don't like the blasted movie…

The world has become a scarier and yet a more and more beautiful place as I grow older. These days I accept that I won't be saving the universe from itself, or rather from its population, for only us humans are a problem. I shall never be a wise man, will not get all I wish for (just as well.) and will never be at peace, because I am as I am, or will be - once I see that movie?

Lucky I am an optimist; I had to become one, but I'm also a realist. It seems that my entire existence will get turned upside down again, joyfully, and painfully as well. What to think or feel now that I am on my way to actually see something real?

Will any of these 'Very Satisfactory Happenings' really turn out to be my 'Special Heirloom'? Would all this answer some of my waiting, like a forever expectant mother who never delivers?

Now, I'm sick of my questions and deep and meaningful thoughts. D&M. It is what I do constantly, and it is tiring, and sometimes it's like piss, has to come out, but it is just waste. Perhaps I do so much thinking because to feel too much, is too much.

Look at where I am going, I reassure myself - no one would be feeling clear and easy in my situation. Now I will get more of my true inheritance! Relief floods me. Soon I will see what a dead man, my father, looked like alive. The idea feels good and yet surreal.

My real inheritance will be the old 8mm movie and the one Andréas is making. That the book was published was good enough. The written word is great, but pictures tell and set into stone the images, my images, the ones I never had! How fantastic is that? That is, if the movie will be good. How bad, if it is not? And what is a good movie anyway but one that people like, true or false the story might be. I am worried about the 'major motion picture event' of our story not being what I want to see.

There is also the old 8mm movie of Andreas took of my father to see. Unbelievable, I keep thinking. A motion picture of him at the age of 37, for me to bed into my brain and heart. No fiction there. He was alive, he was not just Mum's myth, he had a character, strength and he succeeded in many things. Was he happy? Did he also have the same hole in his heart as I have? I imagine from what I already know that he did, and perhaps worse than mine.

I feel pleased and cheated all at once. Why? Because he was alive and we missed each other. Fuck. We could have had him back, except for some awful mistakes, misfortunes and decisions one could never fathom, or even question. Awful bad luck, no one to blame! Though, I do blame myself and even Josef, others too, but that is a stupid waste of energy.

Surely now, all this will be adequate, if not perfect? I keep trying to convince myself that the two movies will bring him to life, at least for me. That surely I will internalize something of all that. Fiction and facts. And to top it all, it seems that some of his papers that no one looked at after he died have been found, thanks to Garibaldi. So more will come to life about him. A few facts, a few ideas, some letters, a few of his dreams I can own. There is an old faded picture of him and his brother, taken at the Russian front by a friend, probably days before the bomb fell on them. What a find for Josef.

Why do I feel touchy and irritated and so close to tears all the time? I never knew the man, that's bloody why, and now I have to let go of my expectation that I ever will.

No more fantasy about the messiah.

Finished, done, puff of smoke, it is gone.

No more waiting and expecting; I've been robbed of my fairy tale well and truly now.

Good, fine.

What a hoot! And yet how rotten to feel this way. To feel one's madness, sadness, gladness all in one messy parcel. For that is what it is, this kind of thinking...Ha ha, ha and ha, ha, ha.

*

Andréas collects me at the airport. He is tall, almost skinny, but holds himself very straight. His face is angular, head covered with wispy blond hairs that flutter everywhere. In his jeans and wide-open neck red shirt he looks like a film director. As soon as I see him, I like him. Josef arrives tomorrow with Juli and Marilyn.

He shakes my hand with both of his, not wanting to let go, tears and smiles in our eyes. On the way to his house we talk about nothing important, as if neither of us has anything else to say. He seems a charming and sensitive man.

Up on a hill, in his handsome home, he shows me to my room. He insisted we stay with him. My bags put down, we move to his study. Andreas makes coffee, puts a plate of sandwiches on the coffee table, and pours a glass of Southern Comfort, putting the bottle next to me. How did he know I like Southern Comfort? A box of Colombian cigars come out of the drawer.

Knowing what I want, he switches on the DVD player, explaining he had the old film restored, and has made several copies. He hands me the remote control and a thick envelope of photos. "I'll be next door if you need me - or anything."

I sit here feeling remarkably calm and comfortable, drinking coffee and the Comfort on ice. I light a cigar, sink back into the chair and feel reluctant to change my mood. I am in no hurry all of a sudden; I really don't want this to be another disappointment. I'm elated and scared. Several feelings, several lives, attack me at once.

The envelope filled with pictures is on the coffee table next to me. I look at it and wait. An old Hungarian tune floats into my head. Mum's favorite tune about an old gypsy.

In front of me the large picture window frames the city of the angels through the usual blue fog. It's a huge room, this study come library, and it is quietly tasteful. It is like an enormous still photo, and yet full of invisible, unseen lives.

The large envelope is in my hand. A few black and white and some color photos tumble out; my father with, I suppose Uncle Carlos, Garibaldi and some children. The color shots are of father amongst a group of very poor looking children. Another shot of a large shed named 'Sari's Gardens' - wow! More pictures of fields growing vegetables and flowers. Another picture of him in shorts, digging the earth, smiling up at the camera.

I can't bear to look at these in detail now... I stuff them back into the envelope.

The remote control is looking at me. ' No hurry,' I tell myself again. I am scared to switch on the film. Scared of my emotions and petrified of what it might bring; or even more fearful of what it may not deliver?

There are two rolls of standard 8mm movies, Andreas said. That means only about six minutes of projection time. Andreas told me he had the movie recorded in an endless loop and that the whole DVD runs for nearly an hour, repeating the same six minutes over and over. He said that he hoped the films would help to add something to our lives. I agreed, feeling grateful.

Outside the sun is turning red and orange, even smog does good work by giving such lovely colors to the sky. It must be around 8pm, the wind is blowing at what looks like gum trees below the pool.

I just sit here feeling variously cautious, comfortable, lost and lonely too, wishing Josef and Marilyn were here. I could wait till tomorrow but I won't.

This is just for me.

What is?

The heartache that will follow?

The ache of never having known a father, grandfather, family, cousins and aunties with moustaches you could dislike kissing. The pain of always feeling like an orphan, in spite of my silly Mum's good intentions. But hold on, I am a good fella, and I have not seriously hurt anyone on purpose. I am holding back a flood of grief with muscle power.

I empty the glass and pour another. My hands tremble. 'Well here comes what there is, be brave, be valiant, growth through adversity…' and I laugh as I push the play button.

The black and white silent movie springs into life. Startlingly, the first shot is of my father smiling with his arm around Wilhelm, I suppose. There are other people standing around looking serious, dressed in black. The film was shot at Oscar's funeral. I cannot make out what my father is saying, so I replay the first scene, realizing that he was most likely speaking German. I watch and see my dad move.

Dad?

It is the first time I think of him as 'dad' instead of father. I've never called anyone 'dad'. I like it when my daughters call me Dad.

Dad looks about as tall as me and about the same build. Mum said he was taller than me. His hair is thinning and he has a moustache just like mine. Is that why I grew one? Do we look alike? Yes, I think so. Ten-year-old Andreas is obviously fond of my dad; he prances around him, entertaining him, and hangs onto him. How I wish it had been me.

Stop the film. I'm unable to continue for a moment. Deep breaths in and out.

Switching it back on, the first reel finishes and the second one comes on. Inside a room, at Oscar's home, I suppose. Old fashioned, heavy furniture lines the space. Again, there are several shots of dad, who, I now think, does not look like anyone's father. He looks calm but his eyes are deeply sad and smiling at once. He moves slowly, sometimes looking uncomfortable, but he often has an arm around someone. But now I see that his attention is mainly on young Andreas. Someone else must have filmed this next bit. Lajos is talking to Andreas as an uncle might, sitting next to him. Andreas is listening intently, radiating, obviously the boy really likes this man.

The movie ends with Wilhelm and dad shaking hands, looking at the camera.

That's it, the end. That's all there is, six minutes of soundless motion about an entire life.

A few still pictures of Oscar follow; a slight, pale looking man, standing there with his wife and a baby. Another of Oscar and my father on a street, arm in arm. Then Uncle Carlos, a jolly rotund looking man, and a bunch of people in a space that looks like a shed, and a few other shots - I'll look again later.

I let the dvd run again and again and the stop it. Standing up, feeling exhausted of emotion. My muscles ache all over, my neck is in a spasm. I shake my arms and legs, but feel numb, and drained.

Sitting down again, feeling dizzy, turning the DVD back on, I look again at what never happened to me. Then my eyes go blank, my focus burns out. I throw the remote away as fury takes over, flooding me.

Where were you, where were you?

Why did you of all people have to die?

Why did you leave me here alone?

Why didn't you come back... why me, why, oh well, why not me?

Why did I have to be left with a silly mother and no one else?

What did I expect from a father, after all, so many have lousy fathers, what if you would have been a rotten dad, but that could not be...?

How do I know you would have helped to keep my soul together, how do I know it would not have been a sad relationship, how do I reconcile all this now, and reconcile it with what? My expectations, my hopes, the deep hole that's missing out of my existence? I know so little of you dad, I had barely bothered to ask Mum about you since the whole father thing was nearly meaningless to me for half my life anyway, and what would we have done together, what could I say to you, what can I have said to you. What? What?

What could we have said to each other? Now you are here in just a small fragment and it's too late, it will never heal me and no matter what I have inherited from you; money or nature, features or moustache, you didn't exist for me, not until now! A stranger, just a stranger who had lost his, and part of my, life.

Were you liberal minded, democratic or deep or shallow or loving or hating...? Were you a man amongst men, or just a canny survivor, hell who cares, you are gone and yet, this movie somehow has to put an end to some part of me that had been alive and hoping for you to come back and...?

What bloody nonsense I have going through me...

What were you like? A very kind man, I hear from what little there is left of you, but we always say that of dead people, and that's what you are, dead and gone.

Ha, but this time for sure, no more doubts about that, you are fucking dead. Twice dead!

I shall never know what wisdoms you may have taught me, or what silly ideas you might have had about how one should live, I had to build all that by myself, with no help really from anyone, I just had to make it all up, make all my life up as I went, keeping straight, holding head up in waters too deep for me, keep from drowning or from going too far, or too close, and I had to restrict myself to the smallness I now find is me. The smallness I am...

The DVD stops. I re-start it again.

But enough, no more for now.

The room is in darkness except for a little light coming in from outside. I am sweating and raging. There are red blotches in front of my eyes. A coughing fit is followed by tears, spit and bile rising, mounting, as if I am full of it! And I am. 'Slow down, slow down, think and be reasonable, slow and gather yourself, don't lose it...' I breathe deep and slow.

Perhaps I am having a heart attack. A gentle little breeze cools my face as I throw myself back into the armchair, worn-out, flat, all energy spent.

It's good it is dark now. The lights of the big city, way down there, blink their radiance up enough to see, so I am reassured; there is not only darkness. I need a cigar.

Andreas must have heard me rage and rant, oh well never mind that. There is that nice breeze again touching my face. I drink a half glass of Comfort, feel groggy; I'm drunk with alcohol or passion? The breeze is blowing harder, from air conditioning? But there is no sound. The windows are shut, it's not a draft - oh well what's it matter? It is not dad's ghost is it?

Funny boy to the end, that's me. I look for a switch on the walls for the air, but there is none. The breeze comes and goes, I'm alternating between boiling hot and cold shivers.

If you can't change the past or the future then what can one change? Oh well, I will go on, as I always have? Not entirely. My life is not so bad, I have people and much love around me. Good. All right, ok, fine. Maybe I will be different?

I hear my voice:
"I have a question for you dad. Why do so many people hate Jews? Why, when we have suffered as much as we have? Why do I feel like I am a Jew, though I neither practice nor care about all the hocus pocus? Who and how would I have been, if you were part of my life and soul? I want these questions answered, but I know nothing much will ever be answered, perhaps it could not have been answered even if you and I were part of each other's lives anyway!"

Not again, give up will ya. Don't start again. Enough already.

I can't see through my eyes, but I hear my obsessed 'recording'. I picture an old 78 record on a turn table, on an old fashioned machine; the old records in my mind playing and replaying the same words and sounds. The needle stuck on the same groove, slipping back to the start of the damned story. In my mind, I step up to the hi fi turntable, hammer in hand raised, smashing down, breaking the record into a million pieces, the smashing sound of an old 78 bakelite record being shattered, and then I pound the pieces smaller and smaller into powder. Then I keep pounding the timber cabinet until it is in also in small pieces.

Hey! The sounds stopped, there is silence, for a moment.

Something within me is cracking open, something is escaping out of my heart, mind and body. A great whoosh of wind, full of sorrow and nothingness, matter blows out of me, spit and fluid shoot out my mouth…poisonous acrid substance. A weight that had me down so heavy all these years rips out of me, it is flying about the room, taken up by a breeze that plays with it;
I can see a blob of black, a gaseous nothing, floating around the room in the darkness, it sparkles, dulls, pulses, moans as if dying… and then it fades away. It has gone out of me, done with forever.
Oh really? Am I really done with it? The pain will not be left behind? It won't be totally finished, cannot ever be. I won't be the man I would have been.
"I am that I am," even God said as much.
I won't be able to redo, relive all my years the way they might have been as if I had not the black hole, the black dog of depression I've always had. And yet. Never will all

of it change - but something has, I've lost emotional weight without dieting.
"Little Weisz, always the joker..." I hear my voice.

I will be better than I have ever been. I have inherited my own life stories, Josef's and my father's stories and so much more. These are what matter most and our lives will become a 'major movie'! What luck and what ever...

L.A sparkles brighter out there down in the valley, the moon ducks behind a cloud, a door slams somewhere. I think something has changed in my world.

A Doubtful Inheritance?

I barely hear the brief speeches before the screening starts in this huge picture show. The four of us are holding hands tight, sitting stiffly, not looking at one another, lest we lose it. The clapping stops, the speaker leaves the stage, the lights dim and fade.
Talking, coughing, rattles stop, an eerie hush fades away, silence seizes the pitch black theatre for what seems like a long time.

Total whiteness blazes onto the screen.
Silent words appear: "Near the Don River, 1945".

The words fade and then little by little transform into a bright, so very bright green field. The absolute silent peace is shattered by the sound of a bomb coming from the left, and then from the right. Then from everywhere. Bombs come whistling, bursting, devastating the empty field, turning over earth, digging deep holes, mixed with machine guns firing, the scene flicks on.
Bodies fly through the air, the ground heaves, splattering sky high, and another bomb crashes into a crowd of running soldiers.

Then, silence again – death. Hush and stillness bring the sound of wind howling through the smoky landscape.

The land seems to have no edges, no end as it winds away toward the horizon. A late afternoon sun casts dark shadows of billowing clouds. The angry wind blows black smoke on the green, brown and barren land. The relentless sound of bombs, shells and gunshots in the distance warns of the ongoing battle and destruction. The cacophony of noises and silence rise, mix, fade, return again; wind and the cries of men mix.

The grassy green field is strewn with ash and rubble, spread out as if the junk of building, machines, torn clothing and blood were meant to be in the fields. The whole world is colored with the gray gunmetal thick mist of the color of war.

The camera zooms in on a timber hut that leans badly to the left. It is just about falling over, but hangs on to that half of itself that is not torn away. It was never more than a shepherd's shed. Brownish timber walls, charcoal black wood still smoking, holds up half a roof, the other half torn away hangs down the back.

Lajos holds his unconscious brother Andor upright, sitting on the dirt, leaning against the hut. Strangled beams, iron and burnt timber contain their aching bodies. Lajos is saying silent words. Perhaps he is praying. Twisting around, looking through an opening in the side of the hut, he sees in the distance what is left of his group of fellow soldiers. They are in retreat, straggling back, moving away from the front line. Dirt-covered tattered uniforms tell the story of lives lost, of all hope gone.

Among the group of retreating soldiers there is one who stops running. He looks back toward the hut as a bomb hits it. He can't see what happened to Lajos and his brother, sees no more than a cloud of dirt and smoke that covers the scene. He turns and staggers away...

THE END

ABOUT THE AUTHOR

DR.TED TODD (PhD) was born in Hungary and escaped in 1956 after the Hungarian revolution. In Australia he established a well known chain of retail stores, TEDS Camera stores. After the sale of that business other businesses followed. In later years Ted decided to go back to tertiary studies. An Arts B.A (Swinburne Univ.) was followed by a Grad Dip of Human Relationships Education (Melbourne Univ.) Eventually a PhD in literary studies/ creative writing (Swinburne Univ.)

Concurrently with his work, business and studies Ted facilitated Human Relationship workshops at the Cairnmillar Institute and other venues, and also ran workshops and lectures in marketing sales, and relationships at the Australian Institute of Management.

*

Previous book: "The Secrets of successful Selling" (Interpersonal selling) How to sell well, easily and stay sane doing it while you enjoy it. Available from Amazon and other book stores, also as an eBook .

To be published late 2016:

Non fiction; Self Help; Philosophy:

"The Software of Your Personality" ™ is about reinventing psych and philosophy and sane thinking for practical and successful living.

Fiction:

"50 Something Male is Looking for a Woman of the Opposite Sex" (reg. Tm applied for). These are connected short stories about looking for and finding a new relationship after a long marriage. It shows the male pattern of relating and emotions, and the stories are as funny as pointed and emotive.